THE FAMILY WORTH

A novel by

JOHN CROSBY

WARNER BOOKS

A Warner Communications Company

WARNER BOOKS EDITION

Copyright © 1987 by John Crosby

Cover design by Rolf Erikson
Cover illustration by David McKelvey

Warner Books, Inc.
666 Fifth Avenue
New York, N.Y. 10103

W A Warner Communications Company

Printed in the United States of America

First Printing: October, 1987

10 9 8 7 6 5 4 3 2 1

To Elaine

"Whoever fights monsters
should see that in the
process he doesn't become
a monster."

—*Friedrich Wilhelm Nietzsche*

BOOK ONE

CHAPTER 1

The naked body hung luminescent in the very center of the submersible's brilliant orange light, like an actor in a spotlight—shouting defiance, mouth open and snarling, eyes wide and angry, arms outflung, widespread feet doing a little tap dance on the bottom of the Gulf of Mexico.

Blaming me for his predicament.

Thus Nicholas at the controls of the little one-man submarine. He uttered a deep sigh that was heard clearly through the intercom on the mother ship seventy fathoms above. "What?" shouted Orin on the mother ship. "I can't hear you, Nicholas."

The sound coming and going as it did underwater.

"I'm not saying anything," said Nicholas. He was twenty-five, slim, dark and sad.

A swarm of red shrimp pranced past the corpse, delighting in the orange light of the submarine, ignoring the body which was not yet dead enough.

"You're not moving!" shouted Orin through the intercom. "Keep moving!"

Not knowing the quest was over.

Nicholas worked the control knob and the manipulator extended its stainless steel claw toward the body until it hung delicately inches over the huge angry head whose widespread mouth was still proclaiming innocence and outrage even at the bottom of the sea.

Not the head, thought Nicholas. He couldn't allow that merciless steel claw to grasp Jasper's head. Jasper wouldn't like that—and why do I give a damn?

The claw poised over the open mouth shouting silent epithets at a passing school of squid who paid no attention.

The leg? No, that, too, would be humiliating. Nicholas brought the steel claw down to the waist and made the grapple around the paunch, tightening slowly until the tentacles had disappeared in the white flesh.

Through the intercom, Orin willed, "Nicholas, say something. *Anything!*"

Dear Orin! A worrier.

"I'm surfacing," called Nicholas. "Bringing the old man up with me. Death hasn't changed him a damn bit. He's as nasty as ever."

The sea heaved, oily and empty, the heat suffocating. From the west came the boom boom boom of the dynamite charge far under the surface. The exploration ship was on the horizon, barely visible, its delicate apparatus listening to the fibrillations which came through the earth's crust, telling where the black oil was.

The other noise was rackety and insistent, coming from the sky. . . .

The body lay on the deck of the mother ship in the blazing late afternoon sunshine, Nicholas bent over it, running his fingers over the flesh, feeling for contusions, abrasions, puncture wounds, anything at all.

Orin was being sick over the side, splattering the bulkhead. Jasper would have been amused, thought Nicholas. Shouting taunts, the bastard.

Nicholas turned the body over, felt down the spine under the bristly black hairs, looking for bullet holes, knife wounds, foul play. . . .

Dake, who was captain of the mother ship, was on the catwalk of the pilothouse, smoking furiously.

Nicholas pushed his index finger up the old pirate's rectum. Overwhelmed with loathing. Laced with affection. Wanting to spit in the old bastard's face. And—Oh, Jesus! —kiss him.

He stood up, defeated. "Why is the exploration ship way over there on the horizon?" he shouted at Dake. "Why isn't it over here?"

Dake said, "I don't know. I'm captain of this ship, not that ship." He disappeared into the pilothouse.

Christ!

Nicholas went to his brother and slipped an arm around his shoulder. "Feeling better?"

"Yeah. Sorry."

"You mustn't apologize for being human, Orin. If I had a spark of decency I'd have thrown up, too—all over the submarine."

Rackety! Rackety! Rackety!

"What the hell is that?" Nicholas asked, noticing the noise for the first time.

Orin was squinting up into the sun. "A chopper! Hanging right in the sun so we can't see it. Are we expecting a chopper?"

"Get him off the deck," roared Nicholas. "Come on, Orin! Give me a hand!"

The brothers hauled the body off the deck, down the forward hatch. Too late, of course.

* * *

In the blood-red helicopter, Robin held the stick in her left hand, the binoculars in her right. The sun was directly behind her.

Jasper, all right.

She watched the brothers lug the body below before turning the little chopper around ninety degrees and heading back toward the line of trees on the distant island just over the horizon.

She switched on the radio, preset to 26.2, and called, "Redbird calling Fishtail. Come in, Fishtail."

There was no answer, and after five minutes she gave it up.

Ten miles from the island she smelled the sulphuric pitch boiling away underground. The smell from hell, Fergie called it. She guided her way in by smell alone, flying low over the endless green of the tropical jungle below.

A very boring jungle.

Robin was twenty-two. Easily bored.

She set the chopper down gently in the clearing, the only clearing big enough to handle the red helicopter, and cut the engine. After the rackety rax of the rotor, the silence was deafening. Across the clearing, her brother Fergie was fiddling with the fire, trying to get it to burn, paying no attention to his big sister. Fergie was seventeen. Seventeen going on a hundred. Very cool.

"What took you?" he asked, not looking up from the blaze.

"They got the body."

Fergie didn't say anything. He nursed the fire until it blazed strong and bright. Finally, he said, "Too bad. I liked Uncle Jasper. And I don't like Elihu."

"Nobody likes Elihu," said his sister.

"Except you," said Fergie. "What's for supper?"

"Beans, mangoes, would you like some bacon? There's some bacon."

The sun was sinking low, fast as it always did on the gulf,

the colors from orange to red, the air cooling, the smell of pitch overpowering.

The smell from hell.

On the mother ship, Nicholas was piling the contents of the refrigerator on the floor of the galley—melons, tomatoes, meat, eggs, fish—Dake roaring his displeasure. "We're three days from Galveston, Misturr Worth," the R's rolling like thunder, "the food will spoil and what will we eat?"

Carefully Nicholas took out the refrigerator shelves, lower and upper, and put them on top of the food. "You eat too much, Mr. Dake. It's not good for you."

"I'm captain of this ship, Misturr Worth," shouted Dake, thrusting his black beard forward, black eyes glittering, "and I'm telling you to put that food back."

Nicholas grinned easily. "You're outnumbered, Dake. May I remind you we are your employers? Or rather, he is . . ." Pointing to the corpse which lay face upward, the angry eyes clouding like a fish out of water. "Or was. If he were alive he'd be giving you hell. Give me a hand, Orin."

Orin, very white, hating the touching, moved forward and picked up the waxen legs.

Dake was shouting, "I'll report this to the Merchant Captains' Association. You'll be reprimanded, Misturr Worth. . . ."

Nicholas and Orin were straining to get the heavy figure into the small refrigerator, Nicholas thinking, Orin was helping because old Jasper—if he were alive—would have *ordered* him to. In that contemptuous, high-pitched, almost girlish voice, "Do your duty, boy, or you won't be able to face yourself in the mirror in the morning."

Orin straining now to bend the stiffening body, both brothers pushing hard to bend the body double. For a moment all three faces—the living and the dead—were aligned, looking startlingly alike.

A minute later it was done, the refrigerator door slammed

shut, Nicholas and Orin puffing like winded athletes. "There you are, Daddy!" gasped Nicholas. "Fully refrigerated, all ready to confront the District Attorney, the judge. . . ."

Orin, very white, sat at the galley table. "Confront them with what? You didn't find anything."

Nicholas sat opposite him at the round galley table. "Anyhow we've got the body. Maybe the coroner can find something. Where's the exploration ship?"

"Over the horizon. Gone." Orin smiled. He was older than Nicholas, twenty-seven, but when he smiled he looked absurdly young. "Very peculiar behavior, don't you think?"

"The whole thing is very peculiar. Where's Dake?"

"Back in the pilothouse, I guess. He says a storm is brewing."

"Storm? The sea is like a lake."

"He says the glass is falling. I didn't notice any difference but I'm not a sea captain."

"I don't trust the bastard, do you?"

"No. He'd throw us overboard and sell the body to Elihu if he could manage it."

"We're two against one," said Nicholas.

"Just watch it, kid." Orin smiled at his younger brother, eyes full of love. Nicholas thinking, He has no defense. Everything just pours out of him—tears, love, hate, his cookies, everything spilling right out on the floor. Always, somebody had to be around to clean up the mess.

Nicholas said, "Wouldn't the old bastard hate this? Can't you hear him roaring in there? 'Let me out of here. Young snot-nosed kids! I'll beat you purple.' "

Both brothers hooted with laughter.

A moment later, Nicholas said, "Still . . . I'll miss him."

"I already miss him." Orin's eyes full of tears.

On the island, the brother and sister were eating side by side next to the little fire, the moon rising orange over the plantain trees, the smell of sulphur over everything.

"It'll take three days for them to sail to Galveston. We can make it in a couple hours."

"I want to fly it," said Fergie.

"Fergie, you can't! You haven't a license. Anyway, I rented it and I get the fun of it."

"Just half an hour, Sis."

"Don't call me Sis."

She'd let him fly it, of course. She always gave way to him. On everything. Since he was two.

Fergie said, "I don't understand why Uncle Jasper was naked. Or why he was in the water. Do you?"

"No."

"Or what we're *doing* here exactly. Are we just here because Elihu wants us to spy on those people?"

Robin didn't want to get into that. She unrolled her sleeping bag. "We scramble at six, kid, so knock it off."

"I want to fly it," he said stubbornly.

Seventeen going on eleven. Jumping from the very serious to the utterly trivial. But then all the Worths did that at all ages, herself included. One minute they'd argue over what family member got more than his share of ice cream and the next they'd be squabbling over a million dollars—how to spend it or invest it—without any change of tone. The rich, thought Robin, had no sense of proportion.

Elihu wouldn't agree. Elihu thought the rich were so above the battle they were the only ones with a proper sense of perspective.

He was weird, was Elihu.

Her lover.

Some of the time. . . .

The brothers climbed the steel ladder to the pilothouse in the onrushing darkness. Dake was at the wheel of the schooner, his eyes on the compass. He didn't look up when the brothers came into the pilothouse.

Nicholas said, "We want to call the exploration ship, Captain Dake."

"You can't." Dake's black beard thrust forward in that nasty way he had. The ship-to-shore hanging up just behind his head.

"Why not?"

"It's out of order." The R's rolling like bowling balls. Dake's eyes gleaming with satisfaction. "Unless you know how to fix it, Misturr Worth."

A nasty crack.

"Since when has it been out of order, Captain Dake? It worked two hours ago."

"It doesn't work now. You can try if you like."

Nicholas lifted the telephone off its carriage and listened. There was no sound, no electronics at all, a dead thing. He put it back.

"Why is it out of order, Captain Dake?"

Dake's eyes were on the compass again. "Maybe the storm, Misturr Worth."

"What storm?"

"There'll be a storm. You'll see."

The two brothers went back to the galley.

Orin said, "Do you think he put it out of commission deliberately?"

"Yes," said Nicholas.

"Why?"

"I don't know."

They had Dake outnumbered, but Dake had them outskilled. He was the skipper; it was his boat, his electronics. They were cut off, and there was very little the Worth wealth could do about that.

Miss Calisher stood with the red phone in her hand, waiting. She was a Texas knob of a woman, gray-haired, solid, tough.

Alec Worth was on the white phone, eyes idly watching

the glittering gulf where an oiler bound for Venezuela rode high past his window. "We are not and never have been that interested in outperforming the market," he was just saying in his casual style, "but we are very anxious to protect the downside. Outperforming is a false goddess, Rupert. You must get over it."

To Miss Calisher without a change of tone, "What is it?"

Miss Calisher put the names written in her strong disapproving hand in front of him. "If we outperformed anyone it is by accident, not design. This is not the Olympics. . . ."

While reading the names: Robin and Fergie Worth.

". . . IBM and Philip Morris. Good growth stocks, Rupert, much better than flying off into high technology. In the stock market it is not patriotism but high technology which is the last refuge of the scoundrel."

Alec put his hand over the mouthpiece and said, "Is she on the phone *now*?" He hadn't seen Robin Worth since she was eleven. "Rupert, hang on a minute!" Alec took the red phone from Miss Calisher. "Robin? Well, *hello*! What are you doing in our backwater. . . You think Galveston's beautiful? How quaint. Of course, we have a bed. Or two beds. How old is Fergie now. . . My God, he was a baby. . . You have no transport? I'll send Absolom. That's his name. Very good man. No, you'd never find it otherwise. Hortense will be overjoyed." What a lie! "Of course, you're not imposing. I insist. . . ."

He got back to Rupert and went on with the sales pitch. "Intrastate pipelines with active exploration programs are in a very strong position, Rupert. . . ."

Meanwhile, writing on his pad for Miss Calisher, "Call Hortense, tell her Robin, Fergie Worth spending night with us. Tell her send Absolom to pick up at airport."

Looking out over the shimmering bay.

All sorts of rumors about the Worth oil stocks. And here were a couple New York Worths who hardly knew Texas existed, much less Galveston. . . very odd . . . Hortense would be, if not overjoyed, intensely interested in what these baby Worths from the fleshpots of Manhattan were doing poking about Texas. His wife who had married into the family had always been far more intrigued by the Worth family than he, a born Worth, had ever been. It was always that way. One of Alec's witticisms was that outsiders were all hot to get into the Worth family and the insiders were all hot to get out—and both were disappointed. Being a Worth was a lifetime sentence. You couldn't get out no matter how hard you tried. As for getting in, you had to be a Worth. The wives of Worths were never quite Worths. He burst out laughing and then he had to explain to Rupert, "I'm not laughing at you, Rupert. I'm laughing at Fate. Yes, I know it's very old-fashioned to laugh at Fate, but then I'm an old-fashioned fellow."

Dinner that night was on the terrace, the weather warm, humid, threatening, thunderheads over the bay. "Storm coming up but we might as well sit here while we can," murmured Alec, fussing with the candles under their glass hurricane shells, the Vietnamese servants in their white coats passing back and forth silently with the tableware.

Robin was in a turquoise floor-length dress of silk chiffon she'd dredged out of the bottom of her duffel bag. (The maid had run over it with an iron.) On her ears were her crystal earrings and on her feet turquoise snakeskin shoes— that was all she had on and it was stunning, Alec quite dazzled.

Looking over the blond, self-confident, quite grown-up . . . Niece? Cousin? He wasn't sure what the relationship was . . . Alec was thinking in his calm analytic way. Soon the Worths will consider marrying only other Worths because no one else measures up. Like the Rothschilds. They weren't as clever as the Rothschilds but they were, God knew, more various and probably, in the aggregate, richer.

He handed her a glass of Chambertin and said, "You look enchanting Robin, but then you always did—even at eleven."

"At eleven I was grotesque."

"Only to yourself. To the rest of us you were quite a ravishing child, though much too intelligent and already giving signs of that arrogance which is the curse of the Worth family. I thought at the time, 'That child is going to cause a lot of trouble—and to no one more than herself.' And have you?"

Robin smiled faintingly. Men were always saying ridiculous things to her, and she delighted in not responding to the pitches. "I never look back," said Robin, "so I don't know how much trouble I leave in my wake." She drank the wine, listening to the sounds. In the darkness a horse whinnied out by the stables and the warm wind smelled of salt hay, stinging her nostrils.

"And you, Alec? My brother says you are the smartest Worth now going—with a fantastic record for pyramiding trust funds or some such thing."

"There is nothing on earth more boring than a trust fund, Robin. Tell me about your love life. Are you in love, and with whom and why?"

That made her laugh. She threw her head back and laughed her throaty gurgling laugh. She might have told him a few lies but just then Hortense came out on the terrace and broke things up. Hortense was thin, dark, not at all pretty, but with such a ravenous interest in everyone and everything that she commanded attention when she walked into a room. She plunged right in, devouring Robin with her curiosity. What on earth was this New York beauty doing in Galveston, the backwater of the Western world? And in a helicopter? Why? How come she brought that beautiful turquoise dress in the bottom of a *duffel* bag. . . .

"Well, you never know," said Robin, "when you're going to need a floor-length turquoise dress, do you?" Fending off Hortense, enjoying herself, going over to the attack when all else failed to hold the lady at bay. "And you were *born* in Galveston, Hortense? How fortunate for Alec."

"Alec was born in Galveston, too. Our two families were almost the only ones who stayed here after the hurricane of 1900 wiped out the city, and consequently we—shall we say—prospered from the timidity and lack of vision of others." Something the Worths had done repeatedly in many lands over the last two centuries. Robin was bored with the tale of her family's success but it was better than answering all those questions.

Fergie came in with Lannie Worth, Hortense and Alec's teenage son, and their other son, Geoffrey, who was twelve. Fergie wore a white jacket he'd borrowed from Lannie; it didn't fit his rangy form but it gave a superficial respectability over his worn jeans and dirty white Nikes.

"Lannie has an FX 4000," Fergie announced. "He can talk to the Pentagon."

"Yes, but what does he *say* to the Pentagon?" asked Robin.

"For God's sake, Sis, that's *not* the point. . . ."

"But it should be."

Robin loved helicopters, detested computers.

Dinner was bouillabaisse full of delightful crustaceans out of the gulf, sharp and hot, musky with brandy. The questioning went on, sharp as a blade. "But how *can* you hop in a helicopter from island to island? What islands? There aren't that many islands. Saugatuck Island and Galveston? What other islands are there? And for what purpose? And why a helicopter? Helicopters are not at all restful! Helicopters are for. . . the police. They have no other decent purpose and not much purpose there either."

Alec listened to his wife's searching curiosity with his own wry inner mixture of amusement and irritation. He would have gone about it much differently. Pretending bland indifference until in exasperation they would blurt out *something* if only to stir him up. That was his technique.

He ate silently, not missing a syllable, admiring how effortlessly Robin fended off his wife's questions. She was a Worth, and the Worths (many of them, anyway) had this supreme indifference to what anyone thought. They never apologized and never explained and they didn't give a damn what you thought, unless you were another Worth, and not even much then, which gave them enormous leverage to shrug off the press, the congressional investigators, or simple probers like Hortense.

Alec himself crawled with curiosity, but he bided his time until the Vietnamese brought the coconut flan.

Then he dropped his little bomb, "I hear Uncle Jasper is in the neighborhood, looking into the continental shelf," in his dusty precise voice, the black eyes sparkling with malice. "All southwest Texas fairly teeming with Worths." Picking away at his flan, not looking at them. "The rumor sent quivers through the energy stocks."

It sent quivers through the dinner table, too. Robin blinking into her flan. Her mouth had fallen open and she instantly stuffed flan into it to give it an excuse for its behavior.

Fergie blurted out, "The gulf is not the continental shelf, Uncle Alec. Geologically the gulf is an insignificant body of water, barely sixty million years old."

Good old Fergie! Robin was thinking. Filling in the empty spaces. She recovered her footing then and said, "Where did you hear all those rumors, Uncle Alec?"

Throw questions when there is nothing else to be said.

Alec, too, was not bad at not answering but asking, "When did you last see Uncle Jasper, Robin?"

She held the spoon mouth level and considered. When had she last seen Uncle Jasper? Wrinkling her alabaster brow, and seeing Uncle Jasper in the back of her plangent mind menacingly dead on the deck of the schooner, "Was it Thanksgiving?"

A question. Not an answer.

She's an amusing little liar, Alec was thinking. Her eyes turn cobalt.

Hortense threw herself into this essentially Worthian game, messing things up like the amateur she was. "We'd heard Uncle Jasper was seriously ill. Didn't we Alec? It was all over the financial sector, that rumor. Wasn't it Alec?"

Wives, Alec thought, are for bearing children. Passing on the sacred flame to the next generation. But what does one do with them in *this* generation?

The wind was rising in the gulf, blowing leaves on the table, making the candles in their hurricane goblets gutter and smoke.

"I'd heard he had a heart condition," fluttered Robin, looking like Camille on the brink of extinction. "Poor Uncle Jasper!"

A truly monumental rock, aimed right at Alec's toe. Nobody said *Poor Uncle Jasper.* It was a little like saying Poor Genghis Khan. One didn't say such a thing unless one was just making fun—and in the circumstance the line was in thoroughly bad taste. That is, *if* they knew. Which was why Robin hurled that particular rock with that particular inflection at that particular time. Looking at Alec with an uplifted eyebrow.

A form of flirtation, this exchange between the dazzling young woman and the middle-aged stock market wizard. Naked blades in the air, both of them enjoying the snicker-snee. In the flickering lamplight under the rising gulf wind.

The night air reeking with sex.

Neither of them giving an inch.

"I think," said Alec, "it's time to go inside. And reconsider our options."

"Oh, one has *options*? How delicious! I've always adored options because I never had any. The rich have everything *except* options. We have nowhere to go except *down*. Don't you agree, Uncle Alec?"

"She always talks like that when she drinks too much," said Fergie gloomily.

The rain came down at that point, driving them inside, drenched and laughing.

Robin dried herself and her turquoise silk dress with a towel, slipped one of her brother's purple shirts over the dress and fell to playing backgammon with Alec at two dollars a point.

Uncle Jasper rising like a hiccup from time to time.

"When did *you* last see Uncle Jasper?" asked Robin. "And why?"

Alec was toying with his options on the board, eyes on the table. "Two years ago. He stayed with us right here. We are a kind of southwest boarding house for touring Worths on the loose from Manhattan. Double," he said vengefully, turning the cube over.

Robin giggled, feeling the sexuality. "Well, we stir things up in your pleasant backwater, don't we? Did Uncle Jasper stir things up?"

"Yes," said Alec. Just yes, leaving her dangling.

She rolled a double six and doubled Alec.

The boys had gone off to play with the FX 4000, and after a while Hortense went up to her bed, leaving the two of them to play on.

CHAPTER 2

The schooner was yawing wildly in the screaming wind, the baby submarine swinging on its davits like a berserk chandelier. The three men were in their safety harnesses clipped to deck stanchions while trying to steady the sub with cables to the ship sides. But the schooner was seriously out of balance with all that weight on the port side. The sub should have been centered before the storm hit, Orin was thinking. Where were Dake's wits?

A gust hit the schooner broadside and it stood on its steel side like a drunken sailor, all three men flattened against the bulkhead, waiting for the damned boat to right itself. *If it righted itself.*

Nicholas was thrown against his brother and he noticed that Orin actually looked much better than he had at any other time during this voyage. His color was fresh and pink, the blue eyes clear and sparkling. "Marvelous!" Orin was saying. Not to Nicholas but to himself. "Bloody marvelous!"

Both brothers flattened out against the bulkhead with the green seawater not two yards away.

"What's bloody marvelous about it?" screamed Nicholas. "The damned boat's about to turn turtle, taking us all to the bottom—and Dad with it!"

"I was just thinking," Orin yelled, "how Dad would be loving this if he were alive! He'd be climbing the mast!"

He'd be throwing Dake overboard for getting us into this mess, Nicholas was thinking. The boat slowly, slowly righted itself.

It might very well *not* right itself the next time, Orin was thinking. He unclipped the safety harness—during a bit of a lull in the wind—and hurled himself on his knees toward the machinery. If he could get the winch going in this breeze.

Dake howling at him some blarney about who did he think was the captain of this ship, a thought which seemed to possess him more than the storm.

The winch cable had a great hook on it and this Orin tossed to his brother. "Slip it over and around the hatch. It's the strongest part of the thing."

The ship went into another of its sideslips, standing on the portside, the water only a foot away from the top of the bulkhead. If water started coming over the side, God help us every one, Orin thought. The boat hanging there trying to make up its mind whether it would plunge to the bottom or not. For the moment steady as a rock.

In that moment of steadiness, Orin flung the heavy hook with its chain around and under the baby sub and hooked it to the balance of the chain.

That would be the worst time to exert pressure. Wait till the schooner rights herself. *If* it decides to right itself. The vessel took its bloody time about that, thinking it over for a very long time, standing there on its portside, the green water beckoning in invitation. Shall I bend to the elements and slip gracefully into the deep, taking these rich idiots along with me? Or shall I fight on, and for what purpose? Long thoughts from an aging schooner.

The gale let up for a couple of seconds and the schooner rocked back upright. Orin pulled the steel lever, the winch snarling to life and inching the baby sub on its davits toward the center of the ship where it should have been all along.

The storm had picked up force again. Force eight? Nine? Somewhere around there, the green sea heaving the schooner from side to side now, back and forth, port to starboard. Dake clambering to the pilothouse to swing the bow into the gale.

"Strictly a smooth-water sailor!" shouted Orin, his blue eyes sparkling.

Orin, who would turn green in a living room when the emotional glass went down, was a miracle of calm in this raging sea. But then Orin had been the sailor of the family. The Bermuda, the Fastnet, he'd done them all. It was a way of dodging the old man, all that ocean racing.

The danger was not over; in fact, just beginning.

As if on cue, one emergency succeeding another, the *Rotterdam* loomed over them in the black raging night. Much too coincidentally. The exploration ship was five times the size of the schooner, bearing down on it from starboard, as if waiting in the wings for just such an opportunity, the damned boat big enough to cut the schooner in half. . . .

The brothers side by side again at the starboard bulkhead looking up at that approaching black mass of ship hanging over them like doom.

"Incest!" murmured Robin, slipping her bare arms around Alec's neck, delighting in the sibilants. Such a delicious word!

"There's a lot of it going around!" Kissing her young breasts under the covers. (They were in her room because it was farthest away from Hortense.)

"*Uncle* Alec!" Bearing down on the uncle to rub it in.

"I'm not really your uncle," said Alec, always the precisionist. "I'm actually your second cousin."

As if that were any excuse.

"Incest!" murmured Robin again, nailing him to the wall with it. She'd tried the incest bit with Fergie once, but they'd both burst out laughing before they got anywhere near pay dirt. But this shattering sexuality was the real article all right, all right... "We're rotten to the core, Uncle Alec, and you damned well know it!" Laughing and shivering with the pleasure of it. She'd hate herself in the morning, but just now it was beyond belief, this storm of red-hot lust she felt for her middle-aged uncle. And why? Because he was her uncle—second cousin be damned! No, there was more to it than that. There were those wizard eyes, that sharp mouth, that snickersnee of a mind, sexy as a bull, in his peculiar way.

"Are you unfaithful to Hortense all the time?"

"You're the first."

"Liar."

Alec was kissing her on the lips now, greedily, delicately, pausing only to say, because it was his turn, "And you! Are you wildly promiscuous?"

She was on the brink of shocking him but drew back because instinct told her this was not the time for it. "Very abstemious," she said, prim as a priest. "I've been waiting for *you*, Uncle Alec, to awaken me."

After which they went at it, hot and heavy and *honest*, which the dialogue wasn't. But then, was dialogue between lovers ever honest? How could it be? One's purpose was to arouse, to delight, to gratify—not to elucidate, and not, God knew, to seek answers to the universal questions. Maybe later, emotion recollected in tranquility.

Not now....

Later, after the raging storm of lust had run its wild way, they lay side by side, reassembling their nerve ends, spent and . . . yes, shamed. Not because it was adultery or incest, not anything like that, but because they were Worths and they had got in over their heads and Worths never liked to get in over their heads. Not ever.

They'd fucked a little flame alive, as D.H. Lawrence had so trenchantly put it, so far ahead of his time, and heaven knew where it would all end.

Alec slipped out of the bed and put on his underwear and then his trousers. "You owe me seven hundred and thirty-two dollars."

Robin burst out laughing. Quietly because it was late and still and who knew how far laughter would carry in the dark?

"You're a shark and you ought to be ashamed of yourself, taking money from a little girl young enough to be your daughter."

"You were never a little girl! Even at eleven!"

"I'm still a little girl, Uncle Alec, first taken for seven hundred and thirty dollars, and then seduced and abandoned. My whole life devastated like a Victorian heroine."

Alec was putting on everything, necktie, jacket, all of it as if he'd never taken it off. He was about to run into a blizzard of questions, about to tell a lot of lies.

He didn't respond to the jokiness.

Instead, he asked, "What are you doing here *really*, Robin?"

"Wouldn't you like to know?"

"I might be helpful."

"Is that why you fucked me? To find out what I'm up to?"

He sat on the bed now fully dressed, looking like a stockbroker. "I fucked you because it was our destiny, yours and mine."

"Oh, that washes away the guilt, does it? Because it was our destiny?"

"No such luck," said Alec, sober as a magistrate. "It

was Oedipus' destiny to fuck his mother but he felt damned badly about it anyway." He kissed her on her sorrowful lips. "See you around, cousin."

He left, closing the door behind him, Robin lying there listening to the howling wind.

Uncle Jasper out there on that schooner in the middle of the storm. . . .

Nicholas would everlastingly give Dake credit for seizing the moment. Dake had thrown the engines full speed astern, almost tearing them apart. The schooner had shuddered under the impact and then the bow had risen and swung off to port, under the urging of the engine and the wind. The big exploration ship bearing down on them, itself not altogether the master of its destiny in the raging sea, had reared up on a vast wave and come crashing down on the precise bit of water the schooner had just vacated.

Nicholas and Orin were glued to the bulkhead, watching the big steamer lurching past them, scarcely twenty feet away. The nose of the schooner swinging back to port barely missed the big rudder of the exploration ship as it rocked into the trough of the very wave that had lifted the schooner's nose. The exploration ship then shuddered forward into the darkness in the wind and the rain.

"Good seamanship," howled Nicholas reluctantly.

"Only thing he could do," shouted Orin the sailor and seaman. "And Dake had to have a bit of luck to get away with it. They tried to run us down, you know. There was no excuse for them being so close. Not with radar and all the navigation gear they have now. Let's go below."

"They'll try again."

Orin shook his head, smiling at his landlubber brother. "It'd take that skipper a mile and a half to turn that bucket around in this sea and we'd be out of sight. Come below."

* * *

In the pilothouse of the exploration ship, its captain, Lemuel Stork, was putting it in a different light, himself at the wheel, the lawyer Francis Graebner bent over the radar screen where the schooner flickered like an expiring Tinker Bell. Graebner had urged the captain to bring the big exploration ship around and head back toward the schooner. Lemuel Stork, in his flinty Maine voice, was explaining a few elemental facts of seamanship to the lawyer.

". . . a force-eight gale you don't go turning a ship this size around lightly or at all unless you have to. Besides, it would take me five miles to do the thing properly in the gale and by then they'd be in Corpus Christi." Captain Stork lit a Gaulois and took a puff deep into his lungs. "Anyway, one might possibly be accident. Twice, they'd take my ticket away. Maybe they will anyway. Damned risky business. . . ."

"I never told you to hit him," said Graebner. "We were searching for the body and keeping the schooner in sight because we had reason to believe—"

"Reason to believe," Stork in his flinty voice, mocking the lawyer. No, Graebner had not indeed told him to hit the other ship. He had merely urged him to get close in this raging sea where an accident would be inevitable. Nudging him into complicity where he'd have to keep his mouth shut, and of course, himself, the lawyer, staying well clear of any wrongdoing that could be proved in court. Lawyers! Bastards, all of them!

"Turn the ship around. Take as long as you please within the bounds of safety, but turn it around," said Graebner.

"The limits of safety, Mr. Graebner? Well, all right then, we'll ride out the storm and then we'll think about turning the ship around. That is the sensible thing."

"I said within the limits of safety," said Graebner. "I said nothing about being sensible."

"I know what you said and I'm following your orders, Mr. Graebner, in the best interests of the safety of the ship and the crew. In the matter of seamanship you'll have to leave it to my judgment, won't you?"

Graebner was a tall, bony man with gray hair and a mouth that hung down on one side as if he'd at some time had a stroke. He tore his gaze away from the radar now and looked at Stork with his icy gaze. Changing course as he had had to do so often in the middle of his court cases.

"Very well," he said. He left the pilothouse and went out on the catwalk where the wind struck hard, driving him into the steel stanchions around the catwalk. He steadied himself and went down the clanging steel ladder, down into the galley where Elihu Worth was drinking coffee, perusing the dead man's papers. He'd hardly left those papers since the accident.

"Stork is getting to be a problem," said Graebner.

Elihu didn't want to talk about Stork. "Five million," said Elihu, flashing his magnificent white teeth like a shark, "for the president of Mexico and the whole thing washed clean in the Bahamas. The old pirate got a hundred million dollars' worth of oil rights in the gulf for a five-million bribe charged off to a now defunct subsidiary in the Bahamas and he never told me a word. I thought he told me everything."

"He never told anyone everything or anything like," said Graebner. "The things he kept from me, his lawyer, would fill the Library of Congress. The things we don't know about him would fill the seven seas. . . ."

In the little gallery of the schooner, Orin and Nicholas had to feel their way around the food they had taken out of the refrigerator to make room for the old man. Melons, slabs of bacon, bits of fish were rolling or sliding about the floor, making the footing slippery. The smell was bad and getting worse.

"Dake hates the mess," said Nicholas. "It'll keep him out of here until we get to Galveston."

"If we get to Galveston," said Orin. "Anything can happen in a force-eight gale, Nicholas."

The ship heaving and lurching under them.

The coffeepot was fastened on the stove by a steel rim around its middle, a clever gadget designed for just such weather. Nicholas poured his brother a cup of overboiled coffee and one for himself and they put their bottoms carefully on the bench that ran around the small galley table, wearily because they were dead tired.

"There's no getting around the fact they must have spotted us or they wouldn't have tried to run us down," said Orin. "That's two of them now, the helicopter people—whoever they were—and the exploration ship. Getting very crowded out here in the Gulf of Mexico."

Nicholas said, "No marks on him. Maybe it's poison, but we'll have to wait for the coroner's report."

Orin said gently, "Maybe he just fell overboard, Nicholas. You know the old man. Maybe he was climbing the rigging to show the world—and especially Elihu—"

"Elihu!" Nicholas spat the name. "The old man was such a good judge of character *most* of the time. . . ."

Orin switched on the radio to get Nicholas off that. There was no point in dwelling on Elihu.

The nine o'clock news from the top. Reagan blaming the truck bombing in Lebanon on Jimmy Carter. His Labor Secretary indicted for one hundred thirty-seven alleged felonies. Various local swindles in the Corpus Christi neighborhood. (It was a Corpus Christi station.) The Cubs won the first game of the playoffs against San Diego, thirteen to zero.

No mention of Jasper Worth. Former Secretary of State. A legend in his time bigger than Howard Hughes and twice as mysterious. He would have been the top of the news.

"Why are they not announcing it?" said Orin. "Lost at sea. A fitting end for the old buccaneer." Orin, who loved his father in spite of everything. Sir Galahad, as they called him at prep school.

"For one thing he isn't lost and they damned well know it. They wish he were."

"It's been hours. They must be in touch with the mainland."

Nicholas' thin, sad face lit up malevolently. "The family's broke. Elihu is keeping the news from the world."

An old family jest. About as likely as the sun rising in the west—the Worths going broke. Still, sometimes in the dark moments, Nicholas and Orin hungered for poverty as one of those unattainable dreams, like a peasant dreaming of being a Rockefeller.

"I don't know, Orin. Elihu is up to something lousy. Deals that have to be concluded. Something..." Trying to keep the hatred out of his voice so Orin—Sir Galahad—wouldn't impale him on it. Nicholas enjoyed his hatred, his motivation. Hating Elihu was what life was all about—at least his life. Orin disagreed. Hatred was wrong. Nicholas should expunge it from his soul. Nicholas had listened to it before many times and he didn't want to listen to it now in this raging storm when he was so exhausted. So Nicholas smiled his sad smile. "We'll just have to wait and see. It'll be interesting to see whether the announcement comes from New York or Washington or Texas. It will tell us a lot—from what quarter the announcement comes, and by whom and in what tone of voice."

The longer the news wasn't announced the fishier the whole thing was. Elihu up to his tricks, many of which he'd learned from Jasper. Too many.

"We could have announced it ourselves. We have the body. But we seem to have a broken ship-to-shore. Isn't that a funny coincidence...."

CHAPTER 3

Alec was in the back seat of the stretch Lincoln dictating into the gadget. Something he didn't do often. He liked to drive his own car to work early but this morning ... well, it had been a late night. Hortense had been asleep, or shamming, when he got to bed, and absent when he got up (at 9 A.M., horrendously late for Alec who was an early riser) and now at 9:45 A.M. Alec had taken the Lincoln with Absolom at the wheel so he could catch up on a bit of correspondence. Not his favorite occupation, correspondence. Alec spent most of his working life on the telephone. Correspondence was for those few uncompromising and uncomfortable communications that had to be put inflexibly on paper so that everyone was absolutely sure that was what had been said and nothing more than this, thus far and no further and no arguments.

"...You must understand," he was dictating now into the mouthpiece of the Diktat, "that in your situation one of the most sensible and most difficult courses to pursue is to do nothing whatsoever. Your portfolio is balanced and beautiful and appreciating harmoniously. Any movement in the market at this point, no matter what the temporary advantage or profit, would only in the long run do you harm, possibly grievous harm..." And so forth.

It wouldn't do any good. Old Lassiter was bored and dying to get out in the mainstream and lose a little money, but Alec had to make his position not only clear but in print where he could summon it up when the old prune rounded on him later and tried—as he had so often in the past—to make Alec responsible for his own indiscretions. Lassiter was monstrously rich and he felt that one of the privileges of the rich was the ability always to blame somebody else. That was what money was for.

Alec closed the Diktat and spoke to Absolom. "Did you take Mrs. Worth anywhere?" He had noticed her car when they passed the garage.

"Miz Worth on her horse," said Absolom. "She was taking a long, long ride."

"Oh."

Alec feeling his way around, as he so often had to do to get information that in an ordinary household would be open to everyone. You couldn't quiz the servants. Very bad form. You had to feel your way. And interpret the signals. A long, long ride on horseback. That meant she'd canceled some appointments (Alec looking at his watch, now almost ten). Georgie Fish had been due at the house with some estimates for the new rock garden they had to make up their mind about. Hortense would have had to cancel that. Or ignore it. Bad news.

"Did she go alone or was Miss Worth with her?"

"She by herself, Mistuh Worth."

In his dry crackerbarrel voice. Alec wished he hadn't brought it up. Absolom knew as well as he that Hortense never went riding by herself unless... There were a lot of unlesses. She was upset. Angry. Wanted to be alone. All three of the above. It was hard to keep these things from the servants who, Alec realized, might even know more about his wife's mood (and the reasons therefore) than he did. That was the problem. The servants who had been with them longest (and Absolom had been with them since they were married and with his father before that) were the best servants but also they knew the most, including a lot of things you wished they didn't know. There was nothing you could do about that.

Absolom said, "I took Miss Worth to the airport very early."

Alec had to call up all the taciturnity he possessed—and he possessed a great deal—to prevent himself from giving vent. He didn't say, "What!" His eyes didn't bug open or his mouth either. He didn't turn red or show anything at all. But inside himself the dismay was very sharp and that scared him. The damned girl had got into his bones, way in.

"Airport?" said Alec. To give Absolom a nudge to embroider that simple naked word.

"Yes, sir!" said Absolom. *Not* embroidering.

Alec blinked and blew his nose and stalled, to see if Absolom, damn his black heart, would vouchsafe just a little something extra. Absolom vouchsafed nothing.

"Did you take her luggage?" Alec very much didn't want to voice anything resembling concern, not in front of the servants, particularly not in front of Absolom who was a very sharp and subtle black man indeed, but dismay had pushed him into this unseemly question.

"No," said Absolom. Nothing more. Just no.

The sunlight piercing Alec's very soul with its brilliance. Alec looking over the green fields that had once grown cotton, where all the money came from, and now harbored thoroughbred horses. The gulf storm had washed the air and left it clear and fresh.

He rolled down the window to get a lungful of that clear

fresh air and only then did he become conscious of the rackety rackety noise. It had been there before but not that loud in the quiet car.

"What's that?" asked Alec.

"That Miss Worth," said Absolom. "She been following us in that machine."

"Stop," said Alec. He got out of the car, folded his arms on the roof and looked up. A red Bell SX 12, fourseater, making the awful noise they all made. It came down, hovering, slowing expertly, just the other side of the fence. The rotors slowed and stopped. Robin stepped out wearing her white overalls, wrinkling her nose in the piercing sunlight.

"Hi!"

"Do you always fly barefoot?"

Robin looked at her brown foot and wiggled her toes at him. "I'd give you a lift but I've got a lunch date with Hortense."

"You saw Hortense?"

"Yes."

Just that. Nothing more. Everyone giving him short answers this morning.

Alec said, "Did you have a nice flight?"

"Very nice. I flew out over the gulf for a hundred miles."

"See anything interesting?"

Robin laughed, looking at him sidewise, taking him all in, all the implications—last night included. And dodged the question. "Do you like my helicopter? I just bought it."

Trying to shock the middle-aged stockbroker and succeeding to the point where—at least for the moment—she silenced him. Robin loved her red helicopter. Such a pretty toy. And she had wanted it immediately. The helicopter people had been very tiresome about that. Wanted to send the thing back to the factory for a thorough overhaul first but she wanted the machine *now* . . . and when you want something *now* and when you're rich. . . .

"You *bought* it? Why?"

"Well, you never know when you're going to need a red helicopter, do you?"

On the exploration ship, Graebner, the lawyer, was feeling his way carefully toward the toilet (which he refused to call *the head*, a loathsome, all-steel cubicle, which stank of urine) when he heard the unmistakable high speed chatter of the tape. He looked at his watch. Seven ten. He pushed his way into the radio shack and there was Elihu feeding the tapes into the machine. No sign of the radioman. Elihu so occupied he didn't notice Graebner standing there.

The lawyer picked up a coil of tape. Coded gibberish. "Applegate stemwind asturias sensivus noster," and much more. Applegate was code for Mercury Oil, but the rest Graebner didn't know.

Elihu flashed his pearly teeth at Graebner and said, "You're up early."

"Not early enough. Who are you sending coded messages to at seven in the morning?"

"Eight in New York." Not saying who.

"What sort of instructions about Mercury Oil at eight in the morning?" Mercury Oil was a ten-billion-dollar corporation. The crown jewel of Jasper's empire.

Elihu didn't bother to answer that, but his smile dimmed. He turned back to the machine which was devouring yards more of tape destined for who knew what high speed receiver in New York. Graebner picked up another bit of tape and read, "Dinosaur apex inter lastfor." Elihu jerked the tape out of the lawyer's hand. The smile had vanished altogether.

Apex was a buy order for dinosaur—whatever that was. Lastfor was a number. Elihu was ordering a buy of . . . what?

Graebner's cold green eyes ran over Elihu quick as a lizard's tongue. The possibilities for this cunning villain were manifold.

"You're exceeding your authority, Elihu."

"You're exceeding yours."

The end of the long coded message was dancing past the lawyer. Graebner grabbed at it and tried to turn the machine off, his hand darting toward the switch—a big red plastic thing that said ON and OFF. Elihu was too quick for him, his white beautiful hand fending off the lawyer's hairy claw even as the last foot of tape was swallowed up by the machine which sent it on its way to the satellite in geosynchronous orbit more than twenty-two thousand miles above the equator.

Elihu breathed a big happy sigh.

Graebner was on his knees in the middle of the pile of spent tape looking for that last significant word which he had half seen. He ran the tape through his fingers until he came to the last word. Thor. Code for Jasper. Elihu had been sending out instructions to buy under Jasper's name.

The printer came to life and chattered, "Acknowledge receipt 0812 end transmission dl."

On his knees Graebner tore off the end of the tape with that word Thor on it and put it in his pocket. He got up awkwardly, and read the initials on the printer. dl. That would be Dora Land, Elihu's personal assistant, conceivably the only person on Wall Street at such an outlandish hour as 0812.

"Jasper's dead," said the lawyer without emphasis.

Elihu had sat down again on the radioman's swivel chair and was sipping cold coffee wearing his gleaming smile.

"Any order signed Jasper Worth or coded to indicate it was signed by Jasper Worth dated after three o'clock yesterday is fraudulent. The SEC would not only nullify them but have your head."

Elihu smiled lazily. "We don't know that Jasper is dead. Only missing."

Graebner licked his lips and took his time. "All transactions on Wall Street are matters of records; their time, date and source. When a man dies, his estate is frozen at that minute to be administered under the supervision of the courts. Any tampering without permission of the courts is a grave offense, Elihu."

Elihu laughed, a gentle mocking laugh. "Graebner, the great liberal lawyer! You know what Jasper said about you, Graebner? He said Graebner covers his ass with liberalism."

Graebner stood his ground. "Jasper Worth never gave you nor anyone else authority to make transactions in his name."

"Oh, but he did!" protested Elihu, smiling infuriatingly. "I'm just carrying out verbal instructions that he gave me just before he so unwisely started to climb to the crow's nest wearing nothing but his misplaced confidence. Are you calling me a liar, Graebner—you who have so much to lose? Let me remind you Graebner, to steal a phrase from Henry Ford—my name's on the building. Yours isn't."

Elihu was a Worth. Graebner wasn't.

That left a hole in the air, a pause—pregnant with indecision.

Elihu gathered up yards of tape and put them in the radioman's iron stove where he set fire to them, Graebner watching. Graebner, the great liberal lawyer, who had successfully defended the five black boys of rape–murder at Teterboro, New Jersey, who had helped found the Civil Liberties Union, was in the forefront of all the Great Society movements, but who had never forgotten that Wall Street was where the money came from.

The fire burning away, Elihu turned the full power of his smile on the lawyer.

He held out his hand. "That piece of tape you have in your pocket, Graebner. May I have it?"

Graebner's face grew even more lopsided. It was decision time, something all lawyers loathed. On the one hand were all those splended principles, on the other—Mercury Oil, a ten-billion-dollar corporation. . . .

He handed the piece of tape over and watched Elihu as he threw it on the fire.

Luncheon was on the terrace but not the same terrace as dinner the night before. Dinner the night before had been on the big terrace overlooking a broad sweep of lawn that fell away sharply to the gulf and the boathouse, where the big and rowdier parties were held and whence the children were banished when their parents wanted them out of the way. That terrace, almost an esplanade, ran the full length of the house and could accommodate an almost infinite number of guests.

The luncheon terrace—it was actually called that—was at the side of the house under the live oak tree whose leaves and gray moss filtered the sunlight onto little dappled pools of brightness. Around the little square wrought-iron table was a bower of greenery and flowers, the table set like a jewel in the very center of this riot of color and chlorophyll.

The table could manage only four lunchers and usually held no more than two. Hortense frequently lunched there by herself when the children were at school. Today there was only Hortense and Robin, the boys all off at the club. Club life loomed large in Texas childhood, some of the country clubs actually running bus service, picking up those children who didn't have chauffeurs, taking them to the club in the morning and bringing them back at night, filling that function in summer that the schools filled in winter, so that mothers were left almost totally free all year long to get into whatever mischief their temperaments demanded.

So thought Robin, a Manhattan child with a large in-grown contempt for country club life and the people who inhabited that life, picking away at the cold salmon which was very good and very fresh. Hortense was picking away at something else. "Alec is a Worth *manqué*," Hortense was saying. "He has all the strong characteristics—the intellectual arrogance, the scorn, the self-confidence—but he isn't, like you eastern Worths, surrounded by relatives to shield him and advise him and keep him from making the big mistakes."

"Alec makes mistakes?" This from Robin. She could see the red helicopter through the encircling greenery. She'd put it down on the lawn to provoke a little comment and it had provoked very little. This, after all, was Texas.

"Not yet," said Hortense in that rushing vibrant voice which implied so much more than it said. "But one is always conscious of the absence of the safety net. When Alec does fall off the edge it's going to be a long fall."

She knows.

Robin eating her salmon greedily because she was very hungry after her early morning flight. She sipped a bit of the Montrachet and summoned Choo Choo, as they called the pretty Vietnamese girl, to give her some more salmon. She knows and she wants me to know she knows. . . .

Hortense prattling on about the Worth family—their strong points, their vulnerabilities.

Vulnerabilities, my God. Why were non-Worths so full of explanations about Worths? We're all different, Robin was thinking, wildly different. We're people like any other. Except she knew that wasn't true.

". . . a different tempo," Hortense was saying. "The rest of us live at a slower pulse beat. Always hurrying to catch up. But we never do . . . catch up."

"I should think it would be the other way around," said Robin distinctly, laying it right on the table. "You have about twenty-five times as much energy as Alec, Hortense. I should think he would be the one who had to do the hurrying."

"You don't know him very well," said Hortense with her bright cold smile.

I'm being rebuked for impertinence for venturing an opinion about her husband after only one night in the sack with him but she feels free to make all sorts of wild generalities about us Worths because we're public property, out there in the open for everyone to take a shot at. Robin smiled, recklessly displaying her faultless teeth and her beauty and—worst of all—her youth to this older, unpretty woman. Answer enough. Perhaps too much.

"I know," said Robin much too meekly, almost a parody of submissiveness. "I know him hardly at all."

Which was, of course, open to all sorts of interpretations. Not the least that Robin intended to know Alec much much better before returning him, after first thoroughly exploring him, knowing the hell out of him. Actually, it wasn't at all what she intended. Robin didn't want Alec all that much (except right at that moment, heated by the wine, she did, very badly), had nothing but very temporary intentions and didn't, God knew, want to alarm or antagonize Hortense because the two of them had to live together in some sort of graceful if artificial amity for the next few days until that damned schooner landed. . . .

All these things passing through Robin's pretty skull, while she ate, and grimaced submissiveness, which wasn't her lay at all. She should be pulling my hair out, not giving me lunch. Food playing so large a role in these rituals of the rich. Dinner the night before had contributed heavily toward— aah, that lovely antique ceremony—her seduction. Or his seduction. Any one of them seducing the other. Or both (being Worths) seducing themselves, and now here was the wife offering me fresh salmon and white wine as introduction to . . . what, abnegation? Not quite. Hortense was calling attention to the fact that she *knew* of this affair (if it could be graced by so stately a term) and she intended forbearance and that this knowledge and forbearance entitled her to some minor participatory share in the delights. We're all in this together! A sort of *ménage à trois* of the mind.

Dear God!

All these polite hyper-civilized signals. She should be throwing the wine in my face! Having a good old-fashioned temper tantrum which is what she would have done if I were a lesser mortal. But because I'm a Worth she's trying to live up to me. And I am supposed to send up a hyper-civilized signal that I recognize her generosity and acknowledge what a marvelous wife and consort she is.

Then it came, the worst possible signal of all.

Against her will—feeling the thing coming and being absolutely unable to control it—fighting it every inch of the way and *losing*, Robin yawned in Hortense's face.

The last thing in the world she wanted to do. My God, what would Mother say? To yawn in the face of a woman whose husband you had laid the night before as if the whole thing were such a bore, and her forbearance an even bigger bore. . . .

"Darling," cried Robin, tears in her lovely eyes. "Forgive me. I was up until four last night! I was up again at six! That delicious lunch and the wine is putting me to *sleep*!"

Each syllable making everything much worse. As Robin stood up, making it even worse, "I've got to go collapse somewhere!"

"Oh," said Hortense, pierced to the marrow, "there's a perfectly marvelous flambé. . . ."

"Might I be forgiven dessert?" Robin kissed Hortense and gave her a little hug, spilling a few tears on Hortense's cheek to show how magnificently sorry she was about *everything*. Off she rushed to her bed, leaving Hortense alone in the beautiful bower of greenery and flowers to eat the flambé by herself.

Might I be forgiven dessert?

Hortense shook her head in wonderment and ate a second helping of flambé because it was delicious.

Might I be forgiven dessert and my beauty and my wealth and my adultery and my bad manners—because what choice have you? The tears on her cheek drying and forming a little tightness on Hortense's skin. My goodness, these Worths cried real tears, like Barbie dolls. They made Hortense smile a tight smile, the rage simmering down. The awful thing was that she was entranced by Robin, by her youth and her beauty and her Worthiness, and she'd miss her terribly when she left.

Choo Choo brought the telephone to the table. "Meez Syd'nam," she said.

Her best friend Margot Sydenham, who usually called at that hour to congratulate or commiserate, sometimes both. "They treat us like innkeepers," said Hortense brightly, bravely. "I don't suppose any of those Eastern Worths has paid a hotel bill in years. They just look up the nearest Worth—and there is one of us somewhere near to every damned city in America. Why do we put up with it, Margot?"

"*Droit du seigneur,*" suggested Margot.

"*Exactement,*" said Hortense. Too damned *exactement*.

It should have been a routine transaction, and normally Alec, as chairman of the finance committee and president of the bank, wouldn't have been bothered with it except that it involved Mercury Oil, and Tomkins knew his chief was always interested in that one.

A five-million-dollar loan to Mercury Oil, a ten-billion-dollar company which should be able to get five million out of petty cash. And for what purpose? To loan in turn to Energy Inc. Energy Inc. was one of Jasper Worth's shell companies which Jasper used for some of his little games of management and control.

Why wouldn't Jasper get the five million out of his own

back pocket? Well, you never knew what Jasper was up to. Sometimes these vast corporations were strapped for petty cash. But why his little First Bank of Texas instead of one of the giants—Citibank, Chase Manhattan? Jasper did that, too. Spread his loans among the little out-of-New York banks to conceal his intentions. Very successfully, too.

If only he weren't so full of questions about Jasper at the moment, his own house full of . . . that damned girl and her brother. All those rumors about Jasper. Robin flying out over the gulf this morning, looking for. . . what?

Alec tapped out a command on his computer. The screen lit up with numbers.

Mercury Oil 37½

Down three points from the day before. Down five and a half from the week before. Alec summoned Tomkins and pointed to the computer screen. "Why?"

Mercury Oil was not only one of the pillars of Jasper's empire (one of many pillars) but also one of Alec's own rock solid stocks.

Tomkins shrugged. "Rumors about Jasper Worth's health, I think."

"Jasper could die this afternoon and it shouldn't affect Mercury Oil. It's not a management company. Its assets are oil, pools of the stuff, ships, oil wells, refineries, all solid brass."

Tomkins knew all that. Like Alec he was thin and young and very Texas. "You know New York. They deal in rumors as if they were fact, and by the time they're through with them they might as well be facts—in fact, they *make* them facts. Lunacy."

The two Texans far from the Big Board and its idiocies shaking their heads over this New York nonsense.

"It went down again this morning," said Tomkins, "at the opening of trading. Down five-eighths. Somebody's dumping shares."

"I'll take them," cried Alec. "These fools, dumping good stocks on bad rumors. Put in a buy order."

"They're already sold," said Tomkins, "so fast we couldn't get in there. The old man dumping his good stock at bargaining rates and buying back with one of his shell companies, impoverishing himself."

"He never impoverishes himself," said Alec. "Never. Which shell company was it?"

"Energy Inc."

The very one borrowing five million that it didn't need from Mercury Oil to . . . buy stocks in Mercury Oil? The SEC would be very interested in that but the SEC would never know because the loan had been made so far from Wall Street. Unless he, Alec, told them.

"Who's CEO of Energy Inc. these days?"

"Jasper."

"Are you sure?"

"Well, he was up until . . . a week ago."

"Look it up."

Tomkins, thin, intense, sandy hair thinning a bit, hesitated at the door. "Are you disapproving the loan? How can you disapprove a loan to Mercury? I mean . . ."

Alec said, "I know what you mean. I'm not disapproving. Just holding it up for a minute. Put it down to the pressure of business, shall we?" Jasper wasn't the only Worth who could play games.

Alec called a distant in-law of his in New York, Abner Drummond, who was married to one of the lesser Worths but was himself a commercial banker of great skill.

"Come off it, Alec. Mercury Oil? They're more liquid than your bank. What's the problem?"

"Why are they borrowing money so far from home?"

"Well, you know Jasper . . ." Still, it was a good question. "Mercury Oil has a line of credit a mile long—perhaps a billion."

"And Energy Inc."

"Well, Energy Inc., uh, no—it's a holding company but it's Jasper's holding company, one of them."

"It's a shell. What's the cash position of Energy Inc.?"

"I don't know who could tell you that. Not anyone here. Jasper doesn't reveal his hand and it's a hundred percent owned by another Jasper holding company, Synergestics, Ltd., which is registered in the Bahamas and is not accountable to the SEC."

"I see," said Alec. Tomkins had reappeared and was laying a memo in front of him. It read: CEO Energy Inc.—Elihu Worth. "Mmmm," said Alec and nodded and waved at Tomkins to get rid of him because he didn't want him in on this telephone conversation. "And how much is Energy Inc. into your bank for in short-term?"

"This is pretty confidential stuff, Alec."

"Not if he's trying to raise five million down here in the boondocks. I should think you'd be interested. How many other little banks is he getting five million from? These five millions add up."

The two bankers sparring back and forth, feeling for each other's vulnerabilities, ticking each other's financial risibilities, trading little snippets of information for other little mutually profitable snippets. Energy Inc., it transpired, had taken out a loan of twenty million just the day before.

"For what reason and who signed the order?"

"Liquidity," said Abner Drummond, "the usual reason, and Jasper signed it himself. It came from down in your area. Jasper's down there, rumor has it, exploring for oil in some ship. Have you heard that?"

"Mmmm," said Alec. "And what sort of security did you get for your twenty million?"

"Mercury Oil stock, good as gold."

"Have you got it, or is it someplace in escrow?"

"It's . . . wait. I'll ask."

A long wait while Alec doodled twenty million in free-flowing figures. Mercury Oil shares were solid gold. To use them as security for cash flow in a minor holding company run by one of Jasper's nephews—or was it a great-nephew? —smelled of cash diversion.

Abner Drummond came back on the telephone and he sounded a bit worried. "Well, we haven't actually got the shares. They're held in a safe deposit box in Switzerland, but we have a piece of paper entitling us—"

"I see," said Alec.

He made more phone calls to friends, contacts, relatives in the banking community in Chicago, Houston, San Franciso, all the lesser money markets, and found, after a bit of badgering, a bit of trading back and forth, a huge cash flow of short-term loans to Energy Inc., all from little banks in out of the way places. And heaven knew how many more there were in the real tricky spots like the Bahamas, the Greater Antilles, the Seychelles and the other little islands which had banks operating with few laws whatsoever.

Tomkins came back. "They're bugging us from New York now for that cash and querying the delay. Why are we doing this, chief?"

"Where did the query came from?"

"New York."

"Signed by who?"

Tomkins showed him the message. It was signed Elihu Worth. "Get me Energy Inc. in New York," said Alec.

It was a long wait. Tomkins had to get information and there seemed to be none about Energy Inc. When he got through it seemed to be on one of Mercury Oil's vast number of lines in the Empire State Building and Alec found himself talking to a self-assured young woman. "Where is Elihu Worth?" he asked.

"I'm not at liberty to divulge that information, sir, but Mr. Elihu—"

Mister Elihu!

"—has asked that the loan be expedited."

"What security are you offering for this loan?"

There was shocked silence on the other end. "Mr. Worth, the loan is backed by Mercury Oil's line of credit which—"

"I know all about Mercury's line of credit but I want to know about Energy Inc.'s line of credit."

"Mr. . . . Worth . . ."

A very interesting divergence in tone between the Mister and the Worth—dripping scorn on the first word, followed by the merest hesitation, and then, in an entirely different tone of voice, realizing that this person she was talking to *was* a Worth, the more respectful, hushed incantatory name. To how many other lesser bankers in the Antilles and the Bahamas, and even in New York to Abner Drummond who didn't have that magic name, had this distant chilly woman dripped scorn at the very hint that some security would be needed to cover a loan to so majestic a client as Energy Inc., a Jasper Worth company?

How many unsecured loans had she (or Elihu Worth) gotten and how many loans secured by Mercury Oil stock not in the hands of the lender, but in Elihu's safe deposit box in Switzerland? And was it Alec's name or his acumen that gave him the courage and the self-confidence to hold off his woman—who was she anyhow?—from overawing him into loaning money without real security?

After all, she'd talked Abner Drummond into this, and how many other able officers of small banks?

"We'd need something more substantial than Mercury Oil's line of credit or," with a faint smile, wishing he could see the woman's face, "Mercury Oil shares in a Swiss bank vault. Under the circumstances we'll have to refuse the loan."

Outraged silence which went on so long that Alec finally said, "Miss . . . uh, I don't believe I have your name."

"Dora Land, Mr. Worth." It summoned up a picture in his mind of a slim, dark, very intelligent middle European woman with furious brown eyes. "We'll have to turn elsewhere, Mr. Worth, not only now but in the future."

Alec couldn't resist saying, "Good luck, Mrs. Land."

An insult, of course, coming from a little bank in Galveston to the fountainhead of money in Manhattan, and what's more an intended insult. Uncle Alec sending a shot over the bow of Elihu Worth . . . to stir him up.

The other work was piling up around Alec, phone calls, appeals for advice, the usual detritus, but Alec was on the hunt now. Something was very rotten in Denmark. He called his friend Jessica Keswick, whose little column in the *Wall Street Journal* was a repository of rumor, gossip and tips of a financial nature. Alec and Jessica had a few flings together when he was in New York. It was a warm relationship.

They exchanged endearments, queries about health and family (Jessica was separated from her husband, had her children living with her), and then got down to trading. "What do you know about Elihu Worth?"

"A nasty piece of work, as the English say. You shouldn't have to ask. You're family."

"Distant family, way out here in the boondocks. Why nasty?"

"He's adopted and he's never got over it."

"Aaah," said Alec.

It was her turn. "Why are you so curious about Elihu Worth at this particular time?"

"What particular time?"

"Right now, there are rumors driving down Mercury Oil."

"That, too. What do you know about that?"

"Alec, love, *you're* not being very forthcoming. What's it to you that you should make long-distance calls all the way from Galveston, which is not even in the Western Hemisphere?"

Alec took a deep breath and said, "You didn't get it from me, I may even deny it, but you have it on good authority that the First Bank of Texas refused Elihu Worth a five-million loan because the bank—not *me*, now, the bank—

didn't like the cash position of Energy Inc. Keep my name out of this thing altogether."

"Well, well," said Jessica, writing it all down. "Sending up a trial balloon, are we?"

"I'm being forthcoming. Isn't that what you wanted me to be—forthcoming? It sounds like I'm having an orgasm, that word. What is the news on the Rialto about Jasper Worth?"

"My God, Alec, asking *me* about all *your* relatives. Can't you keep track of your own family?"

"I just want to know what's being said. It sometimes has very little relation to the truth. What are they *saying* about Jasper?"

"That he's sick or senile. Is he?"

"Not when I saw him last, which was six months ago. He was impossible but then he's always been that. Anyway, I don't know why Jasper's health should affect a ten-billion-dollar corporation. There's something very fishy about a stock whose price keeps going *down* even though it's in great demand. I should think the SEC might ask some questions."

"Darling, the SEC's authority stops at the water's edge. A good many of these transactions are coming from abroad— both the buy orders and the sell orders—from places like Bahrain and the Seychelles. Panicky selling from the institutions in these islands. There's a rumor afloat the Arabs are dumping Mercury stock and *that* has caused grave disquiet, as we say in the *Wall Street Journal*, among American investors."

"Mmmm," said Alec.

Jessica uttered a huge sigh clearly audible all the way to Texas. "Alec, I don't know why I'm telling you all this. I'm a newspaper gal. I'm supposed to be asking the questions. Now you give me a little something in return."

"Not for attribution."

"Not for attribution."

"You know my—uh—second cousin, Robin Worth?"

"I don't move in those circles but of course I know *of* her. The girl who has everything—looks, charm, wit, money and most of the men."

"Well, she had everything except a red helicopter. She now has a red helicopter. Good-bye, love. I'll buy your lunch next time I'm in New York which may be very soon. You've been very helpful and I'm deeply grateful. Save the whales."

He hung up.

CHAPTER 4

The schooner ploughed due east through the blue gulf water, Dake at the wheel in the pilothouse, wrapped in his formidable Scottish silence, a bearded Jehovah. Orin was spread-legged in the bow shooting the sun with his bronze sextant, an activity as quaint as driving oxcarts in the age of satellite navigation.

Nicholas lay atop the tarpaulin over the forward hatch, watching through narrowed lids in the dazzling sunshine. Envying his older brother this antique business with the sextant. Orin holding time and place in the palm of his hand like Vasco da Gama. Beautiful! Himself barely awake in the glimmer and peace. The little battery radio was on his chest tuned to the Corpus Christi station which had nothing on its mind except the next rock number. Nicholas listening for news of Jasper. Or Elihu. Or anything.

I am my brother's keeper. Me the youngest. The older brother and sister would have to be told. Jasper Jr. who lived in Manitoba on his four-thousand-acre ranch with his blooded Herefords (as far away as he could get from the old man) and Louise, who was the Marquise of Hampton, who lived in the drafty old castle in Surrey, both of them with the money from their mother, who was not Orin and Nicholas' mother.

Nicholas, eyes closed, hovering on the edge of sleep where the boogies will get you if you don't watch out. Drifting just short of the abyss. The old man in one of his furies. Nicholas tumbling down the stairs, bang, bang, bang, hitting his head at every step. The old man hurtling after him, screaming, "Oh, dear God, what have I done? What have I done?" Screaming contrition. Bellowing his shame. In all things outsized, even in apology. Gathering the twelve-year-old in his powerful arms, Nicholas saying, "It's all right, Father! It's all right!" It wasn't all right but he had to say it because whatever one's father did must be right or the universe would fall apart. "It's all right! It's all right!" Being thrown down the stairs by one's father.

Orin vomiting all over the carpet. Vomiting because someone else was thrown downstairs.

The red and the black on Nicholas' eyelids.

Himself breathless with anticipation.

Up from the vast deep with great glowing eyes flaming with life, the vast muscular arms pulled back in that characteristic gesture as if he was about to take off into the sky, his Shakespearean vastness of personality filling the air.

Dripping the saltwater all over the deck. Naked as the day he was born and roaring. "I have been slain, Nicholas, by that Satanic monster who is the product of my loins."

Father's prose style grotesquely, unabashedly Elizabethan, as if no other style was large enough for his own outsized personality.

"There were no marks, Father. I looked everywhere, even up your rectum, an area I never thought I'd have to inspect on my father."

Victorian dialogue, no question.

"I was most unkindly flung from the rigging by that monster of ingratitude, Elihu, who owes his very existence to me."

"Did you expect gratitude, Father? You told us to beware gratitude. It poisons the well. Your very words. Have you forgotten your own lessons?"

"Avenge me, Nicholas! It is your destiny. . . ."

Nicholas woke up violently. Orin was kneeling next to him, shaking him. "Nicholas, wake up! You're moaning like the wind."

"Wait!" cried Nicholas. "Wait!" Trying to cling to the dream. The old man, ten feet tall! Jovian in his splendid nakedness! Michelangelo on his great ceiling never painted a more commanding figure!

Avenge me! It is your destiny!

Who else but Jasper ever used such Churchillian prose?

I have been slain, Nicholas, by that Satanic monster. . . .

Nicholas' very own speculation. The dream was just a dream, clothing his own deepest fears in melodrama.

But then. . . .

. . . who is the product of my loins. . . .

Now what was this?

Nicholas sat up abruptly, his eyes wild.

"Nicholas, what on earth is the matter?"

"I have had a vision, Orin. Just like Hamlet on the battlements. Isn't that interesting? Do you believe in visions, Orin?"

"You've had a bad dream. You've been yelling—"

Nicholas laughed a little wildly. "Bad dreams are for ordinary mortals. We Worths have *visions*. Like Joan of Arc. Orin, did you ever hear any whispers that Elihu was our father's son?"

Orin blinked his blue eyes and looked out over the Gulf of Mexico. "Was this part of the dream?"

"Vision," said Nicholas.

"Nicholas, no one takes dreams seriously anymore. Not even the analysts. You're inventing explanations."

Nicholas grabbed his older brother by the shoulder and held him close. "It would explain a lot of things, wouldn't it?"

"Like what?"

"Like why he took a twenty-two-year-old adopted *cousin* into Securities Unlimited and put him over everyone—including us, his two sons."

Orin watched a gull fold its wings and plunge into the blue sea. "Nicholas, Jasper put Elihu in that job because neither you nor I wanted the damn job. You know that."

Nicholas full of glee, "I have never in my whole life seen a human being who looked and acted so *illegitimate* as Elihu. The word was coined to drape around the thin sinister shoulders of Elihu. He is the very incarnation of illegitimacy, Orin. That's what's the matter with him! Not that he's adopted but that he's *illegitimate*! Illegitimacy is in his bloodstream like a virus!"

Orin in his gentle voice, Sir Galahad, "You're grasping at figments of a dream because you don't like Elihu—"

"Don't *like* him? I *loathe* him! Loathing is much more nourishing than dislike. Dislike is for children! Loathing is for the grown-ups. . . ."

"Loathing," said Orin, "is not anything I do because I think it diminishes me more than it does the object of the loathing. I don't loathe out of sheer self-interest."

"And that's the end of the line," said Nicholas, still galvanized by the vision, charged with excitement. "When you cannot loathe properly, you are finished. Your blood is too thin to carry on the line. Me? I am the inheritor of my father's sins and of his vices. I am being visited by his ghosts and infected by his diseases. . . ."

Dake had come down from the pilothouse and was flushing down the deck with the hose, while the gulls wheeled above screaming maledictions.

"Dake, you old pirate, there is a ghost walking on your ship! The ghost of my father, crying out for vengeance—so watch it, you old swindler!"

"Nicholas!" protested Orin.

"I do not take kindly to your language, Misturr Worth." Dake didn't even look up from his hosing. "I shall report it to the Merchant Captains' Association when I land."

"Report the ghost, too, you Scottish windbag! See if I care!"

Orin's blue eyes were full of pain. "Nicholas! Nicholas! You're making an enemy of the man."

"He's already our enemy. They're all our enemies now. When a father dies you inherit his enemies!"

"Nicholas! Nicholas!"

"Those whom the Gods would destroy they first make rich."

In late afternoon the red helicopter came out of the east and passed about five miles to the north of them hugging the shoreline. It flew parallel to their course, in a directly opposite direction, and vanished into the sun in the west.

Robin marked the coordinates on her map, her binoculars to her eyes, bringing in the schooner sharply. There they were, all three of them—that bearded captain at the wheel, and the two brothers standing at the bow looking directly at the helicopter. Almost visibly wondering who she was, thought Robin, with a little grimace of a smile.

Going eighty miles an hour the opposite direction, she hadn't much time. She looked at Nicholas briefly. The one with the thin, sad face. They had met several times as children and quarreled fiercely. Then Nicholas had gone away to Yale and Cambridge and she'd not seen him again until very briefly, at the past Christmas party at her Aunt Hetty's.

Again they'd quarreled. About *genetics*, for Christ's sweet sake.

The glass lingered only a moment on Nicholas and passed quickly on to Orin. She'd never met Orin and she was vastly curious. The saintly one. The quiet, shy one who was a marine biologist, whatever that was.

A beautiful boy. Well, beautiful man, really, but he seemed boylike. Vulnerable. Except those vulnerable ones were really tough as steel.

A *saintly* Worth, my God! Every family threw them up from time to time, every other century or so. There had been another saintly Worth in 1846—one of the Delaware Worths—who was the world's greatest authority on snails. He had lived in a monklike cell, never drank anything stronger than water (not even coffee), and his *Life of the Snail* was still the final word.

In her glass Orin seemed to be looking right at her—right into her soul—which made Robin distinctly uncomfortable because her soul at that hectic moment (or at any other moment, for that matter) was in no shape to be inspected. It was all over in seconds because the helicopter was going so fast.

Robin put the binoculars away and, when it was decently possible, banked sharply to the right and sped back toward the east, this time directly over the inland waterway, passing the big tankers one after another, flying at five hundred feet. She was still bleary eyed from her nap and cantankerous. The call had wakened her from deep sleep at three thirty.

Elihu's silky voice. The bastard!

She had snarled at him and at first refused. "I went out a hundred miles this morning! That thing has only so much range, Elihu! No sign of them! No sign at all! No, I won't! I'm dead on my feet!"

But he had persisted as he always did with his steely silky voice which always sent shivers up and down her spine. "That was this morning at five. It's ten hours later. They'll have come eighty miles closer. I must know."

"I won't! I won't! I can't!"

But here she was in her new red helicopter, her newest toy, cranky and grim, flying savagely along the waterway down Matagorda Island down Espiritu Santo Bay. The exploration ship was tied up at Port O'Connor.

Robin flew the red helicopter over the ship at fifty feet and put it down right outside the little town in the salt bay.

Elihu took his own sweet time. It was half an hour before he appeared at the edge of the town, and then he was sauntering as if he had all the time in the world.

"Elihu!" Robin was simmering with rage. "Hurry *up*! It's six o'clock! I can't fly this thing in the dark."

Elihu smiled—a triumph of dentistry, that smile—and said nothing. When he reached her, he tried to kiss her but she slipped away angrily. She was in no mood for kissing. "Damn you, Elihu! I've flown four hundred miles today and I'm practically out of gas. Can you get me some gas? I've got to get back before dark."

"Why? Spend the night on board with us and get off in the morning."

"I can't do that. What explanation would I give Alec and Hortense? They're full of questions and I have no answers because I don't know the answers."

"Good!" said Elihu with his gleaming smile. "You don't want to know the answers, my darling. You'd be very upset by the answers."

"I'm very upset by the *questions*! What the hell are you up to, Elihu?"

"Exploring for oil to help our balance of payments—a very noble, patriotic, thoroughly admirable activity, as are all my activities, my sweet . . ."

Robin was pulling out the map sullenly, the endearments making her a little sick. She pointed on the map with her pencil. "The schooner is right there." Jabbing the spot with the pencil, she told him the coordinates. "They're traveling about five knots, almost due east toward Galveston, I suppose . . . What's the matter?"

Elihu's smile had vanished. He was looking at her coolly now, the black eyes wary. "I was about to ask you that."

"I'm tired. That's what's the matter. I was up until four A.M. last night and I had to get up at six to do your damned dirty work and you got me out of bed this afternoon when I needed my sleep." She slammed the map into Elihu's hand. "Here, take the damned map. I've marked the time I saw them and their probable speed and you can estimate—"

"Up until four last night?" said Elihu.

Robin didn't want to get into that. Elihu was quick as light about some things. "They've got the body," she said sullenly. "They tried to hide it, but I saw it. There's been no announcement on the news and I wonder why."

"Who knows?" Elihu had gone very still, eyeing her. She didn't like it, didn't like any of it.

"And why aren't *you* announcing it? Uncle Jasper is a world-famous man. What kind of game are you playing, Elihu?"

"We've been searching for the body. It's vital that we know definitely before making an announcement."

"You could have announced he was missing."

"We didn't want to start a panic." Elihu's voice was measured, low, as if the words hurt.

Robin shook her blond head savagely. "You're lying through your teeth, Elihu. You're up to something damned funny and I don't want to have any part of it anymore. I want some gas, and I want to get out of here."

Even as she said it, she knew she had overstepped. Not that it mattered. Robin had overstepped before with other men. When she was fed up, she let them know it and that was just bloody well that. But of course, Elihu was a bit different. Quite a bit different, quicker, sharper, more violent, more malevolent. (And after all, wasn't that what had been the attraction?)

Elihu was looking at her now, the black eyes smoldering

like a volcano, the black eyelashes leveled at her like bayonets. "Well!" he said in his silky voice. "Well!"

Zeroing in on her as if she were a target.

He stepped up to her now, his face not six inches away, testing the chemistry, and she just as quickly stepped back because she could not stand the closeness. That, of course, told him a very great deal.

Not that she gave a damn.

"You were always mercurial," he said in that silky voice that had sunk to a whisper. "You ordered me out of the nursery once when we were six."

"I'm not reviewing our childhood, Elihu! I want some gas! I don't want to argue! I've got to get out of here!"

"The legendary Robin," whispered Elihu, "who always walks out of men's lives without turning around. . . ."

It was more than she could bear. "You're being a sentimental boor, Elihu. . . ."

She would have gone on with it but he hit her hard, a long swinging slap she didn't see coming, didn't expect, couldn't, in fact, *conceive*.

So swift was it, so hard, so *inconceivable*, it knocked her down. Not flat. Sitting up in the Texas dust in her white coveralls, eyes like pear-shaped sapphires, watching Elihu stride away on his little feet. (He had absurdly small feet, something she'd remarked on before, discovering he was very sensitive about his tiny feet.)

Robin astonished.

She wanted to laugh. Not the proper reaction at all. She should be in tears. Or in a rage. Or both. I better not laugh. He'd come back and kill me good. What a scene! She wanted to giggle and because, by this time, he was far enough away, she *did* giggle, puffing out her cheeks comically, playing the clown.

Hitting me! Imagine! People don't do that anymore. He's in the wrong century, this kid.

Robin sitting there in the dust, her arms around her knees

watching Elihu walk off into the sunset. Well, anyway, into town where he disappeared behind the Gulf Stream National Bank.

Who would have thought he'd give way like that? He didn't care for me that much. In fact, I cared more for him than he did for me. Love's not this kid's problem. Something else was eating him. . . .

And other thoughts that occupied a good five minutes. After that, Robin jumped to her feet and walked into the town to the Esso station which was, like so many gas stations in the small villages, the center of intellectual and cultural activity. There she turned all her considerable charm on the loungers, fluttering her eyelashes at a gawky redhead who seemed to be the leader. "I've got a little problem," she breathed at him. "I need gas for my helicopter."

All the men pitched in, as men always did for her, got her the gas, drove her back to her helicopter, put the gas in her tank and stood there waving at her as the red chopper rose in the late afternoon sunshine.

The setting sun behind her, she pushed the Bell top speed all the way (though the man who'd sold her the chopper had cautioned that was a *bad* idea) because she didn't want to be trapped in darkness in this hostile territory (anywhere near Elihu). Just as the sun sank into the gulf she settled the copter down on Alec's lawn.

It caused talk, of course. *Two* trips over the Gulf of Mexico was just one too many for recreation or common sense. Robin was too exhausted to fend off questions. She begged off dinner and went to bed.

Seven minutes later Hortense walked into her room bearing a tray with boiled eggs, toast and coffee, and sat on the edge of the bed as Robin wolfed the food, Hortense *not* asking questions, not saying anything which was in itself an intrusion of absent curiosity, Robin babbling away, gratitude piercing her like a blade. "Thank you! Thank you! That's two meals I've messed up for you today. I'm sorry! I'm sorry!''

The two of them growing closer, wife and rival, sharing, sharing. I don't want this! Still, there it was, this *sharing*, this mental *ménage à trois* that I so devoutly don't wish. . . .

Later, in the moonlight solitude, Robin lay on her back and drew arabesques on her assaulted jaw which was beginning to hurt quite a lot and decided that she was, after all, outraged. Retrospective outrage. The best kind. I have been shamed. Will this change my character? Yes, of course. For the worse? Almost certainly.

Making jokes.

It wasn't altogether funny. Lying there in the darkness she felt the beginnings of a *tremor* of genuine fear. Emotion recalled in tranquility. The ferocity of him! The viciousness!

"I'm *scared*!" she whispered aloud to herself to exorcise the fear. It didn't do any such thing. Just made it worse. Imagine being scared of Elihu, that clown! But he wasn't a clown anymore. If he had ever been.

It was hours before she got to sleep.

At 3 A.M., Alec slipped, naked, into bed beside her and she wakened and buried herself in the warmth of him. Last thing in the world she wanted was sex; what she wanted was a cuddle and warmth.

Alec seemed to be aware of this, though how he knew she couldn't understand. He enfolded her in tenderness very different from the raging lust of the night before, smothering her in kindness. Presently she was in tears, she knew not why—and he didn't ask.

After that—a long while after—came the sex, dreamy, and loving, a far cry from the savagery of the night before, and after that—a long time after—Robin told him everything he had tried to learn the night before.

Including Elihu. All about Elihu.

"I don't know what he's about. I didn't ask and, at the time, I didn't particularly want to know. It was a game, you see. Lots of fun, with the helicopter, all his idea. I was thinking with my spinal cord, a mistake we women make all the time, because it comes naturally. We're much closer to the animals—preprogrammed, don't you know. A smell, a look, turns us on. And turns us off, too. It was only later, well just this evening, really, that the whole thing began to look rather sinister. . . ."

The overarching, overwhelming fact that Jasper was dead.

Jasper the patriarch, the progenitor, the linchpin of empire. Dead.

". . . and they've kept it quiet. Why, Alec?"

Alec's mind was on something else. "Another Worth you've been to bed with. It's quite an obsession, isn't it?"

"It isn't," said Robin fiercely, "the same thing at all. He's not a blood relative. He's adopted."

"Oh!"

"Didn't you know?"

"Should I?"

"We all knew back east. He's always been there, always a little different from the rest of us. . . ."

Alec was thinking, Elihu is twenty-two. So young to be such a villain. Alec had thought villainy itself had been superseded by more scientific concepts, but no, here it was in full flower in the late twentieth century.

Evil had made its reappearance and now here was villainy, fresh as new minted money. Society couldn't manage without villainy any more than it could manage without unicorns. . . .

CHAPTER 5

The first word appeared in Jessica Keswick's column in the *Wall Street Journal* and it was blunt: "Jasper Worth is dead. The financier died in a fall from his exploration ship in the Gulf of Mexico. The body is being brought back to a Texas port. [Alec had warned her to avoid any mention of Galveston.] Meanwhile the story is being kept quiet by the family to protect its worldwide oil, shipping, banking, and commercial interests."

The *Journal* didn't quite know what to do with the story. It belonged on page one, of course, but since Jessica refused to name her source or go into details, the editors left the story where it was, Jessica's lead item, which was read by everyone on Wall Street and financial circles across the country. Everyone was awed by the flat assertion that Jasper Worth was dead. Nothing there about "it was reported," or "rumor in the Street," her usual disclaimers. The man was dead. Flat statement.

The phone rang off the hook but Jessica was not taking

calls, letting her assistant handle the thing. Even to the editors in strictest confidence she said only, "It's true. Trust me." Something she'd never done.

Worth stocks plunged for no very good reason as so often happens on the Street. Alec could have made a quick killing selling short but he didn't. What he did was characteristic of all his operations. As fast as the easterners dumped the shares, he bought them all. "They'll go up again," he said to Miss Calisher. "Fools! Dumping good stocks on bad rumors."

"But it's not a rumor," said Robin, who was in the office. "It's true."

"The very fact it comes out like this—in a gossip column—makes it rumor which has the aura of bad news. Death of a tycoon. End of an era. Actually, it's probably good news. Jasper had outlived his usefulness. He was a buccaneer and this is not the time for buccaneers. Jasper's empire could very well do much better in the next decade by the absence of Jasper—provided somebody takes charge fairly soon."

"Who? You?"

Alec smiled. "I'm a distant cousin. I don't know who he left in charge or if he made any plans. These buccaneers don't like to appoint successors. They don't like to be elbowed aside. They leave everything until too late, and then . . ."

"Then what?" Robin wanted to know. Uncle Jasper was not all that distant to her. Her family's fortune was tied up in Mercury Oil and Worth real estate in Chicago and Denver. Jasper had handled all her father's money and her own and Fergie's.

"If there is not a clear line of succession—or authority—the lawyers settle like vultures on the estate and begin gorging. It could take years and cost the estate several hundred million if it gets into the courts."

"You're still buying Worth stocks."

"Oh, the shares will be all right. It's just the heirs who have the worries. They'll have plenty."

Jessica's story about the death of Jasper remained hers alone until midday when Worth stocks began to weaken. That put the story in everyone's corner since the slump in shares was incontestable. "Worth stocks plunged sharply yesterday morning on a reported rumor in Jessica Keswick's 'News of the Street' column. . . ."

That was picked up by the broadcasters and by one o'clock it was on the air. That led to a general decline in stocks, not as sharp as that in the Worth stocks, but the downward drift pulled Worth stocks even lower which made it a good general news story which appeared the next day on the front pages of the *New York Times*, the *Washington Post* and the *Los Angeles Times*. In the *Wall Street Journal* it moved from Jessica Keswick's column to the front page—and, of course, across the Western world, the *Financial Times* in London, *Figaro* in Paris, and others.

Spreading, not quite panic, but certainly dismay. Stocks going down because Jasper had been such a secretive cuss and bad rumors always drove out the good ones.

On the exploration ship, it was eleven o'clock in the morning when the radio officer heard the news on the radio and brought it to Elihu who was in the cabin bent over his flow charts. "Jasper Worth is dead. It's on the radio."

"Bitch!" said Elihu, spitting it like a curse.

Recovering instantly. Flashing his gleaming smile at the radio officer who was twice his age, a little bald-headed blinking alcoholic named Fence, and saying, "Well, it had to come out eventually, didn't it?" Assuming good nature. Bitch didn't necessarily mean what it said. It was a general imprecation.

Inside, of course, saying Bitch! Bitch! Bitch! Boiling away. Hating her! Hating her!

Meanwhile smiling, "What did the radio say exactly?"

"Just an announcement. There'll be much more. Shall I take it down?"

"Yes. You do that." Ushering him to the door with his gleaming smile to show what a good fellow he was.

Out went the radio officer to the deck and inside Elihu was left to boil away. I must stop! Must get control. Nothing in his life had so undone him as that . . . slap. Himself the slapper, the protagonist, himself the injured. Why did I? Why this boiling hatred? I am a very cool customer. I must, in this situation, be calm. Above all else. How can I think with this boiling . . . and why the boiling. . . .

Jealousy? I never loved her that much. I never loved her as much as I now hate her. Wounded pride? Whatever it was, he had to stifle it, get control because there were decisions to be made. He snapped on the radio and listened for the news which now flooded the air. . . .

"Jasper Worth, patriarch of the family whose wealth stems from a grant of thousands of square miles of American wilderness from Charles II . . ."

Oh, they were pulling out all the stops.

". . . selling gunpowder to the American forces in the Revolutionary War, wheat to the Northern forces in the Civil War, guns and ships to the Allies in both World War I and II, the Worth family has always thrived on wars and languished, though profitably, in peace. Jasper Worth was a loner who had pulled away from his eastern branch of the family and ran his own shop like a nineteenth-century robber baron to whom he had frequently been compared. . . ."

They didn't understand him at all, at all! But he would have loved that robber baron bit, would have howled with glee.

Thus Elihu, storming about his little cabin, damping down his humiliation by recounting to himself his victory. I did it! I did it! My triumph! Drinking it down like alcohol to drown that other incomprehensible sorrow. The rage! I must be calm because there's much to be done.

He stormed out of the cabin and up to the pilothouse.

"You've heard the news?"

"Yes."

"We've got to get out of the inland waterway and into the open gulf. They'll be hovering over us like bats, shooting at us from shore. We're too visible here."

"They have to find us first. We are not all that easy to find. Anyway, you're just postponing—"

"I want to postpone as long as possible. There are reasons."

"I'm sure there are but we cannot just dart out of here. We must await an opening and the next one is not until Matagorda. Twenty miles. You'll have to hold your horses till Matagorda, Mr. Worth."

The ship crawling along at two miles an hour in the ship canal.

"We couldn't go a little faster?"

"It's against the law, but I can speed up a bit," said the captain. "How are we to explain we haven't the body? How are we to explain that we let all this time elapse without an announcement that he fell off this ship. . . ."

If indeed he fell.

Stork didn't say that, but the implication hung in the air between the men, unsaid, nevertheless shrieking. Elihu's sharp black eyes were running over Captain Stork, waiting for him to unsay it, to back away from this shrieking silence. Stork didn't, didn't soften at all.

Never apologize, never explain. The Worths had been doing that for two hundred years. Leave explanation to the historians, Jasper Worth's own grandfather had said. Jasper had drummed it into all the Worths, especially Elihu.

"I think you had best leave explanation to me, Captain Stork," said Elihu.

"So long as it agrees with the ship's log, Mr. Worth. You cannot argue with the ship's log."

Obduracy hanging in the air. Elihu didn't like it. "Perhaps I'd better read the log."

Stork handed it to him silently. The passage was brief:

"Copper wire from the radio antenna on the foremast was torn loose by the wind and flapping wildly, fouling the radar dish. Elihu Worth climbed rigging to attempt to clear it. After fifteen minutes Jasper Worth climbed rigging to help, first stripping off clothes because he said clothes were hindrance. Wind blowing thirty knots, ship heaving. Jasper Worth and Elihu Worth worked together to clear wire. Jasper Worth plunged into the sea at 1425."

Elihu looked at the captain. "Actually, we weren't working together at the exact moment of the accident. I had started down the rigging to get another clamp when Jasper lost his footing."

Again obduracy hung in the air. Captain Stork said nothing but contradiction crossed the stubborn New England features.

Elihu said softly, "Where were you exactly when the tragedy struck?"

"On the bridge," said Captain Stork.

"I see."

Elihu went back to the ship's log. "Brought ship about immediately, searched for Jasper Worth until darkness and after. Wind sharpened to gale force at 1600 hours and by 1800 hours reached force eight. Resumed search for Jasper Worth at daylight."

"We didn't *resume* search. We never abandoned search."

"Nobody is going to believe that in a force-eight gale." Not yielding an inch.

Elihu said, "Hadn't we better put in here something to the effect that at the moment Jasper Worth lost his footing I was on my way down the rigging?"

"You can't tamper with the log, Mr. Worth."

Not quite calling him a liar.

Elihu smiled silkily. "In that case, I think you had better leave all the talking to me when we get to Galveston, Captain Stork."

"If there's an investigation, I must take the witness stand."

"There won't be an investigation, Captain Stork, if you leave the talking to me."

Again that unspoken obduracy hanging in the air. Elihu said in his silky voice, "This ship is owned by Mercury Oil whose chief executive officer is now dead. Mercury Oil is owned in its entirety by the Worth family. I happen to be the only Worth aboard and I will be consulted about all kinds of things by the Mercury directors, including who is or isn't to command this ship. I'm not asking for anything from you, Captain Stork, except silence, something you're very good at. I have been admiring your command of silence ever since I got aboard. You were particularly good at silence when the old man got on your ass when we first got aboard. When he railed and ranted at you about the condition of the ship and especially about the nature and delinquencies of its crew and your, shall we say, derelictions in that regard, you remained magnificently silent. I admired your silence then, Captain Stork. I said to myself, 'Here is a man who knows when to shut up.' That was only five days ago. Surely you couldn't have lost this magnificent talent in only five days."

Captain Stork said nothing.

On the schooner Nicholas listened to the obituary babble on the radio, face screwed up into a knot of distaste that his mother had always hated. "Your face will grow like that, Nicholas," she had said as all mothers had said of their son's twisted faces since the beginning of recorded time. Which brought up the subject of . . . Mother. How was she taking it? This death of a husband who had been so loving, so unfaithful, so brutal, so—as she had always said of Jasper—*interesting*. That had been Rebecca Worth's unfailing defense of Jasper. He was in all things *interesting* and that was, by her lights, the highest praise. She adored him through his desertions, his rages, his silences, his incomprehensibilities, in fact, for those very reasons. He had never bored her. Certainly nothing was less boring than the manner of his death, mysteriously at sea, leaving his great affairs in a princely tangle, leaving succession, inheritance, the condition and even ownership of all his companies up in thin air.

"The news was announced in New York in some column in the *Wall Street Journal*. Tells us nothing. Anyone could have planted it there. Elihu. Graebner. Whoever was in that helicopter. . . ."

"Elihu wouldn't," said Nicholas. "Elihu is as secretive as the old man. He wouldn't give you the right time. In fact, if you asked him the time he'd give you the wrong time just to fox you. Elihu doesn't want to answer questions. He wants to provoke questions that are asked of others. Us, for instance. We have the body. Let us explain what it's doing here, which takes the onus off Elihu explaining why he fell off the exploration ship."

Orin's eyes were on God. That was what others in the family always said when he got that faraway look, when—as they said—he left them for outer space or wherever he went.

"Orin," said Nicholas patiently, "wherever you are—"

"I'm thinking of the others, Louise and Junie, when they hear Dad's dead."

"They'll be delighted."

"The first minute perhaps. After that they'll feel lost."

"Did you feel lost, Orin?"

"I'm getting over it. It's like being born again. It's going to change all of us, you know that, don't you, Nicholas. None of us is going to be quite the same person. Without that vast presence hanging over us, we're all going to change. . . .

"Not necessarily for the better," said his brother.

The Marquise of Hampton was presiding over breakfast for her three daughters in the nursery, one of the few warm rooms in the vast drafty pile of stone called Syddons Castle that had once belonged to Henry VIII, when her husband came into the room (in itself very unusual since he never interrupted her nursery breakfasts).

"Daddy," squealed the littlest one, Deborah, who didn't know any better. The others said nothing.

The marquis, a beefy sardonic Englishman, handed his wife the *Financial Times* and pointed to the front-page story. The marquise unloosed a sharp breath, as if someone had stabbed her. She read the news story in its entirety, mouth open.

"What is it, Mummy?"

"Your grandfather's dead," she said crisply.

The children looked at each other. They hardly knew their grandfather.

"We'd better be getting over there," said the marquis. "Find what's going on. Protect our interests."

"I'll go," said the marquise. "You stay here and take care of the place."

"No, you jolly well won't go alone into that den of sharks—"

"He's my father, not yours. It's my family, not yours. I'm going alone."

She had never spoken to her husband like that in her marriage. He was an older man as brusque, selfish and inconsiderate as her father. (Some said she'd married her father, as so many of them did.) At this fit of wifely temperament he would have been savagely sardonic but for the fact that his wife had dissolved into tears which so astonished him as to drive the sarcasm out of his skull.

"I thought you hated the old bastard!"

"I did! I did! But I miss him! I miss hating him!"

She wished she hadn't said it in front of the children, but there it was right out in the open for all to see. She had defied her father to marry this beefy Englishman who, Jasper said, was just after her money (and wasn't he?). Now there was no one to defy and it took the purpose out of her marriage, out of her very existence. . . .

In Manitoba, the news was brought to Jasper, Jr., by his wife Eleanor, a muscular, capable Canadian woman who was five years older than he. Jasper (whom she never called Junie) was cleaning his shotgun in the gun room, oiling it, caressing it (making love to the damned thing, his wife used to say) when she walked in.

"Your father's dead."

"No!" It came out of him as if shot out of a gun.

"It's all over the radio."

"Never!" His chin jutting out belligerently. He looked, she thought, very much like the old tyrant at that moment.

"Perhaps you'd better come listen, Jasper."

"I don't *believe* it!"

"People die, darling."

"Not Jasper! Not our father! He wouldn't do a thing like that." He bolted into the kitchen where the radio newsman was spouting about the grant of thousands of square miles from Charles II, getting it all wrong as they always did every time a Worth died, compounding an error which grew in dimension with each new dead Worth.

Tears gushing forth because he couldn't stop them. Crying and laughing at the same time. "Fell off a goddamned ship. Wouldn't you know he'd die some crazy way. Looking for oil, for God's sake! As if we needed more oil. Haven't we got enough oil?"

"Your father never had enough of anything," said Eleanor Worth.

CHAPTER 6

"In all systems of law derived from Roman law, the power to dispose property is limited in order to protect the widows and children," intoned Humphrey Worth in his rich baritone. Humphrey sang the law as if it were a sacred hymn, the sound filling the small dining room of the Azure Club. To the headwaiter, who was black and white-haired, Humphrey said, "The sole Albert, George. Green salad with oil and vinegar, the usual. Mr. Settle here will have the same. You will, won't you, Oscar? Very good here, the sole Albert." Humphrey handed George the menu, closing the discussion and after the briefest moment Oscar Settle closed his own menu and handed it to George, yielding the decision.

Humphrey always ordered for his luncheon companions and it took a very powerful personality to stand up for his rights and say, "No, Humphrey, I don't want the sole Albert. I want the *oeufs* Florentine." Some strong-minded judges did and they were never invited back to the Azure

Club. Humphrey hated to be disputed. For one thing it delayed lunch while his companion pored over the menu. For another, Humphrey—like so many lawyers—was quite sure he knew what was best for people. He was accustomed to telling clients what to do and what not to do and he expected them to shut up and do it, combining in his person not only the inherent arrogance of the Worth family but also the acquired arrogance of a lawyer, a dismaying aggregation of chutzpah.

Oscar Settle, who wasn't a lawyer or a Worth, though he'd married one, could hardly stand up to this powerful will and he didn't attempt it. Anyway he was more interested in the law than the food.

"How about nieces?" said Oscar Settle carefully.

"Oh, you can dispose of nieces," said Humphrey gleefully. "Also nephews-in-law." Rubbing it in. Meanwhile poring over the wine list. "The Bollinger, George. You do like champagne with fish, Oscar? Of course, you do." Handing the wine list to George and resuming musically.

"The custom of the will is recognized even in many primitive cultures where there is no such thing as property as we know it. The custom of the will has since earliest times been associated with ancestor worship, and to this very day you'll find a great deal of ancestor worship which has very little to do with the disposal of property. The word heir comes from the Latin *haeres*, a man whose duty it was to carry on the family rites. We've never *quite* got over that. A great deal of the tussling over a man's will revolves not so much about who gets the money—though that is important— as who acquires the *power* and the *position* to command the family. When the family in question is the Worth family, aah, then. . . ."

The grandeur of the concept Humphrey left in midair, himself admiring the edifice as if it were architecture. Oscar sipped the Bollinger sullenly and said, "When do we get the pelf, Humphrey?" Trying to shock the fruity old bastard out of this peroration and get down to the meat of the thing. Humphrey's eyebrows shot up at this *lèse majesté* and Oscar quickly added, "Sylvia wants to know." Throwing it all in the lap of his rich wife who was a Worth.

"Yes," said Humphrey, making it into two syllables, yeah-uss, a rich lawyer's drawl, "I expect she does." Humphrey and Sylvia had not got along since they were four. He looked at Oscar Settle now with naked dislike. So much time lunching people one didn't like because . . . well, because there were very few people Humphrey did like. Had to have this worm to lunch because he was family. I am drowning in Worths, impaled by Worths, suffocated by them. Still Humphrey was far too clever not to acknowledge, if only to himself, that the family was the very fount of his existence, the core, the engine of his being.

This worm of a cousin-in-law married to his wickedly witty, lecherous cousin Sylvia was being stood lunch because he was family. Elucidating law to him was a family rite. Humphrey took family rite very seriously, himself more Roman, more patrician than any Roman had ever been. (Aah, why had togas ever gone out? Humphrey would have loved to wear a toga.)

Humphrey signaled George to fill his champagne glass, wrinkling his nose. "Pelf. Which is to say spoils, booty. The word, you know—no, you probably don't—is related to pillage. You're implying loot when in fact what we're discussing here is inheritance. The one thing is illegal, the other legal. Don't forget that. Actually, we don't even *know* that Jasper is dead."

"We *know,* all right."

"The courts don't. Until we do, we can't go searching for a will, the last *will* and testament. That word last in this case is very important because Jasper made a lot of wills. He loved making wills, loved disinheriting and letting people know it by this means and that. He loved hiring lawyers and firing lawyers. He hired me a half dozen times and fired me a half dozen times. I wrote a number of his wills but I'm sure they're not the last will and testament of Jasper Worth because no matter what lawyer comes up with what he considers the last will and testament, some other lawyer will spring out of the cement with an even later one. He was that kind of man. He wanted to buffalo us after his death, as he buffaloed us during his life."

Humphrey's rubicund face with the ridiculously cherubic lips were wreathed in a triumphant smile. He had outlived the old pirate. Hah! It wasn't living well that was the best revenge—Humphrey had always lived well—it was *outliving* that was the best revenge. I shall dance on his grave—when he has one. He and Jasper had hated each other for most of their lives. Humphrey had actually become a lawyer because he feared Jasper, feared his tyranny and his intelligence and had used the law to hold him at bay. In their middle years they had declared a truce, each recognizing and respecting the other's more spectacularly evil qualities, and had been partners in setting up Mercury Oil. Then the old hostilities had surfaced. Humphrey had sold out most (not all) of his Mercury Oil interests to Jasper (very profitably). Jasper the pirate, Humphrey the shark—that's what Wall Street had called them.

Humphrey showed his shark's teeth to Oscar Settle in a thoroughly nasty smile. "Your wife wasn't mentioned in any of the wills I drew."

Oscar looked mulish. He had been a very handsome fullback (a piece of ass, Humphrey had called him at the time of the marriage) but he was now running to fat. There had been rumors about Jasper and Sylvia, the old man having it off with his niece and flaunting the cuckoldry right in the husband's face.

"She was in the later ones," said Oscar sullenly. "He showed it to her."

"Pity he didn't leave her a copy."

"Perhaps he did." Oscar wasn't going to show his hand.

Humphrey signaled George again. "George, have you any of that delicious cheesecake? I'll have a slice—and Mr. Settle will, too. And two coffees." Then to Oscar, "You don't remember the date on it, do you?"

"Two years ago last August." Muffled tones. Oscar didn't want to admit the cuckoldry had gone on that long but what could he do?

"How much did he leave her?"

A rude question that infuriated Oscar. "A lot!"

"Why don't you go to the lawyer who drew up that will? His name is on the will. Why are you consulting us?"

"Because you're family and he isn't. We want some *family* advice. The shares are plummeting in value and we think somebody should move in and take charge."

"*Sylvia?* Good God!"

"Well, *somebody*! How do we go about implementing the will and bringing in the trustees to guard the inheritance before it all goes down the drain?"

Humphrey smiled his scabrous rubicund smile. "What you need is a nice predatory lawyer who will keep you on the string for years and take you for every penny. You will wind up with nothing, no inheritance and some lovely legal bills. Ho! Ho!" Well, one deserved a little pleasure, didn't one? After all, he was paying for lunch.

Humphrey went on with it to see how far he could go before Oscar Settle erupted. The poor cuckold must have a boiling point and Humphrey was interested in finding out where it was. If you put up with cuckoldry two years at the hands of someone old enough to be your father, well, where was the boiling point? A matter of scientific interest.

"I'm sure somewhere there is a document revoking that will your wife holds. Most recently Jasper has said he had no intention of dying. He was studying all sorts of rubbish about living forever and coming back in different forms. Any swami with a tale about transmigration of souls could get his ear. If he was going to come back in some other body, he wanted the money to be waiting for him somewhere, not in Sylvia's greedy hands, so I'm sure he took measures to see that you wouldn't get any. . . ."

And so forth. Delightful simply to *watch* Oscar's empurpled face listening to this malarkey. The ultimate worm. The rich, thought Humphrey, got all the ultimates—the ultimate houses, ultimate racehorses, ultimate paintings, ultimate fucks and ultimate worms in marriage. The best of everything as well as the worst of everything—the ultimates.

"I think," said Oscar, who had finally had enough, "this isn't getting us anywhere."

"In law you frequently don't get anywhere at great length and expense. That is what makes it such a rewarding occupation for those of us who are in it."

The Worths were exceedingly various. Not all of them were rich. In Cleveland there was a disc jockey who had been born Gerald Worth who had changed his name—noisily and in public—to Tab Epstein (which infuriated all the true Epsteins as well as the Worths) who broadcast from midnight until dawn and specialized in right wing outrage. (He advocated capital punishment, compulsory sterilization of all whose SAT scores fell below 600, etc.) There were bankrupt Worths in Milwaukee and Chicago whose fathers had spent the money or fiddled it away. Still, even most of these Worths were bright or peculiar in distinctive ways. Young Terence Worth hadn't any money at all but he was DeWitt Professor of Law at the University of Michigan and one of the most radical and original legal thinkers in the country. Branch Worth wrote poetry in a loft in Soho where the rent was three months overdue. Jed Worth was Governor of Arkansas, a state, they said, he picked out of a hat. (He wanted to run for governor somewhere out of reach of the eastern branch of the family and their incessant demands. He had been a very capable governor and was now contemplating the presidency.) There were, as everyone knew, two Senator Worths—one from Delaware, one from New York. (Jed Worth considered that quite enough for the Senate.) Besides the Soho poet, there were innumerable writing Worths—Archibald Worth, the distinguished historian who wrote about the Worth family as if they were Caesars; Endicott Worth, who wrote airless novels about rich people who were all thinly disguised Worths; and Serendipity Worth, the eccentric philosopher at the University of Chicago whose cerebrations in print were so profound as to be understood by only a handful of other philosophers. Lots of other Worths sounded off in letters to the editor, magazine articles, lectures, denunciations, diatribes. The Worths were in all things outspoken.

Most of the family had not even met Jasper Worth, but, of course, they all knew of him. The newspapers had decided long ago that Jasper Worth was the head of the family but this had never been recognized—in fact, was seriously disputed—by most of the other Worths. In a family so widespread and individualistic, there was no such thing as a head, but Jasper was probably the richest and the most—at that moment—celebrated.

His death smote them all.

Not the least William Worth, a silver-haired aristocrat, who owned Claystaff Stud, one of the finest racing stables in Virginia (or anywhere), whose habitat was the Brook and the Jockey Club, who presided over Worth Freres (after all, the Worths had been French two hundred years earlier and there were still French Worths), as chilly a stockbrokerage as there was in all the world. (The word around the Street was you had to have not only a hundred million but an *old* hundred million to be allowed in the front door.)

William Worth was a patrician. He had been very fond of Jasper (they were first cousins only a few years different in age) even though their natures were so different. There were not many Worths left to whom William was so close or so intimate. Therefore the death hit him hard, but even harder was the manner of death.

To have one's death announced in a gossip column, my God, had it come to that? Rumor of death—what a blasphemy of death itself. William Worth remembered when the *Wall Street Journal* would never have printed such a line until it had been cleared by the family itself—and of course, it never would have been until the patriarchs (himself in charge) had seen the body and personally supervised the wording of the announcement.

But now there was no respect. No tradition. This was journalism run wild.

The shares sinking, sinking. Good Worth shares. If Jasper hadn't been such a secretive man. If he had confided in him, William, his friend, his cousin. But he hadn't.

Scandal loomed. Not that the Worths were strangers to scandal. No such family as the Worths could avoid it altogether. Worths wanted what they wanted—women, racehorses, emeralds, whatever—and took it, letting the chips to fall where they would.

Financial scandal the family had kept at bay (sometimes only by the skin of their teeth) for two hundred years. But this thing was too flagrant. There would be a demand for investigation and William Worth, chairman of the SEC, would be in the forefront. How could he, a Worth, fail to investigate? If he had not been a Worth he could have done the thing quietly, kept the matter under wraps.

A Worth couldn't do that about a Worth scandal, damn it. The media would be all over him and the implications that one Worth was whitewashing another Worth would be all over the newspapers, the columns, the editorials.

Thus William Worth agonizing alone in his vast office at 44 Wall Street, far in the clouds. (The building had actually once been hit by an airplane which, the wiseacres had said, bloody well deserved it for considering itself so above ordinary buildings.)

"Oh Jasper, why did you get yourself into this—so unlike you!" William Worth actually said that aloud. In a whisper, but nevertheless audible to himself, and it set him to thinking furiously on wholly new and alarming lines.

Jasper would never have done any of this. Jasper would never have siphoned off the good Worth Mercury shares to these foreign exchanges. Why? Jasper was secretive, devious, intricate (in many ways a step and a half ahead of the Street, initiating and inventing what frequently became orthodox procedures ten years later), but this business was worse than that. This smelled to high heaven of fraud.

Thus William Worth, an honorable man. Born and brought up in an age when honor was practiced like scales on the piano. Until it was performed instinctively. Like a reflex.

William Worth was not the world's most intelligent man. He should have surmised what he surmised thirty-six hours earlier, but once the thought occurred, it provoked action immediately (even though he knew so well the consequences, the uproar, the whole ghastly mess).

William Worth, chairman of the SEC, picked up the phone and called the president of the New York Stock Exchange. "Stop trading in Worth shares, all Worth shares—Mercury Oil, Dataflow, Worth Mining and Minerals, All Food Products, United States Bank & Trust, the whole boiling lot. . . ."

Locking the barn after the horse was stolen, he was thinking. He was an old-fashioned man and used only the oldest of metaphors.

CHAPTER 7

News stories grew in America at the speed of the fertilized egg in a woman's womb, first two cells, then four, eight, sixteen; the rush is on. From the little item in Jessica Keswick's column to the slump in shares to the suspension of trading the size of the embryo had multiplied by about a billion. It was now a major news story. Official action had been taken. The window had been slammed down. Anyone owning a Worth share in anything—millions of them—couldn't sell it to his own uncle.

The exploration ship was far out in the open gulf ploughing due west when the news came in on the radio. The radioman was bringing it to Elihu in his cabin and on the way he encountered the lawyer Graebner.

Fence showed the lawyer the bit of tape. SEC HALTS TRADING WORTH SHARES, followed by a list of them. "Then this," said Fence. He gave Graebner another communication. REQUEST INFORMATION JASPER WORTH REPORTED

DEAD AT SEA BENEDICT CALHOUN DISTRICT ATTORNEY HOUSTON.

"Groping for jurisdiction," snarled the lawyer. That's what had held them all at bay, death at sea. A *rumored* death. Not even official. The District Attorney would be fighting over the corpse before they got to land; the publicity value was immense. A world-famous figure, former Secretary of State, mythological character as weird and wonderful and rich as Howard Hughes, dying in mysterious circumstances. What couldn't a district attorney do with *that*? Now that the SEC had acted, it had put the ball in somebody's court. But whose?

"What'll I do?" asked Fence.

"Ignore it," said Graebner. "The Houston DA has no more jurisdiction over a death at sea than the Queen of England."

"He just requests *information*," protested Fence. "Couldn't I give him *information*?"

"No," said Graebner. He pushed into Elihu's cabin with the message in his hand. Elihu was at the little table bolted to the wall, on which were piles of Jasper's papers. Without looking up, Elihu said, "You don't knock, Graebner?" The voice mocking, knowing without looking who it was.

Graebner didn't bother to answer. He put the DA's messages before Elihu, right under his nose. Elihu looked at it with a little smile. "Well! Well!" he said. 'We're pushing along, aren't we?"

Graebner laid the SEC communication down under Elihu's nose. This occupied the young man considerably longer. He looked at the cable, expressionless, gritting his teeth. "Very interesting," he said at long last. "Mr. Graebner, you knew my uncle far longer than I did. Did the SEC ever suspend trading in Worth shares, any kind of Worth shares in his lifetime?"

"Never," said Graebner.

"What do you suppose Uncle Jasper would have done in the event that that had happened?"

"He'd have been on the telephone in five minutes to the chairman of the SEC, who was his cousin and very close friend, William Worth."

"Mmmm," said Elihu.

He rose from the chair, turned his back on the two men and stared out the porthole at the blue gulf. "I don't think I'll do that," he murmured. "Uncle William and I are not close friends."

He turned with his gleaming smile and said, "Thank you, Mr. Fence, for bringing me these communications. There'll be no reply for the moment. Do stay on duty and notify me immediately if there are any others."

It was a dismissal. Fence said, "Thank you, Mr. Worth," and left the two men alone.

Elihu rustled through the papers on the bolted table and brought up a single sheet of paper. "Going through Uncle Jasper's papers—"

"Which you have no right to do," said Graebner. "Those papers should be sealed until the court decides what's to be done."

"Ah, yes, that's precisely why this is so important. Uncle Jasper's last official act."

He handed the single sheet to the lawyer.

LAST WILL AND TESTAMENT OF JASPER WORTH

April 26, 1984

This instrument is intended to revoke all prior wills by my hand.

All my real property, personalty, financial interests, stocks, bonds, and other assets are to be left to the Worth Trust to be administered by Elihu Worth, as trustee, for the benefit of my wife, Rebecca Worth, and my children, Jasper Worth,

Jr., Louise, the Marquise of Hampton, Orin Worth, and Nicholas Worth.

Each of these beneficiaries is to be maintained in the style to which he or she is accustomed according to the discretion of the trustee who is free to invade the principal when such action is necessary for the benefit of the beneficiaries.

The trustee, Elihu Worth, is also free to make such unlimited gifts to those charities which he knows I favor and to make gifts to other beneficiaries who are known to him and me alone in strictest secrecy as prescribed by trust law.

Jasper Worth.

The blatancy of it took Graebner's breath away. It was the kind of thing a child might do. A child of twelve. Or a consummate villain like this villain.

"What do you think, Graebner?"

Graebner took his time. He put the piece of paper down on the desk and withdrew his hand as if from the fire.

He spoke softly. "It doesn't seem to have any witnesses, and a will is not valid without at least two witnesses."

Elihu's smile gleamed like fire. "It's a sailor's will made at sea. Surely you, as a lawyer, know that a sailor's will made at sea requires no witnesses."

Graebner coughed, a dry lawyer's cough. "Mr. Worth was not a sailor in the sense covered by that, uh, ruling. He was a financier as you and I and everyone else knows."

"He would have been the first to dispute you, Graebner. Jasper Worth was a member of the New York Yacht Club for forty years. He was a sailor through and through, boasted of his prowess, spent years passing his sailing skills on to his son Orin, called himself a sailor and on several occasions in front of witnesses actually asked to be buried at sea. He was a *sailor*. He wished to make a sailor's will and he made it and signed it. The signature you'll find is authentic and I can prove it.''

Graebner coughed again, his lawyer's cough. There were all sorts of tricks toward obtaining authentic signatures available to anyone as close to the man as Elihu was to Jasper. The lawyer didn't even look at the paper. What he said was, "I am—or was—Mr. Worth's lawyer. . . .''

"You're *one* of Mr. Worth's lawyers. Jasper Worth had lawyers like a dog has fleas.''

"I happen to be the only one of Mr. Worth's lawyers aboard this vessel. Why wasn't I consulted on the making of the last will and testament?''

"Perhaps you were,'' said Elihu with his gleaming smile. "Think what an embarrassment it would be if you *weren't*. How would you explain it to your partners that so important a document as this was drawn up and signed on this ship—only four days ago as you notice by the date—and you had nothing to do with it? How would that look to the partners? To the legal profession? To the world at large? And just think of the fee you would forfeit by *not* having had a hand in this document. Last will and testament of Jasper Worth. One of the richest men of the world. A fee of one million would not be excessive, would it?''

The jaws of the trap yawning wide. Graebner said dryly, "Even for a man of wealth like Jasper Worth there would never be such a fee for drawing up so simpleminded a document as this. Fifty thousand would be . . . perhaps excessive, but conceivable.''

"Aah, but there is going to be much more than the drawing up of the will. This will is going to have to be defended in court. You and I know there will be lawsuits from all the principals, from Orin, Nicholas, Rebecca—oh, *all* of them—William, dozens of other Worths filing suit. It will be your task to *defend* this will against those others, and a fee of a million is not at all inconceivable for that, now is it?''

"You are asking me to perjure myself, to say that I drew up this document when I didn't."

"Not at all, not at all. I am asking you to state that to the best of your knowledge this is the last will and testament of Jasper Worth. Now honestly, to the best of your knowledge, *isn't* this the last will and testament of Jasper Worth? Certainly the last. What evidence have you that it is not authentic? You knew the man intimately. You knew he drew wills up all the time and revoked them all the time. Didn't you? You knew his, shall we say, variability. How quickly he changed course. How decisive he was when an idea hit him. You knew all that. And this will leaves it all to the proper beneficiaries—the wife, children. . . ."

Yes, and leave you in the driver's seat as trustee to loot and pillage.

"No," said Graebner. "I have no knowledge that this isn't the last will and testament of Jasper Worth." Only common sense, which the legal profession has never recognized. "But I have no knowledge that it *is,* and I could not therefore—"

Elihu was rustling through the papers which covered the small table like snowflakes on a hill, saying in his silky voice, "Well, then you *do* have knowledge of this, don't you, Mr. Graebner? Because it's got your fingerprints all over it. This five-million-dollar bribe to the Mexicans for sole rights to a bit of Mexican sea floor which you personally took down and gave to Huelva de Santo because Jasper wouldn't trust anyone else with that much cash.

"That could get you disbarred, Mr. Graebner, bribery of another country's official to get an advantage in business, now couldn't it?"

First the carrot. Then the stick. The boy had been well taught by Jasper Worth, who had used the same technique many times. . . .

* * *

Alec and Robin strolled the Strand, not touching. "This used to be the Wall Street of the whole southwest—until the hurricane struck in 1900. Back in the 1880's there were five banks on the Strand and eight newspapers." Like so many waterfronts, the Strand had been tidied up with restaurants, gift shops, art studios, reveling in its nineteenth-century architecture. "Waterfront worship," commented Alec dryly. "It struck us first—ahead of Boston, Baltimore and New York. You can charge twice as much for a shrimp cocktail or a porcelain pig if it's within sight of saltwater."

"How about stocks?" asked Robin. "Can you charge twice as much for those?"

"No, but it gives you a sense of solidity and peace watching the ships go by. One of the most difficult things to do in stock trading is nothing. Waiting for the other fellow to make his mistakes. If you have a view of the ships, it passes the time."

Alec steered Robin into the Golliwog and sat her imperiously at the best table on the terrace overlooking the bay. "Is this wise?" murmured Robin.

"Being conspicuous is a form of concealment, sometimes the best device of all." Alec smiled and ordered Bloody Marys. "I think we're entitled," he said.

Robin looked out over the passersby to the sparkling bay. "Hortense knows," she said. "You know that, don't you?"

Alec frowned only slightly and looked at the menu. "No, I can't say that I *know* that. Are you sure you know that?"

"Quite sure."

"She *said* something?"

"Not in so many words. But she knows all right. And she's not going to do anything about it which makes it much worse."

The Bloody Marys came and Alec sipped his, his eyes opaque. "Were you in love with Elihu?"

Robin laughed her throaty laugh. "You're always asking me things like that. It's very impertinent, Alec."

"I know. I'm a Worth. We ask rude questions. Were you?"

"Well, I was attracted. He was a son of a bitch and women are frequently attracted to sons of bitches."

"And are you attracted to me?"

"Not for that reason."

"I could be a son of a bitch if you like."

"You don't have to go to such extravagant lengths. I'm already attracted enough."

"I could be as big a son of a bitch as Elihu if I tried."

"You're quite wicked enough without making any special effort."

Both of them having a good time.

"Are you in love?" persisted Alec.

"Oh, hell, I'm afraid so. Are you?"

"Yes."

"What an awful thing for Hortense. Are you going to have the crayfish? Because I'll have it, too, but only if you have it because today is the day we must share everything— the crayfish, the Rhine wine. . . ."

"It'll cause talk. I never have Rhine wine. I have Moselle, but never mind." He ordered Rhine wine and crayfish.

"I feel marvelous, don't you?" Robin chattered. "I should feel guilty about feeling marvelous, but not now. Later."

Conversation bubbling out of both of them like spring water.

"You're a damned attractive woman, Robin, which is quite unusual for me. I usually fall in love with damned unattractive women. Well, Hortense . . ."

"Darling, Hortense is very attractive in her unbeautiful way. She's *homely* attractive, which is quite the in thing these days. I'm out because I'm," shrugging, "so goddamned beautiful I'm a cliché. But Hortense with that little mouth and big forehead pulls you clear across the room. Should we be discussing your wife like this? It's indecent."

"She'll never know. And it clears the air, emptying out our minds this way."

"Do you think I have a mind, Alec?"

"Oh, *yes!*"

"Most men don't. Elihu certainly didn't. And, you know something, I was inclined to agree. But if you think I have a mind, then I think I do, too. You're like the Wizard of Oz, Alec, you're endowing me with what I most wish to have. . . ."

And so forth until three in the afternoon when Alec was called to the telephone by Miss Calisher who told him that trading had been suspended in Worth shares and then, of course, he had to go back to the office because nothing like that had ever before happened to Worth stock.

The two boys, Fergie and Lannie Worth, were stretched out on the bed with the FX 4000 on the bedspread before them. Lannie was punching up the score. "Is the Ampex connected?"

"Yes."

Lannie typed out the code and the screen lit up. "That's the Big Board. What would you like?"

"Mercury Oil," said Fergie. "That's the bell cow."

Lannie was a dark-haired chunky kid with blue eyes and his mother's broad forehead. He punched the code letters and the screen said: Mercury Oil 37½ (Trading suspended).

"Three points off since yesterday," said Fergie Worth. "And eight points in three days. Bring in some of the other energy stocks—Exxon, Gulf."

All the energy stocks were down, but nothing like eight points.

"Very peculiar," murmured Fergie. "You know what might be fun? If we could get into Grandfather's computer on the Street."

"Now what might that be called?"

"Well, Grandfather had a lot of them, but the top holding company was called Securities Unlimited."

"We'd have to have the code. Wait a minute, Dad might have it in his desk because sometimes he does business at home."

They searched the desk in Alec's bedroom but delicately putting everything back in place. Alec was very neat and the drawers were laid out with mathematical precision. "Here it is," said Lannie. "What was that name again?"

"Securities Unlimited. Grandfather liked names like that. *Big* names. He said they reassured the investors. Did you know my grandfather?"

Lannie was bent over the code book, lips pursed. "He stayed with us a couple of months ago. I was scared to death of him. Were you scared of him?"

"Well, not so much. He scared Mother and Dad more than he scared me or Robin. He was always very nice to me. Said he was going to take me into the firm and show me all the things my dad didn't want to know. Dad's an art historian."

"Why?" Muffled because Lannie was deep in the code book, but listening as kids do, his mind on something else but not missing anything.

"I think he wanted to get as far away from the money as possible. His whole generation. Dad marched through Alabama with all those civil rights people, picketed the White House, all that sort of thing. But I don't know. I don't think money is all that evil, do you? I kind of *like* money. I might have gone into the firm with him and learned his tricks—if he'd lived. . . ."

"Here it is, FLOUNDER. What do you want to know?"

"Stock transactions. Maybe none of this passed through Grandfather's shop, but then maybe it did."

"Mercury Oil?"

"Well, try all of them, Mercury, Dataflow, Worth Mining

& Minerals—that's a big one—United States Bank, All Foods...."

The boys went back to the bed in Lannie's room and played with the FX 4000. Aladdin's lamp. Like Aladdin's lamp it was stubborn, refusing them access again and again because they didn't have the codes quite right. Because they were teenagers, with infinite energy and lots of time, they persisted, trying this combination and that combination until the answers flooded forth, pages and pages of printer paper falling on the floor, masses of figures which stunned Fergie.

"It can't be right. I mean look at it—*millions* of shares! Grandfather wouldn't do that! Not in a million years.... Maybe this is like *years* of trading."

"No, it isn't. It's got the date right there, April 25. Just the other day."

"*Millions* of shares. He wouldn't! My God...."

The computer was showing signs of mutiny, querying their queries, asking who they were, requesting authorization, refusing information.

"We better get out of *here*," said Lannie, "before they track us down."

Both the boys grinning with the mischief of it. Lannie broke off the connection.

That left pages and pages of computer stock paper neatly stacked on the floor. "Couldn't we ask your dad what it means?"

"God *no*! If Dad knew I'd been probing around his desk, he'd *kill* me!"

Fergie gathered up the sheets of paper and detached them from the machine. "Can I keep them? I'll think of something."

"Just so you don't say where you got it."

"I won't. I promise. There are no marks saying what computer this came off of."

Fergie took the computer paper back to his room and put it at the bottom of his duffel bag, underneath his dirty socks.

Lannie said, "Now what'll we do? It's only three o'clock.

Do you like to sail? I got a new spinnaker for the boat and I ought to try it out. It needs stretching before the race on Saturday.''

The boys took the Comet out and broke in the new red, blue and yellow spinnaker, putting it up, taking it down as they came around the practice buoy in the harbor. They got the time down to thirty-eight seconds before they got bored. It took about an hour and a half—a long attention span for a modern teenage boy.

CHAPTER 8

"William," said the imperious voice, "you will come to lunch at 12:30. We must talk."

William Worth, president of the Jockey Club, president of Worth Freres, chairman of the Securities Exchange Commission, age seventy-two, silver-haired aristocrat before whom even U.S. Presidents were extremely deferential, rolled his eyes toward heaven and said, "Mother!"

The ensuing argument took fifteen minutes out of William Worth's exceedingly busy day. He pointed out to the grande dame who was his mother that she was in the Waldorf Tower, a good hour in heavy noontime traffic by limousine from 44 Wall Street, and roughly another hour to get back, that he was up to his ears in work, especially since this unfortunate business about Jasper. . . .

"It's about Jasper I wish to talk. I've called Humphrey, and Estelle and Prudence and Oscar and Sylvia. They're all coming. Unfortunately, Arthur and Constance are in Europe and no one seems to know where Orin and Nicholas are."

A gathering of the clan which would do no good at all. By strenuous argument William Worth succeeded in getting his mother to change the meeting from luncheon to tea which would shorten his day but wouldn't wreck it altogether and at 5:30 (half an hour late) William Worth presented himself at the suite in the Waldorf Tower where Elsie Worth, age ninety-two, had held forth since the death of her husband, William Worth, Sr., twenty-two years earlier. Prior to that time the William Worths had lived in suffocating grandeur in a Renaissance palace of gray stone behind acres of wrought iron which covered doors and windows on East Eighty-sixth Street. (The palace was now the habitation of the tax-free Foundation for Pre-Colombian Indian Art, whose contribution to Western culture has long mystified journalists, scholars and the Internal Revenue Service.)

"I know the way," said William Worth irritably to the aged butler who met him at the door. He picked his way from the exquisite little egg-shaped foyer, its cream walls overlaid by rococo panels covered in blue and gold silk, its crystal chandelier sparkling like diamonds, through the grand salon with its marble columns, cream pilasters, its gloomy works by Velasquez and Rembrandt and Frans Hal (all of which William Worth detested), its gilt rococo furniture, its floors of Breche marble overlaid with Aubusson carpets, to the small salon (so-called though it was about thirty feet square) where his mother was bent over a tea wagon which contained a horrifying collection of scones, cakes, eclairs and sweets. The French furniture was covered with Worths, most of them female; the noise level was very high. His damned family, William Worth thought, was, if nothing else, piercing.

"You're very late, William," said his mother.

William Worth kissed his mother on the top of her head, the only part of her he could get to without crouching. "You're looking well, Mother."

"What a lie!" said his mother, who was pouring tea with intense concentration as if she were measuring out gold bullion, her clawlike hands holding both teacup and silver teapot, the deep blue eyes glittering like dark sapphires. "I'm too damned old. I can't understand why I'm still alive. My friends are dead and most of my children and now Jasper. It's very unkind of God not to take me to my rest." Elsie Worth had been lecturing God about this for twenty years, pleading for surcease and not getting it.

William Worth made the rounds, starting with Sylvia, the cleverest and most cursed of Worths, with her bright predatory smile and her wicked tongue. "Hello, Uncle Bill," she drawled in that marvelous smoky voice. "Welcome to the *Titanic*. Pull up a deck chair and lie down."

William Worth kissed Sylvia's chic and fragrant cheek. "No ship would sink with you on it, Sylvia; it wouldn't dare."

He passed on to Prudence, a widow now for thirty years, drying up like an old apple, kissing her leathery cheek, and then on to Estelle, an old maid of sixty-five who looked eighty-five, shy as a hunted animal, looking, as always, terrified. And, oh my God, Humphrey, that damned pansy, wearing one of his awful Italian suits with their thin lapels and quite inappropriate pockets, to say nothing of those dreadful Gucci shoes.

The two men's dislike of each other had a profoundly sexual basis. William with his little girl friends tucked away discreetly in the East Seventies. Humphrey with his little boy friends he never managed to tuck away discreetly enough. Each made physically ill by the sexual predilections of the other, their aversion so strong they hadn't shaken hands in years.

They nodded to each other like boxers across a ring and that left Oscar Settle, Sylvia's miserable cuckold of a husband, the non-Worth, as they liked to call him. (Alec Worth had once said, "He's unworthy of being a non-Worth.") William nodded at the non-Worth and said, "What is the purpose of this gathering, Mother? We don't even know that Jasper is dead yet. Not really."

"He's dead," said Elsie Worth ferociously. "I feel it in my bones and my bones are never wrong. Poor Jasper is dead and he *hates* it and I'm alive and I don't want to be—we should trade places. William, you must try one of these—Viennese and quite delicious." A mass of whipped cream overlaid with strawberries.

William Worth said, "If you're worried about the shares, I've suspended trading."

Humphrey with his rubicund smile. "I told you long ago, Aunt Elsie, to diversify."

"Quite disloyal of you, Humphrey."

"Just sensible, Auntie." Humphrey cool as a knife. "You should have sold at least half of your Worth shares and you should have got out of Securities Unlimited long ago and put yourself in the hands of Morgan or Lehman Brothers, somebody outside the family, so that you can raise your voice when the time comes."

"Well, we can't undo what's done." Estelle in her expiring voice.

"Can't undo *what*?" William didn't like the sound of that word undo. Lady Macbeth with her sorrowful, "What's done cannot be undone."

"Well, I mean that boy was Jasper's favorite nephew. Jasper was grooming him for... well, to take over, I suppose." This from Prudence. Defiantly as if she'd been accused.

The grande dame sniffed. "Where on earth did Sophie get that name—Elihu? It's not one of our names. We've never had Elihus."

"The smiling hyena," said Humphrey.

Everyone started talking at once, the noise level rising sharply.

Elsie was still fiddling with the tea tray, not missing anything. "Some stockholders were staging a mutiny, William, and Jasper was in a tearing hurry to quell the revolt. Anyway, that young man Elihu said the thing could be revoked by a telephone call. At a moment's notice."

"Revoked? Revoked *what*, Mother?"

"Now, William," said his mother, "Jasper has always run my affairs very well."

In the end the butler and footman were sent scurrying through the fifteen-room suite (which, after the eighty-four rooms in the Renaissance palace, Elsie found quite cramping) in search of the piece of paper she had signed. "Yes, of course I read it. You don't think I'd sign something without reading it. Anyway, Jasper has always had my proxies to vote my shares however he pleased. He enjoyed my fullest confidence. . . ."

When the piece of paper was located in the Louis Seize desk—itself worth half a million—it was discovered that it was not a proxy statement but a power of attorney Elsie had signed and it was made out, not to Jasper Worth, but to Elihu Worth.

The level of self-assertion rose thunderously, even from timid Estelle, a deep fissure appearing in the granitic unity of the Worth family. There was one group consisting of Elsie, Estelle and Prudence (and possibly other Worth women who were not there), who had signed powers of attorney, and there were the others, William, Humphrey and Sylvia, who not only had *not* signed such pieces of paper but had not even been approached. Elihu had known which Worths could be conned and which could not. Even then it had taken someone from inside the family, brandishing the awe-inspiring name and reputation of Jasper to have got to these women who would have called their lawyers if an outsider had attempted such a thing.

The three women had signed power of attorney to Elihu Worth for some thirty million Worth shares valued at roughly two hundred million dollars.

In Galveston it was an hour earlier, five o'clock, when the exploration ship docked accompanied by two helicopters, one hired by CBS news, the other by the *Houston Post*, which had circled overhead for the last hour of the voyage. The deck was now awash with media—radio, press, TV cameramen, reporters, even a few columnists. Buried in this mob were representatives of the District Attorney's office and the coroner's office, both wanting a little piece of the action.

This mob scene produced one of those comedies that so often happens at large, over-covered news events. The DA and the coroner had both staked out a claim to talking to the captain and owner of the exploration ship before the press got to them. The police chief agreed that they were entitled and had so instructed police on the scene.

Then the event itself took charge. As the gangplank went down there was a rush of TV cameramen—all veterans of many such mob scenes where the race went to the swiftest—and they went up the gangway and were on board with cameras churning out color reportage before the much slower coroner and DA's men got to the upper deck.

Elihu Worth was on the catwalk outside the pilothouse, slim, darkly handsome, appropriately grief stricken. (Not too much grief, just enough.) As the very first camera zoomed in on him (the microphone boon just a second behind, losing the opening words) Elihu started to speak.

"...a very sad occasion. It is my grievous duty to report that my distinguished Uncle Jasper has been lost at sea in the great storm, a force-eight gale, winds of hurricane strength during which we kept circling, trying our utmost to rescue...."

During all this the ship was still tying up and Captain

Stork was off the bridge and up forward supervising. He had quite deliberately removed himself from the limelight and reporters and cameramen. He heard the words of Elihu imperfectly; it crossed his mind immediately that this was not the way it happened. Jasper Worth had not been lost *during* a storm but *before* the storm. Just the same Stork was in no position to contradict (being thirty yards behind the cameras and microphone). Also he was uncertain as to whether he had heard right. Elihu had so swiftly garbled the rescue attempts with the actual fall from the rigging that Stork could not tell whether Jasper Worth had indeed got it wrong or whether he, Stork, had got Elihu wrong. In any case, he hesitated too long and lost the chance to correct the story.

The word went out on the air then and there that Jasper Worth had been lost in the great gulf storm rather than before the storm (in quite calm waters as had actually happened). This impression was never corrected. Similarly the coroner's representative, a man named Prentice, and the Assistant DA, named Wainwright, hesitated just one minute too long. The reporters were shouting questions. Why hadn't the exploration ship reported the loss of so important a man? Why had the ship ignored queries from the District Attorney's office? Wasn't it true that the ship had been on the inland waterway and then gone back out into the gulf again? Why?

"These are the questions *we* should be asking," said Wainwright angrily, pushing hard at the crush around the steel stairs which led to the pilothouse.

Prentice, an older, wiser man, said, "Yeah. We should stop the show, shouldn't we? Tell all those cameramen to turn off their cameras until we talk to the guy. Deprive all those listeners—who are also voters—of their fun house. Go ahead! *You* do it!"

Wainwright didn't. He nursed ambitions to be District Attorney himself some day, which meant running for office, which in turn meant he had to curry favor with the very same cameramen and reporters whose attention was now turned on Elihu Worth. Wainwright kept his mouth shut and therefore the story about the death of Jasper Worth was shaped (or rather misshaped) by Elihu Worth from the very outset.

Elihu gave a great performance. "Jasper was a man in the great Worth tradition, an originator, an innovator, keeping always on the very edge of technology, never resting on his fame or his wealth. He insisted always on personally taking part in the exploration for new oil fields, as he insisted on personally involving himself in all new technology, new financial techniques, never resting, always pushing forward, this great man . . ." Elihu's voice throbbing with emotion, love and pity, the words throwing attention on the man who had died, distracting attention from the *way* he had died.

Elihu very telegenic, his dark handsome face convulsed with sorrow and pride in being a Worth (which most Worths thought actually he wasn't). What the media had planned— an accusatory confrontation, pinning Elihu to the deck with hard questions—was transformed by Elihu's eloquence and powerful self-confidence into a long throbbing eulogy of Jasper Worth. . . .

. . . which was listened to on the little radio on the deck of the schooner with total absorption and not a little skepticism by Orin and Nicholas Worth.

"Is that our daddy he's talking about?" said Nicholas. "Our own beloved innovator keeping always on the very edge of new technology?"

From the little radio came Elihu's voice, throbbing away. ". . . he was above all else American, plainspoken, full of old-fashioned virtues—patriotism, love of country, love of his fellow Americans, love of God. . . ."

Said Orin, "Here was a Caesar! When comes such another?"

Nicholas said, "Save it, kid. For opening night."

* * *

The Worth women, sitting on the gilt Louis Seize chairs in the small salon in Elsie Worth's Waldorf Tower suite, were unaccustomedly quiet, even Sylvia's smoky wisecracking voice silenced, while William Worth dictated the letters revoking the power of attorney. (Too late, too late, Sylvia was thinking, everything comes too late.)

Oscar Settle, the despised Worth, took it all down on Elsie Worth's ancient Corona portable because the Worths didn't want outsiders involved in this operation. (Oscar had helped put himself through Michigan typing other people's term papers.)

A heartwarming display of family cooperation in a family renowned for its individual cussedness.

Everything a little peculiar about this scene.

Not the least Estelle, the timid one, the inaudible one, speaking up sharply. "Better late than never." Catastrophe had brought roses to her ordinarily ashen cheeks, a sparkle to her eye.

Twice in this dictation William Worth, the white-mustached, white-maned aristocrat, turned to his detested nephew Humphrey to confer on the proper legal phraseology for these letters, the two of them, putting their heads together and discussing the legal proprieties in low earnest tones. Twice William Worth took Humphrey Worth's *advice*, to the utter amazement of the assembled female Worths who had never thought they would live to see such a thing.

When the meeting broke up, much later than any of them had planned, during the kissing and farewells, and the We-must-have-luncheon and the You-promise-to-come-to-Southampton, Locust Valley, or wherever, William Worth was actually seen to shake *hands* with Humphrey Worth, an astounding sight.

In the stretch limousine, William Worth told Terence O'Reilly, the chauffeur who doubled as bodyguard and routinely packed a .357 in his belt, to head for Sixty-fourth Street and Lexington, and take it slow. William ran up the glass that separated chauffeur from passenger, picked up the telephone (one of two) and rang, not knowing if she were home.

"Lolo," he said. "Could I come up for a minute?"

"Darling, of course."

"I don't like to put you out. You're sure you haven't any plans?" Always exquisitely polite.

Lolo Vanbrugh. Sylvia Worth's best friend and confidante.

But not so confidante that she told Sylvia about William Worth, who was a rather recent acquisition.

CHAPTER 9

Twenty-four hours later the schooner tied up in Galveston harbor. No TV cameras were present, no reporters, no DAs or coroners, no crowd at all.

Only Alec Worth wearing his designer jeans and sweatshirt, looking very slim and intelligent, stood on the dock whose number and location he had got from the harbor master. The ship had barely tied up when Alec leaped from dock to deck, landing almost in Nicholas' arms.

"Hello," he said. "I'm Alec Worth. And you're..."

"Nicholas," said Nicholas. "This is Orin."

The three Worths looking each other over, shaking hands, faces wary. Alec had never met these Worths, but had heard of them vaguely as he'd heard of so many others, not looking them up or anything like that, just filing away what bits of information about other branches of the Worth family drifted his way.

"The news is all over the radio about your father," said Alec easily. "That's why I came."

No news about us, Nicholas not saying it. Just looking. A time to tread softly.

"I come offering condolence and," Alec sighed because the brothers were not welcoming, "sympathy and," waving his arms, feeling his way among these strange, rather hostile Worths, "advice?" Putting a question mark on the last because Worths traditionally shied away from the advice of strangers, even strange Worths.

"How'd you know about us?" asked Orin. The innocent, always asking the dumb questions, Nicholas was thinking, that I don't dare ask.

"A little bird," said Alec.

"A little bird in a red helicopter."

Alec's smooth stockbroker face showed nothing at all. He wandered up the deck to the submersible hanging from its davits at center of the deck and looked it over, openmouthed like a sightseer. Up forward in the bow of the schooner, Dake was repositioning the schooner, the winch pulling the hawsers tight against the jetty. He nodded at Alec, not saying anything.

After a bit Alec wandered back to the brothers. He had given them a chance to confer about him and said, "Well?"

"What kind of advice do you think we need, Mr. Worth?"

"We'd better go below," said Alec.

They all sipped the overboiled coffee which had been simmering too long, seated around the teak table. "The District Attorney is very concerned about the death of your father," said Alec.

"We don't think it's any of his business," said Nicholas. "It happened at sea."

"The body is here. In his jurisdiction," said Alec softly.

"How did you know about the body? The little bird in the red helicopter?"

Alec said, "The DA will want to know why you were

lying at the bottom of the gulf at the very point where your father fell off the exploration ship. A very odd coincidence!''

"It is, isn't it?"

Nicholas not giving anything away.

Alec looking them up and down with his smooth self-confidence. Kids! New York rich kids with that look of aloneness that was a hallmark of New York rich kids. Aloneness was not altogether loneliness (although there was loneliness in it), but a sort of separation from the rest of the species. They surrounded themselves with contemporaries, these New York young rich, but were always apart from them, even in the midst of a crowd, listening to distant drums of their own devising, an outgrowth of their own distrust, many of them born and brought up in big estates surrounded by servants and inferiors never quite part of the human race, resenting that always, always.

Texas rich were not that separate, riding their horses, shooting and hunting with friends and kinsmen and buddies. Arrogant, not separate.

Sipping the bitter terrible coffee, letting the brothers work it out in their minds. It was a little like being an emissary of Venice to the Orient, the Oriental potentates, holding him hostage while fumigating him to get rid of those foreign infections.

Nicholas with his sad handsome face and his keen intelligence living in his deep well of loneliness, yearning for companionship while holding every human being at arm's length. Except this older brother. Very curious. Brothers who loved each other because they were both in the same predicament. Both Worths, both rich, both—and there was the rub—the offspring of that wonderful and terrible old man Jasper Worth.

After he'd waited long enough, Alec said, "I think you better check in with the DA, tell him you have your father's body and, uh, have some sort of interesting explanation as to why you were lying in a submarine—by such a remarkable coincidence—just where you were.''

"It wasn't a coincidence," said Nicholas.

Of course it wasn't a coincidence. Any damned fool would know that, especially any damned DA, but still a great admission to come from this thin, sad-faced, intelligent young man who suffered from inexperience so wide as to amount to a fatal physical defect, like a hole in the heart.

"I suspected as much," commented Alec dryly, "but the DA is going to ask how come. Why?"

"Suppose we don't answer."

"Why should you want to do that?"

"Even the reason for not wanting to is . . ."

Nicholas trailed off to silence.

"Yes, I see what you mean," said Alec very softly, not wanting to scare these shy birds into flight. "But you see, you're giving Elihu a bit too much rope. He's already had his say to the DA and gone off. He's about twenty-four hours ahead of you and that gives him a very great head start. If you're to close that gap, you must get the DA off your neck right away. You must . . . well, I don't know what your plans are, or if you have any. I just know this: Elihu does. I don't know what it is, but I can assure you he's got a plan and it's in operation and, I suspect, doing fine. . . ."

He had their interest now. The two Worth brothers, Orin and Nicholas, both with their dark eyes and their tremendous physical resemblance (their souls, their characters, their inner essence not at all alike, this coming through in their silences, their gestures, their tones of voice). What had gripped the brothers instantly was the name Elihu.

There was now a divergence among the brothers, faint as a whisper. Orin was shifting in his seat slightly, his eyes on his younger brother troubled and questing. Nicholas meanwhile clearing his throat, scowling as if he'd bitten into something foul.

"Elihu," said Nicholas.

"I think we'd better tell him," said Orin.

"No!" said Nicholas violently. Hanging on.

"He's a Worth," said Orin, the trusting one.

"So is Elihu."

"It's not the same thing."

"Red helicopter," said Nicholas warningly.

"Aah," said Alec. "Red helicopter." It put him in the ranks of the enemy. He saw that, saw that clearly. But what to do? Robin was his . . . love. He couldn't . . . without compromising her. And they wouldn't without getting clear about this. . . .

Or at least Nicholas wouldn't. Orin seemed to be under the thumb of the *younger* brother! Very peculiar, that arrangement. But of course, the Worths were always a little peculiar. They had the confidence of their own peculiarities.

We are nothing if not singular. The singularity of the very rich, even among other very rich, singular in the purest sense of separateness, detached, estranged; we are ourselves, unique in a world of increasing uniformity, self-worshipping, mistrustful even of one another, and here I am hung up on loyalties from one Worth to a quite separate bunch of Worths who are in deeper trouble than they realize and I am smitten beyond my depths and quite contrary to my custom. Thus Alec, the cool, confident, surefooted one, for one of the few times in his life at sea in his own uncertainty.

It showed in his face, a bewilderment foreign to his nature so great as to be obvious even to these two brothers who had never before met him.

"You think I'm some part of Elihu's design," he cried. "I'm not. I assure you."

"What sort of assurance can you give us?" asked Nicholas.

"Oh, Nick," said Orin. "Don't you see? He's trying to help. . . ."

"No, I don't see. He's asking a lot of questions. He's not giving much. What was that red helicopter doing, chasing us when we fished Dad out of the gulf? Talk about coincidences! That was an even greater coincidence. How did it get there, hundreds of miles from land?''

Revealing more than he intended. He shut up.

They were cracking open, Alec saw, and he moved in. "She's changed sides. That's all I can tell you. You must trust me.''

"*She!*'' The two brothers said it together, both leaping on the word she, both astonished, full of wonder, and perhaps a little light titillation. "*She!*'' said Nicholas again, breaking into a smile. "We should have known. *She!*''

The game was up. Alec frowned into his bitter coffee and dropped his eyes. He said nothing because he didn't know what to say. Anyway the brothers were full of smiles and self-congratulation.

"Perhaps we'd better call the DA now," said Nicholas. "We can explain *our* coincidence. If she can explain hers.''

Now it was Alec's turn to be alarmed. "You must keep her out of it." There was of course not only the DA. There was Hortense. Robin had said that Hortense knew and didn't *care,* well not exactly didn't care but planned no action, quite a different thing from not caring. If this thing came out in the open . . .

"She's changed sides," said Alec again.

"Why?"

There it was—out in the open.

Alec's face twisted into a grimace: "I should never have come. I was trying to help.''

He stood up.

Orin said, "You have helped, Mr. Worth. Do sit down. Perhaps there's another way.''

"Ah, Orin . . .'' Nicholas unwilling to give up his distrust. If there was one thing Jasper had taught him, it was distrust.

"Sit down, Mr. Worth," said Orin again. "If I could just talk to my brother . . .''

A change of wind. Alec sat down, at least partly because

he was fascinated by the interplay of brotherly authority, passing before his very eyes from one brother to the other.

Orin pulled Nicholas—it took physical strength to do it—out of the little galley into the forecastle where he said, low and urgent, "We *need* him, Nicholas. He's one of the cleverest Worths there is, especially in stock trading."

"Yeah, so clever he's urging us to give ourselves over to the DA."

"We were going to do that anyway, weren't we? We can't keep Dad in that icebox indefinitely."

"Orin . . ."

Orin took his brother's face in his two hands and held it close. "You must trust someone, Nick, or life's not worth living."

It was the touch of hands that did it. Orin could always sway his brother with a touch of flesh better than with argument.

"Ah, Orin, Orin! You're a soft mark."

The brothers went back to the galley where Alec was staring entranced at the sonar, the satellite communications, all the electronic wizardry.

Nicholas sat on the bench opposite Alec, eyeing him. "We're listening," he said.

"Don't tell the DA one word more than he wants to know. Don't volunteer information he doesn't ask for."

"What will he ask for?"

"Why were you lying in a submarine underneath the exploration ship?"

The brothers cracked their knuckles and looked at the planking. Nicholas scratched his head. "It's not a crime, is it?"

Alec spoke carefully and distinctly. "It could be evidence of conspiracy. Not anything the courts or the SEC could do much with, but the press could go wild. Speculative stories in the media could do a lot of damage."

The brothers remained silent. Above they could hear

Dake hosing down the deck, whistling tunelessly. On the jetty the little electric loading lorries ran about noisily.

"The press could make quite a scene over the true facts too. Maybe a bigger splash than conspiracy."

"Perhaps you'd better tell me."

The brothers exchanged glances, full of rue and deep filial currents.

It was Orin who spoke with the unvoiced agreement of his younger brother. "We were where we were because our father told us to be there."

Alec was astonished. The last thing in the world he'd expected. The complications of Jasper Worth!

"Why?"

Nicholas smiled his bitter smile. "He never told us why. Dad didn't believe in explanation. He gave orders."

"Of course," said Orin, "we had our suspicions."

Nicholas said, "We don't intend to tell our suspicions to the District Attorney. We don't think our suspicions are any business of his."

Alec said, "He'll have his own suspicions."

Orin said, "We won't ask him his suspicions if he'll leave us ours."

"He won't."

Later, after all else was said, the time came when Alec had to extend hospitality. Knowing the cost. He couldn't have these Worths in Galveston without making the gesture, hoping they'd refuse, knowing they wouldn't. Still there it was. He had to extend hospitality because failure to do so was unthinkable.

"You'll be here two or three days. The coroner will have to perform an autopsy. You'll be more comfortable at my house and we can plan a strategy. . . ."

Alas, they accepted. Eagerly on the part of Orin. Reluctantly, even a little sullenly, on the part of Nicholas.

Explaining it to Robin was the worst part.

"Throwing me out, Uncle Alec? How very unkind!" Her

bright hurt eyes full of tears. She has the courage of her own tears, Alec was thinking. A lesser woman would have suppressed them but Robin let the tears flow because that's the way she was—outspoken. "After all we've been to each other." Making jokes, not staunching the tears which ran down her bright cheeks.

"You've got to get that damned helicopter out of here. They know all about the red helicopter."

"I've got to get myself out of here is what you mean."

They were standing on the luncheon terrace surrounded by the brilliant flowers, but tight as fiddle strings.

"I didn't want them here," cried Alec. (Was that Hortense in the library? He could see a shape moving in there. Perhaps just one of the Vietnamese.) "I had to. There's a great deal at stake."

"Money," cried Robin, tears splashing down on her white rumpled jumpsuit. (She didn't give a damn what she wore half the time. The other half she was Princess Di.) "Money is what we're all about—the only thing, the guiding thing, the final arbiter in all our decisions."

"Oh, for God's sake, Robin, if you knew how much this is costing me—"

The minute he said it he wished he hadn't.

"*Costing* you. . . ."

The worst word he could have picked.

"I'll see you in New York!" he said miserably. "I'll be there next week."

"What makes you think I'll be there?" But of course she would. She shook the tears out of her eyes with one fierce shake. "Do you know where to call? Where will *you* be? And when? Oh, my God, here comes Hortense. I can't face Hortense."

Hortense came out the French doors leading to the library. So it *was* Hortense. Tears. How would he explain tears?

Robin turned her back to him and strode into the garden and around the side of the white frame house, blond curls bobbing on her neck, her little round bottom churning flashes of concupiscence that pierced Alec to the marrow.

Hortense was at his side with her bright rictus of a smile. "You've made the child cry, Alec. How very unkind!"

Alec thinking. I can't fight both of them! Hortense who never missed anything.

"A couple of other Worths are coming to stay." Alec delivered it straight into her eyes, standing toe to toe with her, always the best way to deal with Hortense. "Orin and Nicholas, Jasper's sons. She's got to go—and Fergie."

"Darling, there's plenty of room for all the Worths—"

"No, there isn't." How to explain this. "These are not Robin's favorite cousins. Some sort of childhood...antagonism I don't understand. There are deep hostilities among the eastern Worths and this business about Jasper has made it much worse. I had to invite Orin and Nicholas here because how could I not? Their mother and my mother were very close friends, though I never met these two before. Oh, hell!"

Hortense standing there, nose upraised, sniffing the air for nuance. Alec watched a bee settle on a white azalea, drinking the nectar, chaste as sunlight. He couldn't leave it at that.

"Orin and Nicholas have their father's body. They're going to have to explain that to the District Attorney."

"Good heavens!" Just that and nothing more. Hortense knew the best way to worm things out of her husband was to leave the air full of unasked questions.

The two of them standing there, husband and wife, very much one flesh, confronting this rich mixture of adultery, hospitality and family as if it were a conjugal problem, one that had to be solved together.

Alec so flooded by his wife's forbearance that he unloosed another fragment, more than he'd planned.

"That red helicopter has got to get out of here. It would

cause a war between the two sets of Worths. Right now we can't afford that."

Hortense ran a finger over her lip, mistress of quietude that she was, and said, "I'm going to go help the child pack."

The second time she had used that word child. Child indeed!

"Pack her duffel bag! She doesn't need..."

Hortense had already flown around the side of the house leaving Alec in the bower of greenery, bereft. Bereft of both of them!

In her room, Robin was thrusting the turquoise silk dress into the canvas duffel bag as if it were a cleaning rag. After it went her cutoff jeans, her crystal earrings and her Tampax. Vengefully.

Her back to the door, she *smelled* Hortense, her astringence, her fragrance. Hortense leaning against the doorjamb, arms folded, amused.

"I've been thrown out!" Violently.

"Not by me."

Robin sat on the edge of the bed, pouting. "Where's Fergie? We've both been thrown out."

Very rude, Robin not allowing herself to be engulfed in Hortense's good manners.

"They're sailing. I've sent Absolom out in the Chris-Craft with the loud hailer. You'd better wash your face. You look quite ridiculous."

Ridiculous!

Robin fled to the bathroom to have a look and, when she saw herself, burst out laughing. Two black lines of mascara down her cheeks like a clown's face. She made a move at herself in the mirror knowing Hortense was right behind her, watching. "I rather like it! Woebegone the Clown. That's me!" She made herself into Raggedy Ann, knees bent inward, elbows in, hands outthrust. "Poor, poor me!" Like the song.

All wrong, Hortense was thinking. She should be singing Rich, rich me!

The rich having their own quite distinctive vulnerabilities and deserving their own special songs. But no one wrote songs about the rich anymore.

Robin had tired of being Woebegone the Clown and now she washed her face in cold water, fiercely, and dried her face vigorously, bringing out in her cheeks a glow of rude red health. It changed the point of view.

She swung around and faced Hortense now, full of energy, determined to take command of the situation. (Worths took command of situations as naturally and ferociously as lionesses leaped on gazelles and for the same reason.) "You must come visit in New York, Hortense. I'll smother you in good manners."

"Have I *smothered* you, darling?"

"You've been an angel." Making it an accusation. Robin leaning against the sink as lazily and self-sufficiently as Hortense leaned against the bathroom doorjamb.

Each of them taking the measure of the other.

Both smiling.

The air radiant with sex.

I'm not ready for this!

. . . thought Robin. But then, neither is she. She doesn't even know she wants me yet. I know it but she doesn't and when she does, oh, wow. . . It's going to cut her in half.

CHAPTER 10

Sylvia Worth was on the telephone with her best friend Lolo Vanbrugh. ". . . gone to Rome for her shoes."

"Trixie Vance? Wears shoes?" Lolo Vanbrugh, rich enough not to give a damn what anyone wore or didn't wear, looked at her own feet encased in snakeskin of deepest blue. "All my shoes are fourteen years old. I have a little leatherworker—"

"Darling, your *own* shoemaker!"

"And I'm not about to share him with you, love. I'd never get him back." The two women enlivening each other with gossip and wit every morning. "Are you telling me Trixie Vance has left her darling jockey for *shoes*?"

"She's fed up with her darling jockey. She said his sole conversation was 'How about it?' Lolo . . . Lolo. . . ."

Sylvia could hear nothing, which sounded as if Lolo had her hand over the mouthpiece, and what did that mean? Ah ha!

At the other end, Lolo was being kissed good-bye by William Worth, his silver bristly moustache tickling her lip,

William smelling of bay shaving soap, looking very much the man of Wall Street, unsexed by money.

"Don't say anything about me to *her*!" said William Worth vigorously.

"Darling, of course not." Lolo Vanbrugh was pushing forty-five and men were hard to find, even elderly gentlemen like William, most of whom went for eighteen-year-olds. It wasn't fair, but then what was? "When will I see you?"

"I'll call when I can. This Jasper business is taking a lot of time. Don't tell Sylvia anything about that either. You're not supposed to know anything."

Lolo had wormed more out of him about Jasper Worth than he wished. My god, the curiosity of women! It was a disease! He kissed Lolo again and walked to the private elevator landing, Lolo's being the only stop on that floor. (At night, when Lolo returned from whatever party she'd been to, she threw a switch by the elevator which prevented the elevator from stopping at the floor for any reason until she herself released it the next morning.)

The lobby was full of uniformed doormen and cleaning men, but mercifully no apartment dwellers, William striding past the flunkies, not responding to their greetings except with curt little nods. Damned awkward, the whole business! Out on East Sixty-fourth Street, the East River gleaming in the sunlight behind him, William Worth walked briskly in the direction of Lexington where there just might be a cab, reveling in the exercise, the early morning air before New York turned muggy.

Back in the apartment, Lolo was fending off her sharpwitted friend Sylvia who was saying, "You're harboring a gentleman, Lolo. Now don't deny it!"

"Oh, don't I wish I had a gentleman!" exclaimed Lolo, who was one of the most skilled liars of the female persuasion. "Darling, I haven't had a lover since Eisenhower. I've forgotten what sex was like. What is it like—ice cream?"

The two women who told each other everything about

everyone else were utterly secretive about their own affairs. Everyone knew about Sylvia's affair with her Uncle Jasper, but Sylvia flatly denied the whole business, and had such a tantrum whenever Lolo mentioned it, even as a gag, that Lolo had given up on that subject.

The two women passed on to other matters. "Marcia's shrink told her to take up painting. He tells them *all* to take up painting. A hundred dollars an hour for that. So anyway, Marcia went out and bought paints and brushes and an easel—the whole works. She was showing Czee Czee all this stuff and she held up the palette knife and said, 'What's that for?' and Czee Czee said, 'That's to cut your ear off with. . . .'"

William Worth caught a cab at Sixty-fourth and Lexington, said, "Forty-four Wall" to the driver, sank back against the tattered backrest and closed his eyes. Jasper sprang at him behind the closed eyelids. Allowing, as he always did in greeting, "What ho, William! What ho!" Like a pirate, which is what he was. William had been the older boy but Jasper was always the leader, the taunter. A wicked polo player! Wickedly aggressive, innovative, always urging William, a classic polo player, into derring-do, which once sent William into the hospital with a head wound that took fourteen stitches and another time killed William's best pony under him.

William running through the play for the ten thousandth time behind the closed lids. Rough but scrupulously within the rules. That was Jasper. Breaking precedent, never the rules. (Bending them a little.) That's why this caper was so uncharacteristic. More than uncharacteristic. Unbelievable. There was, William believed, a signature to stock trading, as recognizable to the expert as an artist's brushstrokes. These brushstrokes were not Jasper's. There was a limit beyond which Jasper never went. A buccaneer but a principled buccaneer.

Jasper.

William's old face crinkled in a sad smile. William had always adored him, forgave him, understood him. Except Elihu. He hadn't understood Elihu. Forgave Elihu but not understood Elihu. Especially since the man had two sons of his own—loyal, decent, intelligent sons like Orin and Nicholas. But then Jasper had never appreciated his own sons. They were not what he'd ordered; they could not be molded into what he wanted.

In Worth Freres' great expanse of a waiting room with its knotty pine paneling (nobody had knotty pine paneling anymore. Worth Freres was definitely out of date) he said, "Good morning," to Miss Digby who had been with the firm twenty-two years and went into the inner office passing Bill Hicks' office. Bill on the phone saying, "The conversion premium is where the play is. That's the difference between the price of the stock when the debentures are offered and . . ." Bill nodding and waving as he passed, talking away, "the fixed price of the shares when they can be converted."

William Worth passed Joe Fratolini's office, the tough little Italian whom William had put through Yale and taken into the firm, waving at him, Joe on the telephone, too. ". . . huge demand in Europe for oil service stocks. There is this rumor floating about that Phillips is going to buy the company, but you'll have to make up your mind *now*."

His own office pine paneled, enormous, the tall windows overlooking the East River and the bay (one of the privileges and prerogatives of the very rich, overlooking the water which the rich and powerful had once scorned, preferring the high ground, the mountains for safety), Miss Trimingham, who had been with him forty years, on the telephone as he entered, saying, "I don't think it's possible today, Mr. Fortescue, but I'll ask him and get back to you."

William Worth leaning over his own desk looking at the calendar which Miss Trimingham had prepared: Board of Directors, Manufacturers Hanover Trust 10:30; lunch Worth

Freres Sigismund Trenc, German Iron and Steel Institute, Harry Van of Rothschild's 12:30 (in Worth Freres own paneled private dining room), 2:30 meeting here, Fratolini, Hicks, etc.

A full day.

Miss Trimingham had hung up on Fortescue and was shuffling memos under his nose, neither of them looking at each other. An old, old relationship, his and Miss Trimingham's. He'd put her into the firm when she was a young girl, a Boston aristocrat down on her luck, and now she was no longer young. The two had grown estranged. Time does not always pull people together, sometimes it has the opposite effect. William didn't even know if she liked him. (She had once, God knew, but now he didn't know what was passing through that white spinsterish, still handsome intelligent head.)

Miss Trimingham was saying, "George Allen has been on the phone twice yesterday, once this morning . . ."

George Allen, executive vice-president of Securities Unlimited, Jasper's top holding company. A bear of a man Jasper had ensconced in Securities Unlimited next to Elihu, the wolf, himself the lion—what a menagerie! Allen would be snarling about the stock trading suspension of Worth shares. "Keep him out of my hair," growled William Worth, seating himself at the desk. "No, maybe not. . . ."

He picked up the phone and called George Allen who launched into an immediate complaint about suspension of trading. William Worth cut him short. "Have you heard from Elihu?"

"He's flying in from Texas today but I don't expect him in the office until tomorrow."

"I want to see him immediately," ordered William Worth. "You've heard, I hope, that we've revoked the power of attorney."

"What power of attorney?"

Dear God! It was worse than he'd imagined! What power

of attorney! "How much of Elihu's operations do you oversee?" asked William. Jasper and his infernal deviousness!

"None of it! We have our separate fiefdoms. Jasper wanted it that way. You must realize, Mr. Worth," the voice dripping sarcasm, "that there are a great many Worth shares *not* owned or controlled by the family and you have suspended trading in all of them—roughly a billion dollars worth. Elihu's fiefdom is the family-owned shares, but mine is far far wider—"

William cut him short. "Have you got Elihu's home phone number?" He pried it out of George Allen who gave it up with the utmost reluctance.

"He's never there," said George Allen. "He's a bachelor, always flitting around at night. You won't find him home."

William Worth got him off and hung up. Miss Trimingham handed him the other phone. "Mrs. Worth," said Miss Trimingham distinctly. She had a separate intonation for William's wife, as if she'd changed keys from B flat to C, just a half note, but the difference in that half note, what an immensity! Marcia Worth, that gentle, proud matriarch who lived an eon away in Old Westbury, that citadel of old money, Marcia that representative of a dying order of womanhood—all this in Miss Trimingham's C natural voice, respect, a touch of envy (not too much) but, above all, an identity of aim.

William Worth grasped the telephone eagerly. "Darling! How are you?"

"I tried to call you at the flat, William. Last night—"

"I was playing poker." An old dodge that she'd long since seen through. "I'll be on the five-fifteen. Meet me."

"Of course."

Miss Trimingham shaking her head violently. "I have the theater tickets for *Cats*. You were going to take that German steel man."

"Give them to Webster. He can have the duty." Speaking

more roughly than he normally would because he, William Worth, wanted suddenly and terribly to spend the evening and the night with his wife of fifty years, to whom he'd been repeatedly and flagrantly unfaithful, to whom he always returned guilty but refreshed, the lone entity in the whole world from whom he had never been alienated.

In Old Westbury, Marcia Worth, as she said of herself, a Helen Hokinson lady long after the Helen Hokinson ladies had departed, ordered the capons for dinner that night, told the cook to do them the Hungarian way her husband loved, and proceeded to the garden overlooking the bay sparkling with white sails. Behind her the big old-fashioned house, hushed and cool, full of space and empty rooms, the children long gone, the grandchildren so seldom there, on her knees before the begonias wearing her old leather gloves, an old lady on her knees in the soft earth (because Rupert the German gardener would replant the begonias if not watched carefully, the German having no faith in her green thumb). Marcia Worth's gentle submissive face very close to the earth, smelling it, taking strength from the earth, fulfilling the basic female urge to create . . . a flower. Feeling creation in her fingertips, so infinitely compelling.

At five o'clock she drove the Mercedes to the Long Island railroad station and was standing on the platform, a plump white-haired lady with a big straw hat. They walked into each other's arms, kissed, and then walked down the long passageway, arm in arm, talking trivialities. "How was it in town?"

"Very hot. Muggy. And here?"

"Quite nice, the breeze coming from the sound. . . ."

"Has Rupert done anything about the hedge?"

"He keeps making excuses."

"I've told him a dozen times."

William drove the Mercedes past the great estates, the shrubbery, the great trees, Marcia saying, "Analie called from Hong Kong." Their elder daughter, now married with two teenage children. "So sorry she missed you. The children are fine but Jade is not doing well in that school and wants to come back to America and go to Madera, where her mother says they do nothing but ride horses. Of course, Analie is flatly opposed. . . ."

Elihu had handled the tickets in his baffling way. Houston to New York with a stopover at Chicago, when quite easily they could have gone nonstop to New York. Francis Graebner, the lawyer, accustomed to asking questions, asked questions. Elihu shut him up with his sharkish grin. They went tourist, which Graebner didn't like at all, and Elihu spent all of the flight asleep. In Chicago, when they might simply have sat in the airplane during the stopover, Elihu hustled the lawyer into the terminal. It wasn't until they got inside that Graebner discovered they weren't to continue to New York.

"You'll stay over, *not* at the Palmer House or any of the big ones where they can track you down. Find a little one. If they do locate you, say nothing at all."

"Locate me?"

"Press. Anyone at all. Just shut up. Lawyer–client confidentiality. The only two words you know are 'no comment.' "

Graebner didn't comment about *that*. Jasper had been the boss. Now it was this . . . shark. Always before Graebner had been contemptuous of Elihu. No more. He was scared to death of him.

TWA Flight 622 from Houston to New York landed in Kennedy at 3 P.M. and was mobbed by the media—TV, radio, press—but the quarry was not there. Elihu landed at La Guardia unnoticed three hours later aboard Central Airlines Flight 12 (which had stopped at Cleveland and Detroit on the way), slipped out of the air terminal and took a cab directly to South Street.

The building was nothing like dignified old 44 Wall; it

was brand new, glass-faced, square. When Elihu got there it was past seven and the financial district was deserted. Elihu had to check in through security, sign the book—in and later out (He'd see to that later.)—and took the automatic elevator to thirty-three, where Securities Unlimited occupied the entire floor. He used his key to get the elevator door to open on that floor.

Elihu stepped out silently into Securities Unlimited's main waiting room, a violent contrast to Worth Freres. It was all windows overlooking the East River; the bit of wall behind the receptionist desk was a vast blown-up line drawing of New York Harbor in 1830 with its sailing ships and wharves. The floor was bare wood; the seats for visitors were little more than polished planks of Swedish blond wood. Jasper Worth had designed the whole place, stark, simple. Alone in the vast waiting room Elihu surveyed his uncle's handiwork, the indirect lighting, the Jasper Johns paintings, the Swedish modern receptionist desk, once so avant garde, now as out of date as hoopskirts. It would all have to go; it would all be changed by *him*. But not yet, not yet. Not until he'd played the grieving nephew for a while longer. The shark smile on his face. Elihu did a little dance in the empty waiting room, a bit of moonwalk like Michael Jackson, a bit of cakewalk like Uncle Jasper, a bit of pure Elihu swooping about, hands on hips. He felt marvelous.

After a bit he went down the long open corridor to Jasper's office which was full of windows, green plants and blond Swedish coffee tables, long and low, brown leather sofas, and no desk. Jasper had operated with his feet up on one of the low coffee tables, a telephone in his hand, a computer terminal on one of the Swedish coffee tables.

Dora Land sat on the brown leather sofa where his uncle had once sat, her legs tucked up under her, eating a turkey sandwich with lots of mayonnaise and lettuce and tomato. On the blond coffee table was a container of coffee. Dora was a trim, slender, taut woman with large brown eyes, and her real name was not Land but Ketchiturian. A refugee from Russian Armenia. "If you want absolute unswerving loyalty," Elihu had said to his Uncle Jasper, "get yourself an Armenian refugee who has no green card and could be sent back at any time. She'll suffocate you in loyalty."

"I'd have got you a sandwich but I didn't know when to expect you." A low musical note in her voice, not quite an accent, just a whiff of foreignness from Mother Russia.

Elihu sat on the sofa next to her, with his shark's grin, and took a swig of her coffee.

"They've revoked the power of attorney on three of those women," said Dora gravely, chewing on her sandwich. "Did you expect that?"

Elihu moved closer to her and kissed her behind her small, neat Armenian ears.

"Wait till I finish my sandwich," she said primly. He liked her to be prim and unwelcoming. One of his peculiarities.

Elihu had picked up the telephone and put it in her lap. "Call your mother," he said. His first words.

The tiniest whisper of a sigh escaped her but she took command of herself and picked up the telephone. She had hoped he'd outgrow the kinky bit but he showed no sign of it. She had no choice.

She dialed her mother in East Islip. Elihu had slipped off the sofa and was on his knees before her, spreading her legs. "Mother mine," said Dora in Armenian, "how are you today? And how is the weather out there? It's hot and humid and rotten here. . . ." Conversation between a mother and daughter, warm, loving, stupendously trivial—about Mama's rubber plant, about daughter's problems with her Frigidaire, about their diets, their digestion, their complexions. All the while Elihu was working his tongue in and out of her she was chatting with her mother as if he wasn't there, as if he didn't exist, which was the way he wanted it to be, and when she came (as she always did), she put her hand over the mouthpiece to exhale a breath only momentarily and went on with it. "Ah, Mother mine, it's a lovely movie, all about small-town American life in the Depression—and you must go see it when it comes to East Islip."

As if nothing had happened.

Later they went to work on the stock transfer, neither of them mentioning the sex again, as if nothing had happened. If Elihu could have arranged that his Uncle Jasper had never existed he would have done that, she was thinking. He was obliterating transactions, blanking out events, erasing history, which was what the Soviets had done in Soviet Armenia and Czechoslovakia. She was an expert at this kind of erasure and, of course, the computer made it much easier; what was needed above all was the intellectual capacity for erasure of memory. It took both skill and will. Elihu himself could do it superbly, deny that the sun was in the sky or had ever been in the sky, looking at *you* as if *you* were crazy. Dora, having suffered much memory erasure at the hands of the Marxists, could play the game almost as well.

They went about the business of blotting out, taking turns at the computer. When Elihu was on the machine, Dora turned her brown eyes on him from behind him where he could not see, looking at him both speculatively and hungrily (two evidences of interest she'd never have allowed herself when he was watching).

She was tremendously aroused by this dark and kinky individual, but by no means in love. She participated not only in this game but in others of Elihu's wildly fertile devising with a mixture of dread and red-hot desire, loving it and hating herself for loving it. She wanted love but she wasn't likely to get it from this man.

She was scared to death of Elihu. That, too, had a strong sexual attraction.

CHAPTER 11

Mortie Wainwright was exceedingly polite to the brothers. The Assistant District Attorney didn't want it thought that he was in any way awed by the famous Worth name. No, it wasn't that. What it was (he kept reassuring himself) was that he wanted to be *correct*. The procedures, the forms, the questions. Everything had to be absolutely *right*, so there would be no kickbacks. He spent an inordinate amount of time on relationships.

"You are the older brother?" To Orin. "How much older? Yes. And what is the relationship with Elihu Worth? Second cousin. Aah, yes. And your relationship with Mercury Oil? Your title? You don't have a title? Well then, what is your *job* at Mercury Oil? No job either? Well then, what exactly was your mission in the submarine? I mean you said it was in connection with the oil exploration of the ship from which your father fell, didn't you?..."

And so on.

Orin was answering each question with total and infuriating honesty, which can be the most baffling rhetoric of all. *The Good Soldier Schweik*, that's what Orin was, taking each question literally and answering it that way.

What a farce the whole judicial process was! Nicholas was thinking.

It was ritual, Nicholas was thinking, and ought to be done in Italian—both questions and answers—the questions changed by the lawyer/priest, and the answers sung in harmony by the brothers Worth, backed up by a choir; someday it would be. Ecclesiastical law which had once been both strong and pertinent had withered away to be replaced by chants and hymns about glory and power and mercy of a God no one believed in any longer. The criminal law would someday go the same way when enough people realized that the courts had no intention of punishing criminals or even determining who was and wasn't guilty (the lawyers and judges, of course, had every intention of holding on to their jobs). The whole thing was a *ceremony,* and as such, it ought more properly to be *sung* if only to hold the interest of the populace. . . .

Robin let her kid brother fly the red helicopter across Iowa.

"Keep an eye on the fuel and wake me if anything goes wrong. Immediately," she shouted.

"How can you sleep in a helicopter?" screamed her brother.

"I can sleep anywhere."

She put the little rubber stoppers in her ears, covered them with the big radio earmuffs, having pulled the plug out, dropped her head on her chest and closed her eyes.

Love. What a mess! Middle-aged man. In *Galveston*! Why? Her uncle! Mess! Mess! Mess! Maybe that was the attraction. The messiness. Or perhaps the unavailability. One shouldn't fall in love with uncles. Especially uncles in Galveston, two thousand miles from civilization. Unavailability was always part of the love game. Romeo and Juliet. Romeo could have had anyone he chose *except* Juliet and she could have had anyone except him so they chose the one unavailable human as the only one they wanted. That made it better, hotter, stronger, more imperishable. I want my uncle because I can't have him and because he's far away! Oh hell!

She fell asleep.

An hour later she was wakened violently.

The helicopter was vibrating wildly, the motion rattling her brains, the noise indescribable. She snatched the controls away from Fergie and dove the screaming beast toward the green winter wheat field five hundred feet below. "What in hell have you done to it?" screamed Robin.

"Nothing! I swear!"

"How long has this been going on?"

At the top of her lungs to get over the rotor racket which was ominously awful.

Diving toward earth before the thing came apart.

Fergie held up two fingers. "Two minutes."

Earth rushing up; Robin leveled at twenty feet, tearing the rotor apart. Robin cut the engine and the helicopter plummeted the last ten feet, the rotor digging a great swathe in the winter wheat.

Then there was silence.

"Fergie!"

"Yeah."

"You alive?"

"Just. You?"

"I think so." She felt herself, legs, breasts, head, feeling for blood, pain, broken bones. Nothing. No blood. No pain. No broken bones.

Only panic. Continuing panic even after it was all over. During the whole fall she'd been horribly, shamefully frightened. Petrified with fear. Still was. She looked at Fergie who was grinning like an actor. "That definitely cleared my arteries," he said. Robin put her blond head on his chest and shook.

"Come on, Sis." Fergie was uncomfortable. "It's all over."

It wasn't. She was trembling like a wild animal. Speechless with terror. *I don't want to die.* A thought that had never before occurred to her. She began to cry.

After a while she stopped crying and mopped her face. She looked up at the splintered rotor. "What went wrong, Fergie?"

Fergie shrugged. "These things take a lot of maintenance, Sis. I told you. The man at the field told you, too. You just had to get away that *minute*. And now look."

They got out of the copter and circled it. The landing gear demolished, the rotor torn off, engine hanging loose. Three hundred and twenty-five thousand dollars. *Mother will kill me.*

"The farmhouse is that way. We passed over it just before the chopper began to shake itself apart."

They trudged down the rows of winter wheat, miles of the stuff.

What a dumb thing to do. Wreck a three-hundred-twenty-five-thousand-dollar helicopter by just dumbness. *Maturity here I come. How boring!*

When they reached the farmhouse, Fergie did all the talking. "We made an awful mess of your wheatfield. We'll pay of course, and we're very sorry."

We always pay and we're always sorry.

The farmer's name was Worrell. A taciturn man who said first, "Are you all right?" and second, "Better show me." He drove them in his pickup to the scene, pulled the two duffel bags out of the chopper and drove the two Worths and their duffel bags to the airport at Des Moines.

Under a milk-white sky.

Worrell wouldn't take any money. "I had to come to town anyway," he said in his flat voice. "To pick up a new condenser for my tractor. And a few other things." He scratched his head. "What you going to do 'bout that chopper?"

"I'll send a man," said Robin faintly. "To see about it."

"Is it insured?"

Insured! Oh my God!

The Marquise of Hampton drove straight from the airport to the big place in Bedford with its polo field (that no one had been on since Jasper gave up the game and the children moved away), its aviary, its stables, its skeet-shooting course, its half mile of greenhouses, its vast tile swimming pool. Andrews met her at the front door, dour, Scottish, capable. "Your mother's in the stable, Lady Hampton. She'll be very pleased to see you."

"How is she taking it?"

Andrews picked up two of the suitcases. "She's bearing up." Andrews had been there for thirty-three years. He took her bags up to Louise's old room where the maid, Laura Ingram, unpacked the bags and put everything away. It was a large high-ceiling, old-fashioned room with three big windows. The wallpaper with its scenes of eighteenth-century milkmaids, horses and dogs was faded and stained. The room smelled of mothballs and must. No one had occupied it for years.

Louise Hampton went out to the stables and found her mother and the groom ministering to her hunter Sarawak. The groom, Jonathan Midge, was holding the horse's head. Rebecca Worth held the hypodermic. She jabbed the needle into the horse's neck and Sarawak reared. "Damn!" said Rebecca. "He's bent the needle again. I have only one more."

She got the spare needle from the manager and only then noticed her daughter. "Darling," she said quietly. "How good to see you. I'll be with you in a minute. Now use the twitch, Jonathan. We can't lose any more needles."

Jonathan twisted the twitch around the horse's nose and

that time Rebecca got the needle in the neck and forced the medicine into the horse.

"Good boy," crooned Rebecca Worth and kissed the horse on his soft nose. "Keep him in all day, Jonathan, and then let him out to graze after his supper."

She joined her daughter just outside the box, held her at arm's length by the shoulders with both hands and gave her a long straight look, as if (Louise was thinking) I was a hunter and she was looking over my hocks, my withers.

"Do I look appropriately grief stricken?" said Louise.

"I don't expect grief from my children," said Rebecca. "I'm looking for signs of nascent common sense."

"Oh, Mother!" said Louise, giggling. She took her mother into her arms, against the older woman's will, and kissed her resoundingly once on each cheek. "The horse got a kiss. I think I'm entitled, Mother."

The two women had tea in the small sitting room with its faded yellow curtains and worn rug. "How is Robert?" asked Rebecca, pouring the tea.

"Impossible, as always. He wanted to come. I wouldn't let him."

"Well! Well!" said Rebecca with a glint of humor. "Striking a blow for women's rights! In merrie England."

"You didn't have all that many women's rights in merrie America," observed her daughter. "Andrews said you were bearing up well, but I think maybe too well. I know you're hurting, Ma."

"How do you know any such thing?"

"Oh, I've always known. You loved the old bastard."

"So did you."

"When I wasn't hating him. Which wasn't often. He was a lot harder on his children than on you, old girl."

"I tried to protect you. You especially. The only girl. The boys . . ." She sighed. "Well, I tried to protect them too but it wasn't easy. They gravitated to Jasper because they were boys. I couldn't . . . fend him off the boys.''

"Where are Orin and Nicholas?"

"In Galveston with the body. They were with him in some kind of capacity. Hunting for more oil."

"As if we needed more oil."

"Your father never had enough of anything, including children. He wanted half a dozen more. I slammed down the window."

Louise Hampton was astounded. She stared at her mother as if she'd never seen her before. "I never thought you slammed down any windows. . . ."

"That was the only one. Actually I thought four were too many. I'd like to have done after you, but . . ." She shrugged. "Don't tell Orin and Nicholas."

Louise Hampton ate her tea cake and let it pass. Orin and Nicholas, the unwanted children of the rich, had grown up surrounded and nurtured by servants, some of whom had loved them.

"Where are you going to bury Dad?"

"Here. He always wanted it here. He always *said* he loved this place above all the other places, but God knows he didn't spend much time here. I guess he figured that if he were going to spend eternity here he might as well see the rest of the world."

Later Louise asked the question. "Will I get some money?"

Her mother took her time answering. "Humphrey has been on the telephone four times, each time to tell us of a new will that has bobbed up. Your father made wills as other men made phone calls—at the spur of the moment and with whatever lawyer happened to be in the vicinity. It will take months, perhaps years, to find the last one. . . ."

But it didn't.

CHAPTER 12

ELIHU COMMANDS WORTH BILLIONS.

Read the *Wall Street Journal* headline. Others were less kind.

A SAILOR'S WILL?

Proclaimed the *Post*, the question mark summing up the general skepticism.

"It is so blatant a forgery that I'm surprised someone doesn't say so," said Humphrey Worth to William Worth. William Worth noted (but not aloud) that Humphrey carefully refrained from saying the word "forgery" in public. Graebner was known as a very fast man with a libel suit and Humphrey was, after all, a lawyer and a good one.

Eight other lawyers had weighed in with other Last Wills and Testaments all signed by Jasper Worth. The press had a field day with the wills. ANOTHER LAST WILL, said one headline, followed the next day by LAST LAST WILL. And finally, after Graebner filed his will, the *Daily News* headlined: LASTEST LAST WILL.

April 26 was clearly the latest will even as it was also the most questionable. What it had going for it were two things: an indubitably authentic signature of Jasper Worth and the presence on the ship of Graebner, who was a much feared (though not greatly respected) lawyer who took refuge in all the lawyer's evasive phraseology.

"I have no reason to believe that. . . ."

"It is not unreasonable to suppose that. . . ."

"I have no evidence to contradict. . . ."

And so forth.

"To draw up a sailor's will at sea," Graebner said at the crowded press conference in his office, "was entirely typical of Jasper Worth. He loved to think of himself as a sailor. He was completely familiar with the law of wills and is the kind of man who would have known that sailors' wills made at sea do not require witnesses and drawn one up for the sheer fun of the thing. As we all know, he delighted in making wills and then revoking them."

Graebner also pointed out that the beneficiaries of the will were all quite properly the widow and the four children, without, of course, making mention of the fact that the beneficiaries were at the mercy of the trustee, Elihu Worth. Everyone else dealt on that at some length.

"The question," wrote Jessica Keswick (who had been thoroughly coached in advance by Alec Worth), "is not who gets the money, but when and where and how much. The big prize is not the wealth but the control of the wealth, and Elihu seems to have that."

Jessica was actually at the famous press conference at Graebner's office and had the temerity (coached by Alec) to ask Graebner to his face, "Do you really believe in the authenticity of this piece of paper?"

Graebner launched into a peroration of whereases and withals and notwithstandings that lasted a minute and a half and answered nothing.

"What he said," commented Jessica dryly over the telephone to Alec the next day, "was that he had no reason to believe that he didn't believe it."

Eight lawyers, one of them Humphrey Worth, filed objections to the Elihu will.

A HARVEST FOR LAWYERS.

Read the headline in the *Wall Street Journal*.

"He's counting on that," Humphrey Worth said over the telephone to William Worth. "He's counting on clogging the courts for years."

"*Years!*" trumpeted William.

"The Lassiter will is the best known of sea will cases. Terence Lassiter died at sea in 1946 after writing a will in his cabin. After thirty-eight years it's still in the courts, and if it ever gets out there'll be no money left. The lawyers will have got it all."

CHAPTER 13

Jasper Worth arrived in New York reposing in a huge bronze casket which horrified that esthete Humphrey Worth as well as many other eastern Worths ("Texas taste at its worst," said Humphrey to William), but delighted the tabloids and TV. The great bronze casket was accompanied by Orin and Nicholas, suitably dressed in black, a marvelous photo opportunity, the sad-faced, handsome young sons standing next to the princely bronze casket ("Out of Michelangelo by Forest Lawn," said Heidi Stroop). This picture alone moved the affair out of gutter level journalism into the realm of high tragedy. A great man dead and his grieving sons. Let us pause a moment with bowed heads and consider Eternity. . . .

The funeral at Saint Thomas' Church was private, but as Heidi Stroop commented it was the most public private funeral ever held. There is no way you can rope off Fifth Avenue even for so powerful a family as the Worths. The curious and the funeral lovers jammed Fifth Avenue from

Forty-fourth Street to Central Park with traffic cops routing all cars straight across the avenue from Fifty-seventh to Forty-eighth.

The TV cameras couldn't get into the church, but they parked, along with hordes of curious, just outside and recorded the arrivals with that sense of wonder that TV manages to inject into the most trivial happening. Only the family and a few close friends were invited (and had to have tickets to get in), but it was a huge family and the Worths used that word *few* with a lavishness that strained definition. Saint Thomas' was jammed with what are always called mourners, though mourning was the last thing most of them were there for. Many of the "friends" were there to praise God that the old pirate was finally and indubitably dead. The family was there less to mourn Jasper, many of whom hated him, than to commemorate the living, to draw sustenance from the ceremony and ritual, and to celebrate the prodigious quantity and quality of one of America's oldest families.

"There are few things more enlivening than a good funeral," whispered Humphrey Worth to Felix Worth who was with him in the third row. Felix was a Chicago Worth, one of the poor Worths. His grandfather had given thirty million dollars' worth of Degas, Rembrandt, and Cezanne paintings to the Chicago Art Institute, but by the time Felix reached manhood the money in his branch had evaporated and he lived in a one-room apartment on the Gold Coast.

Worths filled the first four rows of Saint Thomas' under the Gothic stone tracery. Prudence and Estelle were in the front row, Prudence with her head bowed, not in prayer but in thought. (I'll be next and where has my life gone? It's just slipped past like a television rerun that no one has paid any attention to.) Next to her Estelle was frowning upward at the stained-glass Christ as if she were seeing Him for the first time in His true colors. Next to Estelle was Sylvia, with her husband Oscar Settle, Sylvia unabashedly turning around to see who was there and what they were wearing. "A few friends!" she muttered in high satiric glee to Estelle. "The Vice-President of the United States and the Secretary of State. Jasper despised them both."

The organ playing Johann Sebastian Bach, the only composer vast enough to encompass Jasper Worth with the magnificence he deserved.

Behind Sylvia and Oscar Settle sat the Galveston Worths—Alec and Hortense and their children Lannie and Geoffrey, looking very subdued in this citadel of eastern Episcopal snobbery. Next to them were some of the stuffiest of eastern Worths, the Maryland (Alec called them the softshell Worths) branch of the family from their horsey estates on Chesapeake Bay, and next to them William and Marcia Worth from that other exclusive body of water around Old Westbury.

Out on the crowded sidewalk, Arthur and Constance Worth, who had arrived in the nick of time from Europe, caused a stir when they drove up in their small Bentley with their children, Fergie and—as the gutter press called her—the Golden Girl, Robin, the glamorous one who flew airplanes and played polo and went out with everyone from Warren Beatty to Trudeau. The color cameras zooming in on the Golden Girl looking sullen and withdrawn. Sarah Ventricle, the NBC commentator, explained that Arthur and Constance were known as the liberal Worths, having marched in Selma and sat down in all the great (and now forgotten) sitdowns of the sixties for splendid (now forgotten) causes.

Elsie Worth, the grande dame of the family, age ninety-two, arrived alone and staged a procession down the aisle all by herself, darting glances right and left—counting the house, as she always called it—seeing who was there, the president of Manufacturers Hanover Trust, Jeremy Scott (that awful bore!), the chairman of Chase Manhattan (one of those Rockefeller boys. Now what *was* his name?), the president of Mercury Oil (Jasper had picked him because he was an anti-Semitic Jew, the brains of the Jew and the prejudices of the Gentile, a formidable combination). The usher sat Elsie in the third row next to the distinguished historian, Henry Worth, the writing Worth, as he was known, and his archaeologist wife Henrietta (who called Elsie behind her back "the walking mummy").

The controversial bronze casket arrived outside the church to great acclaim from the crowd and from Ms. Ventricle, who told the NBC audience what it cost (thirty thousand dollars) and what each of the bronze figures which ran around the top of the casket meant and their personal standing—their Neilsen rating, as it were—in Heaven or Hell. In the middle of this peroration, the immediate family, Rebecca, the widow, the children Jasper, Jr., and Eleanor, Nicholas, Orin and Louise, Marquise of Hampton, debouched from their long limousine and scuttled almost unnoticed into the vestry.

The chords on the organ grew portentous, massive, magnificent, summoning from Humphrey one last whisper to Felix. "I am never more alive than at someone else's funeral. I look upon each funeral as a personal victory."

It began.

First of course, the crucifer, the man with the cross in his white surplice, and behind him the rector, the Reverend J. Thomas Stokes, intoning in his rich baritone which vied on equal terms with the organ:

"'I am the Resurrection and the Life,' saith the Lord."

Reminding the assembled Worths and friends (and enemies) that this ritual was not meant to celebrate the great man's wealth or his fame but to launch him into an even more splendid existence: Death. (Belatedly, since Jasper has already been dead for two weeks.)

Behind the Reverend J. Thomas Stokes came the great bronze casket and behind it, the grieving family, Rebecca on the arm of Jasper, Jr., behind them Eleanor on the arm of

Orin and last, Louise, Marquise of Hampton, on the arm of her brother Nicholas.

The Reverend J. Thomas Stokes sounding like a bell. "'He that believeth in me, though he were dead, *yet* shall he live. . . .'"

My God, what an awful thought! Jasper *alive*! occurring simultaneously in a dozen minds.

Nicholas, the sad-faced one, kept his eye on the closed casket, expecting any moment Jasper to push up the lid, roaring, "Stop the music."

"'. . . for none of us liveth to himself and no man dieth to himself.'"

Nicholas thinking, Jasper dieth to himself as he liveth to himself, God notwithstanding.

"Oh, God, whose mercies cannot be numbered, accept our prayers on behalf of Thy servant and grant *him* an entrance into the land of light and joy, in the fellowship of the saints. . . ."

He would *hate* the fellowship of the saints. This thought in Sylvia's iconoclastic skull, which was turned full around to watch the procession, the others around her facing the altar. Sylvia, not wanting to miss anything, was one of the few Worths (Humphrey, himself turned facing the rear, being one of the others) who witnessed the scandalous events that happened.

Elihu Worth, escorting his mother Sophie Worth, entered the church and strode down the aisle behind the immediate family. Elihu with his great gleaming teeth bared in an entirely unsuitable smile (his mousey, reclusive mother was in a black veil which hid her face entirely).

The Prince of Darkness, thought Sylvia, feeling a monstrously unwelcome stirring in her loins.

Humphrey whispering so savagely he could be heard for three rows, "Upstaging the family! Upstaging the corpse! Upstaging God!"

The Devil himself, was Sylvia's thought. Just the sort of

thing Jasper would have done. Taking center stage by pure outrage. The mutterings and whisperings drowned out the Reverend J. Thomas Stokes; all in the church turned center to the preening figure of Elihu with his outrageous smile escorting his black-veiled mother down the center aisle.

This made a shambles of the seating. Space had been reserved for the immediate family in the front row at the left next to Sylvia, but somehow in the confusion the widow, Rebecca, Jasper, Jr., Eleanor, Louise and Orin were seated at left and Elihu and his mother wedged in next to them, leaving no room for Nicholas, who went to the right and found himself seated next to that bane of his childhood—Robin. Robin, the Golden Girl, sat very straight, with hands folded in her lap, eyes front, deigning him not the slightest glance, as if she were posing for a postage stamp. In an instant Nicholas was back in the nursery with this proud and prickly little monster. In childish fury he whispered into the shell-like ear: "Did you fly in in your red helicopter?"

Robin flushed as red as her helicopter and looked him full in the face (which was what Nicholas had wanted, some acknowledgment that he existed), and in that instant Nicholas wished he had kept his mouth shut. Two pairs of eyes locked, Robin's full of hurt, Nicholas' full of remorse, the church, the gathering of family—all these things imposing sanctity and grace on these two young people. The Reverend J. Thomas Stokes intoned the lesson. " 'In My Father's house there are many mansions.' " Then he began the Apostle's Creed. " 'I believe in God the Father, Almighty Maker of heaven and earth.' "

"Amen," said Nicholas and Robin together, both breaking into small, quickly suppressed smiles. They had found themselves for the first time in their whole lives agreeing on something. *Amen*.

On the other side of the aisle Sylvia was pressed, ass to ass, against the Prince of Darkness, feeling again that prickling in the loins that she didn't want to feel, certainly not on this most holy and social occasion, certainly not for this absolute son of a bitch Elihu. (What is this attraction the sons a bitches of the world have for me? Dear Lord, she was praying—this being the House of God—spare me this nasty creature!)

The hymn was that epitome of nineteenth-century seafaring sentimentality always trotted out when anyone was lost at sea.

"Most Holy Spirit who dids't brood
"Upon the chaos dark and rude...."

Robin and Nicholas sharing the hymnal and the hymn, her voice mocking and low, his dry and unbelieving.

"And bid its angry tumult cease
"And give the wild confusion peace...."

Across the aisle Sylvia wasn't singing but she was listening to Elihu singing joyfully (his mood entirely wrong for a funeral), those ridiculous words which were in her case so apt. Tumult and confusion, indeed, oh, give me peace! But there was no peace.

The choir which in Saint Thomas' is always loud enough to pierce the soul, trumpeting.

"Oh, hear us when we cry to Thee
"For those in peril of the sea...."

After that the congregation knelt again—Sylvia pressed to Elihu who was on his knees with head bowed—doing filial grief and piety as if he had invented it. Kneeling next to him, watching from under her lashes, Sylvia could feel the fire in Elihu, the passion of the man filling the church with vapors from Hell. My very own anti-Christ (Sylvia was taking refuge in mockery), for the girl who has everything.

The Reverend J. Thomas Stokes had pulled out all the stops in his organ of a voice. "Wash him we pray Thee in the blood of that Immaculate Lamb...."

If you don't want to, I'll wash him in the blood of that Immaculate Lamb. Thus Sylvia. What am I thinking! My mind should be washed out with soap....

". . . that was slain to take away the sins of the world that whatsoever defilements he may have contracted in the midst of this earthy life. . . ."

Have now been passed on to his sons and heirs. Thus Nicholas on his knees next to the Golden Girl, full of indignation and—yes, grief. He missed his hated father very much.

Riotous thoughts flicking through the heads of so many of those kneeling individuals, paying their disrespects to the monumental man who had mocked them and scorned them and outwitted them in life and now in death had brought them to their knees. . . .

". . . being purged and done away, he may be presented pure and without spot before Thee."

The assembled mourners got off their knees and stood, exhausted, in their places, their eyes darting uneasily about. Enough! Enough! they were feeling. The funeral had reached that turning point when the congregation was drained and restless, wanting to get out of the church, into the open air, to be restored to the living, away from the indecent clutch of the dead.

"Onward Christian soldiers," sang the choir—all those beautiful young boys with their mouths open, like baby robins begging food.

". . . *marching as to war*
"*With the cross of Jee-sus*
"*Marching on before*."

The crucifer with his cross went down the aisle followed by the great bronze casket after which came Reverend J. Thomas Stokes. The ushers led the immediate family down the aisle first after the procession—Rebecca, Jasper, Jr. (who was no longer Junior but who would be called Junie the rest of his life), Louise and Orin. Again Elihu interjected his mother and himself into this group where he had no business and paraded down the aisle. This time Elihu wore a scowl as unsuitable as his earlier smile, again attracting attention and outrage, calling down the lightning on his derisive, defiant head.

Nicholas, who should have been ahead of him, was just behind Elihu, again with Robin at his side. Robin had her eyes on the capering Elihu and felt nothing at all, neither rage nor hatred. I have been washed in the blood of that Immaculate Lamb, Robin was thinking, and cleaned of my defilements. I am at peace.

Behind her came Sylvia, who was not at all at peace and not at all cleansed of her defilements, her unfortunate husband Oscar trailing along, forgotten.

The choir singing in that emptying church.

"Crowns and thrones may perish
"Kingdoms rise and wane
"But the Church of Jesus
"Constant will remain.
"Gates of Hell can never
"'gainst that Church prevail.

Sylvia was not at all sure about that.

CHAPTER 14

They gathered at Elsie's Waldorf Tower apartment, subdued by death and ritual but, because they were Worths, famous, rich, and eccentric, they didn't stay subdued for long, drinking the drinks and soon asserting their loud self-confident opinions of politics, society, and each other. Here without the confines of pew they went their own way, assembling in little groupings of their own choice, mingling with the Worths they picked and most ostentatiously *not* mingling with others for a variety of highly complicated and abstruse reasons.

There were vast divisions in the Worth family, some of them going back for generations, but the vastest division of all was also the most recent. This was the seizure of power by Elihu, the assertion of his will over all others. Elihu was, in fact, being sued by at least four of the other Worths present.

When Elihu and his mother arrived, Elsie was holding

court in her favorite wing chair in the small salon, and she immediately sent a footman to summon Sophie to sit by her side, "just there," while Elsie fussed over her. "My dear, you look ghastly! What on earth have you been doing to yourself?"

Elihu had taken up a position behind his mother's chair and he spoke up now in his commanding voice that could be heard even over the din. "It's Jasper's death. She has taken it very hard, Aunt Elsie."

The old lady scowled. She didn't want to hear from Elihu; she wanted to get the answers from Sophie herself.

Elihu, unheeding the scowl, continued. "Mother was very fond of Uncle Jasper. He's been enormously kind."

"Jasper? Enormously kind?" The old lady sniffed. "I've heard Jasper called many things. Never enormously kind. It's a little like calling a cobra enormously kind."

That was a bit much even for the recessive Sophie. "Oh, Aunt Elsie!" she gasped. "Jasper could be *very* kind. When he wanted to be." She fussed with her fingers in her lap and said, "I thought it was a very nice funeral. Very uplifting. A funeral should *lift* the spirits. It should be a joyous occasion. Reunion with God!"

A long speech for Sophie.

"Run along, Elihu, and get yourself a drink," snapped Elsie Worth. "Your mother and I wish to have a little private talk."

Elihu smiled, showing all his teeth. "Your wish is my command, Aunt Elsie," he said. He moved scarcely six feet thereafter. When someone came to pay court to the old lady and make his exit he ran inevitably into Elihu, who would speak a little piece tailored to each of them. "Aah, Uncle Horace, how are the Irish setters? You were having a little trouble with that last one." Elihu knew all the eccentricities, the enthusiasms of each Worth and this would get his attention. The Worth in question would pause and tell of his trouble with his Irish setters or his racehorses or the Cleveland Museum, whatever it was that commanded his interest.

These small pauses spelled absolution. A good many of those who had paused had taken a stand against Elihu in this family battle, but now they were trapped into discussing their favorite Irish setters (or racehorses or whatever) with this smiling and sympathetic Elihu, their hostilities dissipating. Each new Worth that Elihu added to his little coterie made his presence that much more acceptable. (If the Maryland Worths are seen speaking to Elihu, then everything must be all right—that kind of thinking.) Elihu's little group just the other side of Elsie's soon became larger than hers.

Orin and Nicholas standing across the small salon watched the accumulation of Worths around Elihu, impassive as Indians. "There," murmured Nicholas, "stands the murderer of our father, playing king of the mountain."

"Nicholas!" protested Orin. "You can't go flinging wild charges like that in public."

Nicholas had moved into Elihu's orbit wearing a faint smile. "Good of you to find time for the funeral, Elihu."

"Ah, Captain Courageous himself," said Elihu in high good humor. "Home from the sea! What an extraordinary coincidence—you lying on the floor of the gulf at the precise spot where Uncle Jasper fell from the rigging."

"Or was pushed," said Nicholas.

A very public accusation. Elihu had been talking to a couple of Delaware Worths and a Pennsylvania Worth who were close enough to hear Nicholas.

"How very rude!" said Penelope Worth, the redoubtable horsewoman.

Orin dragged his brother away through the swinging doors into the pantry which was empty. "Why on earth did you say that, Nicholas? You can't charge a man with murder because you had a bad dream!"

Nicholas was pouring himself a drink from a bottle of

Black Label scotch. "How did he know it was me lying on the floor of the gulf, not you? It's usually you in the submarine. How did he know it was me?"

Alec Worth had come through the swinging doors in time to hear that. He took the Black Label from Nicholas and poured himself a drink. "I suspect he got it from the skipper of the schooner, John Dake," said Alec. "John Dake is here in New York, you know. He was summoned here by Elihu."

"How do you know?"

"He was on the airplane with us from Galveston. I had a talk with Mr. Dake. He hates your guts, Nicholas. It wasn't very smart making an enemy of him."

Nicholas frowned impatiently, as if being smart was somehow beneath his notice. "What is Elihu up to with Dake? Why did he summon him to New York?"

"Captain Stork, too, Dake told me. He's got them both here. Well, after all, Elihu is now CEO of Securities Unlimited. He's their boss. I suspect he's covering his ass. I suspect also that he's sowing the suspicion that you and your brother could have saved your father's life if you had moved a little more rapidly. The best defense is a good offense." Alec looked into his drink sorrowfully. "You two brothers have got to move a little more rapidly. Elihu is miles ahead of you."

"What do you suggest?" asked Orin.

"I think you might have a talk with Lemuel Stork who was captain of the ship your father fell off."

"Or was pushed," said Nicholas.

Alec sighed. "I wouldn't go around making accusations until you have a little more proof, Nicholas. Outside the Worths are choosing up sides between you and Elihu—and you're losing."

Outside the party was breaking up, with kisses and vague invitations to Old Westbury, to the Eastern Shore, to Southampton, to all the garden spots of old money, neither the inviters nor the invitees intending them to be taken seriously.

When Nicholas, Orin and Alec emerged from the butler's pantry, Elihu and his mother Sophie had left and so had most of the party.

Nicholas bent to kiss his Great-Aunt Elsie good-bye. She said, "You behaved abominably, Nicholas." But submitted to the kiss anyway because she loved the boy. "I know Elihu is a monster but he is Sophie's adopted son and we mustn't hurt Sophie's feelings. You need a haircut, young man. You look like a roustabout from the oil fields."

Nicholas knelt in front of the old lady and said, "I'd like to have a talk with you, Aunt Elsie, when no one else is around. Might I drop around?"

"Of course, dear boy. What do you want to talk about?"

Nicholas smiled his evil smile. "Scandal."

"Oh, goodie," said the old lady. "I love scandal."

In the grand salon, Robin had been trapped and bombarded with conversation by a lot of Worths she didn't especially care for and had stayed at this party much longer than she'd planned. In the end she used that oldest of devices to escape—the bathroom. She fled to her great-aunt's guestroom lavatory, the one with the peacocks on white rice paper with its little ormolu dressing table in ivory and satin, a haven of peace.

Not for long.

Robin was at the dressing table, looking at her face, not making it up, just looking at it, to see if the tumultuous events of that day had left any marks. I have been washed in the blood of that Immaculate Lamb and I don't deserve it. I feel splendidly at peace. Now why?

Hortense came into the lavatory, filling the mirror on the ivory dressing table with her reflection. Peace fled.

"Lamentation," said Hortense, "is something the Worths don't understand. They make a celebration of it which isn't the idea."

She's not a Worth, thought Robin. She married one. Why does she always go on so about the Worths?

Hortense had moved to the dressing table and stood behind Robin, her hands on Robin's shoulders. "Alec wants me to go back to Galveston tomorrow with the children. I don't want to go."

Oh, God, here it is! "I know what you want," said Robin flatly.

"Do you now? Do you indeed?"

"Yes, I do. And you can't have it. I'm trying to keep you from making a goddamned fool of yourself."

Robin spun around to face her, but Hortense had already left.

When Robin came out of the lavatory the big apartment was empty of Worths except for Elsie, who sat in the small salon. Around her Waldorf footmen were picking up glasses and teacups, sweeping up crumbs, emptying ashtrays. Elsie sat hunched over, her chin on her chest. Robin knelt at her side and kissed the old cheek. "Good-bye, Aunt Elsie. It's been a lovely party."

Elsie stirred. She'd been asleep but now she was awake and she smiled and stroked the girl's face with her old hand.

"Oh, Robin, my dear. How nice of you to say so! You know, I'd fallen asleep in my chair and I was dreaming—of Jasper. I dreamt he walked into the church at his own funeral. Oh, it's going to be very hard to keep Jasper in that coffin. He's going to keep popping out. You just wait and see. Help me up, my dear."

Elsie looked every bit of her ninety-two years, her eyes tragic. "I don't know why I'm alive, child. What have I done to deserve this living death?"

Robin helped the old lady into her bedroom, it too full of servants cleaning up after the party. "I wouldn't call it living death, Aunt Elsie. You are one of the most alive people I know."

"Only when you're around, my dear. Or when someone is." Elsie was taking off her jewelry, her great emerald necklace with the matching emerald bracelet and brooch, throwing them on the dressing table as if they were hairpins. "But there are hours and days and weeks when there is no one around and then we old folks live in a kind of hellish twilight." The old lady was undressing now, dropping her dress on the floor, stepping out of it, talking away. "The memories crowd our minds, old triumphs and old tragedies, the second and third and hundredth time around, repeating themselves until even the triumphs become bitter. Oh, it's horrible to be old, Robin, don't ever get old, you beautiful golden child. You can't tell the people from the phantoms. I sometimes think I died years ago and this is purgatory. I don't even know if you're real or phantom, Robin."

Robin got the old lady into her bed and kissed the old cheek. "I won't sleep, you know, Robin. We don't sleep, we old ones. We just lie here in the darkness and think of all the things that happened that shouldn't have happened and all the things that should have happened and didn't. We want to rearrange our lives, our marriages, our children, our houses, everything—and we can't. We can't. We can't change anything because it happened and we old ones are condemned to relive it again and again until it sickens us night after long night. I want to die, Robin. Why can't I?"

Unexpectedly the old lady fell asleep. Robin tiptoed out, turning out the lights, shutting the door, shooing the footmen away.

She let herself out into the corridor and walked to the elevator. There waiting for her were Nicholas and Orin.

Those handsome young men.

"The Brothers Inseparable," said Robin mockingly. "Are you two never apart? It's neurotic. And why are you still here? You should have been long gone."

"We were waiting for you," said Nicholas. "We're going to take you to dinner."

CHAPTER 15

The brothers helped her into the taxi as if she might break, and sat next to her, one on each side.

"You were in there forever," said Nicholas.

"I was putting Aunt Elsie to bed. She's full of woe—like a Greek chorus."

"Did she tell you about taking horse-drawn trolleys up Fifth Avenue when she was a child?" asked Orin.

"She told me never to get old."

Mario's Bar and Grill at Thirty-seventh off Eleventh was full of young people in jeans and leather jackets, talking very loud to be heard over the Mock Turtle, which played hard rock on the bandstand at the rear. The saloon had burgundy-colored walls, ruffled pink curtains over the windows and was lighted by gas chandeliers. Mario was behind the bar in his white apron and waved at the brothers as they came in.

Young couples were dancing on a square of floor about the size of a billiard table, and it made Robin restless. She pulled at Nicholas. "I want to dance. Get the funeral out of my bones." She dragged him out onto the floor, the two of them in their funeral black, dancing to the hard rock as if it was part of the burial ceremony.

Robin was a splendid dancer, moving as easily as breathing, everything falling away, the past, the future. When Robin danced she was in the present tense. Everything was Right Now. Lighting up the room.

Nicholas danced absently, as if he weren't inhabiting his body, as if he weren't even in the building. Robin wanted to ask, "Where are you?" But she didn't. Remoteness was as much a part of Nicholas as his nose.

Later, after they ate the barbecued duck and drank the beer, Robin asked, "Why did we quarrel so much as children?"

"You were frightfully spoiled," said Nicholas.

"Maybe you were too."

"Jasper's children? Spoiled? Ho ho."

"I hated you," said Robin.

"You didn't notice me at all."

"Oh yes I did."

Robin danced with Orin which was quite a different proposition from dancing with Nicholas. Orin took her in his arms and did swoops and swirls as if he were in Vienna in 1905. With Nicholas, Robin went her own way; with Orin she followed. He was the high priest of old orthodoxies.

Orin the saintly one. What does one do with saintliness in the twentieth century? As useful as crossbows.

"I've had enough of this place," said Nicholas.

They moved to a waterfront bar called Fratonelli's which contained only two customers, both whores. "Past your bedtime, dearie," said one of the whores.

"I know," said Robin.

They ordered beer and Nicholas and Orin played the match game.

Robin watched the brothers, noting ferocity of the eyeballs, the muscles on the cheeks. They hate each other, these brothers. For the moment. Tomorrow they will love each other. Right now...

"Two!" snarled Nicholas.

"Three." Orin won and Nicholas scowled as if it hurt his teeth.

They went to Negelesco's, which was an after-hours club under the sidewalk at Madison near Twenty-second. You could buy your way into it with a fifty-dollar bill. It was full of hubbub and hatcheck girls from the other clubs out having a bit of a lark after their own places closed. A homosexual piano player sang filthy songs he wrote himself and it was very noisy and crowded.

The Worths were very drunk.

Nicholas had to shout over the noise. "What were you doing in a helicopter over the Gulf of Mexico?"

Robin stared glumly into her beer. "It's a question I ask myself many times. Many times I ask myself that question. Many times...."

"And what do you answer yourself?"

"What were you doing at the bottom of the Gulf of Mexico in a submarine?" said Robin carefully. "Answer me that! My mother always warned me about submarines. Stay out of submarines—my mother said. Everybody's mother said that."

In vino veritas.

"I was in a submarine because my father told me to be in a submarine at that precise spot," said Nicholas.

"Why?"

"Because," said the drunken Nicholas, "he knew he was going to be pushed into the sea at that very...Oh my God."

It had popped out of his mouth as easy as a blasphemy and there it lay—a drunken revelation reeking of *veritas*.

"He knew! He knew!" said Orin.

The brothers looking at each other in wild surmise.

"Knew *what*?" Robin very puzzled.

"Elihu was stealing the kingdom."

Orin, very sober, said, "He knew more than that. He knew Elihu was going to kill him. He knew it."

Robin was wakened by her mother at eleven. "Oh, my God, Mom. I just got in. Whoever it is, tell 'em to call back."

Constance put the telephone in Robin's hand. "It's your Uncle Will. He says it's *very* important and won't wait. Now, *talk*!"

"Hello, Uncle Will," whispered Robin.

"Robin, did you buy a helicopter? Three hundred and twenty-five thousand dollars? Your check has bounced all the way from Galveston."

Robin woke up all the way. "Bounced?" She shook her blond curls, blinked her fogged eyes. "Uncle Will, I paid for that chopper with a Securities Unlimited Command check. There are millions in that account. My credit—"

"There's nothing in that account and you have no credit. You'd better get down here."

Elihu Worth walked into the reception room, moving very quickly as he always did, right over to Bates, the SEC lawyer. "Mr. Bates, how are you? Do come in. I hope I haven't kept you waiting too long, but the market took off this morning and things got very tight here."

Bates mumbled that he understood perfectly, that he wasn't at all put out by waiting. No, you go first. . . .

All very exciting! Elihu Worth *never* came out of his office and ushered in the guest. Normally, a secretary showed up and showed the visitor in. It was so thrilling that Sally Quinby, the receptionist, called Ella Wheeler, the assistant to Mr. Ellenbe, and told her.

Ella Wheeler was way ahead of her. "They're giving him an office—Elihu's old office at the corner of the building. Turning it over to him so long as he's here and turning all the records over to him. What a mess! Sarah Tieg in records says they're moving stuff in there by the truckload, they can hardly get the stuff through the door, and when it comes back it'll all have to be refiled and it could take *years*."

Even as she spoke the stainless-steel cars on the four rubber wheels, piled high with documents, were being pushed into Elihu's old office and there the documents—the books, files, ledgers, tapes—were unloaded on the floor to join the piles of papers already there, then the carts promptly turned around to get more.

Bates eyed it all nervously and said, "Mr. Worth, if we could first have a talk. I have some questions. . . ."

"Of course! Of course." Elihu was all geniality, flashing his toothy smile. "First perhaps you'd better run over some of this material. Then anytime! Anytime! My office is wide open! After you familiarize yourself. We are cooperating fully. I have instructed everyone on the staff. Nothing is to be withheld. Nothing!"

Another cart came in piled to the height of six feet with records, which the solemn-faced girls unloaded near Elihu's old desk.

"Now if you'll forgive me, Mr. Bates. I've got to get back. I'm expecting a call from Geneva. Just pop in anytime you have a question. . . ."

Elihu left.

Bates was now alone with the stack of records which were beginning to assume the size and general appearance of a major catastrophe. If a tornado struck a small town library, that is what it would look like afterward. Everything on the floor, piles of it. Bates picked up an account looseleaf and opened it at random.

400 SGCT   20 1/3   Comp PLIC .27   32,947.96
10 units CIF 122 MPS RG   1,267.76
1,003 P. B. RES FD   9.98 net 10,0009.94

*   *   *

"It's called smothering," said William Worth. He was at the small leather-bound bar at the corner of his big office, mixing himself and Alec Worth martinis, pouring a thimbleful of dry sherry into a tiny glass for Robin. "AT&T did it to the government in that antitrust case and now everyone's doing it. You just move all the records you've got—everything from the purchase of a pencil sharpener to the sale of a diamond mine from one room into another room—and say there it is. You snow them under and hope they'll go away. Sometimes they do. Bates is a very persistent little cuss, though. He could find something if it's there—but not tomorrow. Anyway, it probably isn't there."

He handed the thimbleful of dry sherry to Robin and the martini to Alec.

Robin looked white and miserable. She had a king-sized hangover—beer always did that to her—and she was suffering waves of nausea which came and went, leaving her as weak as paper.

"Medicinal Superfund," she was reading off the account statement. "I never heard of it, Uncle Will. I mean, I never paid *too* much attention to what Uncle Jasper did with my money, but I paid *some* attention. I looked over the statements from time to time. I never heard of Medicinal Superfund."

"It's a shell company Jasper established in the Seychelles. Jasper, like all of us, liked to get away from the full-disclosure laws in this country. But Jasper never mixed you up with that kind of shell game."

Alec spoke up. "The blue chips have all been exchanged for this junk. Medicinal Superfund, High Tech Growth Fund. These companies have no assets. Millions of blue chips exchanged for companies that have no assets whatsoever. . . ."

The floor was coming and going, waving about like a sea in a storm. Robin closed her eyes and fought the nausea. I shall *not* be sick in Uncle Will's office. She wished they would shut up.

They didn't. Uncle Will was saying to Alec, "This is not only Robin's but Fergie's command account. The brother and sister inherited roughly eleven million jointly from their grandmother, Jasmine Wentworth, when they were born. . . ."

That was the last Robin heard. A wave of nausea rose from the soles of her feet, rushing up through her thighs, her middle, her head. Her head went into her knees and she rolled out of the chair onto her Uncle Will's Bokassy carpet.

William and Alec picked her up and spread her on the leather sofa. Already she was coming around but she kept her eyes shut, clinging to unconsciousness.

She heard her Uncle Will say, "It's much worse. He's not only plundered her; he's plundered Constance and Arthur. They've got nothing in their portfolios but stock in these worthless companies. . . ."

Alec's voice, "Surely you can pin Elihu to the wall on this. My God, Uncle Bill, all these transfers were made in one day. Plain arrant fraud . . ."

Uncle Will's voice. "Elihu says he had nothing to do with it. That he was as shocked as anyone when we called it to his attention. He says all these transactions were engineered by Jasper and he has the dates to prove it . . . Meanwhile, all the confirmations and the blue ships are sequestered in places like the Seychelles where we can't get at them, can't freeze them, immobilize them, can't even locate them. . . ."

It was a waterfront bar in Brooklyn. Lemuel Stork had chosen it and then only reluctantly. He didn't want to talk to Nicholas Worth, didn't want to get involved in an intramural Worth dispute, but didn't, at the same time, know how he could decently turn aside the son of Jasper Worth.

A very uncomfortable meeting with long silences and much evasion. Nicholas looked at the rugged New England face, so full of the old virtues.

"It's all in the log," Captain Stork said, not for the first time.

"Well, there isn't much in the log," said Nicholas. "What I was interested in finding out was whether you actually *saw* the, uh, mishap, actually witnessed . . . Were you at the wheel?"

Captain Stork's already taut jaw tightened another millimeter. Another of those silences. He didn't lie. He couldn't. "I was on the bridge."

"Looking *up*?"

What else would a ship's captain be doing with two men aloft in a thirty-knot wind?

"The ship was pitching and yawing," muttered Captain Stork. "They were very high. What I'm saying is it's difficult to be sure. . . ."

"Sure of what?" asked Nicholas gently. "I mean . . . you saw *something*?"

Lemuel Stork scowled bleakly. "I'm not at liberty to go into this with you, Mr. Worth. I have spoken to that Assistant District Attorney in Galveston. I have spoken to, uh, the *other* Mr. Worth, Mr. Elihu Worth." The way he said Elihu spoke volumes. Lemuel Stork didn't like the man but was scared to death of him. "I've been advised by both those gentlemen—Mr. Worth and that Assistant District Attorney in Galveston—not to talk about this thing to others because of the possibility of an investigation."

Nicholas spoke between his teeth now, holding himself in. "There isn't going to *be* an investigation unless you speak up, Captain Stork. There is—so far—only a vast cover-up."

Lemuel Stork was looking at his watch then, getting to his feet. "I'm sorry, Mr. Worth. I've got a plane to catch."

Nicholas followed him to the door because he couldn't allow it to trail off into nothing like this. It was a dingy place with a bar that curved from a window next to the door inward. There were two or three drinkers at the wide sweep of bar and a solitary drinker near the door.

Nicholas said, "Suppose the District Attorney of New

York questioned you, Captain Stork? Would you then feel you have a *duty* to speak up?''

Duty was the note to strike. Nicholas could see the word hit the New Englander like a blow. Lemuel Stork could dodge Nicholas' questions, but if duty entered into it . . . And if a District Attorney asked the same questions, duty would certainly enter into it. . . .

CHAPTER 16

Robin lay under Alec and looked at the frescoes on the Waldorf Astoria ceiling. The last hotel to put frescoes on the ceiling because after that came the crash of '29; everyone lost their money and no one could afford ceiling frescoes any longer. It almost gave her the giggles—and that would never do with Alec pumping away on top of her. One of the cardinal rules of womanhood: You can do anything when they're screwing you—bite them, scratch them, curse them— *except* giggle.

She felt nothing. Below the waist. Above the waist, especially in the cerebellum, were the remnants of chaos, the quietening sands of the great emotional storm. What had happened to love? Gone. Evaporated. No money. No love. Ah, woe! Again she suppressed the giggles. Mustn't giggle.

Alec pumping away.

Much later, Alec said bitterly, "You weren't there. You just weren't there."

"No," said Robin sadly.

"Where were you?"

Robin slithered out of the bed and went looking for her panties. "You weren't there either," she said. "Not really." She found her panties and put them on.

Alec had launched into expostulation. It was because of her *absence* that he had, as it were, performed inadequately. And so forth. Robin couldn't make head nor tail of it. She went into the bathroom and looked at herself fiercely in the mirror. Putting her face up close, looking at the eyes, the ears, the mouth, the pores. She felt lightheaded.

Alec loomed behind her, naked and cantankerous. The age difference between them yawned like a canyon. He was old.

"You know what kind of people live in the Po Valley, Uncle Alec?" she said. "Po' people."

That time she didn't suppress the giggle. It was all right to giggle afterward. Not bad sexual manners at all. Afterward.

"I'm po' people, Uncle Alec. You're rich people. Scott Fitzgerald was right. The rich are different from the poor. They have mo' money is why."

She pushed past him and picked her blouse off the floor where Alec had thrown it in an excess of passion. Or haste. Or whatever. Ah passion! Where have you fled? *Adieu, passion! Bonjour tristesse!*

I'm drunk. Or just clearheaded. Perhaps it was the same thing. She and Alec had had a couple of Bloody Marys and that had banished the nausea and brought on the . . . clearheadedness.

Alec was sitting on the foot of the bed, naked and bewildered and miserable. "Why are you doing this, Robin? Fleeing from me. I thought we were . . ."

"Well, we aren't anymore." She was pulling on one stocking. "You're rich people. I'm poor people. We look at each other over an unbridgeable gap, Uncle Alec."

"Stop calling me Uncle Alec!"

"All right." She was looking for the other stocking. Where was her other stocking? "You're the Wizard of Oz and I'm Dorothy and I've got to get back to Kansas." She was on her knees looking under the bed. Aah, there it was. She reached for it.

"*Robin!*" Alec was shocked by the levity. Deeply hurt.

"Oh, for God's sake, Alec. What do you want—*love!* I've just been robbed of eleven million dollars. It changes a girl's point of view. I've got to go home and tell my dear mother and father they're broke. They haven't a bob. My dear father who has never in his whole life earned ten cents or even managed his own money or even known where it *came* from. It came out of the tap like water, an endless stream, and now my poor darling innocent liberal dad is flat on his ass."

"We'll get it back!" cried Alec. And went on with that looney thought—the District Attorney, the SEC, what the law would do. All the time naked as a jaybird, ridiculous. Robin laughing at his nakedness, Alec the brightest Worth of the lot, Alec who'd turned a small fortune into a large fortune, Alec the wizard of Galveston, sitting naked on the foot of a bed, lovelorn, a figure of fun.

But Robin was a warmhearted girl and she couldn't laugh at Alec without a degree of discomfort. Now she put her arms around him, sat next to him, still laughing, but warm and loving laughter, to get a little of the desolation out of him.

"You'd better put some clothes on, Alec, before you talk money. Never talk money without your clothes on because no one will take you seriously."

Light as a feather.

That was what losing eleven million did for a girl. It unburdened her. I'm so light I'll float to the ceiling. If I don't watch out. . . .

Alec was putting his clothes on, talking law, finance,

SEC regulation, all that nonsense while Robin put on lipstick carefully as Alec rambled on. And on. . . .

My helicopter, Robin was thinking. My lovely red helicopter. I'll never see it again. How can I manage?

That gave her the giggles again so that she messed up with the lipstick and had to do it over again.

"Loan me a million will you, Alec? So I can get my helicopter repaired. A girl *needs* a helicopter. To get around in."

Alec didn't think it was funny which just went to show how little a girl knew about a Texas stockbroker until she lost her money. Then the shit hit the fan. . . .

"Go ahead, Alec. Just one lousy little million. You make that in the market in a week. The wizard of Galveston. I just need a little teensie weensie grubstake to keep body and soul together. A jug of wine, a little red helicopter and thou is all I need."

She could see the panic rising in him, his eyes darting away from hers, seeking escape.

The poor relation asking for money!

Hilarious!

She put her right hand out now, palm upward, holding the left hand into her body as she had seen the beggars do in all those pictures of starvation down in Pakistan or Ethiopa or Bulgaria or wherever they were starving at that moment, a ritual attitude, frozen in stone, turning her mouth downward, feeling the starvation in her bones, experiencing impoverishment to the roots of her hair, eyes staring. . . .

It scared the wits out of Alec. He jerked backward as if bitten by a cobra.

That made her laugh. It didn't make *him* laugh. We are a million miles apart, she was thinking. And this is the way it's going to be with all of them. I am a poor relation already and will be treated with the proper scorn, taken to parties, smiled at, and put at the foot of the table because that's where poor relations belonged. There is something automatically reprehensible about poverty. If you haven't any money, you have done something *wrong*; you are an embarrassment. All this and much more thronging the mind. Have I a mind? What grounds have I for supposing...

Alec was putting on his trousers and Robin watched— stared really—as if it were *The Fall of the House of Usher*, mysterious, shocking and shameful all at once. Have I ever watched a man putting on his trousers before? God in heaven, what low comedy is this? First one hairy leg, then the other. He made it! He did it!! And I have shared sex with this...creature! Again and again! How could that be? How could I? "Quoth the Raven: 'Nevermore.'" If indeed the Raven said that, which I have always doubted. I think Edgar Allan Poe made it all up, if you want to know what I think.

Alec had retreated into himself—far, far into himself. Furious. Robin became aware of the fury as one becomes aware of a faucet dripping. It's been going on for a long time until suddenly one is conscious of it. Hell hath no fury like a man scorned....

Robin deeply ashamed. I have hurt poor dear Alec and I didn't want to. Oh, Christ! She searched for something to say, something healing. Nothing came.

He was putting on his necktie now, facing the mirror the way men did, face set in granite. My fault! All my fault! I lost my money....

The telephone sounded its old-fashioned Waldorf Astoria tinkle. "Yes." Alec very gruff, very brief. The Galveston wizard again, now that he had his clothes on. "Ah, Uncle Will. How are you?" Long pause. Alec listening, not liking what he was listening to. Robin picked up her handbag and tore her eyes away. She couldn't bear to look at Alec any longer.

Alec was saying, "You'll have to handle it by yourself, Uncle Will. I've got to get back to Galveston. Something has come up. No, this afternoon. First plane out."

So that was that. Alec was abandoning her to . . . Uncle Will, the District Attorney, the SEC. Alec was taking himself off the Case of the Missing Millions, fleeing back to the warm waters of the gulf, the warm embraces of Hortense. Well, the lukewarm embraces of Hortense who would much rather be embracing me. . . .

Robin looked into her handbag to see if she had the cab fare because, things being as they were, she could no longer ask the butler would he mind paying the cab. Or the doorman. No longer the Golden Girl, me. Little old bankrupt me, without a single red helicopter to my name.

Alec on the phone saying, "Oh, you can handle it all right, Uncle Will, if you want any advice, just call."

Alec the wizard, the smartest Worth of all, especially on stock market swindles, would have come in very handy in the Case of the Missing Millions, but it simply wasn't to be. . . .

Or not to be, that was the question. That was *always* the question. A very old question. What was the answer?

There were several hundred-dollar bills in the wallet; cab drivers hated hundred-dollar bills, didn't they? Oh, well, it was not all that far and the walk would be . . . bracing. A good bracing twenty-two-block walk, chin up, facing the future, come what may, ho ho ho ho. . . .

Robin walked out of the hotel without a backward glance—at Alec, at anything—because she didn't want to turn into a pillar of salt.

CHAPTER 17

It was a standoff between two very stubborn men. Dora Land held her hand over the mouthpiece of the telephone. "Mr. Mauriello doesn't talk on the telephone. This is his chief of staff, Sylvia Vicino."

Elihu grinned his sharkish grin and reached for the phone. "Buttons..." he said, using the nickname though he'd never laid eyes on the man.

"We don't like to use that word on the telephone," said Vicino.

"Tell Mr. M that in a transaction of this size I must talk personally to the top man."

"Mr. M doesn't talk on telephones. Not ever."

That, of course, was why Elihu was so insistent. What a score!

Very softly—knowing Mauriello was listening on another phone—Elihu said, "Just a word. I must know who I'm dealing with from the man himself. Otherwise there's no deal."

A test of wills. Millions involved.

A very long pause.

The voice when it came was silky, whispery, very confident. "Tasio will bring the merchandise, Mr. Worth."

"Where and when?"

"You'll see Tasio when you see him."

The phone went dead.

Elihu laughed shrilly and handed the phone back to Dora. Truly a standoff. He'd got Mauriello on the phone—first time anyone had done that in twenty years—but Mauriello had had the last word. Each man had scored one point.

Dora Land was gathering up her notes, her mouth set.

"You disapprove, Dora?"

"Mauriello needs you. You don't need him. You're doing *him* a favor."

"Bread cast upon the waters, Dora. We may need a favor from him sometime."

Mauriello was the *capo de capo*. "Muscle, Dora."

"Once you mix with those people you never get free."

Elihu walked to the window and looked out over the bay. He felt marvelous. "I wouldn't be the first. Old Joe Kennedy was involved with Frank Costello in the old days when Costello was running the Mob. Kennedy later became first chairman of the SEC and father of a president. The Mob didn't interfere."

Dora Land said, "If they're bringing the money here, someone will have to be here at all hours to receive it, someone who knows how to handle the time lock on the safe."

"Who else but you, Dora?" said Elihu, smiling.

Sylvia Settle was lying in the big bed, listening to Lolo Vanbrugh's delicious scurrilities and wishing Oscar would hurry into his clothes and get the hell out of there. She could never really open up to Lolo with Oscar listening in.

Oscar was slowly putting on his trousers, seated on the bottom of the bed. Sylvia thinking, men who have to sit down to put on their trousers are well past it. And where had she first heard that bit of macho wisdom? Why, from Oscar Settle himself in his earlier, more virile years (a shining example of the level of discourse of Oscar Settle in those years) and here was Oscar Settle sitting down to put on his trousers (the level of discourse not having risen a single inch in recompense). Oh, my God why doesn't he go. . . .

Lolo chattering away. " . . . a tennis player with that locker room smell they all have and the conversation . . . my dear, the *conversation*—his forehand, his foreplay, his foreskin—that's the wrap, the whole magillah. . . ."

Right there Sylvia would have loved to jump in with her own witticisms on the subject of athletes' conversations, having married one but, of course, with Oscar there, she couldn't.

Oscar was buttoning his fly which Sylvia found an indecent sight—a husband buttoning (Oscar had never recognized zippers) his fly. Now he was mouthing, Get off the phone.

She mouthed back, Why?

On the other end Lolo was saying, "Speaking of foreskins, have you heard . . ."

"Not now," said Sylvia warningly. "I'll call you back, Lolo." She hung up and faced her husband with uplifted eyebrows. "I don't want to hear any more about the will, Oscar. I've heard enough. It's my funeral."

That was further than she usually went. She had stopped well short of saying, "It's my money" but "my funeral" was uncomfortably close. Usually she handled Oscar more gently than this, not out of compassion but because he fulfilled a very valued function in her life. He was The Husband. One needed The Husband to accompany one to plays, to dinner parties, to funerals. One didn't want a lover around on those occasions because he interfered with the hunting. Lovers hung around a girl's neck at these affairs; they meddled; they got jealous.

Oscar never did any of those things. He was the model cuckold, never voicing suspicions or jealousy (though he probably felt them), while still performing that valuable symbolism of Husband, whose presence could be brandished when the lover himself grew tiresome and Sylvia wanted to get him out of her bed.

"You *were* interested in the will," said Oscar weakly. "And now suddenly—"

He choked himself off even as she had, because he was getting into a forbidden area. He'd already had this conversation with himself, as he'd had so many others. A form of masturbation. What he had said (to himself) was that there was only one thing that Sylvia loved more than money and that was a good fuck and the fact that she had suddenly fallen so alarmingly silent on a subject about which she had been so stridently vocal—namely, a share in Jasper's millions—could only mean that her interests had shifted from money to fucking. And what's more, to a new lover (Jasper had been the old one. Oscar had known all about Jasper, as had everyone else). Either Sylvia had a new lover or she was eyeing one.

But Oscar was not about to say any of this because it was unsayable. Their marriage was nothing but a succession of unspoken quarrels, silent screams and unvoiced accusations, a cozy if squalid relationship that had worked very well for both of them. She had her lovers, all she could corner (and in her mid-forties, the hunting was getting very poor), and he had the pleasures of cuckoldry, such as they were, and a very good allowance. The consenting cuckold. One couldn't *say* things like that; one could barely think them.

She got rid of Oscar finally and got back to Lolo who went on as if uninterrupted. "Speaking of foreskins, Carrie

Smothers has wrapped her arms around—you'd never guess—
her analyst. And you know why? Because she's run out of
subconscious. She never had very much subconscious to
start with. An hour of Carrie's deepest fears and what's left
to say? So there she was, lying there, saying nothing at a
hundred dollars an hour when love bloomed and now she
has all this fresh guilt to talk about. Have you ever heard
such a thing? She tells him how guilty she feels about *him*
and he has acually raised his listening price from a hundred
to a hundred and a quarter for—I can only assume—providing
all this fresh material. . . ."

Twenty-five minutes more of this entertaining stuff and
Lolo struck a nerve.

". . . Elihu Worth sitting there with Humphrey Worth at
the very same table that Jasper and Humphrey used to sit
at. . . ."

Sylvia felt as if an electric wire had been attached to her
genitals, a *live* electric wire. She came out of the pillows
and sat bolt upright, trying to keep the tension out of her
voice. "Whoa! Back up, Lolo! Humphrey is *suing* Elihu,
charging misfeasance, malfeasance, nonfeasance, and God
knows how many other feasances and they're *lunching*
together?"

"Well," said Lolo merrily, "you Worths have your own,
very original ethical standards, haven't you? I thought that
would grab you, Humphrey and Elihu—"

"Where?" breathed Sylvia, still bolt upright, body as
tense as a spring.

"En Vedette. Wouldn't you know. Elihu is there every
day, leaping from table to table, turning on the charm of
which he has a great deal. Everyone knows he's a crook,
but such a *charming* crook."

"I don't believe it." Throwing the bait.

"Darling, I'll take you there and show you."

"Today?"

"Well, I don't know that Humphrey and Elihu will be

lunching together today. But Elihu will be there with *some-body,* leaping around, exuding his loathsome charm."

"I'll buy lunch," said Sylvia. "One o'clock."

Elihu was there at the center banquette, the best table for exhibitionists in the room. Jasper had put the arm on that table when the place opened, having helped raise the money (even putting in a little of his own) and, they say, having more than a little to do with selecting the name of the restaurant, En Vedette. In the limelight. That, said Jasper, was what diners of the sort the restaurant wanted to attract were looking for—not food, but the limelight, both to be in it and to look at others in it. And, of course, in French which implied good food but also, of course, a good deal of that dear old French quality known as *je ne sais quoi.* En Vedette had a lot of *je ne sais quoi*—softly subtle lime-green walls, green and white draperies, crystal wall brackets, though the light itself came from concealed lamps in the wainscoting. After all, people came there to see and be seen. One didn't go to En Vedette with the little girl (or someone else's wife) one was trying to keep out of sight. You brought the girl you were trying to show everyone you were currently laying. Look what I've landed. That was the substance of it.

"En Vedette," Lolo had said once, "might more properly be called On A Note of Triumph."

"Or," amended Sylvia, "Look At Me, Mom. No Hands. That's really what we're doing our whole long lives—saying, Look, Mom. Especially those of whose moms never never paid any attention. Did your mother ever pay any attention to you, Lolo?"

"She would have considered it bad form."

Just what blackmail Elihu had employed on the maître d', Antoine, who was also the owner, no one quite knew. It must have taken considerable arm twisting because there were innumerable customers of En Vedette—screen stars, writers, old monied names, beautiful women—who were infinitely more entitled to the center table than this twenty-two-year-old upstart. Also Antoine with his oily, always slightly sneering smile, his crafty bleak eyes, his subtle and powerful French mind, was not an easy man to intimidate. He was accustomed to telling bankers, Secretaries of State, captains of industry, anyone at all, to wait right there until he was ready to seat them—and these very important ones would wait until summoned because no one wanted to risk the wrath of Antoine.

Yet there was Elihu in the seat of power, Antoine bowing low—Antoine who rarely bowed to anyone. "Money," hazarded Lolo. "Elihu has waved money at him. Antoine despises all of us and everything—except money. He goes down on his knees to money five times a day like the Arabs facing Mecca."

Elihu was talking, gesturing and smiling—that dazzling toothy smile—around the room, while his companion, a dour middle-aged man, looked at the tablecloth and did a lot of listening.

"No, I don't know who that is. Wait, I'll find out." Lolo waved a finger at Antoine who was passing by and Antoine bent over her with his sneering smile (after all, she was a Vanbrugh. Old, old money, so old Lolo had no idea where it came from or even when). "Who's that with Elihu?" whispered Lolo.

Antoine didn't even look up. He was truly a professional. Knew who was lunching with whom at every table. (And probably why.)

"Gregory Godwin," mouthed Antoine. "Wall Street lawyer. He has never been here before." With the clear implication he'd never be there again unless someone far more important than himself brought him. Antoine passed on to another table farther down the line bearing bottles of two rare aperitifs to the French jeweler who lunched there alone every day. Antoine was very polite to the French because the French who were rich enough and worldly enough to lunch at En Vedette were wise to him and he knew it. It was a truce, each Frenchman saying, Let's not blow the whistle on each other, eh, Monsieur?

"Mean anything to you?" asked Lolo. "Gregory Godwin."

"Oh, my God, yes. He's the lawyer for Henry and Henrietta Worth. They've got their own will they're pushing. Godwin is *suing* Elihu. Why is Elihu lunching all those opposing lawyers?"

"Softening them up, my dear. Bringing the man to a place he's never been and showing how *au courant* Elihu is with Hollywood and Wall Street—how out of his depths he, the lawyer, is. It's very subtle treatment."

"Mmmm," said Sylvia. Nothing more. She doubted that it would work on Gregory Godwin, who was a damned good—well, damned expensive—lawyer, although the two were not necessarily the same thing.

"The opposing lawyers come here and lunch very well and then both charge their clients with the full cost of both lunches—nothing at all is settled. How can you lose?"

"Yeah," said Sylvia, unaccustomedly quiet. She was watching Elihu's flashing eyes, the white teeth, the energy of him. But it wasn't physical, not altogether, not even primarily. He was such a scamp was what it was. Such an *outrageous* scamp! Everyone in the room knew what a crook and scoundrel he was and there he sat, the cynosure of all eyes, and everyone wanted to meet him. (Including me who has already met him.) But then scoundrels always attracted. If Attila the Hun walked in, every woman in the room would be making eyes at him. Including me.

All the time eyeing Elihu and his toothy good looks. But it wasn't the good looks that attracted her. No, it was the downright evil of him. I'm rotten to the core, said Sylvia to herself with great satisfaction, just as rotten as you are, Elihu, so let us begin. . . .

Elihu had bounded out of his chair and table-hopped to the side of a young actress who'd got smash notices only a week or so earlier, smothering the girl in charm, totally ignoring her companion.

"Antoine does *not* like table-hopping," said Lolo. "If I did that he'd be on my neck. 'Madame, we'd rather you didn't,' in that icy voice, but Elihu gets away with it all the time. Of course, I realize Jasper owned part of the restaurant and that mantle has descended on Elihu, but as a matter of fact, Jasper never table-hopped. If he wanted to talk to someone here, he'd send a little note and they'd go to him."

"Oh, what a marvelous idea!" said Sylvia. She dipped her long, many-ringed fingers into her handbag and came up with a notepad and gold Tiffany pencil.

"Sylvia, what on earth are you— Oh, you wouldn't . . . You can't. . . ."

"Why not? What are we here for if not a little amusement? Wave that languid hand of yours at Antoine. I don't want anyone else but Antoine bearing this note to Elihu."

Lolo was craning her neck to see what Sylvia was writing. "What are you going to . . . Oh, Sylvia, you *can't* say that! You can't—"

"Why not?"

What she'd written was: Why have you never tried to plunder *me*? You're scared is why. Sylvia Worth, table twelve.

Both women watched the note being delivered, hawklike, for the reaction which was immediate. A pursing of the full lips, an arch of the eyebrows going skyward like Groucho Marx's. The eyes flicked about until they came to Sylvia, who was looking at him challengingly, full face that she had spent an hour on, showing her teeth.

Immediately he excused himself yet once again to the frequently abandoned lawyer and plunged across the room.

"See?" said Sylvia. "He's the kind that does battle instantly. Throw a glove in his face and there he is."

She extended a hand to Elihu, turning on all the electricity. "Why are you always here with lawyers, Elihu? They're very bad for the digestion, lawyers. Do you know Lolo Vanbrugh? Yes, of course, you do."

Elihu was holding her hand in both of his, directing what used to be called a burning glance deep into her eyes, turning on the full candlepower of his personality: "How nice to see you, Sylvia. I saw you at Elsie's but I didn't have a chance—"

"To tell me any lies? Well, now's your chance to make up for it."

Elihu laughed. "I resent the accusation—not of plunder—but of cowardice."

"I rather thought that would be your priority. How are all the lawsuits coming along?"

"Swimmingly. I'll be in jail before the snow flies. That leaves me just enough time to plunder *you*, Sylvia."

"Oh, good! Shall we say next Tuesday? Right here at En Vendette—in full view of *tout le monde*?"

"One o'clock," said Elihu with his dazzling smile. Without further ado, he went back to the dour Wall Street lawyer.

Lolo shaking her head in total disapproval. "He's too young," snapped Lolo.

"For what?"

"What you have in mind."

"I was just going to show him my backstroke. I rather doubt he knows the backstroke."

"Oh, he knows the backstroke all right. And the footstroke and the sidestroke. He'll stroke you to death, that one. Sylvia Worth, I'm shocked to the core. He's twenty-two and you're—"

"Let's order, Lolo. The waiter has been standing here for five minutes. I'd like the *veau diable*—"

"How very appropriate!"

"... with the wild rice and early peas. Lolo, do you mind champagne?"

"We'll throw the glasses right in Antoine's face," said Lolo. "And do cartwheels across the room. Leave 'em laughing, I always say. ..."

CHAPTER 18

"*Criminal* charges, Mr. Hanagan!" Nicholas was in the office of Louis Hanagan, Assistant District Attorney of New York County, on whose litter-filled desk rested bits and pieces of eleven unfinished prosecutions. "As you know we have seven civil suits pending that will not be tried in this century, if ever, but *criminal* charges might just possibly..."

Hanagan, who had tired Irish eyes and six children, lit a cigar and closed his eyes. This was Nicholas' third visit and he was getting tired of it. "Mr. Worth, we've been over this before. This matter is under investigation by the SEC. If the SEC wants a criminal prosecution, it is empowered to institute suit all by itself in Federal District Court."

"I'm not talking about Elihu stealing a hundred million from us, Mr. Hanagan. I'm talking murder."

Hanagan's eyes flew open then and he said, "Dear Jesus!" Softly and reverently. "A grave charge, Mr. Worth."

"Call me Nicholas."

"Okay, Nicholas. You can call me Louis. Have you any evidence at all?"

Nicholas spoke about Lemuel Stork, about his New England upbringing, his New England integrity. "He dodged and weaved with me because he could quiet that New England conscience by assuring himself he was following the path of rectitude. But if *you* asked him . . ."

"You are asking me to bring this witness—if he is one—two thousand miles at the expense of the taxpayers—"

"I'll buy the round-trip ticket from Galveston and I'll put him up."

". . . on the basis of a suspicion that he *might* have seen something?"

"If he hadn't seen anything he would have said so. It's when he started dodging and weaving that I *knew* he'd seen something."

Louis Hanagan took the cigar out of his mouth and spun it around in his fingers, a trick he had when the chips were down. He took his time, a long time. Finally he said, "What's the name of his ship?"

"The *Saint Elmo*. It's docked in Galveston."

Hanagan lifted the phone. "Miss Simmons, call information and get the phone number of a ship tied up in Galveston, Texas, called the *Saint Elmo*. I want to talk to the captain, Lemuel Stork."

It took Nicholas' breath away. He hadn't expected action, not that swiftly. He was dumbfounded and he looked it. Hanagan had hung up the phone; he rose to his feet and started rustling about in the litter of a nearby table. Presently he brought over a tape recording machine and a spool of tape.

"I want you to listen to something, Nicholas." He was putting the spool of tape in the recording machine. "This is the real reason I'm calling Lemuel Stork, because it may be connected."

Nicholas heard the familiar voice of Elihu. "Tell Mr. M

that in a transaction of this size I must talk personally to the top man."

"Mr. M doesn't talk on telephones. Not ever."

"Just a word. I must know who I'm dealing with from the man himself. Otherwise there's no deal."

A very long pause, the tape recorder winding away. A new voice, silky, whispering, confidant. "Tasio will bring the merchandise, Mr. Worth."

"Where and when?"

"You'll see Tasio when you see him."

Silence.

Hanagan turned the machine off and chewed on his cigar. "That cousin Elihu? You recognize the voice?"

Nicholas nodded.

Hanagan chewed on his cigar and scowled. "You understand this is very confidantial, Nicholas. You must not talk about this to anyone. Not to your brother. Not to anyone?"

"Yes."

"We have a court-approved tap, not on your cousin Elihu, but on Vincent Mauriello, and I'm sure you know who he is. That was taped yesterday and it's important because it's the first time in twenty years anyone has got Mauriello to speak on the telephone. So whatever transaction your cousin is involved in must be *very* important or Mauriello would not get on the telephone."

"What sort of transaction?"

"I can't tell you that. It's part of a continuing investigation that's been going on for months. The reason I let you listen to that phone call is that it makes me a little nervous about *you,* Nicholas."

Nicholas tried to remember when anyone had worried about him last. Orin, maybe. "Why would you worry about me?"

Hanagan stubbed out the cigar and sat up straight. "Nicholas, you've been running around this town sounding off—to the press, to me, to the SEC—accusing your cousin of stealing a hundred million dollars. Pretty serious accusations. I didn't take 'em seriously *until* I heard that phone call. Your cousin Elihu—and he made the call—is talking to the *capo di capo*—a very powerful, very dangerous man. Why?''

Nicholas waited. Hanagan rubbed his chin and took his time. ''We think we know what your cousin could do—and is, in fact, doing—for this *capo de capo*. All sorts of important financial services Mauriello can't do for himself. But why should your cousin, a pillar of the Wall Street community, get mixed up with this mobster? Unless he expects some comparable service in return. You take my meaning?''

''No.''

Hanagan scratched his head in exasperation. The rich! Christ! ''What I'm saying is that we already got more dead bodies in Manhattan than we can handle. That's what I'm saying. In other words, pipe down, Nicholas.''

Nicholas got his meaning then and started to laugh, though, God knew, it wasn't all that funny. In the middle of the laughter, the phone rang and Hanagan picked it up. ''Yeah? . . . Oh, Mr. Stork. I'm glad I caught you before you went to sea. I'm Louis Hanagan, Assistant District Attorney of New York County and we are concerned about the death of Mr. Jasper Worth. There are now implications of homicide in his death—and since you are one of the few witnesses of that unfortunate happening, I would like very much to talk to you.''

Nicholas listened, wishing he could see Captain Stork's granitic New England face on the other end of the line. Hanagan was telling Stork that the District Attorney's office would buy him a round-trip ticket from Galveston and wanted to see him immediately—all very polite, very firm, very legal, and only a little bit threatening, but that little bit quite explicit.

Hanagan hung up. ''He'll be on a plane Tuesday.''

* * *

Robin had gone very quiet. She sat in the leather wing chair, her feet curled up under her and listened to her father, Arthur, the celebrated liberal Worth—the one who had been on all those marches and sitdowns and sit-ins of the sixties for the blacks, the poor, the lame, the halt, the blind—*pleading* . . . this time for himself.

He had called Delaware Worths, Chicago Worths, Texas Worths, all of them overflowing with money, and they had all, with exquisite politeness, superbly expressed compassion, profound and heartfelt and, above all, beautifully modulated sympathy, said no. Sitting there in the wing chair, in the quiet of that beautiful (if unused and slightly archaic) library so full of leather-bound copies of the books nobody had read in forty or fifty years, Robin could hear the modulations, the timbre of the expressions of regret and what she couldn't hear she could imagine from the anguished lineaments of her father's handsome, mobile (archaic like the library) face.

He was suffering visibly, her dear old dad, he who had suffered (visibly) for the blacks, the poor, the lame and the blind was now suffering his own personal deprivation, and it was devastating because he was so unaccustomed to deprivations. The rich, Robin was thinking, knew how to say no with grace and charm because they were asked every day of their lives to part with some of their money and they were constrained to say no again and again and again. A thousand noes for every yes (which was why they stayed rich). They had far more practice at saying no than ordinary people and they got very good at it. On the other hand the rich were very unpracticed at asking for money for themselves because they had never had to ask for a job, a raise, a loan—any of those things the rest of the populace was quite accustomed to. Every time her father dialed, Robin could see the agony in his eyes, and when she could stand it no longer she got out of the leather armchair, moved in her stockinged feet to the Queen Anne chair where her father sat, took the telephone out of his hand in mid-dial, and put it back on its rest and then curled up in her father's lap.

"That's quite enough humiliation, Daddy," said Robin. "I won't permit you to go on. We don't need these people or their money. We've got each other. We don't need this goddamned apartment. It's too big, too expensive, too everything."

Curled up in her father's lap, head nestled against his chest. Thinking all the while, Get me! She had never in her life sat in her daddy's lap, not as a child, not ever. Arthur had been a kind but forbidding father, much too busy with the problems of the blacks, the poor, the lame and the blind to pay much attention to his children (though never cruel or unkind, just absent), and there she was (thought Robin) in his lap, and very nice it was.

Her father saying "... from your grandfather. What would your grandfather say!"

"Who cares?" said Robin. "He's dead, Daddy, and we're alive. Sell the place. You ought to get a million. Maybe a million and a half."

"Sell my *home*, Robin? What are you saying? All I'm asking is a *loan*. A million or two, they've all got it, they know I'll be able to pay them back when we get this thing straightened out."

"No, they don't. They don't think you're ever going to be a rich man again for the very good reason that you have no gift for making money! You've never done it or shown any interest in making more, and, as for the lawsuits, they just don't think you're going to win. So let's go on from there. Sell this place..."

"We won't even get enough to run the place in Sag Harbor."

"Sell that too. Sell all of them, Beaulieu in South Carolina, the Paris flat..."

"Where will we lay our heads, your mother and I?"

Arthur had put his arms around her and now he squeezed her to him, the first time that had ever happened in her whole life. And he did it unconsciously, talking away while drawing comfort from the love of his daughter, who was enjoying a delicious feeling of being needed.

All the time thinking how very conservative her liberal father was. He'd been brought up in the Fifth Avenue apartment; he couldn't imagine living anywhere else, couldn't imagine any other kind of life.

"Best thing in the world for all of us," said Robin (herself astounded at the idea she could voice such heresy). "Think of it as an adventure, Daddy, a change."

"It's not," whimpered her father. "It's disgraceful."

Disgraceful being poor! She shivered with laughter but kept it quiet because she mustn't laugh at dear old dad. "Daddy, count your blessings! You've got your health! Your kids aren't dope addicts." (She'd only flirted with cocaine as who hadn't.) "You've got a wife who loves you."

Constance walked into the library at that point and stopped in the door, amazed. "What are you doing, you two?"

"Having a cuddle," said Robin. "It's all we can afford."

Estelle had lived in her Seventy-second Street apartment for forty years. It was too big for her—fourteen rooms—but she had her adored housekeeper Jessie Abrams, who ran the place for her with the help of a procession of maids that Jessie kept hiring and firing. Nicholas had pleaded with Estelle not to sell the apartment; she'd just have to find another place to live and they were all overpriced. He'd got Uncle Will to agree to pay some of the upkeep cost and he, Nicholas, would take on the rest.

It was Estelle herself who had insisted, with a stubbornness that dumbfounded Nicholas, in putting the apartment on the market. "I'm not going to live in a fourteen-room apartment when I'm broke," she had said with an asperity and a finality that floored him. "Anyway, forty years is enough! Too much!"

Because a fourteen-room apartment on East Seventy-second Street was almost too good to be true, Estelle sold it in a couple of days to one of her own unplundered distant cousins for a very good price without the help or expense of a real estate agent. "Aunt Estelle," said Nicholas to his Uncle Will, "has made a score. Quite a good score. Unassisted. Fancy that! Now, if you'd just help her invest the money, we might have Aunt Estelle home and dry."

"She has refused my help," said William Worth stiffly, his plumage distinctly ruffled. "I've offered. She said no."

That was the reason Nicholas went to his aunt's that day. Partly to help her with the packing, mainly to try to get her to change her mind about Uncle Will. Just because she had been swindled by one Worth didn't mean that she'd be swindled by another. Uncle Will was the soul of integrity. And so forth. Nicholas had prepared quite a speech.

When Nicholas got out of the elevator on the twelfth floor, he was struck instantly by the noise. Ordinarily that floor was as quiet as an empty church. It was inhabited exclusively by old ladies who shuffled about its handsome corridor (decorated with French antique wallpaper of hunting scenes in eighteenth-century France) like timid mice. That day the quiet was broken by two strident voices.

"You are a crook and a bully and you think I didn't know but I did know!" A voice he'd never heard before.

"I'm going to consult my attorney about this." That voice was clearly that of Jessie Abrams, though Nicholas had never heard it raised in anger.

"You haven't got an attorney and you will never bully me again with your damned threats. I have had quite enough."

The door was wide open, all very peculiar, and the two women faced each other hardly two feet apart, screaming like hysterical parrots.

One of them Nicholas' gentle Aunt Estelle.

"You've been stealing from me for years, my money, my jewelry, my furniture."

Thus Aunt Estelle. In a voice that sounded like someone else. Still it was a voice of enormous authority and experience. Not a new voice at all, as if the voice had been there all along, unused.

Jessie Abrams' face (which Nicholas had been accustomed to think of as the soul of sweetness) was contorted with anger, the eyes narrowed to slits. "I have taken care of you, you helpless booby, for forty years! Do you think I did that out of love, you little nincompoop?"

"Ladies! Ladies!" said Nicholas. He stepped between them.

"Get out of my way, Nicholas," screamed Aunt Estelle.

"No," said Nicholas. He lifted his aunt who weighed about a hundred pounds and carried her easily into the living room where he put her down gently in her favorite chair, a high-backed, heavily carved Tudor chair, immensely uncomfortable, of a sort that had gone out of style fifty years ago.

"Bah!" spat gentle Aunt Estelle.

Outside they heard the door slam very hard behind Jessie Abrams.

"I've hated her for decades," said Estelle, suddenly very calm.

"Why didn't you tell us?"

"I didn't even tell myself."

"We all thought you loved Jessie Abrams."

"I hated her but I wouldn't admit it to myself . . . I don't know, Nicholas. I just don't know."

Nicholas expected her to burst into tears; instead she burst into laughter. Hard dry laughter. "You think Elihu is the first to steal from me. They've all been stealing from me for years. All of them—maids, chauffeurs, gardeners—and Jessie Abrams. But you can't tell yourself things like that. Now I can because I haven't any money. Now I can be honest.

We're all victimized by servants, all the rich, Nicholas. Rotten servants, simpering and gushing. You think they love us. They hate us. I had to get it out before she did. I had to tell her how much I hated her before she told me how much she hated me, and by God, I did it. I got there first!''

Gentle old Aunt Estelle burst into hard, dry, slightly hysterical laughter.

She was not gentle or even especially old anymore. It was as if she'd been locked in a cocoon all those years and had now burst out of it, a whole new identity—not, God knew, a butterfly, more like a wasp.

CHAPTER 19

Sophie nibbled her toast, her heart full of love. Opposite her in the breakfast nook was Elihu who had his own apartment but frequently stayed with his mother. The adopted son had never quite cut the umbilical cord. If only he weren't on the telephone so much.

As he was at that moment.

"In West Africa," Elihu was saying with his mordant smile, "it's called dash. Pronounced upbeat with a broad A and bright smile. Daash—like that." Elihu knew all the words for it in all the countries, in South America the bite, in Italy *la bustarella*, in France *pot de vin*, in the U.S. grease. "President Okabi himself, Peter, two hundred thousand in Credit Suisse. He'll tell you the number—and you must leave this afternoon because it's very important."

He hung up. "Mama mia," he crooned. "I'm sorry about the telephone but there are things I can say on the phone here I don't dare say on my own phone."

"You are so secretive, Elihu. I don't understand."

Elihu was looking about him at the immense gloomy bronzes that had been there since his grandfather's day, the green hanging plants, the dark wood paneling, the dusty drapery. "Mother, I'm taking you out of this place. It's too dreary."

Sophie was shocked. "Elihu! You spent your babyhood here! Your childhood!"

Hooker, the English butler, doddering about with the toast rack like a dying hound dog.

"This is the wrong end of Fifth Avenue, Mother. I've bought you a nice big modern place on upper Fifth overlooking the park."

"Elihu, I'm not ever leaving this apartment where your father and I—"

"I paid seven million for the new one."

"Seven million! When people are starving in Africa. . . ."

Elihu took a piece of toast from old Hooker. Cold, as always. Hooker would have to go too.

"The security at the new place is much tighter, Mother. You'll feel safer."

"Why do I need security, Elihu? I've always felt perfectly safe here."

Elihu was on his feet now, behind his mother's chair, putting his arms around her, crooning, his mouth in her hair, reducing her to jelly as he always did. "Mama mia, I'm going to have my own computer room in the new apartment. You'll see much more of me than you ever did. You'll like that, won't you?"

"Oh, Elihu, I'll love it! You are a dear dear boy!" She blinked the tears away because he didn't like tears. "But Elihu, a computer room. Why would you—"

"That's where the secrets are, Mama mia, in the modern corporation. The only one who knows all the fragments of company policy, all the shards of knowledge; they rest deep in the innards of the computer. The computer is the Wizard of Oz who manipulates us all.''

"But, dear boy, why would you want the thing in my home? Wouldn't you need the computer in your own office?''

"Oh, we have another one there, Mama mia, but it's a little too available to too many people. This one we'll keep locked up in *your* apartment, not mine, where no one will think of looking for it.''

The modern corporate mainline computer, Elihu had discovered, was the Wild West before the sheriff arrived. Corporations were so big, so complex, that no one individual could handle the overload. Individuals were cogs manipulated by the computer. But who manipulated the computer? Ah, there was the rub. A mainline computer tucked away in his mother's apartment, to which only he and Dora Land had access, would make him the fastest gun on Wall Street. And the least accountable.

His mother was saying, "Elihu, I don't want to leave this apartment. This has been my home for thirty years. . . .''

But the arms were not around her anymore and when she looked around, Elihu had gone.

They were lying apart in a well of silence and fulfillment with perhaps just a trace of postcoital *tristesse* when the telephone cut into the affair with its bad-mannered noise. Sylvia watched carefully as Elihu lifted the phone to his ear and said, "Yes," in measured neutral tones.

She welcomed the interruption, fearing she had pushed ahead too fast. But it wasn't only herself that had been eager. He'd been as eager for her forty-four-year-old body as she had been for his slim, almost too white, very young, quite delectable (in an odd unhealthy way) frame. Why? When there were clearly so many much younger girls lying in wait for this evil young man?

All the while listening hard. "Yes," he was saying. "Okay. Do that." Giving away nothing. Elihu said very little really; he probed always, made jokes about himself (taking quite a lot of pleasure in his awful reputation), kept it all in. In the sexual act itself, he had been remarkably generous. For so evil and complex and brilliant a character, the sex had been surprisingly naive, and for that very reason powerfully erotic in ways that Sylvia hadn't expected or wanted. *I'm falling for him, very hard, and falling for this bastard is the last thing in the world I want.* What she had wanted was a little adventure, herself keeping her head above water, getting him in over his. It was working out quite the opposite.

Herself lying there quite naked looking at her own forty-four-year-old body in the full-length mirror. *I look like the Naked Maja, quite seductive to a sophisticated man and Elihu is nothing if not sophisticated. We are a pair all right, him twenty-two, me forty-four. . . .*

"Lemuel Stork," Elihu was saying, the muscle play on the much-too-white body, the movement of the much-too-black eyebrows, the set of the chin all betraying that this was a very serious phone conversation. Sylvia, whose sense of curiosity was almost beyond masculine imagining, was wishing—oh, how she wished—she could hear the other end of the conversation.

On the other end, Vicino was explaining that the Capo had a source in the District Attorney's office that kept them informed of these matters. "Your name has been mentioned," said Vicino. "Perhaps we should talk." Vicino was a *consigliere* in the Mob. Very important.

"Yes," said Elihu. "Where? . . . Half an hour okay?"

He hung up and shot out of the bed. "I've got to go," he said, reaching for his shorts. The note of apology was the only surprising bit to Sylvia. Jasper was, after all, the role model upon whom Elihu based his performance, and Jasper had never apologized, never explained. There had been with Jasper the same kind of phone calls—too many times—and Jasper would be out of bed and into his clothes with barely a good-bye. Jasper had treated her like dirt and that, alas, had been part of the attraction.

But Elihu, a much younger man, as ruthless as Jasper, and (the whispers went) much more crooked, felt the need to explain, his dark eyes upon her even as he hustled into his trousers. "There are times when you must catch the moment or it vanishes." Slipping on his shoes as he said this. "I would far prefer..." Buttoning his shirt, not finishing that thought because he was looking for his necktie. "But I can't..." Finding the necktie and putting it on.

Sylvia lying there, the Naked Maja, wearing only a slight smile, watching, saying nothing. Let him run with it. He didn't exactly apologize, but an air of apology hung in the air, and this was more than she expected.

Fully dressed, he sat on the edge of the bed and kissed her, all very surprising. She sat up on the impulse to say, "When will I see you again?" and waited for him to say it. He didn't. What he did say—just as he vanished through the bedroom door—was, "I'll call." She heard him clatter down the corridor (uncarpeted like the whole apartment) and heard the front door close behind him. Bang.

Then she was alone with her naked, forty-four-year-old body, making faces at herself in the mirror that had been built into the wall beside the bed for one purpose only, wondering how many other females had lain there (and what age they were) and feeling nevertheless triumphant. Things had gone far better than she'd hoped. He had the forty-four-year-old body and he wanted more of same. It wasn't simple politeness; the I'll call was not one of those let's have lunch routines. If he wanted to get rid of her, he'd just have plunged out that door without saying anything. He wouldn't have given a damn about manners. No, he had said he'd call because he wanted more of her forty-four-year-old body. Why? (Lying there inspecting it in the mirror. Not bad, slim, tough, well cared for but still forty-four.) Humphrey Worth had said—again and again to anyone who would listen—that Elihu was a classic mother lover (a politer term than mother fucker but meaning much the same thing).

"Am I—Mother *manqué*? God forbid."

She would settle for it if she had to because she was smitten from head to toe with this damned young man. Play with fire. . . .

That made her laugh.

She dressed slowly, thoughtfully, wearing the same slight skeptical smile she had while naked. Afterward she went through the apartment from top to bottom, looking for whatever she could find. She opened every built-in drawer in the closet, looked at the shirts, the socks, the underwear, looking for clues to . . . what? Elihu's black soul. Caressing these mundane objects with her little cat's smile, feeling Elihu in them.

She looked especially in the small drawers at the top of this built-in dresser where a man kept his cast-off cufflinks, his old charge cards, letters from cast-off mistresses, his soul. But Elihu left no traces, no charge cards, no letters, no clues; the cast-offs had been cast clear out of his life.

She went through the entire apartment, room by room, drawer by drawer. Where were his bad habits? Where did he keep the cocaine? The marijuana? She found nothing more heinous than aspirin. There was some booze in a lower kitchen cupboard but it looked as if it were there for others, not for Elihu. All sorts of strange liqueurs no one bought for himself, seduction liqueurs.

She read the titles of the books. A man always gave himself away in his books. Isaac Asimov's *Foundation's Edge* lay next to the bed. Wouldn't you know? Sylvia was always disappointed in her lovers' taste in literature. Asimov was not her dish of tea at all—too childish and outside her range. Next to Asimov lay a Doonesbury comic book and next to that *The Notebooks of Leonardo da Vinci*. She opened that one and found an underlined passage.

"Flatterers or Sirens: The Siren sings so sweetly she lulls

the mariners to sleep; then she climbs upon the ship and kills the sleeping mariners."

Sylvia shivered.

Underneath *Foundation's Edge* she found a magazine she'd never heard of, *Musician*, full of rock articles—one of them about Twisted Sister. Twisted Sister, she discovered, was the name of a heavy-metal rock group that was, according to the magazine, vicious and androgynous.

"They sing about murder, mayhem, insanity, vigilante justice, resisting authority and motorcycles. But they do not sing about poontang."

That made Sylvia laugh aloud. "I sing about poontang, never about vigilante justice."

She read on. "Dee Snyder, leader and singer of Twisted Sister, refers to himself as a dirtbag and is so effective at being one that his father, a cop, keeps no pictures of Dee past the age of twelve."

On the page was a photograph of Dee wearing a dress, long, long hair almost to his waist, his face twisted into a snarl.

Charming!

In the entrance hall was a table she almost passed by. On its top was the *Wall Street Journal* and a few bills and . . .

She almost missed the little drawer altogether. It was on the side of Elihu's bedside table rather than in front, an odd place for it to be and so inconspicuous that she might easily have overlooked it. It was hard to draw open, clearly it hadn't been opened in quite a spell and inside was an object that dumbfounded her. It was a round medallion, a medallion in the shape of a red devil with pointed ears, a tail, devilish grin. Sylvia hadn't seen one in years.

A memento of The Game, that long-ago children's game that had ended so disastrously for little Elihu. Sylvia had not been in that children's game—she was much too old—but she'd been at the party, remembered it well. Why had Elihu kept this memento of his humiliation for all these years? Next to his bed! How very odd!

CHAPTER 20

With the bundle of money she'd made from the sale of her apartment, Estelle Worth bought a four-room, first-floor apartment in a brownstone in the upper West Seventies between Broadway and West End Avenue, over the horrified outcries of her relatives. "You'll get raped!" cried Prudence. "What fun!" snapped the spinster Worth. "No Worth has lived on the West Side since the dawn of history." "You'll get murdered!" said Prudence. "I'll take a few of the killers with me," said Estelle. And so on.

The outcries not only did no good; they reinforced her opinion that she had made a sensible move. "I'm taking no more advice from Worths," the spinster said crisply to Prudence, to all of them. "I spent my life following your terrible advice and look where it's landed me." It was her money and she'd do with it as she chose. She wouldn't even put her money in a Worth bank; she put it in Chase

Manhattan. ("One of those rotten Rockefeller banks," said
William Worth gloomily.)

She went right ahead with the purchase of the West Side
place as she had gone ahead with the sale of her East Side
flat, paying no attention to the outcries. She had less success
fending off the brothers, Nicholas and Orin, who showed up
on her doorstep one day to announce they were going to
help her move.

She protested fiercely that she didn't want any assistance,
but with sunny good humor they ignored her and proceeded
to pick up lamps and tables and move them into the waiting
van of the Friendly Neighborhood Mover (who was distinctly
unfriendly).

"You've never helped me before!" said Estelle.

"You never needed help before," said Nicholas.

"I don't need it now! And I don't want it. You two boys
have ignored me your whole lives..."

"Well," said Orin with a great open smile, "you're much
more interesting now, Aunt Estelle." He had picked up one
of his aunt's dreadful chintz-covered standing lamps and
was carrying it to the door. "You weren't terribly interesting
before this happened."

He disappeared down the hall, carrying the awful lamp.

Nicholas said, "Orin is a scientist, Aunt Estelle—"

"Fishes!" said Estelle ferociously. "He studies fishes.
I'm not a fish!"

"He is fascinated by your crisis behavior, Aunt Estelle.
He plans to write a paper on it for *New World Humanities*."

"I'll sue!" cried Estelle.

When they got over to the West Side and the furniture—
of which there was much too much—was duly deposited,
here, there, everywhere, in the little first-floor apartment
(which had very high ceilings and lots of closets), Estelle
unbent enough to make the brothers tea and buttered toast,
herself unpacking one of the kitchen boxes which contained
a toaster and a teapot. The boys sat on packing boxes in the

living room and watched the schoolchildren from Saint Mary's Parochial School around the corner troop past the first-floor windows.

"You're going to have to get rid of a lot of this stuff, Aunt Estelle," said Nicholas. "You won't have room to turn around in." He was looking over the Tudor oak chairs, the immense oak tables with corkscrew legs, museum stuff. "Where did you get all this junk, Aunt Estelle?"

"From my father, who got it from his father. I don't know where grandfather got it. Maybe from his father. It's been in the family for generations." She laughed unexpectedly, the laugh opening up her tight face in a way the brothers had never before seen. "It is pretty awful, isn't it? Maybe I'll open an antique shop. Worth Antiques. People might buy this junk simply 'cause we once owned it."

The brothers said nothing, let her run with it.

"If that Rockefeller clown can get away with selling reproductions of that deplorable sculpture for ten times what it's worth, simply because he owns the original, why couldn't I sell these originals for... five times what they're worth?"

Ending on a questioning note. Looking savagely at the brothers, prepared to resist any objections.

"We're not arguing, Aunt Estelle," said Nicholas mildly.

Estelle was chewing thoughtfully on a piece of toast, eyes full of dreams. Nicholas, watching her, was struck by the character in his aunt's face, something he'd never before noticed, perhaps because it wasn't there. Or perhaps because he'd never really looked at her. Spinsterhood awakened. Jesus!

"As a matter of fact," said Estelle, "there isn't a Worth house or a Worth apartment anywhere up and down the east coast that isn't full of junk furniture everyone would love to get rid of...."

CHAPTER 21

The item was in Heidi Stroop's column. "Robin Worth, the Golden Girl, has sold her golden smile, her golden hair, her golden charm to GBC for what is known in the trade as an undisclosed sum. Word on Wall Street is that the death of Jasper Worth has left the Golden Girl without enough gold to pay the rent. They say you can't take it with you, but Jasper apparently did—not only Robin's fortune but several other Worth fortunes that had been entrusted to Jasper have vanished into thin air."

The story had been whispered all over Wall Street but never before quite so blatantly in the newspapers.

Nicholas phoned GBC.

"She's on a stakeout." The woman's voice on the telephone was very chilly.

"A what?" said Nicholas.

"Look, who is this? I can't give information—"

"I'm Nicholas Worth. Robin's cousin. Friend since childhood."

"Oh, Gawd!" The voice became even chillier, and then retreated altogether. Nicholas overheard the voice saying, "Some goddamned cousin! Anyone know where the stakeout is?" The woman came back to him. "She's doing stakeout at the Frobisher apartment. Sixty-sixth Street."

"What's a stakeout?" asked Nicholas.

There was no one there. The woman had hung up.

Frobisher? Nicholas ruffled through the *Post* and there on page three it was. Polly Frobisher, lovely, rather haughty looking woman who, it developed, was running a very high priced call house on West Sixty-sixth Street. Frobisher. An old name. The Frobishers had not quite come over on the *Mayflower* but they had, the *Post* writer said, caught the next boat. Or perhaps the one after that. One didn't expect to find them running cathouses on East Sixty-sixth Street. It wasn't that Polly Frobisher was down on her luck or needed the money. She had embarked, said the *Post*, on this enterprise for the sheer adventure of it and was herself one of the call girls.

All of this was highly speculative information coming from unnamed sources. No direct quotes from Polly Frobisher herself, who had apparently barricaded herself in her apartment and was unavailable for comment.

Nicholas caught the Lexington Avenue local at Wall Street, got off at Sixty-eighth and walked two blocks south to Sixty-sixth. He could see the stakeout from the corner of Lexington, a large truck with GBC written all over it. Atop which was the big TV camera; alongside were burly young men with smaller hand-held TV cameras, others holding long metal arms with microphones hanging from them.

Leaning against the side of the truck, arms folded, was Robin. A woman next to her was fiddling with Robin's blond hair, combing out a curl here, fluffing up a curl there. Robin looked as if she were awaiting electrocution.

As Nicholas got within earshot, he heard the other woman say, "Smile a little, Robin.".

"Why?"

"Good for the soul."

"I haven't got one. I sold it to GBC. *Nicholas!*" She'd just caught sight of him. "What are you doing here?"

"Looking for you. Come have a cup of coffee with me and explain what a stakeout is."

"*This* is what a stakeout is," said Robin savagely. "We've been here for two days waiting for that damned woman to come out of her apartment. I can't go have a cup of coffee with you because I must be ready to pursue that bloody whore when she emerges—if she emerges."

"Polly Frobisher?" said Nicholas. "Don't we know Polly Frobisher? I mean, isn't she—"

"Yes, she is. The very one. A hot lay—even at dancing school. She's your generation, Nicholas, not mine. She's three years older. Did you . . ."

"No."

"She was always a kook. I think she's doing this to get her name in the paper."

"Then why does she barricade herself in her apartment? Why doesn't she come down and face the cameras?"

"The book publishers have got to her. Don't say anything for free. Save it all for the book. This is Miss Endicott. My cousin Nicholas."

"So this is what you're doing for a living."

"If you can call it a living. More like dying. I die every time I face the cameras."

"And what are you going to say when you get in front of the cameras?"

Robin pinned on a sour smile and intoned in a high-pitched squeak, "Miss Frobisher, would you mind explaining why you embarked on a career of fornication when there are so many other less strenuous means of making a dishonest dollar?"

Miss Endicott looked pained. "Robin," she said, drawing it out like a moan.

"Where are NBC and CBS?"

"CBS considers prostitutes beneath its dignity. NBC was here yesterday but they chickened out, the sissies. They're off covering fires— Oh my God, there she is!" Robin's voice had risen to a squeak. She bolted toward the marquee, showing a speed of foot Nicholas had never seen in Robin.

Polly Frobisher had emerged from the apartment door and sprinted under the marquee toward the curb. A limousine had snaked past the TV truck toward the end of the marquee, obviously part of some prearranged rendezvous. It didn't quite work. The limousine took a little longer than it had planned threading through the TV truck and crew, leaving Miss Frobisher standing there waiting long enough for Robin Worth and one of the hand-held camera crew to get to her.

Robin thrust the microphone in her hand toward Polly Frobisher and said, "Polly Frobisher, would you tell the TV audience what emotional satisfaction you derive from a career as a call girl?"

"Oh my God!" muttered Miss Endicott.

Polly Frobisher, a slender dark-haired girl, turned a frosty smile on Robin. "Look who's calling the kettle black. Robin Worth, the Golden Girl herself."

The limousine arrived and Polly Frobisher yanked open the door and got in. Before closing the door, she poked her head out just a little and said, "How much did *you* sell out for, dearie?"

The limousine sped away.

Robin waved good-bye with her free hand and, smiling, turned her face to the hand-held camera. "That was Polly Frobisher, folks, showing a quickness at repartee that she didn't have when I last laid eyes on her at Miss Whittingham's Dancing School a good long time ago. We are outside the apartment building from which, the District Attorney alleges, Miss Frobisher has been running a call girl service catering to some of New York's richest and most prominent people. This is Robin Worth for GBC.''

Robin smiled as if she were having the best time and held it until the red light on the camera went off, at which time she turned herself off like an electric light, her whole face sagging into a murderous pout.

''Degrading, isn't it?'' she said to Nicholas. To Miss Endicott, ''Well . . .''

''We can't use any of it. She all but called you a whore to your face—our high-priced Golden Girl. Did you have to antagonize her?''

''Did you expect me to kiss her ass? That whore! I didn't tear her hair out, although if that limousine hadn't moved off . . .''

Miss Endicott shook her head in despair. '' 'Tell us what emotional satisfaction you derive from a career as a call girl?' '' Saying the thing through her teeth. ''Just suppose she had said on camera, 'Yes, I love my career and I urge all red-blooded American girls to follow my example. Whoring is where the big money is.' ''

''You'd have cut it out,'' snapped Robin. ''You always do when they say something honest. The poor crumbs haven't a chance.''

Nicholas thinking, it's Robin who hasn't a chance.

Miss Endicott—what was she? director? producer?—had walked away, stone-faced, back to the crew who were packing away their cameras and sound equipment. She was talking to the camera and sound men, her back to Robin, sharing with them a familiarity, an empathy from which Robin was conspicuously excluded. They're torpedoing her, Nicholas was thinking. Shafting the poor little rich girl.

''Come on, Nicholas,'' said Robin. ''I'll let you buy me that cup of coffee now.''

They went to the Chock Full o' Nuts on Lexington and sat

on stools. The luncheon crowd had largely emptied out and the place was only half full.

Robin looked woeful. She was running her hands through her hair, shaking out the curls Miss Endicott had carefully arranged there as if trying to get her real self back.

"Two whole days with a full crew wasted!" she wailed. "That's the third time in a row I've struck out. I always blurt out something that shocks them to the core."

"I thought you were wonderful, quick, natural, tough."

"They don't *want* me to be tough. They want me to be a lady. Oh, my God, Nicholas, GBC's idea of a lady. They never met one. They just read about them in Jane Austen. They want Jane Pauley with bloodlines. That's what these idiots said! And now they're paying me all of this money...."

"How much *did* you sell out for, dearie?"

Robin laughed. "Three hundred and twenty-five thousand dollars. Over a period of one year. Without options, which means they can't get out of it no matter how many times I blow it. I got a very good agent—Henrietta Mills—a real shark." She made a face. "Well, I've got to pay for that helicopter, Nicholas—three hundred twenty-five thousand..."

"You could have declared bankruptcy. Wiped it out."

"Dad won't let me. He says it isn't honest. My dear darling daddy. He was brought up in Never-Never Land where one does unto others what one wishes others would do unto one."

She had her compact out now and was looking searchingly into the mirror, looking for the real Robin Worth. Nicholas said gently, "You're twenty-two, Robin. You don't really have to do what Daddy says anymore."

She smiled at herself in the mirror and said, "I'm still Daddy's girl, Nicholas. I wouldn't hurt the old darling."

"You're pretty much in Never-Never Land yourself, Robin."

"I suppose we all are—and now the real Worth has crashed in on us Worths and here I am trying to earn a living. They're *changing* me, Nicholas, into this simpering sweet milk and water—''

"No, they're not," said Nicholas. Actually he thought Robin was changing into a tough streetwise cookie full of show-biz smarts. It always happened. "I don't know why they won't show that bit. I thought it was very amusing."

"Darling, you don't know network television. They're scared of their own shadows. One letter and they go over the wall."

Nicholas doubted that very much. It was the upper levels of the network that negotiated that contract, but Robin was now down on the lower level with the working stiffs who didn't make anything like three hundred twenty-five thousand a year and who were having a little fun sinking the Golden Girl forty fathoms deep. It had happened before, the working stiffs out of envy, spite or plain cussedness torpedoing the high-priced stars, some of whom sank. Others, the tougher ones, didn't. But the tougher ones had usually been in the business a long time and knew all the plays, while Robin . . .

Aloud Nicholas said, "Mike Wallace must get letters. And Donahue."

"They all started on independent stations," said Robin bitterly. "When they got famous they got taken over by the networks and they went their own sweet way. But me, I'm supposed to do what I'm told." .

"And what are you told? What are you *supposed* to do?"

Robin turned herself into what she was supposed to be right there on the counter stool. "So you're Nicholas Worth. How marvelous! Look at him, folks, the real genuine, actual, live-in Nicholas Worth—a member of that legendary family! I'm so thrilled I'm likely to fall right through the floor! Tell me, Nicholas, what is it like waking up being you?"

The place had emptied so that Robin's act sounded through it loud and clear, attracting all the counter women.

One of them, a black buxom woman with a face that looked as if it had been carved in stone on a twelfth-century cathedral, was running her cleaning rag over the counter next to Robin.

"You complainin' about yo' lot, Miss Worth? They treatin' you real bad? I'm real sorry! I truly am." In a voice that sounded like it came from a bronze bell.

Robin slid off the stool, muttering, "That's the way it is, folks, in Never-Never Land. Come on, Nicholas."

Nicholas paid the bill and followed her. "They own me now, Nicholas," said Robin savagely, striding down the street. "That's what it's like being on television. Before, they'd nudge each other and say, 'Hey look, that's Robin Worth.' But now that I'm on TV—now that I'm right in their living rooms—they walk right up and say, 'Hey, Robin, you were real lousy last night on that news program.' Very friendly, they are, while they're sticking the knife into me. I've got to get back to GBC. Can you drop me across the park? I've got to tell you something."

In the cab Robin slunk deep into her seat, hands in her pockets, scowling at the floor.

Nicholas said, "How are your mother and father bearing up?"

Robin made a little face. "Graciously. Grace under pressure, all that malarkey. Actually, they're shell-shocked is what they are. Dad has sold the Fifth Avenue place—everyone wanted that—and put Sag Harbor on the market, but it'll take years to sell that white elephant."

She subsided mournfully, looking at the floor as the cab crept across Manhattan. Nicholas had to nudge her. "What were you going to tell me, Robin?"

Robin drew a deep breath into her lungs, let out half of it and said, "We're suing you, Nicholas. Mummy and Daddy and Fergie and me are suing you and Orin and Aunt Rebecca for a hundred million or some such ridiculous sum. Isn't that awful?"

Nicholas said, "Why?"

"Because," wailed Robin, "the goddamned lawyers say that's the only way we'll ever see our money again. They say that Jasper, through fraud, misfeasance, malfeasance, embezzlement, all that stuff, wrongfully exchanged our good stocks for bad stocks."

"Dad would never do such a thing."

"And since you inherited the money, we have to sue the estate which means suing *you*. Oh, Nicholas, I hate it! I didn't want to do it! I said under no circumstances would I sign that piece of paper, but then Mummy had hysterics and Daddy yelled that I'd lose the case for them and—oh God, Nicholas. I hated doing it."

She burst into tears. Nicholas put an arm around her and let her sob away on his new light blue summer suit.

"I'm not a suing person, Nicholas. Neither is Fergie. Or Mummy or Daddy. This would never have occurred to any of us if some goddamned lawyer hadn't thought it up. Why do we let lawyers push us around like this?"

"They're the new priesthood, Robin. We are the most litigious society in history. I sue therefore I am—that's what old Spinoza would have said. We are as lawyer ridden as the Middle Ages was priest ridden. One day we'll get fed up with the bastards and hang 'em all from lampposts."

"Let's go hang one now, shall we? Let's go hang our lawyer. His name is Mandlebaum and I hate him. Is it okay to hate a lawyer named Mandlebaum or will everyone say I'm anti-Semitic?"

"Just don't say it on GBC. You'll get letters."

"Oh, Nicholas, you're so nice! Much too nice—considering the lawsuit."

"Hanagan doesn't think I'm all that nice. Hanagan has been throwing Nietsche at me. 'Whoever fights monsters should see that in the process he doesn't become a monster.' Nietsche according to Hanagan. Another lawyer. Can't hate him either because he's Irish. Can't hate the Irish or the

Jews or the blacks or the browns or the yellows or the reds—anyone else, you can hate away.''

The Worth family, he was reflecting, were splitting into little warring factions, all suing each other, including himself, who had three lawsuits going concerning the will. Alec Worth had said that Elihu had a plan and was pursuing it. Was this the plan? To stir up so such intramural warfare that his own crimes would sink under the surface?

The cab creeping through the sunny choked streets of Manhattan. Nicholas said, ''I think Nietsche had it all wrong. I think whoever fights monsters should damned well see to it that he becomes a monster—or he won't stand a chance.''

BOOK
TWO

CHAPTER 22

The electric blue waters—bluest waters on earth—glowed like fire in the morning sunshine. Orin very hot in his long johns and sweater, checking the CO_2 absorber that lay next to the cramped cockpit, the pilot up forward checking the oxygen intake, the *Pegasus* at ten meters now, fifteen, twenty.

The water outside the ceramic glass window was running its color riot that always pierced Orin to the heart—from electric blue to sapphire to cobalt to purple-blue to deepest purple more regal than a Roman emperor. Orin feeling the elation rising in him, the sinful elation. Going backward in time to the very beginning of primordial existence.

The little deep-diving submarine was now in the Twilight Zone where the world was gray and as perpetual as perpetuity ever gets on this earth—where there is no sun or rain or day or night, where everything is the way it was yesterday and an hour ago and a hundred million years ago, where change is unknown—what a fearful thought, forever and forever. (When Irving Berlin first played his great hit song "Always" to George Kaufman, Kaufman, a cynic in matters of the heart, said: "Irving, always is a long time. Wouldn't the song be better if it went, 'I'll be loving you till Thursday.'?")

Orin rarely saw anything of note at this level, but he kept his eyes fixed on the window because he didn't want to miss it when it happened. Someday an eel would wriggle past that window. No one had ever seen a mature eel in the Sargasso Sea, but everyone knew they were there in the millions. (The Sargasso Sea is the size of the United States so it's easy to miss an eel.) Someday an eel with its huge golden eye, grown to eight times its normal size for this journey, would glide past his window, grinning his dark sinister eel grin guided by his built-in, automatic compass on its way from an American river through thousands of miles of open ocean to its spawning site somewhere in the Sargasso Sea that man with all his electronic gadgets has never been able to find.

There this boy eel with his marvelous round laughing golden eye (the better to appreciate you, my dear) would mate with a girl eel, the two of them passing on to their young the primordial secret of why this long long journey which had gone on unchanged for a hundred million years, way back to when North and South America and Africa and Europe were all one continent, the Atlantic Ocean just a big river in it. Why not accept the facts of change, Mr. Eel, and adapt—have your young in the Chesapeake Bay like everyone else? But no, the eel was a true conservative. The old way was the best, the only way.

Someday Orin would see an eel in his window.

Not that day. At that moment all Orin saw outside his ceramic glass window was a sliver of clay that had blown off an Iowa farm three days ago and, borne by the winds, had fallen into the sea and was sinking now at the rate of three feet a day. It would take ten years to get to the bottom, that bit of clay, and there it would join other bits of clay that, when a thousand years had passed, would reach a thickness the width of his fingernail.

Orin wrote it all down in the diary on his knee. Then he checked the camera which took those marvelous pictures you see in *National Geographic* in four colors and turned up the heat because it was getting cold in the little submarine. Up front in his own little cubicle, Elliott, the pilot, was humming "I Might Have Been Queen," which is almost unhummable, occasionally muttering the words ("I'm a new pair of eyes/Every time I am born/An original mind/Because I just died").

The *Pegasus* was at six hundred fifty meters now, the Deep Scattering Layer where monsters lurked. Not big monsters, most of them half the size of a finger, but monsters nevertheless. The sea at that level was alive with luminescence, lights flashing on and off, beckoning evilly. A dragon fish glided past Orin's window, ablaze with phosphorescence, its teeth so large they wouldn't fit into its mouth, the mouth open, lined inside with a row of lights....

Like the little crocodile in *Alice In Wonderland*.

How cheerfully he seems to grin
How neatly spreads his claws
And welcomes little fishes in
With gently smiling jaws.

The dragonfish disappeared into the murk—to eat or be eaten, perhaps both—and was succeeded by a viper fish, its two rows of photophores glowing red with invitation, a lighted tip on its dorsal fin. When a littler fish, thinking that lighted dorsal fin was a bit of food, reached out to touch it SNAP went the terrible jaws and the backward-pointing teeth of the viper fish would push the littler fish into his stomach. O big fleas have little fleas upon their backs to bit 'em and little fleas have littler fleas and so on ad infinitum.

Gleaming darkness velvety as coal in the Deep Scattering Layer now, the luminescence far away. Orin switched on the searchlight transfixing in its glare a lancet fish six feet long, the gourmand of the Sargasso Sea in whose stomach scientists had found fish not seen anywhere else on earth, a beast of enormously catholic appetite, the lancet, which would eat anything including its own young—the ultimate in child abuse.

The *Pegasus* at eight hundred meters now, the bliss in Orin rising to dangerous levels; he wished—oh, how he wished—to leave the warm confines and go join the tumultuous dangerous life in the depth of the sea. Won't you walk a little faster, said the whiting to the snail, there's a lobster right behind me and he's stepping on my tail.

The luminescence outside the window distant as a star.

Orin turned on the searchlight and in its rays, bearing down on the little deep-diving submarine—furious, as always—was a twelve-foot swordfish, coming at forty miles an hour. It struck the searchlight and glanced off, the encounter shaking the *Pegasus* from keel to sail, as they called the conning tower.

"Monster time!" said Orin.

"Is there ever any other time?" said Elliott.

"He's rounding for another go."

The swordfish swam a long, graceful, angry thrashing circle. Very bad-tempered, the swordfish, because its metabolism doesn't really work. It cannot idle, cannot, like other fish, lie lazily in water, taking its ease. If the swordfish doesn't go about forty miles an hour, it sinks to the bottom. Evolution has not thought things through with this fish; it has a hard life, traveling at high speed morning, noon, and night and this has made him evil tempered.

Orin set the camera for high-speed continuous action as the great fish circled.

At this point the Isistius, a little black, foot-long shark, interjected itself into the action. Ordinarily the swordfish would stay a respectful distance from the knifelike teeth of the Isistius, but the little shark had crept up, flashing its own set of photophores, pretending to be a squid. O never trust a Sargasso fish, con men every one. The Isistius rammed its razor teeth into the attacking, thunderstruck swordfish, scooping out a delicious round ball of flesh, the greatest saltwater delight, and flashed away to eat it, leaving a neat hole like a bullet wound, oozing cold blood.

The swordfish lost concentration and swam off, David beating Goliath yet one more time, the cameras recording it all in four colors. Orin wrote it all down. Eating and being eaten was the primary business in the Deep Scattering Layer, yet there was not that much of it going on. The Sargasso Sea is a desert as seas go, every mouthful prized.

When he looked up from his yellow pad again, Orin saw a jellyfish, so aptly named a Medusa, drifting along upside down (at that level in that sea upside down and right side up had little meaning), its Medusa snakelike locks trailing behind, each containing enough poison to stun a man, each tentacle harboring its own hypodermic gun that could fire at will, its Medusa face grinning a Medusa grin.

The Mock Turtle telling Alice how his Teacher taught him Reeling and Writhing and all the branches of Arithmetic— Ambition and Distraction, Uglification and Derision. . . .

They'd been in the water two and a half hours, the *Pegasus* at fifteen hundred meters now, in the icy blackness. A squid floated past, its sharp eyes gleaming with intelligence (of which the squid has a great deal). Nearby—far too near—a lantern fish with its round bright eye was preening, showing off its luminescence like Cindi Lauper showing off her blue hair, an adorable little show-off fish, the lantern. The squid reached out with its terribly quick arms and embraced the little lantern, its tentacles bringing the morsel to the squid's parrotlike beak which tore off the dear little round head and delicately consumed the rest, silver scales falling to the bottom like snowflakes.

The camera recording it all for posterity.

An hour later *Pegasus* was on the bottom, a mile straight down, the lights shining on the tranquil bottom fish—a crustacean that looked like a flat lobster, a sea cucumber, sea urchins in all their fussy splendor, a tiny red shrimp nosing around the mud—a very peaceful scene next to the homicide of the Deep Scattering Layer.

Orin was murmuring Coleridge to himself.

"For thou art long and lank and brown
As is the ribbed sea sand."

Marvelous lines that Coleridge confessed had actually been written by his friend William Wordsworth.

No one understood the repetitions of the ocean better than Coleridge, whose *Ancient Mariner* was set in the Sargasso Sea.

Alone, alone, all all alone
Alone on a wide wide sea.

The pulse of the ocean in those lines.

I am two hundred million years old. Thus Orin on the bottom of the sea. I am that starfish there. We all crawled out of this sea and someday will all crawl back, looking for our roots.

Like Father.

Who fell or was pushed. Into the silvery sea.

Orin was crooning Coleridge aloud now, the narcosis very strong.

Like one that on a lonesome road
Doth walk in fear and dread
And having once turned round, walks on
And turns no more his head,
Because he knows a frightful fiend
Doth close behind him tread

From up forward Elliott called out, "Did you say something, Orin?"

"No," said Orin. "Nothing."

They'd been down five hours, and it was time to get back on the surface where the Portuguese man of wars floated and where the Sargasso Sea waves were whiter than any other waves on all the seven seas.

Elsie Worth was reading Jessica Keswick's column in the *Wall Street Journal*, something she'd never done before in her whole life. "Warfare has broken out among the many Worths, following the death of Jasper Worth. There are now a total of twelve lawsuits of one Worth against another, a highly unusual scenario for this close-knit, secretive, almost invisible family. . . ."

Nicholas, who had brought the *Journal* and asked his great-aunt to read it, sat opposite her in one of the uncomfortable Louis Seize golden chairs, watching the delicate tracery on Elsie's papery hands.

Elsie lay the paper down on the ormolu coffee table. "Scandalous," she said without heat. "But there have been worse scandals in the family. When I was a little girl, there was a fearful row about Uncle Robert, who'd done something horrifying to a servant girl. I don't think he raped her. One almost never heard that word in 1900, but he had his will of her in some improper way. There was a lot of that kind of scandal in 1900—abuse of servant girls. Now it's abuse of children. Dear boy, you haven't touched your tea."

Nicholas drank dutifully and launched into the other topic, the real reason he was there. This one involved sex, not money. Elsie was far more open about sex than money, loved sex scandal. "Aunt Elsie, have you ever heard any gossip to the effect that Elihu might be my father's child?"

"Good heavens!" Aunt Elsie only faintly titillated. Jasper's robust sex life was not exactly a secret. "Elihu? A natural child of Jasper's! What an idea!'' She was smiling faintly. She had always adored piratical Jasper.

''Why did Aunt Sophie adopt a child? She had two sons of her own.''

''Dear boy, why does any Worth behave as he does? We're all peculiar. Sophie wanted another child and Ellsworth wouldn't—or couldn't—oblige.''

It didn't sound like the timorous Aunt Sophie at all.

''Elihu was always her favorite—even over her own children.''

''He had a lot of charm,'' said Elsie dreamily, ''Elihu did.''

''Where was he born, Aunt Elsie?''

''You'll have to ask Sophie.''

''She'd never tell me. But she might have told you. She was always one of your favorites, Aunt Elsie.''

''She didn't tell me or, if she did, I've forgotten. She brought Elihu back from Europe. Sophie had gone to Switzerland for her health. That's where they went then—not one of those fat farms in Arizona like today—but to Switzerland because the air was so pure and so *thin*. Six months later she came back and there was Elihu in a little blue basket—''

''Six months!''

''I know what you're thinking, Nicholas. Stop it this minute! Sophie Worth is one of the most straitlaced young women I have ever known.''

Nicholas nibbled an almond cookie. ''You must have had letters from Switzerland. Where was Aunt Sophie recuperating?''

''Nicholas, you mustn't think such unkind thoughts. Anyway, I can't believe . . . I think it was Lausanne. Everyone went to Lausanne in those days—though why, I can't imagine. It's an ugly town.''

''Lausanne,'' said Nicholas.

* * *

William Worth was reading the report the little SEC lawyer Bates had brought him. "No one else must see this."

"No one has."

"I never heard of Alvin Worth."

"A California Worth," said Bates, as if that explained a great deal. "He changed his name to Ahmet Ali."

"Changed his name from Alvin Worth to Ahmet Ali? Why would anyone—"

"It's all in there, Mr. Worth."

"I'm not believing what I'm reading. *Ashamed* of being a Worth. Ashamed of his money!" The white eyebrows beetling ferociously.

The fierce features were softening now as William Worth read on. The boy had been very bright, magna cum laude at the University of Chicago. My goodness! A tough school, Chicago. Graduated at twenty. Roustabout in his Uncle Jasper's Texas oil fields which was where Jasper met him. . . .

Two hundred miles south of Woods Hole, the *Pegasus* hung on its cradle aboard the mother ship, the *Serpentine*, bobbing in the endless quiet swell of the Sargasso Sea. The amber light flashed for ten minutes in the pilothouse before anyone noticed. The call was from New York.

Elliott, the pilot of the *Pegasus*, went for Orin who was in the ship's darkroom developing the black and white photographs he'd taken that morning. The red caution light was on so Elliott thumped on the door and shouted, "Orin, telephone from New York. Your cousin Elihu."

In the red light of the darkroom, Orin had just plucked out of the developing tank the negative of a picture of the viper fish blown up to ten times its size and was holding it between thumb and forefinger.

Elihu.

He hadn't seen or talked to Elihu since that gathering at his Great-Aunt Elsie's after Jasper's funeral.

Orin blinked at the negative of the viper fish with its immense curved tusks, so big they wouldn't fit into the fish's mouth. That other viper fish on the telephone. . . .

"Tell him I'll call back."

"Come on, Orin. It must be important or he wouldn't. . ."

Orin put the negative into the fix tank, turned off the red light and went up to the pilothouse. The white telephone stood off its hook on the brass binnacle.

"Hello!" Elihu sang out, the second syllable rising like a woodwind note, full of good cheer. So friendly! This viper fish who had murdered his father and stolen a couple hundred million.

"What is it, Elihu?"

"I do *hate* to interrupt your holiday."

Orin's life was marine biology. Holiday!

"But something extremely unpleasant has arisen. You must know that your brother, Jasper, Jr., is suing me. As part of his suit, Jasper's lawyers are continually asking the court to stop payment on checks which they charge are an unwise drain on the estate. The court has resisted these requests until today. Today the court stopped payment on a check you made out to the Ocean Institute."

The Ocean Institute was Orin's own creation. It was a tax-free foundation that ran all the operations of the *Pegasus*, the *Serpentine*, and its attendant marine biology, financed almost entirely by Orin.

"You understand that this is Jasper, Jr.'s, doing, not mine. As trustee, I don't agree that Ocean Institute is an unwarranted drain on the estate, but since neither you nor your brothers and sister recognize me as trustee, nor recognize the will, there is no way I can come to your rescue on this matter. The check has been stopped by court order. I thought you should know."

The check was for one million, two hundred thousand dollars and was to have financed the entire third quarter, starting almost immediately with the deep-diving exploration Orin was conducting in the Sargasso Sea.

"Thank you," said Orin, always polite, distant as the remotest galaxy.

"Don't hang up, Orin. There is a way out of this. If you and Nicholas withdraw your suit against me, if you recognize the will—even if you alone recognize me as trustee of your father's estate—it would give me some leverage to go to court to overturn this monstrous judicial interference in your affairs. I realize this is not a decision you can easily reach over the telephone, but do think about it."

Orin could picture Elihu on the other end of that telephone call. Baring his white teeth in that great predatory viper fish smile.

"Cheers!" said Elihu over two thousand miles of ocean. He rang off. Orin hung up the white telephone on its cradle.

"Bad news?" asked Elliott.

"Is there any other kind?" said Orin.

CHAPTER 23

William Worth was in the bathroom, gargling noisily, so Lolo Vanbrugh had a moment's freedom to dial. For the first time in a week, Sylvia answered sleepily. "Hullo," in that smoky voice of hers.

"Darling," said Lolo. "You've disappeared. I've left endless messages on your machine and I never get a reply."

That was the trouble with the answering machine. You couldn't say you'd called back and got no reply because they all had machines when they didn't have maids. You had to use other subterfuge.

"Darling Lolo. I am sorry but I've been up to my ears in my damned relatives."

"Have you seen The Young Gentleman?"

As they called him.

"No, actually, I haven't."

A fat lie. Lolo could smell intercourse on her friend's breath—even over the telephone. But there was no point in accusation. Sylvia would just deny it, as for that matter Lolo denied the presence of William Worth who was there in her bathroom, gargling away.

"Darling, I haven't a minute. I've got to fly. The wedding, you know, the Worth–Dalrymple affair. I have to get a present and throw a dinner. 'Bye, love. I'll call when I can."

She was gone.

Lolo hung up the white telephone, furious. Sylvia had never rung off so abruptly. Besides, Lolo simply didn't believe any of it. Sylvia didn't give a damn about her relatives or their weddings. Lolo had simply been brushed off and she hated it.

William Worth came out of the bathroom and started to dress. "She's having an affair with Elihu," said Lolo vengefully. The moment she said it she wished she hadn't.

"Who?" said William Worth.

"Sylvia."

Now why did I say that?

William was all over her. When? How? How long has this been going on? Does Oscar know? And so forth.

Lolo bitterly regretting she'd ever spoken up.

Meanwhile, on the other end, Sylvia was having her own disquiet. She had hung up abruptly, cut off her old friend for one reason only: she was terribly afraid that if she hadn't she would open up and spill the works. She was dying to tell someone—but not, for God's sake, Lolo, who couldn't keep a secret across a room.

This playing of games. How very, very. . . extraordinary! They had played—well, what hadn't they played? Isolde and Tristan, in the original dialect, a kind of Nordic German that seemed to send Elihu into transports. Sylvia (age forty-four) had been—God save the Queen!—Lolita (age twelve) while Elihu (age twenty-two) had been Humbert Humbert (age forty-four). Lately the games had gone very wild indeed. She had had to play Marilyn Monroe confessing infidelity in the very act of having sex with her husband Arthur Miller, and then—just for the hell of it—she had to be Arthur Miller and *he* played Marilyn Monroe—still confessing infidelity.

The fucking during all this role playing was absolutely marvelous, but Sylvia would have liked to dispense with all the dialogue which seemed to turn her partner on. She was exhilarated but lonesome. There was never—and she had said this openly the last time—a time when they were just Sylvia and Elihu. When one role ended, another role began, or the whole game ended. He'd look at his watch and be into his clothes and out of his apartment. There she'd be with her forty-four-year-old body and the remnants of Isolde's or Marilyn's personality still clinging to her like perfume and no one to talk to.

A few mornings later, very early, so early the sun cast long black shadows across Manhattan's tall buildings, Estelle, the spinster Worth, stood in the very center of Fifth Avenue contemplating B. Altman's great windows. On the other side of the windows Jeremy Quilp was arranging a mannequin—a slim, pouting beauty of a mannequin—on one of Estelle's worn Tudor chairs which stood before her large Tudor table, the one with the corkscrew legs. When he had finished arranging the mannequin, Jeremy Quilp stepped back, put his hands on his hips, and contemplated his workmanship with enormous self-satisfaction. Jeremy was always his own greatest admirer. He looked at Estelle in the middle of Fifth Avenue and blew her a kiss, followed by an extremely obscene gesture.

Estelle burst out laughing as she always did when Jeremy did things like that. He was so *outrageous*, that naughty Jeremy. I'm becoming a fag hag, she thought. What would Mother have said?

Jeremy was working the window again, piling green plants around the table, obscuring its harsh edges with foliage. Next to the table and chair was defiantly non-Tudor furniture: a Chinese mandarin red and gold chest with great filigreed locks, a bit of Charles X statuary, and, of course, lots of Biedemier without which no ensemble was quite complete. At the front of the window, written in large hand script, was the legend, "From The Worth Collection."

Not all of it was, of course. Certainly not that Chinese chest or that Charles X statuary, but who would know? The greenery was pulling it all together, making the window into a room that looked so livable. Dear Jeremy! He had such style, such flair!

It was so early the city had not awakened. Estelle loved the early morning air, sharp and clean, the hard oyster white light. She had Fifth Avenue all to herself. Well, almost to herself; busses rumbled down the avenue even at that hour and so rapt was Estelle that she didn't notice one until it bore down on her, the bus driver who was black and female shaking her woolly head at her with such contempt it made Estelle shiver.

Within seconds, Jeremy Quilp emerged magically from the Altman window and stood at her side. "You'll get run over, you silly old frump!" he shrilled at her. And in the next breath, shouting after the departing bus driver, "Up yours, you black witch! Why don't you watch where you're going?" Accompanied by that same obscene gesture he'd used a moment before on Estelle.

Estelle shrieking with laughter. "Jeremy, you disgusting little faggot, you'll get us arrested."

That's the way it was with them. He called her a silly old frump and she called him a disgusting little faggot and they'd both hoot with laughter. A very warm relationship. Jeremy delighted in telling anyone who would listen that he was a classic faggot of the old school; he minced, he pranced, he stamped his little foot, his conversation flamed with rococo epithets and epicene obloquy.

"These new faggots all *claim* to be bisexual! What a

laugh! About as bisexual as a cow!'' The word faggot itself had gone out of style, but Jeremy said he was bringing it back singlehandedly. And he'd stamp his little foot with glee.

Now his attention was on his own window. ''Oh, that *delicious* Tudor chair! I *must* have it!''

Estelle choking with laughter. ''It's a hunk of junk, Jeremy. You said so yourself. You've sold yourself again!''

Jeremy was always doing things like that. He'd transform perfectly ordinary furniture into collector's items by his genius for arrangement.

''I pluck some stupid little gewgaw out of an attic and glamorize it with my own superb touch, and presto, who is fooled by this magic? Myself! The ultimate in salesmanship! To fool yourself! I *must* have that chair, Estelle. I know just where I'll put it—in my front hall right next to my Roman head of Augustus.''

He turned his little hand outward—a coup d'état.

Estelle had been rejected by every store she'd approached with her Worth Collection—until Jeremy swooped down on her. (He always swooped, like a great hawk.) Instantly everyone wanted her furniture because Jeremy was one of the best and certainly most autocratic decorators in New York. Jeremy had selected Altman's because the windows were so large and he needed the space to work his magic in.

Now her old junk furniture was decorating Fifth Avenue, nobody admiring it more than Jeremy. ''Don't I have the most divine outrance? No one else has my outrance, wouldn't you say?''

''No one,'' agreed Estelle. ''Twenty-two thousand for that table! You crazy faggot!''

''Twenty-two thousand six hundred eighty-one,'' corrected Jeremy Quilp. ''It sounds so authentic. You must never give the suckers even numbers. They think you're robbing them.''

''Where did that bit of Biedermier come from?''

''My own attic.'' Jeremy shivered with laughter. ''We

faggots have had Biedermier for *ages*. We're bored to *tears* with it and we're all unloading it on you tiresome straights at ridiculous prices."

That's the way the wheel of fashion went, Estelle was thinking, keeping it to herself. Biedermier was unloaded on the straights and the straights unloaded their junkie old bric-a-brac on the queers. That Tudor chair Jeremy so lusted after had been for decades in her maid's room.

Aloud she said, "I haven't even begun to empty the Worth attics. There are Worth attics up and down the eastern seaboard groaning with furniture—Victorian mostly, I'm afraid. You said Victorian is out."

"We'll bring it back!"

After Jeremy had finished the Altman windows, still very early in the morning, Estelle took Jeremy back to her own new nest in the West Seventies and made him coffee to his own exacting standards. ("Swill!" he'd squealed the first time. "Are you trying to poison me?" And he'd taken her to Veronica's and told her exactly what quality of Colombian to buy and how to have it ground.) Now, as she made coffee, he prowled her apartment, shoving this bit of furniture there, and that bit over there—stopping to contemplate, moving it all someplace else, gradually transforming her own dingy abode with his flamboyant and famous outrance. "They'll all be stealing from it! My genius! My outrance! And getting it quite *wrong!*"

After the coffee, during which they bickered amiably over her Scheherazade lamps which he wanted to sell and with which she was loath to part, he took her to a furniture opening on Madison, to an antique store on Second Avenue, and to a hardware store also on Second where he bought masses of brass wall fittings for an apartment he was decorating in the nineties. That done, she accompanied him back to his own wildly imaginative house on Gramarcy Park and waited while he dressed—all in white flannel with a broad-brimmed hat and white shoes—to wear at the Worth–

Dalrymple wedding on Long Island that he'd never have managed to get into without her Worth name. In short they fed on one another, he taking her to chic gatherings, full of actors and writers and artists that she'd never have seen otherwise, and she took him to upper-crust affairs that she'd never have gone to without his reassuring and witty presence, affairs he'd never have got into without her.

"It's a symbiotic relationship," Jeremy would tell anyone. "Disgusting, like all relationships, but intrinsically basic."

Actually, it was much more than that. He loved the old bag, frumpy clothes and all. He was a snob, the supreme snob, and she was a Worth. He needed a Worth to go with his head of Augustus, and to have a live Worth to whom he could scream joyous insults (and receive joyous insults right back) was bliss beyond measure.

His name wasn't Jeremy Quilp at all, of course. It was Peter Feinstein. "Which is not *me*! Not me at all! Peter Feinstein, indeed! Sounds like a Jewish dentist!" He was an anti-Semitic Jew with a mind as sharp as a razor blade and as quick as lightning. He had made up the name Jeremy Quilp, letter by letter, syllable by syllable, to suit his own fey personality and no one pronounced it with the crisp authority and snap that Jeremy Quilp himself pronounced it.

"*Moi est* Jeremy Quilp," he would say, "and Jeremy Quilp *est moi! Cela!*"

Stamping his little foot.

CHAPTER 24

It was Ashley Worth who was getting married to Montagu Dalrymple IV, and they were both, everyone agreed, much too young—Ashley nineteen, Monty only twenty. But weddings were back in style again, big lavish weddings, young weddings. There had been that unfortunate period when the kids didn't get married at all or waited until they were past thirty and had had a career (or *something*—a fling, an adventure, a war). Not anymore. Pure unadulterated matrimony was back in fashion and it was very like Ashley to want to get in on the ground floor.

She was sharp-faced, beautiful (if you liked foxy faces which were much admired at the moment), slender, tough, athletic—played a hell of a game of basketball and was a real menace on a polo field—bright, foul-mouthed and thoroughly spoiled as even her mother Rory (especially her mother) would be the first to admit. Ashley was accustomed to having everything and now she wanted a husband (much as she might want another polo pony) because some of the other girls had them. She had proposed one night to Monty Dalrymple (who was a bit of a wimp) because she was a little drunk and he was *there*. He was not a bad match, rich, socially eminent and—well, he'd been there since she was about eight years old. So why not?

This was the wedding toward which many of the eastern Worths were assembling on that beautiful Saturday in late June. Rory and Algie Worth's place was at Seraph Point the other side of Oyster Bay on the sound. It was an enormous sprawling Gothic structure, hideously ugly everyone agreed, that some robber baron in the nineteenth century (*not* a Worth) had bought in France and had shipped to America to put up again; according to Humphrey Worth, they got it all wrong. Either someone had misnumbered the pieces or they'd slipped the robber baron some spare pieces of a lot of other castles. Nothing fit very well. Algie Worth bought the place for the view and had never quite got around to tearing it down and building something else.

The place had a broad reach of marvelous lawn with a superb high view of the sound which on that bright Saturday was full of white sails, the water blue as heaven. The wedding was at 11:30 that morning, but many got there a half hour early to look at the wedding presents— Ashley and Monty had looted not only Manhattan and Long Island but Philadelphia, Baltimore, and much of Delaware—and also, of course, to look at each other to see who was with whom and who was wearing what. The presents were in the long hall of the hideous Gothic house, acres of silver, polo fields full of cut glass and crystal, forests of mahogany. The very sight of it made Ashley slightly ill. "I've got to write polite letters about all this fucking shit," she moaned.

Estelle Worth and Jeremy Quilp drove down to the wedding in a hired Cary Cadillac (neither of them could drive) and passed the time jovially hurling insults at one another.

"You look like something discarded by the Second Empire, my dear, in that unspeakable brown dress. I'm positively ashamed to be seen with you," sniffed Jeremy.

Estelle sniffed right back. "And you, my darling, look like a little fat pansy which is what you are. How am I going to explain you to my friends?"

"Are you sure you have any? Why don't you buy a dress sometime?"

"I'm a Worth, darling. We don't have to buy dresses. I could show up stark naked."

"You'd look much better than you do now."

And so on. Both of them having the best time.

In the long hall Sylvia Worth was looking over the wedding presents with her basilisk eye, dripping scorn.

"That bowl—that Chinesey thing with the dragon handles and the green insides—has been given to at least three brides I know of and each one has bundled it up in the same tissue paper and passed it on. So here it is again."

"It has gone over the threshold of dreadfulness," said Humphrey. "It is so dreadful I rather like it."

"Just get married, Humphrey. Someone will give it to you."

The long hall was full of other guests eyeing each other as well as the presents, the air full of little cries. "Darling Wilma!" "James—how are you?" "Veronica!" An exercise in instant recall the social Worths were very good at.

The encounter between Humphrey and Jeremy was epochal.

"We are two homosexuals of different gender," Jeremy was to say later—an aphorism that got passed around. They hated each other on sight. "A closet queer. Ashamed of his sexual convictions. How utterly utter," said Jeremy. Humphrey felt nothing but horror to be seen in the same room with this little round pincushion.

Orin deflected attention from this chilly encounter by saying, "Look who's here," and pointing. At the entrance arch stood a gaunt lady in blue gabardine, writing away with a gold pencil on a leather-bound tablet.

"Who's that?" asked Sylvia.

"Heidi Stroop."

"That gossip columnist!"

Sylvia said, "I thought she was a mythological beast—like unicorns."

This same rumble was being heard at that moment upstairs in Ashley's bedroom where Ashley, in her white satin, was standing in a sea of white tulle, surrounded by bridesmaids, trying on her veil when her mother stormed in.

"Ashley! Heidi Stroop is down there taking *notes* and she says you—"

"I invited her, Mom." Ashley was looking at her foxy discontented face in the mirror. "My God, I'm beautiful. But I don't look happy. Now why is that?"

"Ashley, how could you? That *gossip* columnist! Here, in my house!"

Ashley couldn't tear her eyes away from her own face. "Why not, Mom? She's invited to the parties."

"Not to weddings. Not to *our* weddings."

Ashley turned away from the mirror reluctantly, loved looking at herself, turning her head this way and that, admiring herself—pixilated, she liked to say, by her own face.

"How could I say no to Heidi when I'd said yes to Robin?" She was kicking away at the clouds of tulle on the floor as she said this, taking off the tight-fitting clochelike veil and handing it to her maid of honor, Marilee Livingston.

"Ashley," shrieked her mother, "*will* you pay some attention! I am your mother!"

"I know, Mom." Still not looking at her because Mom was not going to like this. "I invited Robin because she's having a very tough time at GBC and this would be a big coup for her." Ashley, age nineteen, worshipped Robin, age twenty-two. Robin was what Ashley wanted to become and never would become because there would never be another Golden Girl like Robin.

"Robin is family."

"Also," said Ashley calmly, "GBC, the cameras—"

"Television! Ashley, you haven't—"

"It's my wedding, Mom. They're out there now." A casual wave at the windows. Ashley's room faced down the broad sweep of lawn which overlooked the sound, and through those windows Rory now saw the GBC trucks, the cables, the booms, the cameras—and their crews in sweatshirts, jeans, Nikes.

From the window Rory could see Robin, who was in a Chinese red linen suit, microphone in hand, already at work. Robin had stationed herself cunningly beside the stone steps leading down from the long flagstone terrace. The guests had to use those steps to get to the lawn, had to pass by Robin who grabbed those she wanted to talk to.

At that very moment she was pointing her microphone at Alec and Hortense Worth. Alec very proper in navy blue gabardine, Hortense vivid in white cotton edged with rose.

Both of them thunderstruck by a Robin they'd never before seen.

"And here," quoth Robin into her microphone, with her brightly pinned on smile, wearing (Hortense thought) far too much makeup and especially too much eye shadow, "are Alec and Hortense Worth from Galveston, Texas. Alec is known in the family as the Wizard of Galveston because he works such magic on the stock market." The gurgle in Robin's voice much too professional, much too studied, too mannered as if Robin was *playing* Robin rather than being Robin. "Could you say a word or two about this wedding?"

Alec could summon up only a beautiful day for a wedding, nice to be here with so many members of the family, Ashley was a lovely bride . . . .

Alec the acrid stockbroker who barely allowed TV in his house, Alec, who was suffering torments of love for this

Golden Girl who was tossing him to the TV audience like a Roman emperor tossing a Christian to the lions (and for the same purpose, to entertain the great unwashed multitude out there).

Hortense with her tight little smile intervened to rescue her husband from his sea of platitudes. "And when you get married, Robin, will we see it all on television?"

Robin laughed professionally, a flash of teeth, a glitter of eye, and grabbed for Elsie Worth, who was feeling her way down the stone steps with her stick.

"Aunt Elsie," she cried, "let me help."

An affecting sight, the beautiful young woman helping the old lady down the stairs. Upstaging Hortense and dismissing her at the same time.

Back at GBC headquarters, Gerald Fisher, executive vice-president of the network, was watching in his office with Jimmy Wechsburg, the station manager of WGBC. "Weddings, Jimmy?" he was saying.

"Well," said Jimmy, "it's a Worth wedding no other TV station could get into, and anyway, nothing else is on. The baseball hasn't started and the kids' programs are over. I wanted you to watch Robin."

Robin on the screen was saying brightly, "And here is the matriarch of the family, Elsie Worth, who is ninety-two years old."

"Is nothing sacred, Robin?" shrilled Elsie in her high-pitched old lady's voice. But she was smiling because Robin was smiling and because Elsie loved Robin.

Robin held the other Worths at arm's length, herself the TV personality, but old Elsie she kissed on both cheeks, saying, "Aunt Elsie you look divine in that tawny silk outfit. Where did you get it?"

"Out of my closet," snapped Elsie. "At my age you don't think I *buy* anything anymore. You're looking beautiful as always, Robin, but you're wearing much too much makeup and now I'm going on down and get a good seat. I don't like to miss anything at weddings."

She hobbled off.

Inside the house, Nicholas had found the GBC assistant director, Webley Foster. He and Webley had been at Choate together and here was Webley with a clipboard, eyes on his stop watch and on the TV screen. "Hi," said Webley, not taking his eye off Robin.

Nicholas said, "Last time I saw Robin doing her act, Sue Endicott was sticking it to her—in fact, the whole crew was giving her the business."

. Webley Foster didn't even look around. "That so? Well, the shoe's on the other foot. Can't talk now." He sped away with his clipboard to collar the best man, Orin, and the groom, who had just shown up at the end of the terrace.

Robin was facing the cameras with her bright smile, saying, "Elsie Worth is the oldest living member of the Worth family and still one of its most tireless. Just last year she went around the world by herself because she wanted to see it before she died."

At GBC headquarters, Gerald Fisher was saying, "She's damned good at improvising, Jimmy. Why have we seen so little of her?"

"Robin says Sue Endicott has been killing her stuff—which has all been on tape. That's why we're doing this live. Robin's idea, this whole operation. Robin is not exactly a shrinking violet."

The two men laughed. "Who is stabbing whose back?" asked Gerald Fisher.

Robin, still interviewing Worths at the foot of the stone steps, had grabbed Humphrey Worth, with Sylvia on his arm, for an interview that reverberated up and down the GBC corridors as well as the length and breadth of the Worth family for weeks afterward.

"Humphrey, the Worth family, this close-knit, almost secretive family, for the first time in its long life seems to be rent by lawsuits, many members of the family suing each other. Will these lawsuits not do permanent damage to the Worth mystique?''

Humphrey, wriggling like a beetle on a pin.

Nicholas, watching the thing on TV in the sitting room, was thinking, she has become Mike Wallace. And her own Uncle Humphrey is the victim. Even Mike Wallace didn't skewer his own uncles.

On the other end of the lawn, near the altar of white carnations, another drama was taking place. One of the GBC trucks had taken up a position directly behind the altar. The Reverend J. Thomas Stokes, vicar of Saint Thomas' Church, who was to officiate, had just come upon the scene and was livid with fury.

"You're *not* going to televise the ceremony,''' he was saying to Webley Foster.

Webley Foster said, "Ashley Worth has given her permission, Reverend.''

"Yes, but *I* haven't,'' said Reverend Stokes. "I absolutely refuse to perform a marriage ceremony in front of a television camera, young man. Remove that truck this minute!''

This attitude had been foreseen and plans had been made. Webley Foster raised his right arm over his head, fist clenched, to indicate to Robin that there was a flag on the play. Robin hurriedly disengaged herself from Humphrey Worth, saving him from answering that last rude question. She punched the button on her microphone which cut her off the air and put her in touch with the lead truck. "Mike,'' she said to the director, "go to a long shot of the lawn. I've got to see Webley. There's trouble.''

Whereupon she tripped across the great lawn (on which she had played croquet and where she'd partied and flirted and drunk champagne in the old days when she was a Worth, not a TV commentator).

"The reverend says he won't perform the ceremony until we get the cameras out of here,'' exclaimed Webley Foster in exquisitely neutral tones as if to say to the rector: I am neither for nor against you in this matter, I'm just a hired hand.

Robin turned on her too-bright smile and said, "Well, we'll have to explain that to the TV audience then, Reverend Stokes."

The same Reverend Stokes who had held her in his arms at her christening, and before whom she, as a little girl in a white dress, had knelt to receive the wafer at their confirmation in the Episcopal Church.

"We'll have to explain to our audience that you consider them unworthy to witness the sacraments. Is there some reason, Reverend Stokes, why a TV audience is excluded from the sacraments? If so, I think you should explain it to our audience."

Robin had become one of the People, a member of the proletariat, outraged from being shut out from a Worth wedding (herself a Worth).

It would have been one of the great television confrontations (television, like the law, must be confrontational) if it had been played out in front of the cameras. Here was a Worth—as elite as elite ever got—allying herself with the common people which is to say the TV audience and opposite her was the Reverend J. Thomas Stokes, himself one of the great masters of public relations. (You didn't get the job of rector of Saint Thomas' unless you knew how to manipulate the media.)

A good director would have zeroed in on the Reverend J. Thomas Stokes' rotund face as he pondered the uncomfortable proposition—how to keep the unwashed in their proper place (which is to say, outside) without appearing undemocratic, to say nothing of being un-Christian (in its modern implications as important and unsolvable a dilemma as how many fairies could dance on the point of a pin). It took the Reverend J. Thomas Stokes, who was no fool, only about five seconds to realize that, if any of this argument got on

TV, his goose was cooked (already the TV lens was zooming in on him). It was a credit to his common sense that he surrendered skillfully and quickly to this formidable young lady he'd once dandled on his knee.

"Let the ceremony begin," he said with no further talk about the presence of the cameras; he turned and walked to the altar as if he had never brought the subject up. With great dignity he took the play away from Robin and brought it back to himself.

In the fourth row, that cynical philosopher Humphrey Worth whispered to Sylvia Worth, "It has been my observation that the more splendid the wedding, the quicker the marriage breaks up."

At the altar of white flowers stood Montagu Dalrymple IV with his best man, Orin Worth. "The distinguished marine biologist," whispered Robin. How grave and handsome and intelligent he looks, she was thinking, as if she had never before noticed.

"Dearly beloved, we are gathered here today in the sight of God. . . ."

"And in the sight of GBC," said Nicholas wryly.

The GBC crew was decent enough to hold their peace until the ceremony itself was over—but not one moment longer. The bride and groom, now one flesh, turned their backs and started up the aisle—Mendelssohn again thundering down—and the crew immediately started rolling up the cables, putting away the boom, dismantling the camera on top of the truck.

All this brought to the wedding a discordant note of anticlimax which changed the tone. The sight of the grips rolling up cables, of trucks beating it for the exits, contributed powerfully to the downrush of feeling that enveloped this particular wedding and helped cause the violent mood shifts that took place.

Ashley, now a Dalrymple (no longer a Worth), played the radiant bride all the way down the improvised aisle, smiling at all the assembled Worths with bridelike intensity up the stone steps and into the house. There she abruptly deserted her new husband whom she had not once looked at after the ceremonial kiss, pelted up the great curving staircase to her room, locked the door and fell on the bed sobbing.

"I don't know why I did it! I don't *want* to be married and I especially don't want to be married to Monty Dalrymple! I don't love him! I don't respect him! I don't know why I did this! I don't want to leave my home and my family for Monty Dalrymple! What the hell are we going to talk about for the rest of our lives...."

Robin drenched a washcloth with cold water, bathed the bride's face, especially her red eyes, and let Ashley run on and on until she finally subsided into low moans.

Only then did Robin speak up. "Ashley, a lot of brides go through this. You're not the first. Pull yourself together, kid. Heidi Stroop is down there—you invited her—dying to have a great big nasty scandal and the Worth family has enough scandal on its hands at the moment. So pull up your socks, love, and face the music. You've got to go down those stairs and get kissed by about seven hundred people and smile and smile and smile and dance with your new husband and smile at him, too."

Even as she was delivering this locker-room oration, Robin was slightly stunned to find herself doing such a thing. Not her style at all, she would have thought. Yet here she was advocating the stiff upper lip, the value of appearance, good manners, noblesse oblige—she who had just been skewering her own relatives with her microphone.

Still, she persisted, and because Ashley so helplessly worshipped at Robin's shrine, she succeeded in pulling the bride together, washing her face, making her up suitably (Robin being very good at makeup long before she got on TV) and propelling Ashley downstairs and into the receiving line where she was indeed kissed by about seven hundred people with whom she laughed and joked and was outrageously visibly *happy*, dancing ceremoniously with Monty, looking up into his eyes, chatting away as if there would never be a dearth of things to say.

In fact, from there on, Ashley had a very good time at her wedding.

It was Robin who didn't.

The show was over, and there she was with that emptiness that assaults the TV performer when he goes off the air, the deflation, the nothingness, the abandonment.

Robin, leaning against the stone balustrade, was passed by groups of wedding guests, most of whom she knew, going into and out of the house. They eddied past her, giving her little nods, sometimes not looking at her at all, but, in any case, giving her a wide berth.

Very hurtful.

She felt out of place at a Worth wedding, herself a Worth. The show was over and she should have departed with the cameras and crew, with the other clowns.

Presently Nicholas stood next to her, bringing her a glass of champagne, her own being empty. "You look sad, Robin," he said. "On this bright, beautiful, glorious occasion."

"They're avoiding me as if I had leprosy," said Robin very low. "You're the first person who has stopped to say hello, Nicholas."

"Well," said Nicholas uncomfortably, "you've left the family. You've become one of Them—the great communicators."

"Ho!" said Robin bitterly. "Left the family, my ass! You can't leave this family, Nicholas! It isn't me that's left the family. It's the family that has left me."

Night had fallen on Seraph Point and the old folks—even some young folks—were dancing to Cole Porter under the red-and-white-striped canopy where the wedding had taken place. Under the blue-and-white-striped tent a whole new wedding feast had appeared, hot hams and turkeys replacing the cold lobster and shrimp of the afternoon feast. Round tables with pink tablecloths and candles had appeared magically on the lawn, and over the smell of baked ham wafted the sharp odors of salt and rotting seaweed from the Long Island Sound.

Nicholas was trying to get through to Orin how serious it was—and not succeeding. "Don't you see, Orin? Elihu's trying to split us—you and me—as he has split all the others."

They were talking about Elihu's phone call that had brought Orin back from the Sargasso Sea in a rush. They were as close to a quarrel as the two brothers ever got.

"If the institute shuts down, all the research we have begun on sea agriculture goes down the drain. Research has to be continuous or it loses validity. You can't just interrupt it like that," Orin was saying. The two brothers were seated at one of the pink tables.

Sea agriculture was going to be the green revolution of the next century. Raising fish and edible grasses in the great wastes of empty ocean to feed, not the starving millions in Ethiopia now, but the starving billions of the twenty-first century. Very big stuff indeed. Orin, the idealist.

Nicholas exasperated. "Oh, for heaven's sake, Orin, we don't even know if there'll *be* a twenty-first century. I'm talking about right *now*. If you take this *bribe* from Elihu—"

"It's not a bribe," said Orin passionately, "it's my own money."

"It's a bribe! You can keep playing games with your damned submarine if you recognize that phony will of Elihu's. You're being seduced by Elihu, the murderer of our father."

"Oh, Nicholas." Orin had to talk loudly to get over the singer who was singing "Just One of Those Things." "We don't *know* that Elihu murdered our father. We're supposing."

A very large break in brotherly solidarity. The two of them had never before questioned the complicity of Elihu.

Nicholas was staggered by this betrayal. Orin was staring at him angrily.

"And I'm not playing games with that damned submarine," added Orin bitterly. "We're doing important marine biology. If you can't see the difference, Nicholas..."

Oh, he could see the difference all right. But Nicholas had always been a little jealous of the importance of marine biology in Orin's life. It had slipped out, that unkind remark. Too late Nicholas tried to repair things.

"Orin, listen! Lemuel Stork saw that business in the rigging. He won't talk about it to me but he might just talk to the District Attorney. Stork is coming to New York to talk to the Assistant District Attorney, Louis Hanagan."

That's as far as he got. Robin was standing at the table then and she bore off Orin to the dance floor, leaving Nicholas alone at the pink-topped table. Nicholas watched the two of them swooping about the dance floor in each other's arms, consumed by loneliness.

A great many things happened at that wedding as they do at most big fashionable weddings. Marilee Livingston met a Harvard boy who introduced her to cocaine and other bad habits. Hortense Worth was sized up in the ladies' room by Annalee Marples who took Hortense's pointed face in her hand and kissed her on the lips. "Not here," murmured Hortense, who decided at that moment that she had waited long enough for Robin. Madeline Forbes had a little too much champagne and left her husband to go off with Randy Tillinghast and that was the end of that marriage.

The bride and groom had gone off long before most of these things happened. The marriage which Robin had predicted would last ten years actually lasted twenty-five and didn't break up until all three children had left home.

But of all the consequences the most serious was the rupture between the brothers Worth. When Robin returned to the pink-topped table twenty minutes later, she was alone.

"Where's Orin?" asked Nicholas.

"Gone," said Robin.

"Where?"

"The Sargasso Sea," said Robin blankly. "Imagine! I thought I had more sex appeal than the Sargasso Sea, but it seems I don't." Robin sipped a bit of Nicholas' champagne. "I gather you two had words. What on earth did you say to him?"

"It isn't what I said to him," said Nicholas savagely. "It's what Elihu said to him."

"Elihu has split the Brothers Inseparable? That *is* serious. . . ."

CHAPTER 25

Sylvia was standing naked next to the horizontal mirror as Elihu buggered her brutally while whispering Buddhist philosophy in her right ear. Very intellectualized high kink. She was being Gandhi while he was Nehru, Sylvia playing not only a male but a homosexual male (which she doubted Gandhi was). In any case, a historic personage. If we have to do all this role playing, Sylvia had asked Elihu, why can't I just once be a nameless black whore? Must I always be the empress? (Of course, she wasn't always the empress; frequently she was the emperor—spread eagled and crying for mercy.)

Sylvia, besotted, played the game because Elihu wanted it and it was her hold on him, maybe her only hold. Sylvia had never subscribed to that sexist theory that love to a man is a thing apart, 'tis a woman's whole existence. Elihu wasn't her whole existence; she had husband, friends, social life, but at the moment he was the most important thing, whereas she wasn't anything like the most important thing in Elihu's life.

The telephone rang (as it did often during these jousts). Elihu, without a pause in his buggery—in fact, thrusting even more savagely—picked up the phone with one hand while holding her to himself with the other and said, "Yes?" With a rising inflection.

It was an exercise he enjoyed, talking on the telephone while, at the same time screwing (or buggering, as the case might be), engaging one end of himself in carnality, the other in some other, more cerebral knavery. While buggering her or screwing her, Elihu had ordered stock market speculation on the telephone; he had once flirted outrageously with some other woman while the bottom half of him disported with Sylvia. It was a mark of Sylvia's infatuation that she didn't pull his cock out of her on that occasion and bite it off.

Elihu was acutely aware of the effect of these phone calls on Sylvia. It was part of his pleasure to—as it were—displeasure her, part of the dominance, part of the game which, to her distress, Sylvia enjoyed as much as he did.

This telephone call was different. All motion stopped in the hindquarters as Elihu listened. He was a very good listener and this time he listened motionless; when he spoke it was with high glee; "Marvelous!" he said, hitting every syllable. Marv-e-lous! "Tell Mauriello thank you, thank you, thank you!"

With each thank-you came a powerful thrust into her hind end culminating in so sweeping an orgasm that Sylvia had one too.

Mauriello!

Thank you! Thank you! Thank you!

For what was he thanking the *capo di capo*?

It sent a chill of fear through Sylvia which left her weak and trembling. Later, when she was getting dressed—the sessions were getting shorter and shorter—she asked him (casting about for anything to hold him there a little longer), "Why didn't you come to the wedding? You would have found much to amuse you."

He shrugged, buttoning his shirt. "Weddings make me nervous. They're so emotional."

"William Worth was there with a very strange young man named Ahmet Ali." Sylvia watching Elihu closely.

Elihu stopped the buttoning and looked Sylvia full in the face. "Yes?" he said.

I've got his full attention, thought Sylvia. "I just thought you might be interested. I was dancing with Uncle Will and he was being very mysterious about this young man. In the next breath he was asking why you weren't at the wedding and I thought to myself there is some connection between this young man and Elihu. So there you are. I am the master spy Mata Hari and I expect a little appreciation."

She had certainly struck a nerve. Elihu was standing there half dressed, without his shoes and socks, his shirt half buttoned, his eyes smoldering. He was furious. Or so she thought. She had never seen him furious before. It was always Sylvia who got mad and it was Elihu who soothed her with endearments and his toothy smile. Elihu who remained above it all, too damned far above it all.

Here he was furious.

Saying nothing. Twisting the ring on his left hand with the thumb and forefinger of the right hand, back and forth, a mannerism he had when he was thinking. He's right here in the room with me, Sylvia was thinking, maybe for the first time, the whole man. Always before she had got the distinct impression Elihu was playing her as an angler might play a fish—full of talk, bright talk, but (like the sex) a role, a game, a form of relaxation, like shuffleboard.

Now Elihu was fully engaged, body, mind and soul, all of him. All because she'd mentioned Ahmet Ali.

"He's a Worth," said Sylvia, fanning the flames, "who changed his name to Ahmet Ali and became a Moslem."

"Is he staying with Uncle Will?"

"I don't know where he's staying."

"Uncle Will brought him to the wedding?" Elihu was hammering away at her, hot-eyed, sullen. He looked like a teenage hoodlum. For the first time Sylvia realized how young he was. This brilliant twenty-two-year-old with his keen mind was an emotional six-year-old!

It was the next day at breakfast that Sylvia stumbled across the item. Sylvia was not a great newspaper reader and in fact she wasn't reading the paper, she was looking at an advertisement for linens at Bloomingdale's. Next to the ad was the news item—a D head, fifteen lines long, and it struck Sylvia only because her name was in the headline.

WORTH CAPTAIN KILLED

GALVESTON, Texas—Lemuel Stork, captain of the oil exploration ship *Saint Elmo*, was killed last night when he fell from his ship to the dock where the ship was tied up. Captain Stork was directing the loading of cargo from the upper deck when he plunged to the dock on his head.

The *Saint Elmo*, part of the Worth Oil fleet, is the ship from which the financier Jasper Worth fell to his death a month ago.

Captain Stork, a Worth ship's captain for the last twenty years, had graduated from the Merchant Seaman's Academy in 1943. During World War II, he saw service in the Pacific...

Sylvia felt the world move a little under her.

"Marv-e-lous! Tell Mauriello thank you, thank you, thank you."

Sylvia could feel again each separate pelvic thrust after each gleeful thank-you.

There could be absolutely no connection between a ship's captain she didn't know plunging to his death in Galveston, Texas, and her own depraved sexual amusements. So why was she so absolutely convinced that there was?

Louis Hanagan found out about it from his own Miss Simmons. His secretary had called the ship to inform Captain Stork that a round-trip prepaid airplane ticket was awaiting him at the airport, only to be told Lem Stork was no longer among the living. She laid that information on Louis Hanagan flippantly, as was the custom in that harassed and often frustrated headquarters.

"Another witness!" she said with her tired smile. "They do fall dead in interesting ways, don't they?"

Hanagan was sorting into some sort of coherence one of his eleven prosecutions, but he found time to call Nicholas Worth. "I think perhaps you'd better stay out of tall buildings for a while," he suggested.

"Did you call Galveston? There's a fellow in the DA's office called Mortie Wainwright."

"I just spoke to Mr. Wainwright. They violently reject the idea that foul play might be involved in this thing because accidental death is so very convenient to overworked district attorneys. In the meantime, Nicholas, be careful."

He hung up.

CHAPTER 26

Alec Worth's head lay on Jessica Keswick's naked breast, Jessica stroking it tenderly. "Somebody has bruised you badly, Alec. You have whip marks all over your soul."

"How clever of you to notice," said Alec.

"That's me," said Jessica wryly, "the comforter of middle-aged men who are in love with somebody else. Do you want to talk about it?"

Alec didn't want to talk about Robin or even think about Robin. Instead he told her about Ahmet Ali. "Ahmet Ali is worth your attention as a journalist. He's a very cool guy. He says Jasper was just on the verge of throwing over Elihu and putting himself in there when the old man fell or was pushed . . ."

For all the wrong reasons, Jessica got out of bed, stark naked, walked to her portable typewriter and wrote something that was to have enormous consequences, none of which she foresaw.

What she wrote was: The Street is abuzz with speculations about the appearance here of Ahmet Ali who is—of all things—a California member of that distinguished family Worth who has changed his name and become a Moslem. Ahmet Ali, it is whispered, was to have become Number Two in Securities Unlimited, but instead he is out of a job. What's he doing here and has it anything to do with all these Worth lawsuits?

The column appeared in Jessica's column in the *Wall Street Journal* the next day, and among its many readers was Gerald Fisher, the executive vice-president of GBC in charge of news.

He summoned Robin to his office and showed it to her. Robin read the piece, her face a blank, and put it back carefully on Gerald Fisher's desk. She didn't know what was expected of her, didn't even know what she was doing in Gerald Fisher's office. She was employed by the local station; Gerald Fisher was network, not widely liked, in fact widely feared. A very tough cookie.

"I don't know Ahmet Ali—or anything about any of that," said Robin flatly.

"There's a great deal unsaid in that article, and you're a Worth."

"Are you asking me to dig up the dirt in my own family?"

"You did the wedding the other day—and, I might say, did it very well. I was especially impressed by the way you put away the Reverend J. Stokes, who is not an easy man to handle."

Robin shrugged, unsmiling. "A wedding is a wedding. This is different. This is . . ."

Murder. But she wasn't going to say that.

Gerald Fisher was on his feet now, pacing around his big office restlessly, his pale eyes stabbing into Robin. "You were very good at the wedding—very relaxed, thoroughly in command. For a beginner, you were marvelous but . . ." Here he turned on the smile for which he was infamous.

The word around GBC was when he smiled, hide under the table. ". . . you're still fantastically overpaid. You are being paid not because you're a performer but a performing Worth."

"Like a performing seal!" snapped Robin. "We don't have to be good. The very fact we perform at all—"

Gerald Fisher was pacing clear around his desk, waving his hands expressively. I'm asking you to justify the very large sum of money we're paying you, Robin, by bringing your specialized inside knowledge into play here to help us uncover what may be one of the great news stories."

"You're asking me to rat on my family," snarled Robin.

"Oh, no no no no no no no no!" Gerald Fisher was horrified, his hands straight out in front of him, disclaiming any such intent. "I wouldn't even *let* you do such a thing, Robin. It would severely damage your name and, after all, we have a large investment in your name. We don't want to damage the property. No, what I'm asking is simply that, since you have been hurt worst by this embezzlement—or whatever it is—"

"That's now being threshed out in the courts."

"That's *not* being threshed out in the courts," said Gerald Fisher. "That is the problem."

"What do you want me to do?" Even as she said it she wished she hadn't, wished she'd just said no and walked out.

Gerald Fisher was very smooth. "All I want you to do is call your Uncle Will and say 'Hey, what's all this about Ahmet Ali? What's the score? What's going on?' "

Gerald Fisher had not gotten where he was by scruples. He had inched his way up the ladder at GBC by pushing hard wherever an opening, no matter how small, was visible. He understood inches. Robin had given an inch and here Gerald Fisher took another.

"Call your Uncle Will and set up a lunch date with him and Ahmet Ali. Tell him we're terribly interested in . . . Islam.

How did a Worth become interested in Islam, and when did he become a Moslem and why? I mean, this is a very interesting thing—a Worth becoming a Moslem—and what is he doing *here*?"

That was the real nugget Gerald Fisher was after. What's he doing *here* with the chairman of the SEC and all these lawsuits?

"We might do a piece on American Moslems—Mohammed Ali, Jabbar El What's-his-name, that basketball player, you know...and now here is a white convert to Islam."

Gerald Fisher's getting his foot in the door, Robin was thinking. Just getting me to know the guy and the next meeting will be why is he here and what has this to do with Jasper's death and all the real dirt. She'd stepped one rung up the slippery ladder by doing the wedding (which was not the station's idea at all, which happened to be Robin's idea as a device to get free of Sue Endicott, and now look where it led).

Robin said, "Would this be a network assignment?" She wanted at all costs to get away from Sue Endicott.

"Absolutely," said Gerald Fisher silkily. "Your salary, Robin, can't be justified at the local level anyway. But right here I'd like to urge you to keep GBC's name out of it, at least at first. Call your Uncle Will in your own name and in your own interest. After all, your fortune has been stolen, Robin. You have every right to be interested. Find out what the man is doing here."

There it was. Deception. Gerald Fisher taking his final inch. It was immoral, it was filthy. It was also very interesting. Robin Worth had been a TV reporter just long enough to acquire a taste for blood, and this story had a lot of blood to it. Her bloodhound instincts were aroused. She was a journalist on the scent, damn it.

She'd caught a glimpse of Ahmet Ali sitting with her Uncle Will at the wedding, this laid-back California character with the gold granny glasses. She was interested if only because he wasn't. He'd glanced at her through those gold glasses and then looked away, bored. Robin was one of those girls who was turned on by indifference if only because she got so little of it. Any man who could turn away from the Golden Girl that casually must be turned on by something else. What? Religion? Every woman wanted to fuck a priest, if only for the difficulty of the thing, as the old saying went.

"Okay," said Robin. "I'll call Uncle Will."

CHAPTER 27

"Until the beginning of the sixteenth century, Moslem thinkers were far ahead of ours in medicine, in astronomy, in mathematics, in lots of other things. The Moslem Emperor Aurangzeb created his own welfare state in India in the seventeenth century—free kitchens, free places to sleep for the poor. He outlawed prostitution and tried to cure corruption and superstition, although, of course, he didn't have any better luck at that than the other reformers."

In the bright June early-morning sunshine as Robin trotted at Ahmet Ali's heels around the reservoir in Central Park. *Not* jogging. Ahmet Ali didn't believe in jogging. Ruined the instep, damaged the tendons, overstressed the heart muscle. But he walked very fast indeed, this slim California Moslem, and Robin had to come close to jogging to keep up.

"Aurangzeb wanted to change the very nature of the human beast. He tried to cure alcoholism among his subjects, to curb their sexual vices."

"No sexual vices?" panted Robin. Ahmet Ali didn't appear to have any of those either. She had turned on all her charms and had succeeded only in increasing the flow of talk. Entrancing talk, but still . . .

"If you're really interested in this stuff, you must read up on Shah Wahliullah, probably the greatest Moslem intellectual of India. He was wise to the whole class structure of society—the ruling class, and all that—in the eighteenth century. A hundred years before Karl Marx he pointed out that labor was the basis of all wealth and that the laboring classes did all the work and got none of the wealth."

They were off the reservoir path now, on to the Promenade, at his six-mile-an-hour pace, and then on to the Great Lawn where Robin maneuvered him to a park bench and sat him down, interrupting the monologue, making Ahmet Ali pay some attention, if only briefly, to her. He was actually looking at her now, as if she were some rare kind of bug, as she fiddled with her tape recorder which might or might not be taking all this down. It was revolving away, recording the silence. She turned it off. It was sometimes the best way to get people to open up.

"Let's go back a bit, Ahmet," she said, still fiddling with the tape recorder, feeling his gaze on her through his granny glasses, the weight of his indifference. "What got you on to Islam in the first place?"

He shrugged. "School, I guess." Ahmet, then known as Alexander Worth, had gone to Mount Hebron Academy, a school for incredibly gifted children, all of them with astonishing IQs. "I did a term paper and then I got emotionally involved. I was pissed off with the Worth family."

"Many of us are," commented Robin dryly. "We don't become Moslems."

"I'd gone through, you know, the usual junk, Marxism, socialism when I was ten. I hated the materialism of all that. Marxism is murder. Socialism is slavery."

He came out with these sweeping indictments with unimpassioned certitude. "Marxism is murder! Socialism is slavery!" said Robin faintly. "I have never heard those phrases before."

"My own," said Ahmet Ali negligibly. "No other phrases fit the facts quite that snugly."

He had the Worth self-confidence all right, this laid-back Californian who was pissed off at the Worth family.

"I'm sure Uncle Jasper must have been entranced with those phrases. How did he come upon you?"

"He spent the night at our house. Just dropped in and invited himself for the night. Dad and Mother didn't even know him."

Robin remembered what Alec had said—that the eastern Worths used the western Worths as a kind of boardinghouse whenever they were in the vicinity.

"We talked Islam half through the night. He was a very shrewd old cuss. Very interested in the Arabs in California because they're all into oil but also fascinated by the Moslem use of power, their philosophy *about* power which is so much different from ours. Islam means *surrender*—surrender to God. There has never been any of this nonsense about separation of church and state in Moslem society because Islam *is* a state. Mohammed wasn't founding a church; he was founding a state."

The discourse flowed on and on like that so long as the subject was Islam, but when Robin tried to interject a more personal note, tried to get Ahmet Ali to talk about himself as a Worth, about his role in seducing the local sheikhs out of the Bank of America and into Securities Unlimited, the golden flow stopped. Ahmet Ali went as silent as a rock.

Sitting there on a park bench, Robin said, "Surely you couldn't have been altogether uninterested in materialism if Uncle Jasper was going to make you number-two man at Securities Unlimited."

Ahmet Ali looked at the blue sky; he looked at the

squeaking children in the playground; he looked at his feet. It was an *active* silence, crawling with meaning and thunderous with disapproval.

Robin had tried talking him out of these silences and had got nowhere. This time she closed her eyes, leaned back on the park bench and listened to the birds. I'm as much Worth as he is; I can be just as stubborn, just as indifferent. The sunlight on her eyelids turning her interior world into slashes of purple and red and velvety black.

It was Ahmet Ali who broke the silence. The words were unyielding. "The Koran demands that Moslems be honorable. It forbids dishonor."

Robin with her eyes closed turned to the sun and had trouble keeping a straight face. The Koran forbids dishonor. Wow! That along with Marxism is murder; Socialism is slavery.

"Dishonor is what this is all about," said Robin, eyes still closed. She would have had difficulty saying that line with her eyes open. Dishonor was not an easy word to cope with in ordinary conversation. "Some of us Worths feel that a great dishonor has been already committed and that it ought to be..." She hesitated before coming up with another word she would have had difficulty saying with her eyes open. "Avenged. Or punished. Or rectified. Or something."

She opened her eyes and smiled at him and stood up. "Would it be dishonorable if I bought you lunch? I'm famished."

"I'm a vegetarian," said Ahmet Ali.

"The GBC expense account is extraordinarily permissive. It embraces all races, creeds, colors—even vegetarians."

She took him to Aspic on Columbus Avenue where they both feasted on cottage cheese, raw vegetables and a green salad washed down with goat's milk. Somewhere in the middle of all this health food, Ahmet Ali actually smiled at her, as if he found her pleasing. Robin smiled back. "What are you really doing here—so far from California, Ahmet?"

"Am I talking to a Worth—or a journalist?"

Both. That was the great problem. Robin was turning into a journalist, willy-nilly, almost against her will, yielding to the siren call of journalism like an addict to cocaine. She couldn't reveal her own disapproval of her own actions to this unflinching (and very young) Moslem so she said, "A Worth." Hoping it was true.

"In my religion, we have nothing like vengeance is mine saith the Lord. Our Lord doesn't say any such thing. Vengeance is honorable and the Koran bids honor."

"Welcome to the club," said Robin.

Ahmet Ali looked at her sternly through the gold granny glasses. "The Koran doesn't say anything about broadcasting this on GBC. That would be dishonorable. Also self-defeating."

Robin reported all this back to the Great White Shark (as she had come to call Gerald Fisher, though not to his face), but heavily edited. "He will talk your arm off about the Moslems, about American Moslems—Muhammed Ali and all that crowd—but he clams up when you interject the name Worth in there."

Knowing full well that the Worth name was what Gerald Fisher was mostly interested in. "We combed the sixteenth century. Also the seventeenth. Do you want a nice oration on the Moslem sixteenth and seventeenth centuries?"

Gerald Fisher scarcely aware such centuries existed. Anything later than an hour ago was too late. "What about Moslem cash flow? Into the country? Out of the country? Are they bankrupting the U.S.A.? What about Moslem sex life in this country? Are they ravishing American teenagers?"

There began what Robin called The Crawl—Gerald Fisher's chair getting closer and closer to hers, his foot suggestively touching hers. Robin moved her foot out of range and said, "We discussed Shah Wahliullah, the greatest Moslem intellectual of India, who was way ahead of Karl Marx on the class struggle. Would you like a nice documentary on that?''

"Oh, for Christ's sake!"

Gerald Fisher wanted some hot blood in the story. (So did Robin.) Gerald Fisher also wanted a little hot blood right there in the office and Robin was not about to let him have that.

He hadn't quite got to the point where he chased her around the desk, but that day was approaching. She reported it to her agent, Henrietta Mills, a very tough cookie. "Can I belt him? Or would I get the heave?"

"You wouldn't get the heave because the contract wouldn't permit it but you'd get the old freeze. You would never get another assignment and when contract time came around, you'd be out on your little fastidious ass."

"Are you telling me I have to sleep with this bastard?"

"No, I'm saying handle him. You've handled men before, Robin. Between the mattress and a belt in the kisser there are other alternatives. String him along."

Robin had never strung anyone along because she'd never had to. She belted them. Or leaped into their arms. She'd never had to play games, because why? Now the situation was different. Gerald Fisher was a very powerful man at the network and she loved her job, loved the smell of news, the excitement, the challenge, the whole bit.

At the same time, she hadn't done enough on the air to be able to walk out of one network and right into another. Handle the Great White Shark! What fun!

"Keep in touch," said Henrietta Mills. "I don't know what I can do. I could warn him off but if I did, *I'd* be in the deep freeze—and I've got a lot of clients over there. Still, I'd like to know what's up."

"Yeah," said Robin.

She was playing a double game with Gerald Fisher in more ways than one. She had said nothing to him about vengeance in the family circle. That was the very heart of the story and she hadn't mentioned it and wouldn't. She couldn't. She wished it were some other family because what a story it would be! But, of course, if it were some other family, she wouldn't be handling it, wouldn't be at GBC at all probably. So there she was: she owed her job to being a member of the Worth family, didn't want to betray the family and was torn in half by the journalistic urge to Tell All. (An impulse in journalists much stronger than hunger or sex.)

The very next day a story appeared discreetly in the business section of the *New York Times* to the effect that Orin Worth was withdrawing from the lawsuit challenging what had become known as the Elihu Will, the Jasper Worth will which made Elihu trustee of the whole inheritance. Since there were a raft of other Worths still suing Elihu, the *Times* couldn't say what this withdrawal meant or if it meant anything at all.

Robin tried to call Orin to find out and discovered he had returned to the Sargasso Sea—his submarine, the viper fish, his absorption in feeding the unborn. From her Uncle Will Robin discovered Orin had made some kind of deal with Elihu which freed a million and a half to support the Ocean Institute. "In other words, Orin is free to spend his own money on the Ocean Institute. That's very generous of Elihu—letting Orin spend his money."

William Worth's white eyebrows flared dangerously. "Elihu is still trustee of Orin's fortune. Also Nicholas' and all Jasper's children's. It gives him great scope to perform his mischief—and he's a very clever operator. The first to really understand the role of the computer. The word is he's installed a mainframe computer in that new apartment he's bought his mother. God knows what he's up to. He might be trying to beggar Nicholas and Orin as he has beggared you."

"Why? He's very rich in his own right. Why?"

William Worth shook his silvery mane. He didn't know. "He's splitting the family into little warring fragments—among other things Nicholas versus Orin, which I never thought would happen. But why?" He sighed. "What did you children do to him? Whatever it was he's getting back at you. . . ."

Robin called Nicholas and discovered he was out of the country. Doing what? Robin had no idea and in an attempt to find out she dropped in on her Aunt Estelle whose Worth Collection furniture was now in display windows all over New York. Estelle had looted a half dozen Worth attics and warehouses—and the stuff, insanely overpriced, was selling like Coca-Cola.

Venetian walnut chairs of the late seventeenth century, Dutch ebony washstands, English bedsteads of carved oak dating from the fifteenth century, Spanish sideboards from the thirteenth century, Moorish doors with iron hinges designed to repel battering rams—all of it, according to Robin, hideous and totally impractical. She could well understand why the stuff had been consigned to Worth attics, couldn't understand why anyone wanted this junk.

Robin found her Aunt Estelle in her West Side apartment working a hand press and singing "There's No Business Like Show Business"—those words she could remember—in a cracked falsetto, over and over and over, her face wreathed in a slightly manic smile.

"What on earth are you doing, Aunt Estelle?"

Estelle was bearing down hard on the handle. She brought the handle up sharply and removed from the hand press a beautifully lettered document.

"Forgery," said Estelle, and laughed her cracked laugh.

It wasn't quite forgery. What she had just turned out was a document which attested to the fact that a sixteenth-century Belgian washstand had indubitably come from a Worth atelier. (Atelier, what a word!) It didn't say that the washstand was indubitably sixteenth-century Belgian (though—of course, it clearly implied that) but that it was indubitably once owned by a member of the Worth family which was incontestable but hardly hot news since there were hundreds of Worths, many of them without taste or distinction of any kind.

"How can you sleep nights turning out waffle like that?"

"I sleep beautifully. Taking the suckers for all they've got. When have the Worths done otherwise?" Estelle was shifting the type on the hand press, her hands covered with black ink. "We've always taken the suckers, honey. You think we gave honest measure when we sold 'em all that gunpowder in the Revolutionary War? Go on!" She bore down on the handle, singing in her cracked falsetto:

"Yesterday they said you would not go far!
"Last night you opened and they were right!"

Which isn't quite the way Irving Berlin wrote that song.

"I'm making the customers happy is what I'm doing, Robin. They want a document, they shall have a document. What's the matter with that? I tell you something, Robin. You and I are the lucky ones. We've been kicked out of the nest and we both had to go out and make it on our own and I have found—and I think you have too—that life is much more zestful, much more surprising, much more satisfying."

She came up with another dubious document of beautifully printed waffle.

"You don't thirst for revenge, Aunt Estelle?"

"Revenge for what? You think I want to go back to my old spinster existence, plodding along in the wake of Prudence, living on the emotional crumbs from her table? Being stolen blind by my servants? I'm alive, Robin. A living breathing swindler in the furniture trade which is just one great big swindle anyway. How badly were the Worths swindled when they originally bought all this trash?"

Robin doubted the Worths were swindled very much. There were the swindlers, born that way, with a lot of swindle in their genes. Then there were the swindlees whom nature put on earth to be the natural prey of the swindlers, like bugs devoured by birds. The swindlees went about begging to be swindled. It was their natural function, their purpose in life.

Listen to me, thought Robin, listening to herself. I would never have had ideas like this before . . . Before what? Before being swindled, before journalism, before the Great White Shark had come into her life.

"You're looking positively evil, Robin. What is crossing your little mind?"

Robin smiled her professional smile, the one she used on the air just before she stuck the knife in. "Aunt Estelle, how do you . . . deliver the furniture after you sell it to the suckers? You do deliver, don't you?"

"Jeremy takes care of all that. MacLean Movers are the only ones he trusts to treat the furniture decently."

"I suppose they can get in anywhere—furniture movers?"

"What did you have in mind, Robin?"

Robin laughed. "I don't know yet." She kissed the leathery cheek. "I'll let you know when I know what I'm up to, you old swindler."

CHAPTER 28

Elihu was fucking Sylvia very slowly, the way she loved it best, nothing kinky at all, which was highly unusual, caressing her lips with soft kisses, making her moan with rapture. All too good to be true, of course, because even while she hovered on the very brink of orgasm, he was whispering to her, "I want you to do something for me, my darling!"

Not the time to be asking favors, her arms and legs writhing around Elihu like convulsive snakes. "Will you, my darling?" Holding her thrashing body off from its magnificent climax. "Anything! Anything!" Sylvia was gasping. "Oh, Elihu! Elihu! Elihu!" But he was holding back now, keeping her from it, depriving her of her ecstasy, and through a blur of pleasure–pain she could see his face twisted in one of his great evil grins.

" 'Anything! Anything!' I'll hold you to it," said Elihu, himself not carried away at all, watching her writhe as if she were an exercise in chemistry, making her wait and wait for it, tormenting her which ordinarily she loved, but not this, not this . . . reptilian abnegation. . . .

She had played every kind of game, submitted in every type of posture, all of it to increase his pleasure and her own, but this, this was different, and after he had finally released her torment, made her come magnificently, and she lay spent and heaving, he repeated, "I shall hold you to it." Always before the sex games had ended with climax but not now. This time he was pulling the sex fantasy into post-coital reality. And that she didn't like at all.

" 'Anything! Anything!' " he repeated, as she lay there, wishing he'd shut up and leave her alone. She closed her eyes and was silent, hoping. It was no good. He was all over with his hands and his smile and his silky voice.

"I want you to find out where Ahmet Ali is staying. A very simple request."

Very simple indeed. So simple that he could manage it himself very easily. There were all sorts of agencies in New York that could run down the address and telephone number of anyone up to and including Mafia hoodlums—and a barracuda like Elihu knew them all. There could be no other reason for his demanding such a thing from her except . . . what? Continuance of the sexual bondage? No, Elihu wasn't like that. When the sex games were over they were over, and Elihu was usually dressed and out of there in five minutes. This request had some deeper and more sinister purpose.

Complicity?

Lovely word, complicity. With her eyes closed, Sylvia said, in loving tones because she didn't want to anger him, "Darling, Dora Land could find Ahmet Ali for you in five minutes."

"But I want *you* to do it."

There it was. The thumbscrew, the chain.

"I'm not a tracer agency, Elihu. I wouldn't know where to begin."

"Call your Uncle Will. He knows."

"You could call Uncle Will."

"But I want *you* to do it. You said you'd do anything."

She opened her eyes then and faced him. "Why do you want me to do it?"

Immediately she wished she hadn't. He went into one of his terrible silences and began pulling on his clothes. "Oh, Elihu! Elihu!" Pleading with him now, trying to coax him out of the sulks. But he would say nothing, the face in fury. Sylvia, devastated, said, "I'll do it! I'll do it! I'll do it *now*."

She grabbed the white phone which was on a long, long cord next to the bed and was never very far from Elihu, no matter what wild sexual calisthenics they were performing, dialed William Worth's office. Elihu dressing, the eyes molten.

Uncle Will was not in his office and Miss Trimingham didn't know when he'd be back.

"I'll try him later," said Sylvia. "I'll get him at home this evening if I don't get him—"

Elihu walked out of the apartment without looking at her.

Sylvia in tears, which both frightened and astonished her. She, Sylvia Settle, the mocking, witty, worldly veteran of a thousand amours—*crying!* Over this bastard!

Not the first time either. The second. The day before he'd—teasingly—said she should transfer her portfolio from Morgan Guaranty which had looked after her fortune since she was a little girl to Securities Unlimited and she had—teasingly (keeping it light and amusing)—said she wouldn't dream of having a crook like himself handling her affairs. He'd gone into a towering rage—scary and astonishing. After all, she'd called him a crook many times, and he'd laughed and topped her joke with better ones at his own expense, taking delight in his own knavery. But not yesterday. Yesterday the mood change had been volcanic; he'd been into his clothes and out of the apartment in minutes, leaving Sylvia in tears. She hadn't expected to hear from him again, maybe for weeks, but he'd been on the telephone that morning.

hard to be executive vice-president of Robin Worth. The creeping chair bit, the little interplay with the toes, had developed into open pursuit around and around the desk, around Gerald's vast office with all its impedimenta—coffee tables, leather chair, end tables.

The Great White Shark had quite accurately assessed Robin's need—her need of the money, her even greater need and love of the job with its excitement and challenge—and was cold-bloodedly trying to exact his price. Robin was having none of it. She was a warm-blooded woman, normally very casual about sex, but not this, not this! Gerald Fisher didn't love her, didn't even desire her really, wanted only to possess the Golden Girl, wanted to humiliate her, wanted to own her.

There was no talk during these pursuits which started almost the moment she got into the office. There was not anything to discuss, as if language had not been invented, just this mindless athleticism, around the desk, over the chair, around the coffee table, feint this way, that way, him snatching, Robin evading, wordless, ridiculous (rather fun in its ridiculousness). Robin was a natural athlete, had always kept herself in shape, with tennis, swimming, and kung fu lessons—and she won these exercises every time, outlasting Gerald Fisher until he finally collapsed at his desk, breathing heavily.

Robin would sit primly in the leather chair in front of his vast desk (where he couldn't spring at her) and wait until the heavy breathing subsided. Then she'd talk about Ahmet Ali, an assignment that wasn't going well. She had learned more about Islam than she wanted to know (and far more than Gerald wanted to know). When she tried to question Ahmet about his personal life, she ran into a blank wall.

"We know—or think we do—that Jasper was going to replace Elihu with Ahmet Ali. Ahmet has said this to several people. He won't go public with it. His Moslem honor is at stake."

Gerald Fisher would suggest questions to ask, angles to take; he was very shrewd about openings, about vulnerabilities, about soft spots in the psyche, about visual possibilities.

There'd be no mention of the chase by either of them. None at all.

The next day she'd confer with Gerald again and the pursuit would resume.

Ridiculous.

That day she'd appeared at the outer office where Jane Fox, a very pretty twenty-year-old receptionist who—it was said—was screwing the Great White Shark in addition to her other duties, greeted her with her little vixen grin (as if she knew what was going on in there) and waved her into the huge office with its fine view of Central Park.

There was no one in it.

Robin closed the door behind her and leaned against it, listening. No sound. She looked at the great American flag which hung from its pole behind Gerald's head (Gerald asserting his and GBC's passionate Americanism), at the six monitors on the south wall (none turned on) which gave Gerald access to the newscasts of his rivals, at the leather sofa (the ultimate destination she was so determined to avoid).

No Gerald. This was some new ploy in the ridiculous game. Robin sighed and drifted along the wall, looking at Gerald's collection of photographs. Gerald shaking hands with Harry Truman, exchanging grins with Eisenhower, arm around Mick Jagger, face to face with the Pope—all those intimate family snapshots of the man on the make.

Robin not knowing what was coming but knowing something was. Now she'd passed the door to Gerald Fisher's personal toilet (you had to be very important to get your very own private toilet) and was looking at a photograph of Gerald lecturing Khrushchev when she heard the toilet door open behind her. She spun around to face him and there was Gerald Fisher, executive vice-president in charge of news, wearing his great shark grin and nothing else.

If you don't count the erection.

He was a foot away from her, far closer than he'd ever got in those silly chases. Just for a second she was paralyzed with astonishment (which was perhaps the idea) and in that moment his right hand caught her left hand and yanked—the worst thing he could have done. All her kung fu training exploded at once, involuntarily, mindlessly, instinctively. She grasped his right wrist with both hands, spun on her heels which turned his right arm over and placed it on her shoulder, his arm outstretched, palm uppermost. In the same motion, she bent her upper body sharply at the waist, both arms pulling down on Gerald Fisher's right arm, shattering it, and propelling him over her back, head first into the floor where he lay very still.

She wished she hadn't. Wished it hadn't happened. Wished it were five minutes ago. Gerald lying there face up, blood running out of nose and mouth.

Robin on her knees now, feeling the pulse, head on the chest, listening. Why in God's name had she pulled the rough stuff! She hadn't meant to! Hadn't wanted this! She'd practiced this movement again and again until it got to be second nature to protect her against *rapists*. But not Gerald (though, of course, rapist was what he was).

There was some pulse, some breath. Not very much.

Robin got off the floor and picked up the phone.

"Jane," she said to Jane Fox. "I think you'd better come in here."

Jane Fox came and said, "Oh, my God." Taking it all in, sharp little twenty-year-old that she was, knowing what had probably happened, what was at stake, what had to be done, what—above all—needed *not* to be done, what—at all costs—must be avoided.

"Is he alive?"

"Just."

Jane Fox picked up the phone, dialing New York Hospital

and while waiting for the ring, very cool, "What did you hit him with?"

"I didn't. It's a kung fu trick, over the shoulder and—oh *God* I wish I hadn't!"

"You didn't," said Miss Fox. "He fell." Then into the phone. "New York Hospital? We need an ambulance and it's an emergency. GBC will pay but you must make it fast. Internal bleeding! Come to the West Eighty-second Street entrance and take the elevator to the twenty-fifth floor. Room 2560. Got that? Okay!"

She hung up.

"We've got to get his clothes on," said little Miss Fox, age twenty, cool as spring water. "The clothes will be in the john. Get them."

The shirt was the hardest part because the right arm was shattered at the elbow and getting that arm into the sleeve, the bone grinding on the elbow socket, stabbed Robin to her very bottom.

Not Miss Fox, who said, "Nice trick. You must teach it to me."

"Never!"

Robin was buttoning up the shirt while Jane Fox was pulling on the shorts. "There'll be questions if he has no shorts on," she said. "He was demonstrating kung fu to you—he does things like that—always showing off, and he got it wrong and fell."

"Nobody'll believe that. Not with that shattered arm, that knock on the head."

"If you can think of a better explanation..." The two women pulling on the trousers now, Gerald on his back, blood dribbling from the mouth.

"Something fell on him," said Robin. "Something heavy." She was pulling on Gerald's socks, followed by his shoes. Gerald was dressed now, far enough. The two women were looking about the office for an alibi, following that most ancient law of journalism which is that news is what happens to other people—never to journalists. (And certainly never to an executive vice-president in charge of network news.)

"The monitors," said Jane Fox. "Come on."

The six monitors were set in a wooden frame that had been built to the left of Gerald's desk. They were very heavy and there was no way they could lay the thing down carefully. In the end, the two women had to push it over, sending it crashing to the floor, hoping the crash wouldn't be heard anywhere else, glass flying all over the place.

"He was demonstrating kung fu—flying through the air— and he miscalculated and hit the bottom rung and that tipped it over on him, breaking his arm and his head," said Jane Fox. "We got him out from under there and called the hospital."

It made very little sense. It might even be possible to prove physically it couldn't happen. Still, they had to go with it because they had nothing else. When the interns came, they were occupied solely with shooting plasma into Gerald, getting him onto a stretcher and into the ambulance— in short, with saving his life, not with what had caused this predicament. They were specialists in accident treatment, not in investigation.

Robin, overwhelmed by contrition, insisted on going along to the hospital, but before she left, Jane Fox dragged her into the private toilet where Gerald had undressed and told her fiercely, "Don't tell them anything about that busted arm. Let *them* find it. Don't say anything at all. Just shake your head and say you don't remember, you don't know. Stay out of it." As if she'd been in the alibi business all her life.

Actually, no one paid much attention to Robin at the hospital; the doctors concentrated their attentions on Gerald, who had lapsed into a coma which was to last two years.

CHAPTER 29

Sylvia stood as stiff as a board before the receptionist on the fifteenth floor of the GBC newsroom where an aged woman named Ella Mae Barnes stood guard implacably. Ella Mae Barnes was typing a memo, not even looking at Sylvia. "Nobody is allowed in there without an appointment, madam."

"I am her Aunt Sylvia." It cost Sylvia dearly to make any such admission. She hated being an aunt.

"It makes no—" Ella Mae broke off and looked up at Sylvia, who didn't look like anyone's aunt. "Robin's *aunt*!" Grumbling, Ella Mae picked up the phone and dialed. "Robin. Your Aunt Sylvia is here. Shall I send her in?"

"God no! She'll get lost! I'll come get her."

Robin kissed Sylvia on the cheek, not asking why on earth she was there, not in front of Ella Mae, and led her through the maze, through the wire room with its almost silent printers spewing out news from all over the world, through the newsroom with its whispering word processors,

down a back iron circular stairs, and then—very quietly—
through the back end of Studio Four where a newswoman
named Hildy Beck was interviewing Marilee Selzer on her
plans to run for Mayor of New York which was being taped
in advance, then up another set of iron steps to a cubbyhole
with a typewriter, filing cabinets and a telephone.

"This is your *office*?"

"They're trying to find me another one. I only went
network a couple of weeks ago. Sit there, Aunt Sylvia. My
God, aren't you elegant in that gray check!" *Not* saying
what the hell are you doing here? Robin had just come from
the hospital. It was ten days after Gerald Fisher had taken
the fall.

Sylvia fussed with her handbag (something she never
did), ill at ease (which she never was). "I should have
called. I didn't want to say it on the telephone."

Good heavens! Her self-possessed Aunt Sylvia, coolest of
icebergs, in this state of disarray. Robin sat at her desk and
waited, hands folded in her lap. She'd learned how to wait,
the hardest lesson in interviewing. Aunt Sylvia looked (for
the first time in Robin's experience) vulnerable. Also furious. The two things together, vulnerable and furious.

"Ahmet Ali," said Sylvia finally, fiddling with her bag.
"Uncle Will said you know more about him than anyone
else. Where's he staying?"

"At the Harvard Club. Why?"

There followed a long silence, Sylvia fiddling with the
bag, big eyes tormented. Again Robin waited. A very long
time.

"Get him out of there!" Sylvia had to force it out of her,
and when she finally did, she uttered a deep sigh that
seemed to come from her ankles upwards. "Get him out of
there! Put him somewhere that no one knows about, somebody else's place, but keep it a secret."

"I don't know that he'd go," said Robin calmly. "He's a
very independent young man. What's this all about, Auntie?"

Sylvia hated being called Auntie even worse than Aunt Sylvia. She stopped fiddling with her handbag and glared at Robin. "I can't tell you that! But I think the boy's in danger! Get him out of the Harvard Club or there'll be another one of those accidents." She stood up abruptly. "Like the one that happened to that poor Captain Stork." Sylvia marched to the door. "You mustn't tell anyone I told you this or you'll put me in danger."

She walked out of the cubbyhole and down the iron circular steps, tap tap tap tap. Robin didn't ask for explanations. If her formidable aunt had wanted to give explanations, she would have given them.

Instead Robin pulled out her typewriter and typed on a plain sheet of white paper, "June 14. Sylvia Settle visits me here, tells me Ahmet Ali must move out of Harvard Club or he'll have same kind of accident happened to Lemuel Stork. I'm not to tell anyone this warning comes from Sylvia or she'll be in danger too. From whom? Elihu? Is Sylvia having it off with Elihu? She's a lecherous lady. She had it off for years with Jasper and Elihu is much the same stripe. A fourteen-karat bastard."

That was enough of that. Robin herself had had it off with Elihu for much the same reason. She took the white paper out of the typewriter and put it in the yellow folder along with all the other bits she'd written down lately. Too much was happening, too rapidly. She wanted a record of exactly what happened and when it happened and to whom. She didn't know why she wanted this record or what use she'd put it to, but it comforted her to get it down on paper as if it solved the many problems that had come into her life recently.

It was more than a record; it was therapy when she wrote it down, coldly, unemotionally. It took the poison out. Like lancing a boil. Whenever anger crept into her prose, she pulled the white sheet out of the typewriter, rolled it into a tight ball. Did the whole thing over—the anecdote, the thought, whatever—in prose as cold as rolled steel. Then the anger, the panic, subsided deep into the bottom of her. It didn't disappear, the emotion, oh no, she wasn't going to get off that easy. But it sank into her depths, and there it lay. Until the next time.

Added to the affair Worth was now the affair Gerald Fisher which was not strictly a family matter except that it had happened to Robin. And left its mark. Daily Robin went to New York Hospital where Gerald Fisher lay expensively in a coma. She stayed only a few minutes, every other day bringing yellow roses which she knew he loved. She sat quietly looking at Gerald's handsome face which in the coma lost all its sharkish viciousness and seemed remarkably innocent. There alone and quiet Robin expiated; an exercise like pushups (only harder) for a deed that was not all that reprehensible but for which she felt a monumental guilt as if it represented the totality of all the other guilts she should have felt but had never felt for all her rich, useless, self-indulgent life (this being the nature and prosody of Robin's self-reproach). Some went to church; Robin did her penance at Gerald's bedside.

That morning she did something she hadn't done before. Sitting there alone with the unconscious man, she had spoken aloud for the first time. "I'm bad luck, Gerald. A real bad-luck girl. It follows me around like a rain cloud and rains on whoever I happen to be with." A wholly new thought that had never before struck her. It struck her again, sitting at the typewriter, and she wrote it down with its date and how it came to be uttered.

That reminded her of her Aunt Sylvia—that cool, chic, witty, imperturbable woman storming into Robin's office in a state that could only be described as uncool, unchic, unwitty and highly perturbed. In her whole life, Robin had never seen her Aunt Sylvia perturbed about anything—wars, financial panics, death in the family. Nothing panicked Sylvia.

Except this.

Robin picked up the telephone and called the Harvard Club. "Ahmet," she said. "We've got to talk."

That is how it came about that, an hour later, Ahmet Ali moved into the little two-bedroom apartment on West Sixty-second that Robin was subletting from her friend Gilian Ray while Gilian was in Tangier. Robin shared the flat with Fergie when he was there which was almost never; Fergie disappearing in the summertime into the North Shore homes of his friends for weeks on end.

Robin had expected a fight from Ahmet, that cool young man, so she made the pitch very strong. "You are in danger," she said. "You must get out of the Harvard Club and you must be quiet about where you are living."

Ahmet Ali blinked his pale eyes behind the gold glasses and said only, "Let's go." Just like that. Robin was left with a whole lot of talk she'd prepared to persuade Ahmet to move and no need for it. She could never quite figure this cool young genius child who was so stubborn about some things and so pliant about others.

In the cab on the way to West Sixty-second, he said abruptly a single word. "Elihu." It wasn't a question; it was a flat statement.

He smiled at her absently, the glimmer of intelligence behind those gold glasses almost menacing. "Who told you I was in danger, Robin?"

"I can't tell you that. It would put my informant in danger as well, and we don't want that, do we?"

Silence then in the taxi all the way to West Sixty-second Street. Ahmet Ali was wearing his soiled white trousers, his rope-soled espadrilles, his short-sleeved cotton shirt of much washed blue.

At West Sixty-second Street Ahmet paid for the cab and took his canvas carryall up the stairs to the third-floor walkup. Robin ushered Ahmet into Fergie's room which was a mess, as always, Fergie's clothes, his books, his

Apple 2E and printer, his white socks and jeans, in a tangle all over the room. "I'm sorry," said Robin, "but this is the way my brother lives."

The Californian smiled—as if this were the way he, too, lived, as if this was the way everyone ought to live— dropped his carryall on Fergie's unmade bed and went straight to the Apple 2E, slipped in a disc, turned on the power. The screen lit up with Madcap Louise, a pursuit game that Ahmet Ali played with intense concentration, forgetting Robin altogether.

Robin watched him, a small smile on her face. He reminded her of her brother who played with his Apple with the same ferocious concentration, sometimes half through the night.

"I have to get back to work," said Robin distinctly, loudly, trying to get his attention.

He didn't take his eyes off the screen but he did hear because he raised his right hand and waggled his fingers to say good-bye. She was being dismissed.

Robin went back to the street and caught a cab back to GBC, thinking more about Ahmet Ali than she cared to, feeling (again, reluctantly) sexual for the first time in weeks. She hadn't had any sex since that unfortunate bout with Alec in the Waldorf, hadn't wanted any, and now this laid-back Californian was arousing her with his damned indifference.

Was it only that? No, it wasn't. Into her mind floated that conversation of long ago in Central Park: "The Koran demands that Moslems be honorable. It forbids dishonor." She had found that funny the first time she heard it. She didn't find it funny now. And why didn't she? Did this mark a difference in *her?* Had she lost her sense of humor? Or perhaps just gained. . . .

She didn't know what she'd gained. A sense of *honor!* Good God.

She remembered something else from that conversation.

"In my religion we have nothing like vengeance is mine saith the Lord. Our Lord doesn't say any such thing. Vengeance is honorable and the Koran bids honor."

What was Ahmet Ali, who was so California as to be in New York almost a fish out of water, actually doing in New York? Her Uncle Will had summoned him but he had come and he had stayed. Why? She didn't know, but maybe Elihu, that monster, did. "Vengeance is honorable and the Koran bids honor."

Back in her cubbyhole, the light was blinking furiously on her telephone. She was wanted in Gerald Fisher's office, which was being run temporarily by Webley Foster. Foster was putting her on the van Ruysdale death, which was all over that afternoon's *Post* like smallpox. Hendrik van Ruysdale was one of the last of an old Dutch family. He was very rich, very old and had shed a wife of twenty-five years to marry a toothsome young girl named Estee. He hadn't even survived his wedding night. Been found dead in bed with smears of blood here and there.

Sensational story and Robin, herself an aristocrat, was being put on the story to—as it were—desensationalize it, make it fit for ordinary network use. Foster wanted a minute and a half, maybe even a minute more, for the six o'clock news, which meant she had to get off her ass fast.

"I've got the crew all ready—Post on the camera, Peters directing, who do you want as producer, Harrison?"

"Not Harrison," said Robin firmly. "Jane Fox."

Webley Foster blinked and sat back on his revolving chair slowly. "Jane Fox? You mean that little girl—out there?" Vaguely pointing toward the reception room.

"She's wasted out there," said Robin briskly. "She's got more brains, more competence, and more *speed* than all six of your producers added together, Webley. She's been taught the business by Gerald Fisher," Gerald Fisher at that moment being in no condition to contradict this, "and she knows where all the bodies are and I want her."

The two young women had shared the Gerald Fisher catastrophe, had worked together as a team so smoothly, with such speed and empathy that their partnership had formed almost without their realizing it. The idea of making Jane Fox her producer had come to Robin on one of her visits to Gerald Fisher's bedside, and now she made her move on a story where GBC could hardly manage without her. There was a good deal of self-interest in this. Robin was protecting her own flanks, putting into place a young woman who would have her undying gratitude. (They were to become a team that was to endure a long time, to make TV history, but that's getting ahead of the story.)

That afternoon they worked together as if they'd been at it for years. "Get to Miriam van Ruysdale. She's Hendrik's first wife—a bitter old trout—and she's full of resentment toward Estee and she'll talk your arm off. Tell her we want her on camera."

Robin herself tackled Louis Hanagan at the District Attorney's office. "I know it's an ongoing investigation, Louis, but what is the District Attorney's office doing there at all? Because you were *seen* up there. Couldn't you give us thirty seconds on camera just to say what the death looks like or, if you like, say you have nothing at all to say—but in a meaningful way that says to the viewer you do have something to say but you can't say it yet?"

Robin forgot all about Ahmet Ali, all about sex. A hot breaking news story was its own sexual fulfillment. Robin adored the speed, the bite, the emotional rush, the mental stimulation, all of it, getting on camera, turning on her lazy half-smile, biting off her sentences with the upper-class lilt and drawl a girl only got after years at Miss Madeira's, loved it, and was very good at it, and damned well knew she was good at it.

There was the letdown afterward, always the letdown. She and Jane Fox were sitting in the cubbyhole feeling the glow fade. "We beat CBS and NBC to everything." Jane Fox with her little vixen smile saying, "I'll want a raise." Robin murmuring, "Of course." Both feeling the letdown.

The telephone rang.

Robin answered, thinking it was Webley to compliment her on how well she'd done. It wasn't Webley; it was Nicholas.

"Where the hell have you been, Nicholas?"

"Lausanne. Could we have dinner?"

"Could I bring my new producer? Very pretty girl named Jane Fox?"

"No," said Nicholas. "Family business. Very private." Nicholas sounded full of grievance.

They ate at Lacklustre on Christopher Street in the old Village, the kind of place Nicholas would choose, ostentatiously unostentatious. The place was full of nonentities who were meat and drink to Nicholas. He loved nonentities as others loved celebrities; the trouble was that when Nicholas discovered such a place, he began bringing his friends and soon entities started crowding out the nonentities and then Nicholas would have to find a new place. But that night the place was crowded with ordinary people, most of them young, and Robin and Nicholas were dumped at a small table next to the wall. The hubbub was very great.

Nicholas was full of fury and ferment and silence. He looked pale in the dark restaurant and Robin thought that his eyes had changed color from bright blue to deep purple. Troubled eyes, almost tormented. Nicholas who had always been so sardonic, so sure of himself. Not that now. Like her Aunt Sylvia. We're all changing, twisting in the maelstrom. Nicholas had always been hard to understand, biting off his thoughts so shortly you had to invent the rest. The air was full of unspoken understanding between these two childhood enemies.

Orin, guessed Robin.

"Orin is in the Sargasso Sea," said Nicholas. You had to

hear it to grasp the enormity of his despair. He's foundering in his brother's apostasy, Robin guessed, and I'm to fill the void. I can't and I won't. I haven't the time nor the energy nor the will of it. Still Robin felt it keenly, as if it were happening to her. The two inseparable brothers separated by a sea and by a betrayal. At least that's the way Nicholas saw it. Not, of course, Orin. Orin would say it was a choice of betrayals—whether to sacrifice the family or the planet. Orin would think his Ocean Institute was the savior of life itself. A brother was small change. That was the trouble with these Sir Galahads; as between you and humanity, it was humanity that got the nod and you who got fucked.

Nicholas showed her the sheet of official paper which had cost him ten thousand dollars to steal. A baby's footprint.

"They're like fingerprints. Unmistakably your own. You're never free of your baby footprints," said Nicholas sardonically. "This one is the only baby footprint that is positively evil—evil emanating from every whorl."

"Nicholas," said Robin, "it's a baby's footprint. Where did you get it?"

"Lausanne—where Sophie went to have Elihu. She is his real mother, Sophie is. And guess who the father is?"

Robin nibbled at her salad, not wanting to know.

"Jasper. My very own father. I am half brother to that son of a bitch. I am accursed."

Robin being a good listener listened. She was a creative listener, one of those who drew out of the talkers their own innermost fears, some so secret the talker himself never suspected them until Robin drew them out.

"It's at the bottom of his quest for legitimacy. He is trying to swallow us—the whole family—as a tribesman swallows the balls of his enemy, to acquire his virility."

"Nicholas," said Robin, "you're raving."

"He has killed his own father and arranged the murder of the only witness, Lemuel Stork. He is now screwing his own aunt and has turned my own brother against me. He will pull down the whole family unless . . ."

"Unless what?"

"Unless we stop him. And I mean you and me. Nobody else is going to do it. I have a plan." He outlined it.

"Nicholas, you're mad!"

Retribution so fanciful she couldn't imagine Nicholas thinking it up. A new Nicholas, a wholly different human being.

"It's not fair to Aunt Sophie, even if it worked and it won't—"

"Adulteress!" thundered Nicholas.

"Oh, Nicholas, really!" Robin had difficulty keeping her face straight. Adulteress! My God. Nicholas piling lunacy on lunacy. She wanted to tell him about Sylvia and Ahmet Ali but she couldn't. It would just fan the paranoia.

The two of them rode in silence in a taxicab to her sublet apartment on West Sixty-second Street. Nicholas looked so alone, so desperate, so at the end of his tether she wanted to take him in her arms and say, "It's all *right*, Nicholas. Don't fret so!" Orin had his Ocean Institute and all humanity to feed and she had bankruptcy and her job and now Gerald Fisher on her plate. Nicholas had nothing but his obsession and it was driving him around the bend.

Nicholas was looking constantly behind him, turning and twisting in the cab. "We're being followed!" said Nicholas. "That yellow Rabbit. On our tail ever since Lacklustre."

"Oh, Nicholas!" said Robin sadly. She felt so badly about leaving him alone that night—this on top of Orin's defection—that she thought briefly about inviting him up. But then he'd meet Ahmet and that would have to be explained, fanning the flames of obsession, and oh God . . .

Instead she kissed him on the lips (something she had never before done) and clung to him a moment, overwhelmed by love—cousinly love, family love—for this tormented Worth she felt she was abandoning.

Nicholas twisted out of her embrace and said, "There it goes, the yellow Rabbit that's been following us!"

Raving. Robin got out of the cab. "Call me tomorrow, Nicholas. You must keep in touch! I've got my own private phone number at GBC now. Wait a minute, cabbie!" She fished into her handbag for the little pad and the Bic pen and wrote it down for him; out of the corner of her eye she saw the yellow Rabbit Nicholas was raving about round the corner of Sixty-second, vanishing in the direction of Central Park West.

CHAPTER 30

It was an old building, its vast lobby covered with faded Oriental carpets, on which were huge oak chairs no one ever sat on, and a great oak table where they had once deposited the mail—that was before they put it in the boxes—which now served no purpose at all except to collect dust. The old black man named Fred who was the night doorman and all-purpose handyman was waxing the tile floor when Robin came in, his back to Robin.

"Good evening," said Robin, and smiled as she always did to Fred though he never smiled back.

"Evenin'," said Fred without looking up.

That was important as she was later to explain to Louis Hanagan, the Assistant District Attorney. Fred didn't look up and he was so occupied with waxing the floor that she could have walked clear to the elevator on those faded Oriental carpets without his ever noticing; anyone could sneak past old Fred who was supposed to keep the building locked at night and personally let people in only after looking them over. But sometimes he forgot. That was important, too.

The elevator was automatic, but Fred sometimes—depending on how bored he was—showed the people into the elevator and ran them to their own floors and said good night like a proper elevatorman, but that night he had floors to wax and he didn't. Robin took herself upstairs and let herself into the sublet apartment with her key. The apartment had an entrance hallway as many of those old-fashioned apartments did. Robin dumped her handbag on the hall table and went into the overfurnished living room. Ahmet Ali was seated cross-legged on the floor reading computer printouts, masses of computer printouts, all interconnected, that stretched on the floor beside him almost to the door.

He had a little smile on his face and behind those gold-rimmed glasses the intelligence that always glimmered in those pale eyes now positively radiated glee. High glee! His mouth slightly open, a bit of tongue sticking out!

He didn't look at her, but he seemed to absorb the fact that she had entered the room through his pores.

"April twenty-sixth," he said in high excitement as if it were a magic talisman. "Look at this, Robin. April twenty-sixth."

She knelt beside him and looked at the printout in his hand. It was covered with figures and letters, masses of them, yards of them.

MO NY, S A+ 100 = 11   14095   39¼ 34

He was reading this gibberish as if it were a comic strip, grinning all over.

"April twenty-sixth. Don't you know when that was? That's the day *after* Uncle Jasper died. *Very* interesting!"

"Why?"

He read it to her. MO was Mercury Oil, Jasper's bellwether stock, traded on the New York and Singapore Stock Exchanges (that's what the NY and S stood for), an A+ stock whose par value was one hundred, eleven was the number in thousands of shares held by institutions like insurance companies, merchant banks, educational institutions, fourteen thousand ninety-five the number of shares in hundreds traded that day with a high of thirty-nine and a half and a low of thirty-four.

"An incredible range for a solid gold stock like Mercury Oil and it was traded in Singapore. Why Singapore? He sold a million and a half shares. Nobody would do that, sell a million and a half shares in one day, and *drove* the price down. Some of that was your stock. But don't you see? It couldn't have been Jasper doing this trading. In the first place he would never do such a dumb thing. In the second place he was dead.

"Now look at this. PCB—that's the ticker symbol for Energy Inc., a shell company somebody's buying in at Singapore for twenty-five, which is a tremendously inflated price. Elihu's own stock—he's driving it up, selling Jasper's good stock at whatever he could get and buying this junk in Singapore and pocketing the money because Energy Inc. was his shell company. It had no assets at all."

Robin had never before heard this young Californian open up like this, speak so quickly in his light high voice, the words pouring out of him, much of it incomprehensible to Robin. For the first time she understood why Jasper had picked this bright young Moslem to be his next Number Two in Securities Unlimited. Ahmet read numbers like music, trilling them in that high voice, throbbing with passion and glee. "I told Jasper he was being robbed by Elihu! I *told* him! The numbers were all wrong and I knew it, but I couldn't pin it down. Couldn't prove it but this does it!"

"Where did you get all this?"

"In Fergie's duffel bag! I was using it as a pillow and watching MTV—Prince prancing about—and this stuff was digging into my neck so I reached in to get it out and I began reading it and I thought, my God, this is it! I *told*

Jasper before that last trip on the oil exploration ship. I *told* him he shouldn't go. He should send Elihu and I'd show him, but you know your Uncle Jasper! You couldn't tell him anything! He said wait until I get back—and, of course, he never got back. I said to him, I said it again and again, don't whisper any of this to Elihu, keep away from Elihu, but you know Uncle Jasper, you couldn't tell him what to do and what not to do. He must have said something."

The words tumbling out, the eyes flashing, the glee in him filling the room. Robin was sitting on her heels. *Glee!* Why *glee*? It was not a gleeful thing he was saying. He was talking about the murder of her Uncle Jasper and *his* Uncle Jasper, but of course it wasn't murder. Not to Ahmet Ali and his sharp mind. It was a game, a numbers game, infinitely complex and exciting. The face and the tone of voice, the whole mood, was exactly that of Ahmet Ali playing that silly game on the Apple 2E when she left.

Elihu was a bouncing ball, or an incoming rocket ship. You shot him down or he shot you down—if you were quicker and brighter.

Ahmet Ali bubbling on all the while. "It's not the smoking gun because, of course, anyone could run all this off on a computer—make it all up, really—but it tells us where it happened and when it happened and that's important. We could go to the Singapore stock market and the Hong Kong market—a lot of it happened on the Hong Kong market—and replicate all this. Now we know where to look. I don't know how Fergie got this but he must have latched on to a Securities Unlimited computer memory before Elihu got a chance to rub the stuff out or change it. It's not evidence, you understand, but with these leads we could *find* the evidence."

Robin on her knees now, sitting back, shoes off, on her own legs, drinking it all in, drinking *him* in because that was where the excitement was—in Ahmet himself, that intelligent *gleeful* young Californian with his golden hair and his bubbling mind, intelligence spilling out of him like water out of a spring. Robin had always been turned on by intelligence; it was aphrodisiac. Some women were turned on by money, sexually aroused almost to the point of orgasm by standing next to a man with a hundred million; not Robin, who came from a family accustomed to fortune as ordinary mortals are accustomed to breathing air. Robin was sexually aroused by the workings of the mind; and now she lay on her back, looking at this young California Moslem with his sparkling gaze behind those gold-rimmed glasses, fascinated by his total absorption in this game of numbers which was really the theft of maybe a hundred million dollars as if the money didn't count for anything but the *numbers* did, the beautiful mathematics of it.

She let him babble on until she couldn't stand it anymore and then she reached up with her strong arms and pulled him down on top of her and kissed him on his young lips, Ahmet protesting a little bit and for a little while, but only a little while—wanting her to *listen* while he explained the quadratic equations—but she had had enough of listening and after a bit he'd had enough of talking. They threw off their clothes in all directions and made it right there on the floor. With glee, Ahmet being as gleeful about sex as he was about numbers.

After the first raptures, they got off the floor which was not all that comfortable and repaired to Robin's bed where they had further raptures (because they were young and healthy) again, and again. Between these sexual transports there was much talk.

Robin was now deeply in love, more in love than she had ever been in her whole short life, and she wanted to plumb this young man from—as it were—head to toe, not simply sexually because there were limits to what she wanted to do sexually with him (Robin who had explored just about everything there was to explore with other men but with Ahmet there were limits), but his mind and soul. She was fascinated by his commitment to God and Islam if only to know how much she had to share him with those institutions so they talked about God, the Moslem God—and Honor, Moslem Honor.

He was a very honorable young man, honor like beauty being much in the eyes of the beholder, changing like the quality of light, one man's honor being another's dishonor—at least that's how it sounded to Robin—the talk getting very abstract indeed.

All this interspersed with much lovemaking.

Along about one-thirty in the morning Robin asked for the first time what she had been trying to get out of Ahmet all along. What on earth was this young California Moslem doing in this wicked, decadent non-Californian New York? He was a very purposive young man; everything about him, his every motion, reeked of purpose. But what *was* the purpose? Robin felt she knew him now—after their many couplings—well enough to ask and he, for the first time, knew her well enough to answer.

But he didn't. Not in the specifics which she, a journalist, wanted. What he wanted in the east was to confirm what he had suspected (though suspected didn't nearly define the certainty of his suspicions), to know absolutely that his Uncle Jasper, who had befriended him and toward whom he felt almost paternal love and pride, had been truly murdered and by whom.

Beyond that Ahmet closed down. He was not, Robin felt, at all vague or uncertain about what he was going to do, but he wasn't telling. What he had in mind—and this was largely supposition because he didn't exactly say it in so many words—was revenge.

Not (as she was wearily and again and again to say to Louis Hanagan, the Assistant District Attorney) justice, not law, but some sort of Moslem retribution which would fit the very large crime far beyond murder and the theft of a hundred million—relatively minor transgressions to Ahmet—

of dishonor, dishonoring not only his benefactor (who was also his father though Elihu did not know that) but the Worth family. It was dishonor of gigantic dimension, Oedipal in size and complexity, and it demanded gigantic retribution, but just what that was to be (as she was to tell Louis Hanagan again and again) she didn't know (and was never to know) because Ahmet didn't tell her.

He fell asleep in the middle of one of his seething electric sentences, after very much sex and very much talk, at about two in the morning, and Robin soon after that, the end of a very long night full of meanings that were not to become clear to Robin for years, and too much activity. Much too much. There had been the six o'clock news in which she had glowed brighter than the anchorman himself; then dinner with Nicholas when she had played Mother Superior radiant with compassion; finally the seduction of Ahmet Ali wherein she was lover and wanton and, yes, wife, all together, instinctively, effortlessly, all of those things for the first time and the last time in her life.

The horror came later.

She awoke at six-thirty because the telephone was making an awful racket and she picked it up off its cradle on her night table without opening her eyes. It was Jane Fox full of chatter. "There's been a big break on the van Ruysdale story. Estee's lover has been arrested in New Jersey with a suitcase full of the old man's jewelry. Get out of bed. . . ."

Somewhere in the midst of this bright chatter, Robin felt the blood, sticky and still warm, against her skin and opened her eyes and saw the dear body torn to shreds, the bed full of blood, and gave vent to the gibbering scream which even all those years at Miss Madeira's could not civilize. That brought Jane Fox to West Sixty-second Street in the first taxicab and thank God (as Robin was to say months later) for Jane Fox on the scene so early because it took all of that young twenty-year-old's cool vixen intelligence to get her out of that one.

When Jane Fox arrived she found Robin cradling the dear body, slashed to ribbons, the knife still lying there which had stabbed again and again and she not having heard a sound, Robin crooning over the dead Ahmet, herself covered with blood from cranium to instep. Jane Fox stripped herself to the buff (the only way to avoid bloodstains on her own clothes) and dragged the moaning Robin into the shower where she washed the woman, every inch, including the pubic hair, especially the pubic hair.

Over and over Robin moaning, "Why him? Why didn't they kill me too?"

"Because," said little Miss Fox practically, "they're trying to pin it on you and if you don't stop moaning and help out, they'll succeed."

CHAPTER 31

It was Nicholas really who saved her bacon.

"A yellow Rabbit," said Nicholas to Louis Hanagan, that overworked Irish Assistant DA whose desk and nearby worktable were piled even higher with the detritus of the unsolved and insoluble. "A yellow Rabbit that followed us from—now get this, Louis—from the Lacklustre on Christopher Street. . . ."

Nicholas had spread out a New York City street map over the litter on Louis Hanagan's desk and he forced the man to follow the route which he demonstrated with the point of a pencil—from Christopher Street not far from the West Side docks, up Hudson which turned into Ninth Avenue at Fourteenth Street and then up Ninth until it turned into Columbus and then right on West Sixty-second Street across Broadway to the apartment.

"It's not exactly a widely traveled route at ten o'clock at night. In fact, there was only one car back there most of the way. It's a very funny coincidence, Louis, for a yellow

Rabbit to follow our footsteps from Christopher Street all the way to West Sixty-second Street, wouldn't you say?''

Introducing the element of doubt.

''Wait right here,'' said Louis Hanagan severely. ''Don't move. Just stay right here.'' Louis Hanagan left Nicholas in his cluttered office and went down the hall, past three other Assistant District Attorneys' offices, past the Law Library and the drinking fountain to the Interrogation Room (one of three) which was a totally different scene from Louis Hanagan's cluttered office—a table, two chairs and four walls. Robin was seated on one of the chairs, stiff as a broom. Another Assistant DA named Jerry Goldstein was on the other chair and a tape recorder was on the table. Louis Hanagan listened to the questioning for a while and then tapped Jerry Goldstein on the shoulder. Goldstein left. Louis Hanagan picked up where he left off, which was about what had gone on between her and Ahmet Ali before that evening, way back to when she first met him. After ten minutes Louis Hanagan shifted to the evening in question, to her dinner with Nicholas, to the taxi ride home.

Robin talking mechanically because they had been over all this so many times.

''What did you talk about in the taxi?''

''Nothing.''

''No talk in the taxi at all?''

''No. None . . . Oh.'' Louis could hardly hear her and he was sure the tape recorder couldn't. ''There was some nonsense about a yellow Rabbit.''

''What about the yellow Rabbit?''

''Nicholas thought a yellow Rabbit was following us.''

''Did you see the yellow Rabbit?''

Robin sighed and ran her hands over her face. ''Yes, it passed us as I got out of the taxi and went off . . . I don't know . . . toward Central Park. . . .''

That let just a little air in a case that had seemed to Louis

Hanagan airtight. Not enough air to get Robin out of custody. Just enough to sow a seed of doubt in Louis Hanagan's mind.

He was grumpy when he went back to his office and Nicholas. "I don't know that you two didn't concoct this yellow Rabbit between you. You Worths stick together."

"Oh, no," said Nicholas sadly. "We Worths don't stick together. That's what this is all about, Louis. The Worths *not* sticking together. If you don't understand that, you're on the wrong foot altogether. What you've got to find out is who is sticking and who is betraying."

Nicholas was sprawled on the worn-out chair in Louis Hanagan's office, very relaxed, his little sardonic smile flashing again. A very different Nicholas from the tormented young man of the evening before. Nicholas had found his own role in this business. The murder of Ahmet had sharpened his purpose wonderfully. He showed his teeth in a sharkish smile because he had pushed Louis Hanagan off base and he knew it.

"Robin got a warning that that young man, Ahmet Ali—who is a Worth in spite of that name—was in danger. Has she told you that? You go back and ask her who told her that, who warned her about danger, because she wouldn't tell me."

Little motes in the yellow air dancing in the splash of sunshine next to the law books.

Hanagan went back to Robin who was now alone. Even the tape recorder had left. "Who told you Ahmet Ali was in danger and why haven't you told us?"

Robin burst into tears, her first. "You're talking to Nicholas, aren't you? He promised he wouldn't. . . ."

Later she whispered, "You'll put her in danger."

"She's already in danger."

"You must keep it out of the papers. She must not be implicated. You'll get her killed as Ahmet was. Couldn't we go up there after office hours? Get her at home after all those reporters have left for the night and only then. . . ."

Robin, herself a reporter, counseling him on how to outwit the media.

"You had better take me along, Louis, because I am a Worth and you're not. I can get things out of Aunt Sylvia that you never could."

Robin's role, too, had shifted all in a trice, before she grasped what was happening. She was not any longer Robin the defendant, the questioned. Now, all in a moment, she became Robin the questioner, the pursuer, no longer the pursued. She had a very large emotional stake in this matter.

The media had parked in the outer office with their cameras, their tripods, their junk. Louis Hanagan emerged from time to time to tell them nothing except that the investigation was ongoing but there was nothing to report. No, there was no charge against Robin Worth. She was cooperating with the investigation. . . .

The media never went home for supper that night, so they had to slip out the lower cellar way which was not often used. At the storied Park Avenue apartment, the doorman had been instructed to say that Mrs. Settle was not at home, not even in the country, was abroad. It might have worked except that Robin knew the doorman and the building manager, and they knew her. The lie stuck in their throats with Robin there. Quite wordlessly they let Robin use the phone in the lobby. "You'd better let us up, Aunt Sylvia, because otherwise Mr. Hanagan will call in the police with a search warrant and it'll be very messy."

So they broached the citadel, which is what the New York apartments of the very rich have become, citadels with medieval moats and drawbridges, and when they got up to Sylvia's abode on the twenty-second floor, it was almost as if they had broached Sylvia herself who had lived so long in her high embrasure enclosed behind her money and her high wit above reproach, well above it, that this invasion seriously eroded not only her confidence but her very personality, as if the chemistry of Sylvia Settle, the very arrangement of her genes, had been altered and perhaps permanently damaged.

Her little amusements, these trifling escapades, which she liked to call her *affaires d' corps* (not *affaires d' coeur* at all, at all) were her own private artifacts, a girl's toy beads, to be held up to the sun and examined one by one, with a gurgle of laughter in the throat, not meant for public display at all, at all. No matter how delicately Louis Hanagan put the questions or she framed the answers there was no getting around the fact that this little escapade consisted of her, Sylvia Settle, age forty-four, screwing her twenty-two-year-old nephew, and it stank to high heaven. (Sylvia Settle didn't believe in high heaven but in high stink, yes, she believed, her nostrils full of it. It was just as well the high stink got into her nostrils because it turned her against Elihu physically, turned that lechery anyway, into abomination.)

It changed the chemistry, all the chemistry.

None of this was very satisfying to Louis Hanagan. He unpeeled a little more of the onion but not nearly enough. "Did Elihu say the boy would be in danger?"

"He would hardly do that, would he? He just wanted to know where Ahmet was staying, something he could have found out himself. What he wanted to do really was to implicate me to ... uh 'neutralize' me."

But of course, Louis Hanagan, not being a Worth, didn't see it that way. "He just wanted the man's address. What made you think that put the man in danger? Perhaps he just wanted to have lunch with him?"

She couldn't explain that to a non-Worth. (In fact, there were a lot of Worths she couldn't explain it to either, a lot of Worths who found Elihu the very pinnacle of probity, an upstanding young man.)

Louis Hanagan was not made happy by any of this. Sylvia was providing—reluctantly, angrily, even fearfully (her own safety now at issue)—confirmation for what Robin had said. Sylvia had warned her to get Ahmet Ali to a place of safety, that the man was in danger, and that was why he was in Robin's apartment. This loosened Hanagan's bonds on Robin without forging any on Elihu. Sylvia provided motivation which didn't altogether exonerate Robin but explained her.

It didn't implicate Elihu. Nothing did. The computer printouts had disappeared. The killer had left the knife to implicate Robin and taken the computer printouts which implicated Elihu who, insofar as Louis Hanagan was concerned, vanished into the mists of legend. (Hanagan had never even laid eyes on Elihu.) Robin tried to explain the significance of the computer printouts, but she could barely remember the gibberish—numerals and initials, mostly—on the printouts. She had never really understood the intricate financial skulduggery that Ahmet's keen mind had detected; she had only, alas, fallen in love with the keen mind, now forever stilled, and while trying to explain the computer printouts to Louis Hanagan, Robin stumbled and paused and grew incoherent because the sexual associations of the printouts which had, after all, led to such bliss and such sorrow overwhelmed her. She could feel the storm coming but she was too exhausted to control it and she dissolved into hysterical sobs, the last thing in the world she wanted because she had never admitted to any personal involvement with Ahmet Ali.

Sylvia wrapped her long arms around the sobbing girl and said severely to Louis Hanagan, "I think that's quite enough." As if it were his fault, the whole mess. She was Aunt Sylvia now, no longer the glamorous wicked adulterous Sylvia Settle, but Auntie, everyone's auntie, taking charge. "I'm going to put you to bed here, Robin. The security here is much better than at the place you're in."

Ignoring Louis Hanagan altogether, Sylvia pulled Robin to her feet and maneuvered her into the little downstairs guest room, the nearest bed of all, shutting the door in

Louis Hanagan's face. Sylvia slipped the brocaded velvet Charivari jacket, the Oscar de La Renta blouse, the Gucci snakeskin shoes off the sobbing girl, threw a quilt over her and kissed her on the cheek. "I'll be back."

She returned to Louis Hanagan who was in a rage of impotence. "You Worths think you are above the law; you think your wealth and distinction puts you in some special niche the law can't touch; that you are exempt from the rules and regulations the rest of us have to live by." He was on his feet, ranting and prowling. Sylvia plumped cushions on the sofa. "What makes you think that girl can stay here? She is a prime suspect in a murder case."

"You said she was just a witness," said Sylvia, plumping cushions. "I watched you on television. Robin is helping with the investigation is what you said."

I've been sucker punched, Louis Hanagan was saying to himself. He had been maneuvered out of his turf, the District Attorney's office, where he knew all the plays, to this high eyrie of the very rich, this sanctuary, where he, Louis Hanagan, was a bum. It made him mad, and what he was was mad at himself.

The superrich lived in their own high treetop, well above the rest of the rain forest, their dangers highly specialized and difficult to explain to lesser mortals like Assistant DAs. You had to be born in the family to feel your way through the vapors, the mystique. Louis Hanagan was aware for the first time how powerless he was in these flickering shadows.

That left nothing more to be said. Sylvia showed him out to her private elevator landing. The elevator was turned off so that it would under no circumstances stop at her floor unless she pulled the proper switch. She showed Louis Hanagan the switch and pulled it.

The elevator arrived; the door opened, showing its carpeted, wainscoted, mirrored interior with the little red tufted seat in the rear in case you couldn't bear to stand for a minute and a half.

Louis Hanagan said dryly, "She seems safe enough here behind all these ramparts, Mrs. Settle—unless you kill her."

"Oh, I wouldn't do a thing like that."

"Yes, it would be very hard to alibi your way out of that, Mrs. Settle," said Louis Hanagan, and released the elevator door in order to give himself the last word. He was entitled to the last word.

Sylvia climbed the curving staircase which led from the twenty-second floor to the twenty-third (designed by Esteban, who flew all the way from Madrid to design her staircase) to pluck one of the long soft cotton nighties with the blue cornflowers out of the amusing drawers (which looked like *trompe l'oeil* so cleverly had Olemandre painted them) and took it downstairs to Robin who was sitting up in the bed, dry-eyed, naked between the sheets. Sylvia slipped the nightie on over Robin's head, pulling and tugging her arms through the armholes until the nightie fell properly over her shoulders, fussing over the much younger woman, loving her auntwise.

Both women silent because there was nothing to be said, much to be felt. Outside of the window they could hear the pulse beat of the city, rubber tires on Park Avenue, the toot of car horns, the whistles, the bleat of taxis, all of it far far down where dwelt the commoners.

Sylvia holding Robin's two hands in her own two hands, sitting on the edge of the bed. We Worths are our own worst enemies, virtually our only enemies. But what enemies! Our own private Furies to run us down, shrieking implacably.

The telephone rang.

They both knew instantly who was on the other end and responded in individualistic grimaces—Sylvia with her eloquent eyebrows, Robin with her marvelous downward-twisting mouth. Neither made any move to answer the phone which rang four times.

The answering machine took over.

Sylvia's bright inappropriate voice. "This is Sylvia Settle. I'm elsewhere, bringing sunshine into some other poor wretch's life; you'll just have to wait your turn. Speak up!'' Sylvia's little joke which she changed from time to time.

Elihu's voice filled the room, bubbling over with high glee. ''Sylvia, dar-r-r-ling.'' Drawling the *darling* in a way that made Sylvia's flesh shudder. ''Our dear cousin Robin has left the District Attorney's office. I suspect she's with you. Do tell her to call me. I'm the only one who can get her out of this mess.''

I! Me! Myself!

Triumph resounding through the bedroom like a wild woodwind note! A paean! *I! I! I!*

The two women who had both lain with this dark satyr (and both knew it) were chilled to the marrow by this wild woodwind note, a wholly new note.

''He's slipped his tether,'' said Sylvia, whispering it low.

Sylvia kicked off her shoes and swung her legs up on the bed, the two women lying against the pillows shoulder to shoulder.

''If Elihu can hire a killer, as he must have done, why can't the rest of us? . . .''

Robin the newswoman knew why, knew the angles.

''He's laundering Mafia money. A lot of the big brokers are doing that under the table. They owe him and he has access to the hired guns which we haven't got.''

She thought of Nicholas and his wild words. ''He's trying to swallow us—the whole family—as a tribesman swallows the balls of his enemy, to acquire his virility.'' Lunacy, she had thought then. She no longer thought so.

''We'll have to do it ourselves, the trustworthy Worths. Nicholas has a plan. It's mad.''

''It would have to be.''

BOOK
THREE

CHAPTER 32

The murder was splashed across the naked face of the hot city like a summer shower, a marvelous diversion for the lower orders, as are all murders in the upper registers. So satisfying to discover the rich bleed and die like everyone else, this murder especially being especially gory and nasty, how marvelous! The *Post* asked pointedly and loudly—in full view of the cameras, "Is she a suspect?" and Louis Hanagan had said, after a perceptible hesitation, "No." He had hesitated because he had considered saying not yet, which would have been a quite different box of worms, opening the press up to all sorts of fruitful speculation. No closed the door on that line of improvisation perhaps a little more thoroughly than Louis Hanagan had intended. But what was done was done and Robin went back to GBC a heroine, not a villainess (the difference between the two in the media being so slight, so unstable, as to be only a matter of tone, and sometimes of hours).

GBC was now ripe for anything Robin had on Ahmet Ali

and what she fed the network were all those tapes about Islam that Gerald Fisher had been so superbly interested in, about all the Moslem beliefs and mysteries. By telling this on the air, Robin—her ready smile now dimmed, her eyes deep as pools—threw suspicion for the murder on every Moslem for miles around for who knew why those peculiar people killed one another? It was recalled that no one had ever satisfactorily explained who had killed Malcolm X or why and wasn't he one of Them?

Hostility against Robin had vanished. The spoiled little rich girl taking bread out of the mouths of more deserving females was now seen to be a no-longer-rich girl deserving of admiration, not scorn. Tragedy had changed the look of her, given her gravity and depth, erased altogether the flippancy; this also sat well with the middle-aged lumps who were TV's primary audience. The women especially worshipped the Golden Girl who had weathered so much, who had survived the buffetings of Fate and still managed to be so beautiful, well spoken, such a *lady*, my goodness! (Where before she'd been a bit of a hoyden.)

All this skillfully managed by Jane Fox, advising on every move, every inflection, and above all advising what must *not* be done, young Miss Fox having a sublimely sensitive nose to the prejudices and peculiarities of the great American heartland. One thing Jane Fox buried forty fathoms deep was the romance between Ahmet Ali and Robin. Even while scrubbing her in the shower, Jane Fox had hissed, "You are cousins, nothing more! Lovers kill each other! Cousins don't! Not a whisper! Not a word!"

So that had been that. Robin had grieved (she who had never known grief!) in private, right down at the bottom of her soul, and this too changed her personality, gave her a conspicuous vulnerability, turned her into the kind of girl everyone wanted to help across the street. Ahmet went to his grave not altogether unmourned. A young California girl, very blond, tanned, healthy, white-toothed, came out of the West, claimed the body and bore it back to California, but not before being interviewed on the air by Robin, who wanted to scratch her eyes out but instead smiled her sad smile and was immensely kind and cousinly, her greatest performance.

She was now a star, that American phenomenon which meant she hardly owned her own soul anymore, could barely appear on the street without being torn to pieces by the admiring multitude. Underneath it all she was bottomlessly sad. She was also petrified with fear. Elihu had not succeeded in pinning the murder on her; he would try something else.

That she knew in her bones, as did Sylvia, the two women who had partaken of that deadly Elihu flesh and had to take the consequences.

Robin had now moved in altogether to Sylvia's Park Avenue duplex and presently, because there was lots of room and it was convenient, Jane Fox joined them, the three women forming an unlikely triumvirate.

Oscar Settle, the husband of the hostess, was still in Oklahoma with his polo ponies. Just to stir the pot a little more, word drifted back east that it wasn't just the polo ponies that were occupying Oscar Settle's attention. Manhattan's most conspicuous, most long-suffering cuckold—so the whispers went—had found himself a woman and was at long last turning the tables on Manhattan's most renowned adulteress. Even more comical—so the whispers went—it was the lady, not Oscar, who had initiated all this. She was a female polo player of awe-inspiring sinew (went the whispers), and she had hurled Oscar to the floor and leaped on him, howling like a wolf.

"Well!" said Sylvia when she heard all this (from, of course, her dearest friend Lolo). "Well!"

The letter from Lausanne bore nothing on the envelope, no return address, no identification at all, except the postmark Lausanne, which itself sent shivers down Sophie's spine. They said mothers forgot the birth pains almost immediately, but she had not forgotten a single spasm even after twenty-two years, which was why she loved him so much because what was love but pain?

The object of her love at the moment sat just opposite her at the square glass table Sophie so loathed (as she loathed everything else in that new apartment). Elihu was tormenting her little dachsund Pandemonium (Pandy for short) under the guise of playing with him.

"Do stop tormenting him, Elihu," said his mother faintly.

"He loves it," said Elihu, showing his teeth. He was holding the little piece of meat close to Pandy's nose and then snatching it just out of reach.

"No, he doesn't," said Sophie mechanically. Pulling the letter from the white envelope carefully as if it might explode, which, in a sense, it did. She drew in just a little bit of air, but it was enough to alert Elihu who knew his mother very well.

He tossed the bit of meat to Pandy and snatched the letter out of his mother's hand because he knew from the nature of that small gasp that she would not show it to him, not ever.

"Oh, Elihu! You mustn't read other people's mail! It's not nice!" An old lecture that had never done any good.

The letter was very short and, to Elihu, mystifying. "Stolen my baby footprints, Mother!" With his high bleating laugh. "It's like something out of Peter Pan. Remember? Peter Pan lost his shadow and he went back to the nursery to look for it."

The sharkish smile now turning into a frown because this wasn't like Peter Pan at all. "Stolen my baby footprints. How very... Who is Madeline Jasper, Mother?"

Sophie vented a small moan, her only reply.

"My real mother? So that's her name, Madeline Jasper."

Sophie rose from the glass table in the vast dining room which looked out over the ugliness of Manhattan so expensively. She wandered into the huge square living room with

windows on three sides (one of the principal reasons why
the apartment had cost Elihu seven million dollars) and sat
at one of the aseptic blond wood tables that Elihu so
adored and Sophie so disliked. Elihu, she thought, had
gotten rid of all her dear shabby Restoration oak (much of it
now being sold by Estelle for a great deal of money) for all
this hideous modern debris. He had actually made her, a
Worth, appear nouveau riche. Fancy that! And yet she loved
Elihu very much for who else had she to love? Looking out
over the appalling rooftops. Why was it that rooftops were
so beautiful everywhere except in America?

Elihu had pursued her into the vast empty living room.
(Emptiness being so chic now and so heartless). "What was
my mother like, Mother? Is it from her I got my beauty?
And my brains? And my..." And here he laughed because,
of course, the other things were not all that commendable
and no one knew that better than Elihu, who knew what he
was very well but didn't know why, had never known why.

"I am not going to tell you anything at all about Madeline
Jasper because I have promised not to, Elihu. You know that."

Of course he knew that. He had tried many times and
failed, his only failure. He could get anything at all out of
Sophie except information of his real father and real mother.
That was Sophie's very private shame and glory.

"You said I'd get used to this place, Elihu. I'm not
getting used to it at all. It's too high and too empty and too
big."

"You're much safer here, Mother." Elihu was staring at
the envelope now, frowning.

"Safer? I lived on Seventy-sixth Street thirty years and I
was safe enough."

Elihu said, "Did you notice where this envelope is addressed,
Mother? It's addressed *here*! Your new apartment which you
moved into less than a month ago. Why should they know
your new address in Lausanne?"

He put an arm around his seated mother and caressed her

cheek thoughtfully with the tip of his finger, a little trick he'd used to quiet his mother since childhood. Sophie grasped the finger that gave her so much pleasure and kissed it and closed her eyes.

Elihu kissed the top of his mother's head absently, both arms around her now, holding her tight. "Why would anyone want my baby footprints, Mama mia?"

"I don't know, darling boy."

So overwhelmed by the bliss of being held by Elihu she didn't care. At least not then.

"It's not like Peter Pan at all, Mama. Not a single bit!"

He kissed her again on the top of her head, unwrapped his arms from around her and walked out of the big duplex, waggling his fingers at her. . . .

"Elihu, where are you going with my letter . . . Elihu—"

He was gone. She had hardly read the letter. Just glanced at it before he had snatched it away. *Now* she felt the alarm bells ringing in her mind. How very sinister it was! That someone should steal her baby's footprints! That someone in Lausanne should know her new address! How very puzzling! How alarming!

They had not known her *old* address in Lausanne. They had not even known her real name. She had gone into the clinic as Madeline Jasper. Only Jasper had known and Jasper was dead.

"I thought I was an American boy, Francis." Elihu used Graebner's first name only when he badly wanted something. Always an ominous sign.

Graebner pulled his lips back in what, in anyone else, would have been a smile. "You *are* an American. Madeline Jasper was an American woman. That's all I know and I wasn't supposed to tell you even that much, but obviously someone else has. That absolves me."

Graebner always sought absolution, rarely found it. Elihu didn't believe that was all the lawyer knew.

"Why was she in Switzerland?"

"It's where women went—if they had the money—for privacy and excellent care." Graebner was sweating visibly in the air-conditioned office.

"You're not being honest with me, Francis." The first name again, Elihu insulting the lawyer with a smile. Graebner sweated some more.

"There are professional ethics involved."

Elihu chortled. "Ethics, Francis? *You?*" Sticking the knife into him but not twisting it because Elihu was well aware you could push Graebner only so far. Graebner was greedy, yes, and his retainer as attorney for Securities Unlimited was preposterous enough to keep him in line through most insults, but there was a point beyond which he couldn't be bullied. He was, after all, very rich and he was getting old. The trick was to torment him so far, no further, because Elihu needed the wily old crook as much as Graebner needed the money. Elihu went on with it, but softly, softly, turning on the charm. "Why were you involved at all, Francis? You weren't my mother's lawyer. Nor my father's. You were . . ." Then it struck Elihu in the pit of the stomach. "You were *Jasper's* lawyer. What a funny coincidence! Madeline *Jasper*! *Jasper* Worth! Isn't that a funny coincidence, Francis?"

"It wasn't her real name—Madeline Jasper," croaked Graebner. "It was a made-up name."

"But why did she make up *that* name? Jasper? It's not a name that springs readily to mind unless . . . Why was Uncle Jasper involved in this?"

"Who said he was involved?"

"You'll have to do better than that, Francis. *You* were involved and you never involve yourself in anything unless you get A, money, or B, publicity. Usually both. You were my uncle's lawyer. My uncle must have *ordered* you to handle this thing because a little pissant business about a woman having an illegitimate baby is nothing you would bother with unless ordered to do so by a really important client like Uncle Jasper. But why would Uncle Jasper do that? And why would she—my real mother—take the name of Jasper unless . . ."

Right there the other thought exploded in Elihu's brain. He had been leaning against Graebner's desk (Graebner hated his doing that) and the idea blew Elihu upright, his skin showing white under his tan. His hands flew to his throat as if he could feel fingers around it, gasping as if there were no air in the world.

Graebner was deeply impressed. He hadn't thought a little thing like patricide would affect Elihu so deeply. Or at all.

"You should have told me!" whispered Elihu.

"Why? You wouldn't have behaved any differently."

"You son of a bitch!"

Elihu's fist hit the lawyer's gray face squarely in the middle, blood spurting out of the nose all over Graebner's old-fashioned leather desk set. Elihu regretted it—oh how he regretted it!—even in mid-punch, tried to recall the punch but couldn't stop it. Oh, his ungovernable temper! Elihu, who hated being ungovernable. He had regretted slapping Robin—again in midair, as it were—but couldn't stop that slap any more than he could stop this punch. There it was! *Splat!* Irrecoverable! It would end this relationship as it had ended that with Robin. Just when he needed all his resources! Oh hell!

Graebner had risen from his leather chair, patting at his bloodied nose with his handkerchief. He was backing away from Elihu, his eyes darting like bats on a summer night, backing all the way to the door which led to the outer office where reposed his secretary and all those law books in their leather bindings. Graebner went out the door, closing it after him, saying nothing at all, leaving Elihu to face his patricide alone.

CHAPTER 33

The session was closed even to Jane Fox. "A family matter," Nicholas had explained with his polished manner and gleaming smile. Not many of them. Nicholas, Robin, Sylvia and Estelle.

They met in Sylvia's upstairs sitting room, off her bedroom, that very feminine room full of Louis Quinze settees with their suggestive curves and pale colors, and Sylvia's painted Italian rococo, so stimulating to look at, so uncomfortable to sit on. Nicholas took charge, this handsome, rich, young dilettante who had never been noted for grand strategy or, in fact, for any entrepreneurial skills at all. Still, the women admitted privately to each other when the session was over, this Nicholas was a different article from the normal carefree Nicholas. Even his appearance had changed. His eyes were darker; the lines of the face were deeper, more inexorable. He was more formidable, less human. That happens, Robin was thinking. It's happening to all of us. We're adapting to a new circumstance. It's coarsened all of us, not necessarily for the worse. She stole a glance at Sylvia, who was sitting up very straight in the rococo chair, her hands folded in her lap as if she were being painted by Vermeer, the very picture of domestic virtue and strength—my God, Sylvia, who had expended her wit and toughness on a boundless pursuit of bedmates, now engaged in a darker enterprise.

Next to her sat Estelle, lighting a cigarette and pulling on it viciously, her latest vice. She had never smoked in her life, but had recently taken it up as part of her personality transformation, the cigarette dangling from the right corner of her lip like Peter Lorre in all those Humphrey Bogart movies.

Estelle was interrupting Nicholas. "Robin can't engage in anything like that. She's too conspicuous now."

"She's our decoy," said Nicholas calmly.

"Oh," said Robin faintly. "Not *again*!"

"The common weal is at stake," said Nicholas. "Family honor. Perhaps even family existence."

"I'll do whatever's required," said Robin. "Once."

"Oh, we'll only get one shot at it."

In another Manhattan apartment, not far away, Elihu was lying in Humphrey's naked arms, smiling his sharkish smile, when he sprang his little surprise. Humphrey sat up abruptly, his rubicund jowls quivering. "I don't deal on that level."

He sprang out of the bed with surprising agility considering the girth of him and minced across the room toward his pile of clothes, close to tears. Much too close.

Elihu lifted himself up on one elbow and smiled lazily. "I have you on tape. Would you like to hear it?"

Humphrey kept his back turned because the tears were beginning to splash down. He hated to cry! Hated it! But he always did when betrayed; he was often betrayed.

"You'd be disbarred. Telling a client's secrets to an

opponent. You'd be tossed right out of the Brook and the Links."

Humphrey's beloved clubs, his most vulnerable point. He was standing next to the wall, waiting for the tears to stop, his mind churning. I'm as smart as he is but not so...vicious. Presenting his naked portly ass to Elihu as his editorial comment on this obscene suggestion.

"You bastard!" said Humphrey when the tears stopped.

"Oh, yes," said Elihu. "Everyone knows that." It was the very root of him—his bastardy. His sinew, really.

He went on with it because he detected the weakening of resolve, went right to the heart of the matter. "Graebner dealt with Mauriello before. Not directly, of course. Through layers and layers of go-betweens, but Graebner did the bargaining. Mauriello will deal. He has to." Anyone with a nose for gossip as keen as Humphrey's would know about the laundering—a hundred million or so. Powerful incentive.

The tears were dry on his cheek now. "I cannot be seen with Mafia mobsters."

"Graebner never laid eyes on the man. You must have someone to fetch and carry, don't you? Someone you've, shall we say, befriended? Not anyone you're too fond of."

Humphrey's features had assumed a dead implacability he used in court when the going got tough. He was thinking, Nothing has changed since the twelfth century B.C. The messengers got killed because they were an embarrassment. Not because they knew too much but simply because one didn't want to be reminded of the function they performed. They were buried like excrement.

Graebner had performed this miserable business before, but now, for reasons Humphrey didn't know and was not likely to find out, Graebner had walked out on Elihu because...because...Elihu didn't have the leverage on Graebner he had on Humphrey. Graebner, that slimebag, had wriggled off the hook. That leaves me, Humphrey was thinking. I'm not so slimy as Graebner, but I suppose I could learn to be slimy and, with a little practice, to enjoy it.

He thought of Petronius, the end of virtue, vice triumphant as the Roman Empire sank into the mire. The splendor of decay! For there was a kind of splendor to it. Oh, those orgies! That *submission*!

He turned his portly nakedness round now and faced Elihu with a little frown, not looking Elihu in the eye because he couldn't bear to do so. "What do you want, Elihu?"

Elihu told him. Fetching and carrying was what it amounted to. Elihu would do the thinking. He, Humphrey Worth, one of the highest-priced lawyers in the land, would be the law clerk. Oh, the delicious humiliation of it! I have never been so thoroughly *plumbed*, Humphrey was thinking. I'm stabbed to the bone! Oh, the pain of it! The bliss of it!

"Yes, master!" said Humphrey—and dropped a curtsey, his plump ass bobbing comically, down and up, *comme ça*. One had to be comical because what else was left?

Robin got Fergie back to Manhattan only by pleading and threatening. He was a very sullen young man when he appeared. He and Augie Winchester were defending the Belmont Cup for six-meter sloops and he was badly needed on Long Island, but the family need, said Robin, was even more desperate. She had gotten him into her downstairs bedroom in Sylvia's flat and had to let him in on some of it, as little as possible.

"All those printouts at the bottom of your duffel bag— they've disappeared. Where did you get them and how?"

Fergie told her. "I'd need an RX 4000 like Lannie had. Even then there's no assurance all that stuff is still there, or that they haven't changed the code."

It was Nicholas who bought an RX 4000 and planted it in Sylvia's music room which was soundproof. Fergie swarmed all over it in minutes, setting it up, putting it through its paces, Robin and Nicholas hanging over him. "They've changed the code. I'll have to call Lannie in Galveston. He got it from his father's desk."

"No," said Nicholas violently. "You mustn't call Lannie. Mustn't tell Lannie or anyone else what we're up to."

"I don't know what we're up to."

"Good," said Nicholas. "I'll get the access code from Uncle Will."

It would be on file somewhere at Worth Freres, but getting it out of Uncle Will was not easy. "We're dealing in trust, Nicholas," said the old silver-haired, silver-moustached aristocrat. "If we forfeit trust, we have lost our good name."

"If we don't," said Nicholas grimly, "we are likely to lose more than that." He had his own refrain now. Family honor. Family survival. Sacred texts to Uncle Will. William Worth conceded these were high altars indeed, but he wanted to know what was going on. Nicholas wouldn't tell him.

"It would just disturb your sleep, Uncle Will."

"It already does."

Nicholas had to hammer away for an hour on Uncle Will's unbending integrity and the arguments he used were emotional and not at all scrupulous. "It was you who brought Ahmet Ali here, Uncle Will. He was murdered because he was *here* and his presence alarmed Elihu. You bear a responsibility."

A fearful charge to hurl at this kindly, honorable man. Nicholas made it even worse. "It will not be the last murder. Now that Elihu has the taste—and knows how to lay his hands on the hit men—how many more murders will be committed? And after each one, Uncle Will, you will have to tell yourself, I could have prevented it and I didn't."

A wholly new Nicholas. Implacable.

He got the access code finally, William Worth getting it

for him personally and writing it down for him with his gold pencil in a shaky hand. "This represents a coarsening of the moral fiber of the whole family. You realize that, Nicholas."

"Yes," said Nicholas crisply.

"What do you want this for?"

"You wouldn't want to know, Uncle Will," said Nicholas and straightaway changed the subject to that other event that loomed large in the plan: Uncle Will's Fourth of July party. A huge family party that attracted Worths by the score from all over the eastern seaboard—Maryland, Delaware, Pennsylvania—for marvelous food, marvelous fireworks, marvelous fun. It was the family's oldest party and it stretched back for decades, no one knew how far back, perhaps a hundred years. No one even knew who had started the Fourth of July party, but all the eastern Worths remembered the party from earliest childhood. It was the children who were the heart of the party for the games, the fireworks, the food, and all Worths harbored childhood memories—some tender, some painful, some awful—of events at the Party. It was at the Party that Orin and Nicholas had first met Robin and, for that matter, Elihu. This was before Uncle Will gave it, back when Elsie Worth gave the Party at the Manhasset place she'd long since sold. It was at the Manhasset party that they played The Game, and Elihu had gotten . . . mislaid. It was at the same party that Robin had told Nicholas he was Beyond the Pale (her strongest epithet at the time). Or perhaps at some earlier party. Because all the Fourth of July parties of their childhood merged into one big party—the misadventures, the burns, the slights, the tears, the fun, the hurts, the excitement, the sicknesses—all merged together in Worth childhood consciousness as if it had all been one unforgettable ancestral memory that was to shape their attitudes toward each other for years to come.

"You'll ask Elihu and Sophie, of course," said Nicholas.

"I always do. They haven't come for years."

"I think they will this year."

* * *

Sylvia frowned, closed her eyes and rubbed her forehead as if it hurt. She had turned into a middle-aged woman before Nicholas' very eyes.

"I think we're out of our depth, Nicholas."

Nicholas grinned his lopsided grin. "We started with gunpowder. Remember?"

"No, I don't remember. Neither do you. None of us remembers. I think you'd better get Orin out of that submarine. We need all the manpower we can get."

In the music room, Fergie was wholly absorbed with his FX 4000. He had the call letters now and he was deep into the Securities Unlimited computer, producing yards and yards of figures, all about money. That was what Nicholas was mostly interested in, money movements. "It's what makes the world go round—money," said Nicholas. "What I want to find out is where it's going round to."

"I'd have to know all the call letters."

Nicholas got the call letters of all those offshore banks from William Worth and hung over Fergie's shoulder as he played with his new toy (which had driven all thought of the six-meter race out of his skull). The stuff piled in and Fergie translated it for him. The Seychelles. The Bahamas, Guernsey. "All the islands where they don't have any banking laws at all."

The stuff was falling into a regular pattern—amounts, destinations, and return of the money, freshly laundered and respectable. "Those offshore banks don't have anything like the security that big banks do," said Nicholas. "Could you plant a Trojan horse?"

Fergie tore his eyes off the computer screen for the very first time and looked at Nicholas. "Judas Priest, Nicholas! I could get into big trouble!"

"I doubt they could trace it—or would want to. This is pretty crooked stuff to start out with."

Fergie was examining the tips of his fingers as if he were

looking for clues. "You know what they call that when you do that offshore? Piracy."

"Piracy is how the Worth family started. Even before the gunpowder."

Fergie examined the tips of his fingers some more. "Could I ask Robin?"

"No," said Nicholas. "Robin's got too much on her plate already. You'll have to take this on your own broad seventeen-year-old shoulders and grow up fast."

Fergie grew up fast.

Mauriello was (he felt) a much misunderstood man. He was seventy-eight and he'd survived not only all the wars but the changes in direction—from booze to rackets to loansharking to heroin to real estate, and even the cancer that had mowed down so many of his contemporaries. He was a very tough but (he thought) gentle man (unless there was some good reason for not being gentle), and that day he was tending his chrysanthemums. It would have made a nice picture, a *capo di capo* snipping dead leaves off his mums, but Mauriello would have no truck with the media and perhaps that was why he was so profoundly misunderstood. It was a dilemma, no question about it. Mauriello, who was widely read, remembered the advice of a British diplomat: Don't worry about what is on the back of the inscrutable Oriental mind, but let there be no mistake about what is on the back of *your* mind. This, in the age of public relations, was increasingly difficult unless you invited in the press, which was wholly abhorrent to an old Sicilian like Mauriello. So there you were. Mauriello, the much misunderstood man.

Snip. Snip. Snip.

Buttons Vicino, who was forty years younger and college trained, stood there, hands at his sides, saying nothing. The old man didn't like to be rushed.

Snip. Snip. Snip.

"He's crazy," said Mauriello finally. "The girl's famous. She's well liked. It would cause an uproar. And why? It's not necessary. It's not *business*."

There had been no uproar over the death of Lemuel Stork because no one gave a damn about Lemuel Stork. There had been a huge outcry over the Ahmet Ali killing which Mauriello had hated. No one had told Mauriello Ahmet Ali was a Worth. If he had been told, it would have been handled quite differently. Only after the event had Mauriello become aware that the man he was dealing with, Elihu Worth (whom he'd never met), harbored quite different philosophies from his own. It was ridiculous, this young genius of finance being so *un*businesslike. Ahmet Ali had been a threat to Elihu and had to be dealt with. The old Sicilian knew that much (though how he knew he would never have said). But this girl was no threat. Killing her was not *business*; it was . . . emotion. It was childish.

The old man put down his scissors and rubbed the sweat off his face with his red bandana. "The man is crazy—and getting crazier. I don't want to . . ." But then Mauriello remembered the sum of money involved, which like the deed itself was crazy. He didn't like to deal in craziness, but for that amount of money . . .

"We'll do it our way, Buttons. Not his way. He is to know nothing."

Vicino nodded. "There's a big family party. Fourth of July. They have it every year." He explained about the party.

Mauriello listened impassively. He was a good listener.

"Insanity," he said. He sat down in the wicker chair on the old-fashioned cushion and wiped his face with the bandana. "A big place you say? A hundred acres? Can we get into the place?"

Buttons explained the scam. Mauriello didn't like it.

"A *waiter*? How do we get him in with these people?"

Buttons explained about Humphrey Worth; that is, as well

as he *could* explain Humphrey Worth. To a Sicilian, Humphrey Worth was pretty inexplicable, but Buttons did his best. Mauriello's mind was on another aspect. "Pirelli's got to be a *good* waiter. He must not attract any attention at all...."

"Pirelli's been a waiter. He knows all the business and he's teaching it to Soldier Ghardelli."

"Soldier Ghardelli is much too big. He'll attract attention."

It couldn't be helped. There had to be a strong man to do what was required and Soldier Ghardelli could lift mountains.

"Bring him here, bring them both here," said Mauriello.

"No, no, *capo*," cried Buttons. "You shouldn't be involved in this business. Not with these punks. They talk."

Mauriello waved him quiet with his big hand, with a little smile to soften the rebuke. He was fond of Buttons, his nephew, a good boy, but Mauriello wanted to attend to these details himself because it was important, much more important than Buttons realized.

The fact was, Mauriello saw an opening. If there was this kind of craziness at the very apex of the Worth family, then with a little swift movement, he, Mauriello, could move in all the way. He could *own* Elihu and, with Elihu, the whole Worth family.

That was the prize, the whole family, and Mauriello wanted to tend to it himself.

CHAPTER 34

Robin lay in the salt grass, shivering. On the Fourth of July! Certainly not from cold. Nor from fear either (Worth children were not permitted fear), but from simple loneliness out there in the tall grass by herself in the darkening night. Far, far away the party howled as parties did when the grown-ups drank. Robin could tell how much they'd drunk, even how long they'd been drinking, by the timbre of the howl, which had risen to a high keening note of hilarity which meant they'd been drinking for hours.

The Game had started at dusk, as it always did, but, because of the wrangling over the rules, it was now quite dark. Robin lay on her back, her yellow dress a ruin, watching the stars come out. Sirius, the Dog Star, winked at her and she winked back. A firefly flew past her nose and it too winked at her and Robin winked at the firefly, feeling a little less lonely. The wind stirred her blond hair, and she smelled the salt. Twenty yards away, waves lapped softly on the pebbled beach.

They called it simply The Game, and the Worth children had evolved it from a lot of other games—Prisoner's Base, Hide and Seek, Run My Good Sheep Run, French and English (introduced by their Canadian cousins and much rougher than the other ones), games that had been played by children since the beginning of human history. The Worth children (simply because they were Worth children) had insisted on shaping and changing the play, creating a game that was uniquely their own, so challenging and difficult that non-Worth children not only wouldn't play it (they felt), but couldn't.

The arguments that year had gone on longer and louder than usual. Why were the boys always changing the rules? Why not play with the same rules as last year? (The year before that Robin couldn't remember and probably wasn't even in The Game since she would have been only three.) This year Nicholas—that derp! (Robin's very own word, a combination of drip and jerk embracing the worst qualities of both)—had insisted on introducing something he called the sacred truce which he said was not at all a new rule and had actually been used by the Greeks at the Olympic Games four thousand years ago.

Robin rolled over on her stomach. Now she could see the gray-shingled hulk of Great-Aunt Elsie's boathouse looming through the darkness, full of mystery and menace, with its marvelous smells of creosote and tar and salt and soap and pine. Peeping out from the slip was the nose of Great-Aunt Elsie's electric launch (one of the few surviving electric launches still running), its nose and pilothouse covered with canvas. The boathouse had always been the center of The Game because it was a long distance from the grown-ups and because it was so huge and there were so many places to hide. The second floor over the slips where the boats were housed was an enormous ballroom which in about 1905 had actually been the scene of many formal balls, but now, dusty and silent, was full of abandoned furniture from the big house, spars and masts from long-forgotten sailboats, buoys, cables, nylon ropes, boat fenders and all the other detritus of boathouses. Above the ballroom were a series of small chambers that had once been the living quarters for Great-Aunt Elsie's gardeners (back when Great-Aunt Elsie had about thirty gardeners) but were now used as storehouses for pool furniture, gardening tools, bits of machinery whose purpose had been long forgotten, all heavy with dust.

Up the hill, on the terrace overlooking the bay, the band was playing Beatles songs and some women were singing "I Want to Hold Your hand" so loud Robin almost missed the signal. Whoo! Whoo! Whoo! It was supposed to be a screech owl but it sounded more like Nicholas trying to imitate a screech owl, seeming to float right out of the water. Robin had no idea where Nicholas was hidden.

She rose to her feet, quaking a little—this was the fun part but it was also scary—and crept forward to the very edge of the pier which was No Man's Land. At the end of the pier was the stockade of the Red Devils (the enemy). Also their prison in which languished Orin.

Robin took a deep breath, closed her eyes and sang out.

"Monkey in the zoo! Monkey in the zoo!

'Afraid to come out and fight are you.'

Robin was the decoy, the lure, to tempt a Red Devil out of the safety of the stockade to where he or she could be captured by the Green Warriors, who were hidden Robin knew not where. (They didn't tell the girls much.)

Silence from the end of the pier. Robin danced out a little farther on the pier (keeping close to the edge as she'd been instructed), singing.

"Cowardy, cowardy custard pie!

'Afraid to fight! Afraid you'll die.'

Herself ready to flee at the first sign of pursuit. Now she could hear whispering and a scraping of feet. Someone was coming out toward her. Out of the darkness a tiny fierce voice trilled.

"Dast you do! Dast you don't!

"Bet you can't! Bet you won't."

Robin couldn't quite see the little figure, but she recognized the voice. It was Elihu, who was only four and hardly worth capturing. The Red Devils were sending out an expendable (like Robin), behind whom would be the heavy artillery, which is to say the bigger boys ready to pounce on whoever pounced on Elihu. That was the way the game was played.

Robin danced backward a little, shouting rhyming taunts, luring Elihu toward the edge of the pier, and now out of the darkness she could actually see Elihu's fierce little face. (Elihu was a werp, which was even more insignificant than a derp.) Suddenly from under the canvas on Great-Aunt Elsie's launch an arm snaked out and caught Elihu by the ankles and pulled him down. Immediately there was a rattle of much larger feet on the pier. The bigger Red Devils who had been following after Elihu came charging to the rescue and there ensued a tug of war, the Red Devils (Jasper, Jr., and a big girl called Peggy Worth) were pulling at Elihu's arms while Nicholas, hidden in the launch and another Worth boy, Michael, were tugging at his feet.

Robin scampered off the pier, charged into the boathouse and into the launch itself to help out. Now came one of the great moments of The Game. The head Green Warrior, Jeremiah Worth, and two other Green Warriors attacked the stockade itself—a seaborne assault from a canoe (the Worth children claimed to be the only ones capable of so sophisticated a maneuver as a combined sea–land operation), and there were howls from the Red Devils left in the stockade.

Jasper, Jr., and Peggy Worth immediately abandoned Elihu and went to the aid of the stockaded Red Devils.

"No fair! No fair!" Elihu screamed.

"Of course it's fair, you little ninny." Robin was sitting on Elihu's legs. "Stop biting! That's not fair."

But Elihu did bite and kick and struggle and it took all three Green Warriors to get him down into the launch's paint locker and lock him in, after which the three Green Warriors—Nicholas, Robin and Michael—scurried out to the end of the pier to join the glorious struggle afoot out there. By this time the Red Devils had launched their own navy—a skiff which promptly turned over and sank. Nicholas wrestled with an older Red Devil, then they both fell off the pier into the water. The Green Warrior's war canoe had also tipped over so that there were actually more combatants in the water than on the pier when the first star shell burst in the heavens which meant the fireworks were started.

"Truce of God! Truce of God!" Nicholas yelled. (He had earlier told them that the Spartans laid aside their arms even with the Persians at the gate rather than incur the wrath of the Gods.) So everyone gave up the fight and scuttled up the hill to the fireworks which that year were glorious— pinwheels of many colors, bombs that shook the earth, zigzagging rockets that lit the Long Island sky for miles, parachute rockets that spelled out Fourth of July in reds and greens and orange—oh, it was a grand show—and the children oohed and aaahed and giggled through the whole thing until the final great starburst (with the phonograph playing "Stars and Stripes Forever") which meant the show was over.

Then the grown-ups started rounding up children they hadn't seen for hours and launching into the long and very sentimental Worth good-byes with all those promises to write and come visit and all that bit the children, fidgeting and now sleepy, hated.

Worth good-byes were not only very long but very noisy, so that it was quite a while before the thin falsetto scream registered on any of the grown-ups. It was a high electric screech, so full of rage as to be hardly a child's scream at all.

In the excitement of the fireworks, the children had forgotten Elihu altogether. That was the worst of it, the forgetting. Sophie flew down the hill, ahead of all the

*others, guided by that high metallic scream, unlocked the
paint locker and enfolded her little boy in her arms, crooning,
"My baby! My baby!" which Elihu wasn't, being four years
old. (Nicholas always claimed that Elihu had never been a
baby at all, that he had sprung from his mother's womb
fully clothed and angry.)*

*Robin never forgot the sight of Elihu's face convulsed
with a fury that wasn't quite human. Werp, she decided,
was not the word for Elihu. He was better than that.*

Or worse.

Marcia Worth had been nagging William to give up the
Fourth of July party for a very long time. "We've done our
share, William, it's someone else's turn." She didn't dare
mention her real concern, that William was too old for the
strain of the party, that it took too much out of him, an
accusation he'd so bitterly resent he'd keep going out of
sheer bravado.

"One last party," said William. He didn't say why. He
couldn't. Nicholas had sworn him to secrecy.

It would be a memorable party, said William. Marvelous
food. A good band a man could dance to. None of these pop
outfits that simply made noise. Nicholas had taken over
control of the fireworks which, he told William, would be
very noisy this year, very bright, very surprising, altogether
Worthian.

The invitations were Marcia's department, but William
insisted on looking over her shoulder, personally inspecting
all the replies to see who was coming and who was not.

"Elihu has declined," said William. "So has Sophie."

"They'll be there," promised Nicholas, his blue eyes
deep as a well.

Worths were coming from all over the eastern seaboard
because William called personally and said it was his last
Fourth of July party and please . . . There would be several
Chicago Worths, Felix and Waddington, Humphrey's twin

brother, the actor Worth. There were the Galveston Worths—
Alec and Hortense. Almost half again as many people
as last year, said William to Nicholas. "Good," said Nicholas.
"It will help the confusion."

Fergie was at the FX 4000 as long as seventeen hours a
day because Nicholas said they were running out of time.
Nicholas got the access codes from a very reluctant William
Worth for computers in all those faraway, almost nonregulated
banks in Bahrain, the Seychelles, the Bahamas. Fergie planted
his little time bombs in these distant spots, timed to go off
July second or July third, depending on which side of the
international dateline they were on.

"When the shit hits the fan, I'll go to jail for a hundred
years," he said.

"I'll send birthday cards every year," said Nicholas.

Robin Worth and Jane Fox now traveled to the network
and back in an armored car. Jane Fox had insisted on the
armored car. "She's been set up," said little Jane Fox to
Webley Foster. "It didn't work so they'll try something
else."

"Why?" inquired Webley Foster.

"Why is the earth round?"

So that was that.

Robin was now picking her own assignments and the
assignment she picked for July third astounded Webley
Foster. "You don't know anything about finance!" he
said.

Robin smiled glacially. "You must never tell a Worth she
doesn't know anything about finance. Finance is what we're
all about."

Nicholas had primed her with astonishing questions, but
in the end, as Robin herself bluntly pointed out, it was
going to be Robin who was out there in front of the
cameras, and it was Robin who did her own research and it

was Robin who made the phone call to the Secretary of the Treasury. Nicholas had not wanted the Secretary of the Treasury; he'd wanted the director of the FBI. "You'd never get him," Robin told him, "and if you did, he's too cagey to be pushed into a corner. Schrader's an idiot. I can handle Schrader."

Secretary of the Treasury Schrader was a big beefy Republican with friends in high places and a very limited knowledge of finance. He was overjoyed to be noticed by this sexy glamor girl, Robin Worth, but he was less than overjoyed about the date of the interview, July third. Like everyone else he wanted to be well away from Washington that night. Robin sweetly, caressingly, insisted that it was that night or none at all. So naturally...

Things were shaping up.

Nicholas had not managed to lure Waddington Worth to New York. In fact, it was difficult to get him to come at all because Waddington was deep into rehearsals with the Wisconsin Players in Milwaukee of *Edward, My Son*. Waddington was directing it and also starring in the old Robert Morley part and he was, everyone in the Midwest agreed, brilliant in the part. (He also played Oscar Wilde, another old Robert Morley part, with even greater authority, his admirers said, than Wilde himself could have managed. Waddington was a portly man and there were not all that many parts for him. These were his favorites.)

In the end Nicholas flew to Milwaukee and laid the proposition at Waddington's feet. "You are the only Worth actor."

Waddington didn't like any of it. "Why must it be a Worth?"

"We'd be blackmailed until the end of time if this got out and it would get out if we brought in a non-Worth. This is an all-Worth operation. It's got to be."

"I hate all of it," said Waddington. He was storming up

and down his Pfister Hotel suite. "Sophie Worth is one of the dearest, sweetest, most innocent people on earth. We could drive her right out of her mind."

Nicholas trotted out all the arguments he'd honed on William Worth. Honor of the family, *survival* of the family, plus a good deal of gung ho history of the Worths in which he pointed out that the family had gotten out of tight spots again and again only by its own united efforts, that when the going got tough, the Worths got even tougher and would not have survived as a family—certainly not as a rich family—if they had not.

In the end, though, it was not these arguments but something quite different that swayed Waddington. The operation was a one-man show, Nicholas said. Waddington would be not only the star and the director but the lighting expert, the makeup man, the prop man, the sound man (especially that), everything. It was the theatrical challenge which was irresistible. Waddington loved painting the scenery, designing the sets, all the technical end of theater, and was very good at it.

The medical part he didn't like. "It won't work without it," said Nicholas. "You're a great actor, Waddington, but not *that* great. She'd never accept it without the Cliomyazene. She's got to be a little dopey to buy it and it won't be any problem getting it into her. Sophie has always taken sleeping pills. She'll be sound asleep and there is a way—I'll show you—of introducing the needle into a sleeping person. . . ."

Sylvia was a problem. When Nicholas broached the proposition she reacted as if stung by a wasp. "I *loathe* him!" She drew the word *loathe* into a long, shuddering whisper like a fingernail being drawn against a blackboard.

"Don't we all?" said Nicholas.

"I couldn't *bear* to touch his flesh." This from the

woman who had kissed it, licked it, caressed it, lusted after it. "I couldn't *bear* it!"

"I think you could."

"My flesh would crawl. . . ."

"You are the supreme mistress of artifice, Aunt Sylvia. You could deceive a cobra into thinking he was a mongoose."

"No, Nicholas, *no*!"

"Elihu must not under any circumstance go back to his mother's place that night and you are the only one—"

"There are limits, Nicholas, beyond which. . ."

It took an hour of Nicholas' special pleading, during which he used every argument, fair and foul, that he could muster. So relentless, so implacable was he, that at one point Sylvia cried out, "I don't recognize you anymore, Nicholas. You've changed into a new person and not a better one!"

"Nicest thing you've ever said to me."

Ultimately, she whispered, "I'm terrified of him, Nicholas! Terrified!"

"Grace under pressure is what we're asking, Aunt Sylvia, and you, being a Worth. . ."

The unfairest argument of all.

The worst part of it for Sylvia was making the phone call. "I've tried not to miss you, Elihu! Oh God, how I've tried! I'm so hungry for your dear body I could scream with anguish."

Nicholas had written all these lines which Sylvia gagged on when she first read but which Nicholas forced down her throat like castor oil. "I'm out of my mind, Elihu! I'm *possessed*!"

Giving the words all the passion she had in her, summoning it all out of the very bottom of her.

Silence on the other end of the phone, sinister frightening silence. . . .

Sylvia seated on the twin bed in Robin's room as she made the pitch. Nicholas stood over her, his hands waving upward, pulling the emotion out of her, directing her like Toscanini directing the *Ninth*.

On the next bed sat Robin, herself an old lover of Elihu, her mouth a little round o. Sylvia had wanted an audience, had insisted on it, to charge her, to get *performance*.

When she hung up she was drained dry, her shoulders curved down, eyes on the floor.

"Well!" said Nicholas.

She shrugged listlessly. "He'll . . . be there. Oh, he'll be there." She looked at Nicholas. "But it's not me he wants. Not my *body*, love. He wants something else. He's a game player, Nicholas."

"We all are."

"He plays very hard. I could get killed."

"You mustn't let him," said Robin. "I'd miss you, Aunt Sylvia."

"You're such a comfort, dear."

"You will become a legend, Aunt Sylvia, to be handed down from one generation of Worths to another," said Nicholas.

"You mustn't inter me quite yet, Nicholas, I haven't gone." She smiled a little cat's smile, her humor seeping back. It was, after all, her strongest fiber, the humor in her. She'd need all of it to simulate what needed simulating. . . .

At the bottom of Manhattan, Elihu hung up the phone and walked over to the huge plate-glass window overlooking the bay and stared out, rubbing his chin. Dora Land watched him for clues since he had said almost nothing except, "Well, Sylvia," at the beginning, "Yes" (several times with a rising inflection), "What time?" and finally, "All right." Not much to work with. Dora Land knew about Sylvia, of course, because Elihu had told her—even while copulating with her—exactly what he and Sylvia had done, every exquisite detail, while making Dora keep her eyes open and listen and react to these prurient details. It was one of his little refinements, of which he had so many that Dora had lost count.

"You're going to her place?" Dora had guessed this from the rising inflection. There was surprise in this rising inflection. If it had been his place there would be no surprise, at least not that much. She knew him well, at least the voice of him. There were large areas of Elihu that were unknowable, but the voice she knew. . . .

"She's playing games," said Elihu, staring out at the glittering bay. "Imagine that, Dora! Playing games! With *me*!" Somebody had put her up to it. Sylvia wouldn't embark on this by herself. He knew her inside out—the inside of her, the outside of her—her quickness, her cleverness, her limitations, all of her.

And he still lusted after that forty-four-year-old body because it *was* forty-four; he loved the forty-fourness of it, the strength of it, the experience of it, the wisdom of it. He had relished listening to Sylvia's passionate utterance about his own body without believing a single damned syllable.

He would love to *watch* her at this game, as well as listen. Her place. Not his. Why?

Dora Land was gathering up her papers. "Robin Worth is living there. Will she. . . ."

"I don't know. I'll just have to go find out, won't I?" Because Dora Land knew about Robin, too.

"The place is like a fortress," said Dora. "You won't be able to summon assistance."

Elihu laughed, his whole face lighting up. "Assistance? My goodness! *Assistance!* Perhaps you'd like to come watch, Dora."

That ended the dialogue. Dora Land gathered her notebooks and left him to his daydreams.

Estelle was put in charge of the delivery and of making the very large box that would be needed, Estelle not having any idea what the box was needed for. "I must consult

Jeremy Quilp both about making the box and about the delivery," she rasped. "I've always consulted Jeremy."

"Not this time, Aunt Estelle. This time you're on your own. We can't have any non-Worths in on this. This is a Worth production—a hundred percent Worth. No substitutes. Those cigarettes are going to kill you, Aunt Estelle."

The cigarette hung from the right corner of her mouth, the smoke curling upward, the right eye closed, the left one staring at him malevolently. "You look like a riverboat gambler."

"It's just a lark, Nicholas. The old lady's last flourish." The smoke curling up from the tip of the cigarette, Estelle smiling evilly. "I can see you thinking it's the old lady's *first* flourish but it isn't. I had a flourish once before—when I was nineteen. I was quite a pretty girl when I was nineteen."

"What happened?"

"He went away. He said, 'You're too rich, Estelle. I'd suffocate on all that money.' And off he went. Now that I'm decently poor, he's," she took a drag on the cigarette and blew the smoke out in a great burst, "married to somebody else. Rich girls attract the most godawful men—like Oscar Settle—and repel all the good ones."

Nicholas pulled out the sketch. Estelle had seen it earlier, but Waddington had added his own improvements which made Estelle sputter, "Does it have to be so *big*? How will we get it in the elevator?"

"How do you get grand pianos in the elevator? He needs all this stuff—lighting equipment, sound effects, smoke effects, recording equipment. It's Waddington's greatest production."

"It's demented!" said Estelle.

"So's Elihu. We're fighting dementia with dementia."

Estelle's reply to that was a burst of coughing that wracked her fragile body for minutes. "I don't think you *like* cigarettes, Aunt Estelle. Why in God's name—"

"It focuses attention on me, silly boy. I've not had much. Now I'm the center of the room. People can't tear their eyes away from this evil old woman, puffing away on her fag."

She cackled like the Witch of Endor.

Nicholas kissed her on the top of her head. "Get on with it, Auntie. It's got to be finished July first and ready for occupancy July second."

"I thought it was July third."

"We're having a rehearsal at Sylvia's the night before. It's all too complicated to leave to last-minute improvisation. Waddington is going to have to run through it—all of it. Getting into the box. Traveling, opening the box from the inside, setting up, all of it. We've made it long and narrow so it'll go through ordinary doors and we've measured elevators. . . ."

Estelle wasn't permitted at the dress rehearsal, which was just as well because everything went wrong that could go wrong. MacLean Movers (the only ones Jeremy Quilp trusted) had trouble getting the box into the elevator and turned it upside down, which wreaked havoc on Waddington, to say nothing of the sound equipment. Waddington had trouble opening the box from inside. The sound equipment had three-pronged plugs which wouldn't fit and needed adaptors. The smoke bombs would have burned the place down and had to be abandoned in favor of dry ice, which actually worked better and was much safer. Waddington forgot his lines. . . .

The audience was Sylvia (playing Sophie), Nicholas and Robin. (Jane Fox was sent elsewhere, not being a Worth.) All of them were appalled and dismayed. Not Waddington.

"Darlings," crooned Waddington, "most dress rehearsals are a disaster and when they're not it means opening night will be a disaster. It'll play like a dream."

That was what it was supposed to do—play like a dream.

CHAPTER 35

Over the ferocious objections of her network boss, Webley Foster, and also those of Secretary Schrader, Robin insisted on holding the interview back for the eleven o'clock news. "If a cabinet officer is worth interviewing at all—and most of them aren't—he should be on the six o'clock news," snarled Webley Foster.

Robin said no. Seated in Webley's office, wearing her fire engine red linen suit, her eyes deep as pools, the cheeks sunken, the mouth now permanently downturned, Robin had never looked lovelier. Or sadder. Or more inflexible. "I'm going to throw a few high hard ones at him, Webley. They're eleven o'clock questions, not six o'clock questions."

"Christ on a raft, Robin, a question is a question is a question. Six o'clock, seven o'clock . . ."

"No," said Robin. "Trust my instinct." Already she had developed the full star temperament. Demanding everything she wanted (or Jane Fox wanted) and getting it. Webley

Foster bared his teeth like the MGM lion. He was still only acting director but, seated in Gerald Fisher's vast office, he was acquiring the mannerisms, the arrogance and even—looking at Robin—some of the same lusts of his predecessor.

"I'll have to, won't I?"

Robin was halfway to the door when Webley threw his own high hard one at her retreating back. "Robin, are you happy?"

Robin turned with her little wry smile. Webley Foster had himself once been a much feared interviewer and this was the kind of question he used to throw at his victims to discomfit them, to unmask them, to draw a little blood.

"No!" trilled Robin—with a big smile.

"Why not? You're young. Famous. Healthy. Beautiful. Admired. Why in *hell* not?"

"The answer is still no," said Robin and left him.

Never apologize, never explain.

It was a very strange encounter. Elihu had never before set foot in Sylvia's Park Avenue flat despite the fact that she'd lived there for years. Sylvia answered the door herself and waved him in with a small smile. Neither of them said anything, which made the encounter even stranger. Elihu was looking around at everything in the reception room, the crystal wall brackets, the Directoire table, the Bokkara carpets, as if he was cataloguing them for Sotheby's. His eyes darted here and there—at the marvelously curved staircase, the antique mirrors, the small Picasso drawing—everywhere except at Sylvia, who never took her eyes off Elihu, not knowing what the play was, knowing only that she was in uncharted seas.

Both of them as tight as fiddle strings.

She led the way into the sitting room with its soft carpets, its sea of flowered chintz, all of which he would loathe. (His own floors bare wood, his chairs canvas and stainless steel.) She was thinking, he wasn't fooled by all that passionate utterance, not Elihu, no, not Elihu. Her heart was cold within her, but there was no fear, she'd outgrown the fear, thank God for that, anyway.

Who's going to speak first? This silence is . . . Well, it wasn't unbearable. It was . . . interesting, the silence. He's as buffaloed as I am. She didn't know why she thought this, why she was so sure of it, but she was, and that loosened her up a little bit. Loosened him up a bit too. She could feel the unloosening of him. He has come (she guessed) not for my tight experienced body (which he'd had many times in many different ways), but to see what I'm up to and in that case I'm one up on him because I know what I'm up to and he doesn't.

She waved him now into the flower-decked sofa before the mirrored fireplace and he sat down. Directly before his eyes was the huge book, lying open in all its magnificent gilt decadence.

"Pornography?" said Elihu. "You?"

She'd got him to speak first and that loosened her altogether.

"Japanese pornography. I thought it would amuse you because it is so ridiculous."

Some forgotten lover had brought the stuff, fearfully expensive, and Sylvia, who had never needed stimulation, had brought it out that night because that night she *did* need stimulation, that night her loins were as cold as a Siberian icicle and she had looked at the marvelous Japanese graphics, trying to arouse herself and not succeeding. Now Elihu was bent over the big book turning the pages, mouth open. He's as cold as I am; he's trying to turn on like me and not succeeding.

The thought made her giggle and he, turning the pages, looking at all those beautiful impassive Japanese screwing each other in such outlandish ways began to giggle too. She dropped onto the sofa next to him laughing, not giggling now, Elihu laughing too, a little. Just a little.

"It's so comical, isn't it, love?"

"Very comical." He turned away from the book. "Why did you ask me here, Sylvia?"

"I told you on the phone, I'm perishing with lust!"

"So perishing you had to resort to Japanese pornography?"

He was very bright. One had to count on that. "A girl's moods change, Elihu. It's been a while, hasn't it?"

He was leaning back on the flowered sofa looking at her for the first time. "Where's Robin?"

"She's got a show tonight. An interview with the Secretary of the Treasury. At eleven. We can watch if you like."

He leaned his head against the back of the sofa, looking at her. "Are you afraid of me, Sylvia?"

"It's part of the attraction." She smiled. A damned lie. It *had* been part of the attraction, but there wasn't any attraction now. It was going to be the hardest thing she had ever done. How the hell did prostitutes manage? She slithered toward him on the sofa, faking it. "And you, darling, are you lusting after me?"

He didn't answer, just smiled, running his hand over her stomach, her breast, her cheek. He's just trying it on, she thought. She waited for the flesh to crawl but it didn't. It didn't! I am a bit of a prostitute after all, she was thinking. I can manage. Perhaps even enjoy.

She kissed him then experimentally, to see what he would do, what he would feel, to see whether there was any fire there at all. Both of us, she was thinking. Both trying it on. Neither of us wants the other and yet we're stuck with it because how can we break it off and anyway I have to keep him here. I have to. . . .

The network had had to give the Treasury some idea of what its secretary was being interviewed about so as to prepare his answers. Robin had answered that one personally. Overseas investment, she wrote, the outflow of money from the United States—its use and misuse. Even as colossal an idiot as Secretary Schrader could hardly miss the implications. The staff gave him his answers—good answers—written on little white cards he could hold just under camera range on his lap.

At first blush—the red eye of the camera winking on, the lights pouring into his very soul—Secretary Schrader was very good because Robin willed that he be. She turned on her beauty like an electric light, wooing him, encouraging him, telling him with her large beckoning smile like a modern Circe how wonderful, how plausible, how *intelligent* he was.

"We are aware," said Secretary Schrader easily (reading the lines written by somebody else), "that the movement of money into and out of foreign markets has been used to launder drug money. We have kept a close watch on the situation for years and in fact the Treasury Department has helped write a bill now before the Senate and House to tighten control of the overseas money flow. However, we must be careful not to choke off legitimate overseas investment. . . ."

Ten minutes after eleven P.M. July third.

Sylvia and Elihu were lying stark naked across her enormous bed watching Robin in her fire engine red linen suit draw the Secretary of the Treasury into the net.

Elihu had emitted a little hiss, like escaping steam, when the word launder was uttered (by Robin even before Secretary Schrader). Elihu had been lying flat, nose to the comforter, and now he came up on his elbows and drew in a long breath.

Like a cobra about to strike. Sylvia in her splendid nakedness watched Elihu, not Robin, herself coldly cerebral. Like the sex with which it had been preceded. She had *entertained* (no other word for it!) Elihu like those sacred prostitutes in the temples of Venus. A high calling. Very strenuous exercise, no doubt of it, but *interesting*. Coldly cerebral. Perhaps sacred prostitution, myself in the service of the godlike family of Worth, is what I'm truly for. I performed very well. After all, I have kept him here, and what is even more *interesting* I have kept myself here. My flesh has not crawled embracing this loathsome creature because I am in the service of a higher power.

Watching him through narrowed eyes, her head on her arm, Sylvia lay flat, loathing Elihu with all her soul and even at the same time contemplating (after the TV program was over) further sexual transports with Elihu without a tremor of revulsion because she was now a priestess at the sacred fountain, performing her sacred duties. . . .

On the screen the questioning had taken a darker turn, and now Elihu rose to a sitting position, his legs dangling over the big bed. . . .

Robin had let Secretary Schrader run with it—blah, blah, blah—for a minute and a half, too long, really, before dropping her bombshell.

"Yes, but don't you find it alarming that Mob money is being laundered by such respectable institutions as Boston banks, which have up to this time been the very symbol of financial integrity?"

"Well," said Secretary Schrader, beginning to blubber a little.

That's as far as Robin let him go. She went on. "Just this afternoon the Chairman of the SEC, William Worth, has accused one of the largest and most respectable of all brokerage houses—Securities Unlimited—of transferring fifty million dollars in Mob drug profits to an offshore bank it controls in Bahrain. What is your comment on that?"

Secretary Schrader's mouth flew open. "I . . . I . . . This is the first I've heard of such a thing. . . ."

It was the first anyone had heard such a thing. Seated on Sylvia's bed, stark naked, the chairman of Securities Unlimited howled as if impaled. "A goddamned *lie*!"

On the screen Robin was pulling Secretary Schrader apart like a little girl pulling the wings off a butterfly. "This collaboration between the very highest element of our society—the pillars of our community—and the very lowest—the Mob—would it be too much to say that in this horrifying union we are seeing the moral integrity of the republic crumbling away?"

Sylvia was thinking, She's moving into the vacuum left by Edward R. Murrow as the conscience of America! God in heaven—little sexy Robin!

Elihu had the telephone in his hands and was dialing away, paying no attention to Sylvia. "Dora! Dora!" he screamed. "Did you watch it? What in hell is it about? Have we transferred any money to Bahrain? Fifty *million*, for Christ sake! Well, I didn't think so either. Where in hell has this come from?"

A moment later he'd hung up and turned on Sylvia, who saw (still coldly cerebral like the priestess she was) the rage in him. His vulnerability is his rage, Nicholas had said, Elihu's only vulnerability since he is both more clever and more unscrupulous than any of us could hope to be, but in his rage we can bring him down to our level. And here was the rage. He might, Sylvia was thinking, just kill me because there's no one else around to kill. It should have terrified her, but it didn't, enwrapped as she was in her priestesshood.

"William Worth's telephone number. He'll be in the country. . . ." Elihu had cooled a little.

Sylvia gave him the Old Westbury number and he dialed it. Marcia took the call. "Elihu! How nice to hear your voice! No, William isn't here. He's on his yacht with his cronies. They're playing poker. No, you can't get him on the yacht. That's why he gets on it, because he doesn't want to be disturbed. Well, of course he'll be here tomorrow. We're giving the Fourth of July party. You must come to the party. William says it's going to be quite marvelous. The best fireworks and food we've ever had because this is going to be our swan song, our very last Fourth of July party. Do come, Elihu. I'd love to see you again. I haven't seen you for so long. . . .''

William sat opposite his wife on the loveseat in the sitting room, the TV set on with the sound turned off, listening to Marcia tell all these lies. She lied very well, did Marcia, and it bothered him, as it bothers all husbands.

On Park Avenue Elihu hung up and began prowling around Sylvia's bedroom silently from the bed to the window to the door, back and forth, like a caged lion. If he had a tail, it would be thrashing around, Sylvia was thinking.

"Where in hell did Robin get that . . . misinformation?'' Elihu was quite calm now and in his calmness much more formidable. "What in hell is she up to?''

Sylvia, the priestess, fielded the pitch coolly. "Darling, Robin's not *up* to anything. She does what the network tells her to do. She's just reading her lines.''

"Oh no she isn't. I know Robin inside out. I know when she's reading her own lines and when she's reading somebody else's. These are her own lines—and what I want to know is why? When will she be home?''

Sylvia yawned, a superb production that yawn. "Darling, who knows? Robin likes to cool out after a performance like any performer. She and Jane Fox will have a drink somewhere with friends. She might not be in for hours. Come to bed.''

She had to keep him there until dawn at least because uptown, in Sylvia's new much-hated apartment, the other performance was about to begin and Elihu mustn't interrupt that. Robin would not return to Sylvia's that night at all, but Elihu was not to know that.

"Come to bed, my darling. I'll comfort you with lust. Would you like to whip me, Elihu? I need a whipping badly to purge me of my many sins and you are just the man to make me swoon with the delicious pain of it. . . .''

Sylvia the high priestess in the exercise of her sacred calling. . . .

Sylvia had had supper brought to her on a tray before the TV set in the small alcove off the main dining room the designer had intended to be a bar but which Sophie had converted into a cozy breakfast room and library, the only cozy room in the apartment. There she ate her steak bearnaise and salad and watched reruns of "The Waltons," that fairy tale from Virginia she found so comforting. Her much loved Hooker had been retired against his will and hers by Elihu and replaced by Travis, a coldly proper English butler who intimidated her. Elihu had been expected for dinner that night, but he had called to say he couldn't make it so there she was with Travis and his propriety. Sophie used to have quite decent conversations with old Hooker, who had known her since she was a young married woman. With Travis speech was out of the question.

At nine P.M. Sophie was in bed watching *A Man for All Seasons*—why didn't they make movies like that anymore? —on the VCR in the vast bedroom where waking was still a terrifying and lonely experience, watching for the eleventh time Paul Scofield perform his magic—that marvelous face, that superb diction!—when the house phone began blinking away. Sophie turned off the VCR and answered it because Travis had gone to his home. (It was impossible to get the butlers to live in anymore, even the English ones.)

A package! At this hour!

Sophie slipped out of bed, put on her old Japanese kimono and went to the back service door because the object which, she was told, was large was coming up the back service elevator. It was more than large; it was immense and MacLean Movers, everyone's favorite movers, in their white coats with the little green enormously reassuring lettering saying MacLean's, were very apologetic. "Sorry to trouble you at this hour, madam, but we were delayed."

"Another one," said Sophie, dismayed.

Elihu was inundating her with furniture all of which she hated—soulless slabs of Swedish modern or Danish art deco or—worst of all—American contemporary.

They deposited the huge crate in the kitchen. Sophie went back to her bed and surrendered her soul to Paul Scofield. At ten P.M. she popped the Valium and Paul Scofield dimmed and presently shivered into illogicality as dreams do. She and Paul Scofield, hand in hand, plunged into the deep green sea and there consorted with the fishes, one of which bit her on the arm, provoking a pain so sharp she cried out.

In and out of the cool green caves beneath the sea, Paul Scofield being ever so courteous and literate, Sophie exhilarated—oh, this was a marvelous dream! It couldn't last, they never did. Presently she was back in her vast and lonely bed, the lights shining up out of the floor. How very odd! Even odder the bedroom curtains drawn. She always threw them open to let in the good night air. Clearly this was still a dream.

Aah, there was dear old Paul Scofield, smiling at her . . . lecherously. No, it wasn't Paul Scofield at all. He wouldn't smile in that lecherous way. It was . . . my goodness. . . .

"Jasper!"

Sophie was giggling, though heaven knew this was not a time for giggling, but she felt a little light-headed, quite carried away. . . .

"Jasper, you're . . . naked! What have you done with your . . . *clothes*?"

Not simply the clothes. Jasper himself came and went, dissolving and materializing, materializing and dissolving like an object in a kaleidoscope, always quite naughtily naked—her wicked, beloved Jasper, the love of her life, her only love. Jasper with his bold assertive smile (he'd bequeathed it to his son, Elihu). Jasper hung there as if suspended from the ceiling, a roseate mist encircling the lower half of him, obscuring but by no means blotting out the pendulous penis which had so tormented and enchanted her.

"Jasper!" Sophie giggling again, she felt seventeen... "Whatever are you doing in my bedroom...naked?" Because they had never done it in her bedroom, always in his....

"Dead, you know." The voice sepulchral. Waddington had played all the distinguished dramatic corpses, reveled in the sepulchral.

That brought forth from Sophie a little preliminary scream, just a little one. (Waddington had not only drawn the curtains, he had closed the windows to keep the screams intramural.)

"You have not faced up to the fact that I'm dead, Sophie. You are in the presence of *Death*." Waddington rolling the word off his tongue with enormous glee. That provoked a loud shuddering scream from Sophie, who rose to a full sitting position, her hand over her mouth to choke back the terror.

"Dear Sophie, am I the first dead person you have met? There are millions of us. The air is alive with the dead—a pun, my dear."

"Jasper!" moaned Sophie. She had shrunk into herself until she was just a pair of huge eyes.

Waddington reached down into the mist encircling his knees and came forth with the document. "Our baby's footprints, Sophie. Dear Elihu's baby footprints." He waved them gently in the encircling light.

"*You* took them, Jasper! It was you who stole Elihu's footprints." Sophie forcing the words out. She was having great difficulty controlling her voice. This was a dream, of course. Had to be! The terror welling up in her like a balloon!

"*Why*, Jasper? *Why?*" The voice out of control now. Screeching!

"I wanted to see if the little monster was truly my child!" Jasper's smile had disappeared. He was glaring at her with hatred, the voice thunderous. He tore the footprints in half and cast them aside.

"No, Jasper, *no!*" A loud and piteous wail.

"He killed me, Sophie! Your son! My son! *Our* son! Murdered his own father!"

Sophie was out of the bed now, her arms around Jasper's naked knees, screaming. "He didn't! He didn't! You fell, Jasper, you fell!"

Waddington's great moment and he rose to it like Brando, the great organ of a voice thundering *basso profundo*. "He *pushed* me from the rigging with malice aforethought. Deliberate murder, Sophie!"

"No!" howled Sophie, because it was unutterable what he was uttering.

"He murdered his own father and then he stole the business—a patricide and a thief. Your son! Damned for all eternity."

Then came Sophie's great scream. "El-i-hu!" Three long howling syllables, a great name for screaming. And again and again.

"El-i-hu! El-i-hu! Where are you, El-i-hu? Your father says you *murdered* him! Say it's not true! *El-i-hu!*"

It was fortunate that the new seven-million-dollar apartment had boasted of its soundproofing.

Waddington had other provocative lines designed to bring forth even louder screams, but he never got the chance. Sophie pitched forward at his feet and lay still, scaring the wits out of Waddington. This was no simple faint. He felt her pulse, looked under her eyelids. She was breathing stentoriously, frighteningly. Waddington lifted her back into the bed, and listened to her heart thumping away, much too loud. He switched off the recording machine.

It all had to be put back into the big crate—recorder, lights, dry ice. After that Waddington washed off the make-up, transforming himself from Jasper back into Waddington, put on his clothes, locked up the crate, and reopened the curtains and windows in Sophie's room.

He put the tape into his pocket, took the elevator to the lobby and sauntered out into the night. Nicholas awaited him at his apartment and the two of them spent an hour editing the tape.

Very early the next morning—on July Fourth!—MacLean Movers appeared at the apartment full of apologies. It had been a terrible mistake but not, they told Travis, the butler, *their* mistake. It had been the mistake of Estelle Worth, who had gotten things muddled and sent the crate to the wrong apartment. They took it away.

"The mistress is still asleep," Travis told them.

Very odd because Sophie didn't usually sleep that long. That day she slept until noon and was so disoriented when she awoke that Travis called the doctor who, because she was a Worth, actually came to her on July Fourth, and felt her pulse and listened to her heart (which had calmed) and, skeptically, to her excuses.

"It was just a dream. A bad dream!"

She clung to that because she had little else to cling to. She didn't tell the doctor what the bad dream was. She wasn't even going to tell Elihu. She was going to keep that bad dream to herself forevermore.

CHAPTER 36

There were more young children than there had been at the preceding three Fourth of July parties. Louise Hampton brought her three from England—Deborah, Abigail and Robert, rosy-cheeked outspoken English children, more Worthian than Hamptons (Abigail with the red ribbon in her hair, high Worth cheekbones and mischievous eyes, the image of Robin at eleven. "Trouble," her mother said grimly). Jasper, Jr., and Eleanor brought their three from Canada, Jasper III (known as Threep), Martin and Susan; Alec and Hortense brought Lannie and Geoffrey from Galveston and the archeological Worths brought their stately Sarah, the brightest eleven-year-old in Chicago (or perhaps anywhere).

All in all there were fourteen young Worths ranging in age from four to fifteen scattered around William Worth's big lawn when Robin arrived at eleven in the stretch Cadillac with the tinted windows you couldn't see through that didn't look like a Worth car, that looked, in fact, so much like a Mob car that Robin was ashamed of it. A gaggle of Worth children gathered around it, hooting and jeering when Robin stepped out. Robin's TV celebrity was considered by other Worth children to be strictly ridiculous, and they were not about to let her forget it. "Can I have your autograph, lady?" said Robert (age seven). Robin put her arms around him, lifted him off the ground and bit his ear, hard. "Ouch," said Robert. "That's better than an autograph." The others grabbing at Robin shouting, "Can I touch you, lady?" "Autograph! Autograph!"

Nicholas shooed the children away and led Robin firmly down the lawn toward the big boathouse.

"I promised Marcia I'd help in the kitchen," protested Robin.

"Later," said Nicholas.

He led Robin down the great lawn past Susan and Daisy Worth playing skipping games, chanting scatalogical rhymes of their own devising, past Arthur (son of the senator from Delaware) and Threep trying to fly a kite and not managing it, to the huge shingled nineteenth-century extravagance of a boathouse that had once harbored William Worth's great racing sloops and now held only a decrepit Chris-Craft and two rowboats.

Nicholas guided Robin up the rickety wooden stairs past the little loo on the landing that overlooked the lawn up to the broad balcony that overlooked the sound with its white sails. There he pulled the snub-nosed .38 out of his back pocket and closed Robin's protesting hands around its butt. "I've never fired a gun in my life, Nicholas!"

"That's why," said Nicholas. He made her hold it, made her fire at a Coca-Cola can she missed by three feet from three yards, made her fire it again, making quite sure she wasn't aiming anywhere near the sailboats, finally reloaded it and put it in her shoulder bag. "Why?" asked Robin for the twelfth time.

He didn't tell her much. "Louis Hanagan says we might have company."

"At Uncle Will's Fourth of July party?" It was absurd. Non-family were never allowed at the Fourth of July party although Worths never stopped trying. Robin herself had tried to bring Jane Fox and Estelle had wanted to bring Jeremy Quilp. Both were firmly turned down with the ancient argument that if anyone started bringing in non-family where would it end?

"Just carry it around in your shoulder bag all day long. I know it's a nuisance. Just *do* it."

Louis Hanagan had called the day before. "For reasons that don't concern you, we have had a tail on a man named Buttons Vicino, one of Mauriello's bright young men." Hanagan didn't go into details about the directional mikes or the other gadgetry they had employed. All he said was, "Mauriello and company are awfully interested in that party your uncle gives every year. We'd like to plant a couple of men there to keep an eye on things."

"Absolutely not," said Nicholas. The last thing in the world he wanted was to have the DA's men underfoot while the plan was going forth.

"For your own protection."

"The Worths have always managed their own protection, Louis. It's a family party."

"Is Robin going to be there? You should keep her away."

But they couldn't keep her away. Robin was part of the master plan. Hence the gun. To still Nicholas' raging doubts. Which it didn't do.

Louis Hanagan didn't give up easily. "We'll be just down the road in case you need us. I'll give you a radio and set it to the right channel."

"Thanks."

The Assistant DA couldn't resist a final thrust. "That was quite a piece of cheese Robin threw onto Elihu's plate on her TV show."

Nicholas grunted. He didn't like the metaphor at all. Piece of cheese? How much did Louis Hanagan suspect? And if he suspected, would Elihu be far behind?

The directional mikes and the other bits of electronic wizardry had by no means brought in all of Mauriello's conversation. The DA's men had missed the tactics as well as much of the homespun wisdom of that old philosopher Binkie Mauriello. Among other pearls dropped by Binkie to his young nephew Buttons Vicino, Mauriello had said, "Drowning's as American as apple pie on the Fourth of July. Nobody thinks twice about a mark drowning on that day because it's the proper American way to go."

Mauriello was a great one for the American proprieties. Always had been.

Nicholas and Robin walked up the lawn to the house, passing a group of the older children and many of the adults, choosing up sides for the baseball game. Uncle Will was doing the counting. "Eenie meenie, minie mo, catch a nigger by the toe."

"Great-Uncle Will!" said Sarah, scandalized. "We don't *say* that anymore!"

"I don't know how to count off any other way."

Sarah showed him. "Bumpety, clumpety, bimpity him. You go out and you go in."

On the big screen porch, there was already an early line of drinkers.

Robin said, "Where's Orin?"

Nicholas was staring off at the swimming pool at the side of the house. Endicott Worth's two big girls were doing their annual trick, riding the mares bareback in their bathing suits at a soft canter—leaping off into the pool from the backs of the horses, which always got a big hand from the kids and a groan from their parents.

"Orin's not coming," said Nicholas.

"*Not* coming!" gasped Robin.

"He's becalmed in the Sargasso Sea," said Nicholas. "Like the ancient mariner."

"But we need . . ." Stunned by Orin's betrayal.

Nicholas strode off, his back to her, without saying another word.

No Orin. Robin had counted on Orin. More than she realized. . . .

Marcia had wanted to use the immense second-story room of the old boathouse for backup for the food, but William had said no. "But, darling, suppose it rains!"

"It never rains on the Fourth of July," said William. "It wouldn't dare." (He was wrong about that. It poured. But then, many things went wrong that Fourth of July to the most carefully laid plans.)

The food would be served, said William, from the Chinese summer house—all red and gold lacquer—on the wooded headland where the fireworks would be.

"The summer house is not nearly big enough," protested his wife. "What's gotten into you, Will? You have never pushed me around like this before."

"My last Fourth of July party," said William, and kissed her.

It didn't explain anything. Or mollify her.

Sylvia, exhausted to the outermost extremity, drove Elihu out in her air-conditioned Mercedes, the two of them exchanging not a single word during the whole drive. Elihu had slept until ten-thirty (very unusual). When he awoke, he leapt on the telephone immediately, ignoring even the coffee Sylvia brought him.

"It's the Fourth of July," said Sylvia. "No time for business."

He called Dora Land at her home and from her he got all those overseas numbers. He called Bahrain. He called Zurich. He called London. To all those places he spoke a sort of high financial gobbledygook consisting mostly of numbers and not, from the sound of him, getting any satisfaction.

Twice he called his mother and both times he got Travis, the new butler, who told him madam was still asleep. On the third call when he did get through to his mother, she sounded waterlogged and vague as if she had difficulty remembering who he was. . . .

Again and again Elihu called William Worth, only to get either the butler or Marcia.

"Darling Elihu!" gushed Marcia. "It's party day. You know you can't get William on the phone on party day."

In the end there was nothing for it except to go to a party he'd avoided for years, a party of many many painful memories and snubs and hurts, and here they were driving up William Worth's long driveway under the cedars past larking Worth children, entirely too self-confident as Worth children always were. Sylvia thinking, I promised to deliver Elihu and here I am delivering him to whatever fate Nicholas has planned about which I have been told nothing. . . .

"There's Uncle Will," snarled Elihu. "Stop the car."

Uncle Will was umpiring the baseball game between the Reds and the Greens on the wide sloping lawn. Sylvia didn't stop immediately. She pulled the Mercedes up under the trees next to the swimming pool and there Elihu, without saying thank you, without saying good-bye, without saying anything, plunged out of the car and darted around the swimming pool. He didn't escape unscathed. Abigail Worth— she of the high cheekbones and the merry mischievous eyes—was on the ten-meter board waiting for just such a victim. She leaped off the high board, forming her tight little body into a round cannonball that sent a great wave of water all over Elihu. After the wave of water came the wave of laughter from the other children and even, in the Mercedes, from Sylvia. Sylvia had had no laughs for days, was dying for a laugh, and laughed. There was Elihu drenched with water and with laughter. It wasn't fair. But then, that party had never been fair to Elihu.

Jasper, Jr., was pitching underhand—very hard—to his own son, Threep, Susan on second, a very tense moment, when Elihu, dripping wet, strode out to his Uncle Will who was crouched behind the catcher.

"Uncle Will," said Elihu.

"Get off the playing field," said Uncle Will crisply.

Jasper, Jr., threw the pitch and Threep connected for a long fly to right field which brought loud groans from the Greens because Amy Worth was in right field and Amy had never caught a fly ball in her life and didn't catch that one either. It went for three bases.

"Would you like to play right field, Elihu?" asked Jasper, Jr. "You can supplement Amy."

Two or even three right fielders were not at all unusual in Worth baseball games. They played by their own rules.

Elihu didn't have much choice. On the big wide front porch were dozens of Worths he didn't want to talk to. At the pool were all those larking laughing children who had drenched him. Elihu trotted out to right field where Amy said critically, "You aren't dressed for baseball, Uncle Elihu, or even for a picnic."

Sylvia found Robin in the kitchen sitting on a high stool wearing an apron emblazoned with the words *Bread And Flesh In The Morning—Kings 17-6* on it filling the hard-boiled whites of eggs with deviled yolks.

"Glamor in the kitchen," said Sylvia. "How very womanly!"

Robin spooned a bit of yellow into the round egg white. "Doris could use a little help with the cucumber sandwiches."

"I'm a sacred prostitute. We don't *do* cucumber sandwiches. Where's Nicholas?"

"Somewhere."

"And Orin?"

"In the Sargasso Sea. He's not coming."

"Crikey!" said Sylvia. She had picked up one of Robin's deviled eggs and had it halfway to her mouth and there it stood, suspended, while Sylvia thought of the enormity of this desertion. "Can we manage?"

Robin shrugged. "It's Nicholas' show. I don't know."

Out on the wide wooden porch overlooking the sound, Elsie Worth was standing very straight, propped up on her stick, telling Endicott Worth (who wrote all those novels with the thinly disguised Worths in them) and George and Delphine Worth (the Pennsylvania Worths) she was going around the world in October at age ninety-three because she was afraid they'd tear down the Taj Mahal ("They've torn everything else down") before she got there unless she hurried up. Felix was standing next to her, holding her elbow. "Felix is coming with me—to open all those doors and to help me down the ramps."

Poor Felix.

Up on the headland around the Chinese summer house, the big tables were being laid out by the servants, two of them Marcia's own, but the others borrowed, as she always did, from other Worths. Hugh Dorset who had been butler to Arthur and Constance and was now Marcia's butler was supervising with the help of Andrews, Rebecca's butler. "That big fellow and his friend," said Dorset to Andrews. "Where did they come from? I've not seen them before."

"Mr. Humphrey brought them from one of his clubs," said Andrews. The big man was carrying a table by one leg in one hand as if it were a teaspoon. "He's wasted as a waiter," said Dorset. "He should be pouring concrete somewhere."

On the porch, Sylvia was telling Louise Hampton she looked ravishing in that flowered pink cotton dress. It wasn't the dress. The smile, the gleaming complexion, the sparkling eyes. She's taken a lover, guessed Sylvia. The expert.

Up in the huge old-fashioned bathroom on the second floor Lannie Worth was sharing a joint with Deborah Worth, age thirteen. "I don't feel a thing," complained Deborah.

"You will. Wait."

Robin had been told to stay out of sight, way out of sight, especially now that Elihu was there. Her part was later in the day. However, she had slipped out of the kitchen to get a breath of fresh air. Just for a moment, she told herself. She was standing there in her yellow trousers with their electric vibrance. (She had been told to wear clothes that could be seen in the dark), her blond hair blowing in the wind, looking spectacularly beautiful when Elihu, out in right field, caught a glimpse which he wasn't supposed to do until later, much later.

Geoffrey Worth had just hit a long ball over the head of the third baseman, Ashley, right at the new right fielder, Elihu. Elihu's mind was elsewhere.

"Robin!" he shouted. "Robin! Wait!"

He galloped off the field toward the house, the ball going right past him.

"You stink, Elihu!" howled Ashley. "You just positively stink on ice."

When Elihu got to the porch, Robin had disappeared.

"Where did she go?" he demanded of Waddington, who leaned against the balustrade.

"Who?"

"Robin!"

"I haven't seen Robin. Is she here?"

A very good actor was Waddington.

Elihu darted into the house, ignoring the greetings of Great-Aunt Elsie and the others on the porch. He walked through the big old-fashioned living room with its masses of flowers, empty because everyone was outside, through the dim dining room, perennially cool and dark, shielded as it was from the sun by huge trees and by the side porch, through Uncle Will's gun room and the big sun porch with its white wicker furniture and potted plants—all of them empty.

He went into the kitchen, but that too was empty now, the food having been taken out-of-doors to the serving tables.

Elihu was alone, fearfully alone, in the midst of these surging, noisy, multitudinous Worths, his mind clamoring, I am the son of Jasper, as much Worth as any of you!

The baseball game had broken up for the food which was being served in two places, the kids eating at the big round table by the swimming pool, the grown-ups (or those who considered themselves grown-ups and there were always those like Lannie, fifteen, who were sort of in-between) by the Chinese summer house where the enormous waiter that Humphrey had brought from one of his clubs was ladling out potato salad with uncommon delicacy.

Oh, it was a bright gay party and with the food and drink it gained extra electricity, familial intensity, sometimes too much intensity. This was when the quarrels broke out, when the tears began.

After the food, dusk descended like a shroud and the Worth children began choosing up sides for The Game.

Elihu had stalked William Worth as if stalking a lion from the ball game to the Chinese red summer house where William chattered with the guests and served drinks and was so very much a host that Elihu thought, He's ducking me, they're all ducking me, and why is that? Because William Worth, the Chairman of the SEC, was not being Chairman of the SEC at all; he was being a host, more a host than Elihu had ever seen him be, or perhaps he had never paid proper attention before, perhaps he was being unnecessarily sensitive. . . .

Then Uncle Will disappeared as Robin had disappeared. One moment he was there playing host at the Chinese summer house, the next he wasn't there, was nowhere to be seen in the encroaching darkness. The fireflies winking mockingly, the stars bright in the sky. A perfect night for Fourth of July. No moon because, of course, you didn't want a moon on Fourth of July to compete with the fireworks.

Elihu walked under the big trees, the party swirling around him, the young children (too young for The Game), the young adults (too old for The Game), alive with electricity and noise from the food and alcohol, showing their white teeth through the dusky light, the party gaining momentum, getting its second wind, as parties do. Oh, this was a party like no other party because they were Worths, because they were cousins and aunts and uncles and brothers and sisters, because they were rich, because they were what they were.

All except Elihu, who walked among them as separate as a tree and as ignored, the rage in him mounting. . . .

Sylvia and Hortense were in tête-à-tête on the wide, otherwise empty verandah, Sylvia saying, "Well, darling, there have been rumors. You are aware, aren't you?" Herself thinking, I have always been avid for gossip, but am I passing into that realm where gossip about others replaces my own delightful tumult, where I talk scandal rather than cause it? How frightening! Not, however, losing the thread.

Hortense tightly emitting, "And what are they saying exactly?"

"That you've become a switch-hitter. I believe that's the current phrase. What does Alec think of all this?"

"It seems to have awakened his interest, which had flagged."

"Is that what happens to husbands?"

"That's what happened to *mine*," said Hortense, reproaching Sylvia for thinking her husband was like all others. "My husband and my lover keep each other in a state of tumescence—each afraid that I will lapse altogether into . . . hitting right, or hitting left. It's exhausting."

"It's done wonders for your skin, all that exhaustion," said Sylvia.

Elihu walked up the steps heavily. Sylvia felt her sphincter tighten into a hard knot; he's about to explode and it mustn't be here. Oh, where is Robin? This is Robin's play! She forced a bright smile: "Elihu, do sit down and—"

"Where's Uncle Will?"

"Probably resting. The party tires him dreadfully. He's getting old, you know. . . ."

Elihu pushed past them into the house, banging the screen door behind him. He knew now where William Worth was and went straight to it, pushing up the stairs to the little choked room on the landing, Uncle Will's den. No one had dens anymore—except Uncle Will—this den like so many nineteenth-century dens on the first landing of a big wooden house when they had so much space they didn't know what to do with it all and made the master of the house a little cluttered spot he could call his own.

Elihu pushed into the little room without knocking, a venial sin, and there was William Worth slumped in the big black leather revolving chair, his chin on his chest, having a little nap. But not alone. At the room's lone window which looked down the lawn to the sound, Terence O'Reilly, William's chauffeur (and bodyguard), leaned against the windowsill, expressionless. Standing guard.

William Worth's eyes blinked open and stared woodenly at Elihu who said, "Uncle Will, I'm sorry. But it's important. That information about the Bahrain bank is false! I have been betrayed by you and by Robin—two Worths betraying another Worth."

William Worth stirred like an ancient crocodile. "You talk about betrayal as if you owned it, Elihu."

Elihu's voice rising now, almost to a falsetto. "You have left me no alternative. I have instructed my attorney to file suit against you, against the SEC, against the network, against Robin. Where in hell did you get all that misinformation?"

"Why don't you ask Robin?"

"Because I can't find her. I've been looking for her since the party began."

Terence O'Reilly spoke up. "She's down there on the lawn." He pointed out the window. Elihu looked.

There was Robin in her bright yellow trousers looking up at Elihu bewitchingly. Now she smiled and waved, the shrieks of the children playing The Game sounding around her like the Pilgrim's Chorus, the awful sound of inevitability. . . .

I'll kill her myself. One killing is not enough. Not nearly enough. He was going down the stairs, two at a time. I'd have done in Uncle Will but for that damned bodyguard. All this ringing in his head, his very own Anvil Chorus. . . .

Robin could see the glimmer of Elihu, not his dun-colored trousers but the white shirt he was wearing that was all wrong for picnics as Amy had so bluntly pointed out. Everything about Elihu was wrong for picnics. He was not a picnic person. Robin sliding along backward, toward the boathouse, keeping Elihu in view. He was coming fast.

Robin bumped square into Amy singing out, "Dare you to. Bet you don't. I can do what you won't." Rhyming games to lure a Red Devil out of the shrubbery.

"The boathouse is out of bounds," whispered Robin. The Game was getting too close to the other game, the big game. . . .

There was a scuffle and a shriek from the hedge, some luckless Red Devil trapped; Amy flew off to join the group.

Elihu flying down the hill at Robin, the white shirt proclaiming its whiteness through the gloom.

Robin scrambled into the boathouse, passing a waiter, two waiters in their white jackets. What on earth were waiters doing there? She had no time to speculate. She tore up the stairs to the little loo on the landing and closed the door, her heart thudding. The Decoy. Decoy to what? She had no idea because Nicholas was playing his cards very close, very close. . . .

Out the little round window, Robin could see Elihu standing on the edge of the lawn, stock still. He had been running hard and now he had stopped altogether. Elihu in his white unsuitable shirt and his dun-colored trousers and his ferocious concentration, concentrating . . . Oh, he would never go into a boathouse, even *near* one—not after what had happened back when he was four, not in the dark . . . Where was Nicholas?

The first star shell exploded, sending a shower of red, green, purple and white streamers across the sky, lighting up the lawn, lighting up Abigail and Sarah who were dragging a screaming Robert to the Prison Stockade in the pines, lighting up the wide verandah where Sylvia and Hortense sat trading sexual badinage, lighting up Elihu in his dun-colored trousers and white shirt, standing there, frozen, remembering long ago. . . .

The star shell was followed by an aerial torpedo—Nicholas had bought the largest he could find—which made a tremendous bang, followed by the machine gun rattle of smaller firecrackers. During that racket—cutting right through it, at least in the vicinity of the boathouse—came the high violin scream of a despairing woman:

"*El-i-hu! El-i-hu!*"

Each syllable a half note higher than the preceding one.

"*El-i-hu! El-i-hu!* Where are you, *El-i-hu*?"

In the bright light of an exploding star shell, Robin saw

the convulsed snarl of rage that was, Nicholas had always said, Elihu's vulnerability, the moment when judgment stopped.

The scream came from the end of the pier and Elihu thundered down the slope and onto the pier, which put him out of Robin's vision. She turned from the window, sick with unknowing. I don't *want* to know! But will I ever have peace. . . .

It was dark as the bottom of Othello in that little loo. Then the door opened and in came the white shirts, *two* white shirts, and what were two white shirts doing there in the loo? The big hand over her whole face with the sweetish sickening smell. I am far too intelligent to breathe ether if you think I'll do that, but it was that or no breath at all; her lungs were bursting, struggling kicking against this massive shape these massive arms her mind exploding like the star shell the gun in her handbag no use at all. . . .

"*El-i-hu! El-i-hu!* Your father says you murdered him! *El-i-hu!*"

Like Circe's song, his mother's sexual screams, irresistible. . . .

It was dark on the end of the pier only momentarily. Another star shell lit the sky, lit the pier, lit the sound, and there was Nicholas crouched over the electronic equipment, baring his teeth in a parody of Elihu's very own smile.

"Welcome to The Game, Elihu," whispered Nicholas. "It's been a long time."

It was a trap like that other trap so long ago. Elihu's intelligence flooded back, his tremendous mental agility returning not quite soon enough. The great bronze claw came out of the sound, right out of the dark water, even as Elihu turned to flee, grasped him from the back around his waist as it had once grasped his father (also Nicholas' father) and held him there against the starlit sky, his arms and legs threshing about like a berserk spider.

The great claw shook him once, twice, thrice, and then,

as Elihu opened his mouth to scream—he had disdained screaming until that very moment, but just as he succumbed finally to the humiliation of a scream—the great bronze claw pulled him under the dark waters, extinguishing the scream like a burnt match.

"Good-bye, brother," said Nicholas very low.

And then, "Oh, my God!"

Sarah, the brightest eleven-year-old in Chicago or perhaps anywhere, was standing on the pier, her mouth open, having seen it all.

"Out of bounds!" grasped Nicholas. "Out of bounds!"

Too late! Always too late!

"What was *that*, Uncle Nicholas?"

"A figment of your imagination," said Nicholas.

"Oh no it wasn't!" said the brightest eleven-year-old in Chicago. "It was . . . Excalibur!"

"Excalibur?" said Nicholas.

"King Arthur's sword. You know, when the knight threw it in the lake, a hand came out of the water and grasped it and brandished it three times and then pulled it under!"

The brightest eleven-year-old in Chicago, Nicholas suddenly remembered, had very poor vision and was too proud to wear glasses. He slipped an arm around Sarah's shoulders. "Your mother will never believe that."

"Nobody will ever believe it," said Sarah glumly.

"It'll be our little secret, Sarah. We'll share it forever."

"Oh *yes*!" said Sarah, full of her secret, her marvelous secret. She reached up and pulled Nicholas down and kissed him, eyes shining. "I've got to get back to the Stockade before I'm caught." She vanished into the gloom.

Actually, The Game was over. It always ended with the fireworks the star shells lighting the sky. Nicholas packed up the Sony and carried it up to the house.

Little Willie Pirelli had come down the rickety wooden stairs softly, softly, Soldier Ghardelli, the big man with the girl over his shoulder behind him, treading not softly enough. Pirelli held up his hand because Nicholas was walking down the pier toward the shore, and the two men in the waiter outfits stopped, listening to the footfalls on the wooden pier. The girl was snuffling a little stentoriously, but they couldn't interfere with that. They had been told very sternly about that by Mauriello, who was a perfectionist in these matters. The girl must be alive when put in the water; she must drown, not suffocate. So they had been careful. They waited a good five minutes. Little Willie went to the door of the boathouse and watched Nicholas as he climbed the hill to the big house.

Only then did they carry the girl out to the end of the pier with the sash weights around her legs that would drop off after eight hours and put her in the water.

Gently. They watched her sink in the black water until the blond hair could not be seen and then went back up the bluff to the summer house where the other waiters were clearing away.

In the little submarine, Orin had expected to be sick, as he always was, and worried about it because there was no room to be sick in the little submersible. But the fact was he wasn't sick. That, he knew, would worry him later, that he had done this deed and not been sick, but at the moment he was too busy operating the claw. Elihu had thrashed wildly, twice almost slipping out of the clutch of the claw—and that would never do because he'd never get him back in the darkness. Nicholas had warned no lights, no lights at all, so Orin had had to make the grab and do the seamanship by starlight and then by the intermittent flare of rockets. In its way this was a blessing because he had had only intermittent glimpses of that contorted face, the wide staring eyes, the round convulsive mouth.

For the last three minutes there had been no movement at

all from the figure in the clutch of the claw, the man in the dun-colored trousers, the white shirt.

Orin locked the claw on Elihu and turned to seamanship. The submarine had to be kept in the channel that had been dug long ago for the deep keels of his uncle's sloops. Orin knew where the channel was because he had sailed in there many times, but without lights he had to position himself by reference to the boathouse itself and that meant using the periscope.

He pushed up the periscope and adjusted it to his vision. The next bit was not in the script, not in the script at all. On the pier walking out toward him were two men, one small, one very large. A brilliant burst of fire in the heavens revealed an object over the shoulder of the big man. Yellow trousers, very bright yellow. Where had he seen those trousers before? The big man had shaken the object off his shoulder, held it now in his two outstretched arms, and in the blue and red and green light of the exploding rockets Orin saw the blond hair, the white face, watched as the two men fixed weights around the legs, watched them lower the figure into the water.

Orin pulled the periscope back into its base and lunged forward on his knees to the submarine tube which had not been designed for human beings, had been designed for fishes, some of them the size of a fingernail. He hoped it was big enough.

But then Robin was quite slender, had always been very thin.

It was an abstract dream in color, bright flashes of color—greens and purples and reds and yellows—interspersed with blackness, tremendous blackness, the blackest of blackness, no story line at all, an awful dream, the brightness of the colors not mitigating in any way the blackness of despair.

Pain. Lots of pain, her chest bursting. Her head splitting in four colors.

She was swimming upward in the midst of streaking multicolored light and broke the surface, her lungs bursting, and there was this man, heavy on her body, kissing her, very hot for kissing, or for raping, if this was rape. She opened her eyes, and choked a bit, the saltwater pouring out of her mouth and there was . . . Orin!

Orin, who hadn't come to the party.

"I'm sorry." Orin always had the best manners. Sir Galahad himself. "When I designed this submarine, I didn't have mouth-to-mouth resuscitation in mind."

Robin closed his eyes and let a little more seawater flow out of her mouth. She felt giggly, the sweetly sickish smell of ether still in her nostrils.

She opened her eyes again and there was Orin, inches away, the closest she had ever been to Sir Galahad. "I thought . . . you weren't coming to the party."

"I didn't. At this very moment I'm in the Sargasso Sea. You never saw me here, Robin. It's very important."

Robin giggled, still full of the sweetish fumes. "If you say so, darling."

Just my luck, she was thinking, when I thought I had Orin all to myself in a submarine, he's not here. He's in the Sargasso Sea. . . .

EPILOGUE

There were no endings in the Worth family, old Elsie used to say, only new directions, fresh beginnings with a new cast of Worths.

Elihu was never seen again, alive or dead, and the disappearance added all sorts of new wrinkles to the Worth legend. The most fashionable theory was that he had fled with a lot of Mob money to Bolivia or Paraguay—anyway, one of those distant Latin American jungles where the Nazis always took refuge—and there he lived with a private army and platoons of fresh girls to amuse him. No one who knew Elihu believed this, but then few journalists knew Elihu, so they rehashed this tale again and again in the paperbacks. Louis Hanagan came sniffing around, of course, but his theories were just as wide off the mark as the journalists'. Elihu had been laundering Mob money and the Mob was very experienced at making people disappear. Ergo . . .

The disappearance left an enormous hole in the fabric of

the Worth family and into this vacuum Nicholas reluctantly stepped because no one else wanted to and also, for some reason, the other Worths looked to Nicholas to take over, all very surprising. Guided by his wily Uncle Alec and his Great-Uncle William, Nicholas took over Securities Unlimited where everyone expected his first act would be to fire Dora Land. Instead he made her Vice-President because (as he was later to tell Robin) she knew where all the bodies were buried and because he knew where *her* body was buried. "We both have each other by the short hairs."

Uncle Will's last Fourth of July added its own fresh scribblings on the Worth legend. Sarah's secret didn't remain a secret very long. She couldn't resist telling about the mysterious mailed hand brandishing Excalibur over the water. The Worth children, of course, jeered, but still it was a good story and throwing a sword into the sound off the pier became part of The Game, adding a fresh complication to a game already much too complicated for any other children except Worth children.

Oh, it was a wow, that last Fourth of July party, and everyone stayed much later than usual, many of the grownups getting quite drunk which was just as well for Robin. Robin made an astounding appearance (most of the Worths could not remember seeing Robin at that party at all up to then) in the Chinese summer house on the headland, dripping wet, about eleven o'clock. By that time the rains had come and those late stayers—the Worths with young children had long since gone home—had fled into the summer house to get out of the rain. Suddenly there was Robin, in their midst, dripping wet, smelling faintly of ether, and giggling a little too much. Ether sniffing, the others whispered, was just the sort of wild thing you might expect from that wild girl.

At another Worth party in September—this one celebrating the imminent departure of Great-Aunt Elsie around the world—Robin and Nicholas got engaged which came as a great surprise.

"Engaged!" squeaked Jane Fox when Robin got home that night very late. *"Why?"*

"Well," said Robin, "you never know when you might need a husband." She smiled her sad smile, now her trademark on TV. "We're only fourth cousins, you know, so genetically it'll be very sound." She couldn't imagine marrying a non-Worth.

"And what about me?" wailed little Jane Fox.

Robin stroked the dark head and kissed her on the mouth, the two women in bed, quite naked. "We'll have to be discreet, but then we always have been."

Herself thinking, I'm in love with one Worth, Orin; pregnant by another, Ahmet Ali; and about to marry still another, Nicholas; myself a Worth! And Nicholas, that idiot, said I had deserted the family! He laid a curse on me with that statement and he bloody well deserved to be stuck with me. Dear Nicholas! He'll make a splendid husband and a good father, and I shouldn't have unkind thoughts about him.

Robin sighed and surrendered to Jane Fox's hot young body. But not altogether. She was not nearly as lesbian as Jane Fox. Always she kept a bit of herself separate. That night in the midst of the kisses, she was thinking of her baby. It would be a boy, she was convinced of that; her firstborn would be a boy, son of the smartest Worth of them all, and raised by two other Worths, herself and Nicholas.

How marvelous!

She'd call him Alexander. After the emperor who conquered the whole world.